MW00635513

Madam
PRESIDENT

Other works by Jordan Wells

LOGGED OFF: MY JOURNEY OF ESCAPING
THE SOCIAL MEDIA WORLD

MIRRORS AND REFLECTIONS

THE HEALING

A LONELY ROSE

THE RING PACK (*Part 1*)

IT'S FUN BEING A HUMAN BEING

THE RING PACK (*Part 2*) Coming *soon 2022*

(*Baby Record Books; Exclusively on Barnes & Noble*)

HE'S HERE: LET'S CHERISH HIS FIRST YEAR

SHE'S HERE: LET'S CHERISH HER FIRST YEAR

MY BABY BOY IS HERE

MY BABY GIRL IS HER

MY BABY BOY

MY BABY GIRL'S FIRST YEAR

A PRINCESS HAS COME: LET'S CHERISH HER FIRST YEAR

A PRINCE HAS COME: LET'S CHERISH HIS FIRST YEAR

A KING IS BORN

A QUEEN IS BORN

My 2nd Novel

Signature

For Dr. Groisser,

Thanks for your help.

With peace and love!

Stay Blessed

Jordan Wells

Wed.

9:14 am

11/23/22

A Novel
By
Jordan Wells

Scott and Scholars Press
East Orange, New Jersey 07017

Scott and Scholars Press® is a registered trademark of
Jordan Wells Publishing

Publisher's Cataloging-in-Publication data

Names: Wells, Jordan, author.
Title: Madam President / by Jordan Wells.
Description: East Orange, NJ: Scott and Scholars Press, 2022.
Identifiers: LCCN 2022902550 | ISBN 978-1-955975-28-5 (hardcover) | 978-1-955975-29-2 (paperback) | 978-1-955975-30-8 (paperback) | 978-1-955975-31-5 (paperback) | 978-1-955975-32-2 (Kindle)
Subjects: LCSH United States. President--Fiction. | Women--Fiction. | Marital violence--Fiction. | Family violence--Fiction. | Thriller fiction. | Psychological fiction. | BISAC FICTION / Thrillers / General | FICTION / Thrillers / Domestic | FICTION / Thrillers / Political | FICTION / Thrillers / Suspense | FICTION / Thrillers / Psychological
Classification: LCC PS3623.E4698 M33 2022 | DDC 813.6--dc23

First Edition 2022
Jacket design by Jordan Wells
Cover photograph by Hakeem James Hausley/Pexels.com

For special inquiries, please email us at scottandscholarspress@yahoo.com

Printed in the United States of America
10 9 8 7 6 5 4 3 2 1

CONTENTS

Introduction: Friday Early Morning, February 14th, 2025
A Valentine's Day Massacre Occurs

Chapter 1: Saturday Morning, January 20th, 2024
Inauguration Day Celebration: History Has Been Made Page... 1

Chapter 2: Saturday Afternoon, January 20th, 2024
Inauguration Day Celebration: The Arrival to The Capitol. Page... 7

Chapter 3: Saturday Evening, January 20th, 2024
The Morrison Family Moves into The White House Page... 15

Chapter 4: Monday Morning, February 5th, 2024
Air Force One Page... 25

Chapter 5: Monday Morning, February 5th, 2024
Air Force One-Press Play Page... 35

Chapter 6: Monday Afternoon, February 5th, 2024
The Eagle Has Landed Page... 41

Chapter 7: Monday Evening, February 5th, 2024
This Has to Stop Page... 53

Chapter 8: Monday Evening, February 5th, 2024
A Pain in the Neck Page... 59

Chapter 9: Tuesday Morning, February 6th, 2024
Midnight with a knife Page... 61

Chapter 10: Tuesday Morning, February 6th, 2024

An American Dream Page… 71

Chapter 11: Tuesday Morning, February 6th, 2024

Bad Morning to You Page… 77

Chapter 12: Tuesday Evening, February 6th, 2024

Dear Journal Page… 91

Chapter 13: Wednesday Evening, February 14th, 2024

Spitting Image Page… 105

Chapter 14: Thursday Afternoon, March 14th, 2024

The Conversation She Feared Page… 117

Chapter 15: Thursday Afternoon, March 14th, 2024

The Interview Page… 125

Chapter 16: Thursday evening, March 14th, 2024

A Letter from A Soldier-less Mother Page… 141

Chapter 17: Thursday evening, March 14th, 2024

Don't Drown Me Page… 149

Chapter 18: Sunday Evening, March 31st, 2024

A Daughter's Secrets Page… 163

Chapter 19: Thursday Afternoon, April 4th, 2024

The Stone of Hope Page… 169

Chapter 20: Thursday Evening, April 4th, 2024

Table For Two Page… 173

Chapter 21: Friday Early Morning, April 5th, 2024

Nightmare Husband Page… 187

Chapter 22: Thursday Afternoon, April 11th, 2024

The Cabinet Room Page… 199

Chapter 23: Friday Early Morning, May 31st, 2024

Time for A Vacation Page… 219

Chapter 24: Thursday Evening, June 11th, 2024

For He's a Jolly Good Fellow Page… 229

Chapter 25: Wednesday Afternoon, July 31st, 2024

An Escape to Paradise Page… 239

Chapter 26: Thursday Early Morning, August 1st, 2024

A Moment of Gratitude Page… 247

Chapter 27: Thursday Morning, August 1st, 2024

What an Actor Page… 253

Chapter 28: Sunday Evening, August 11th, 2024

Sad Birthday, Kelissa! Page… 261

Chapter 29: Monday Early morning, August 12th, 2024

Don't Do It, Kelissa! Page… 271

Chapter 30: Monday Late Morning, August 26th, 2024

He's Leaving the White House Page… 281

Chapter 31: Tuesday Afternoon, September 3rd, 2024

Darling Boy, I love you Page… 291

Chapter 32: Wednesday Morning, September 11th, 2024

A Day of Remembrance Page… 303

Chapter 33: Wednesday Late Evening, September 11th, 2024

Late Night in the Private Office Page… 309

Chapter 34: Thursday Evening, October 31st, 2024

A Halloween to Never Forget Page… 315

Chapter 35: Thursday Evening, November 7th, 2024

A Night in the Sky Page… 325

Chapter 36: Friday Evening, November 15th, 2024

The Act Page… 335

Chapter 37: Sunday Evening, December 1st, 2024

Ted's Got Her Back Page… 345

Chapter 38: Saturday Evening, December 7th, 2024

Hell of a Party Page… 361

Chapter 39: Friday Evening, December 13th, 2024

Camp David Page… 381

Chapter 40: Friday Evening, January 3rd, 2025

The Moment of Truth Page… 387

Chapter 41: Thursday Evening, January 16th, 2025

No Ted Thursday Page… 395

Chapter 42: Saturday Evening, January 18th, 2025

Kelissa's Sympathy Page… 403

Chapter 43: Tuesday Evening, January 21st, 2025

State of The Union Address Page… 409

Chapter 44: Tuesday afternoon, February 11th, 2025

A Mother's Closure Page… 417

Chapter 45: Friday evening, February 14th, 2025

Oh No! Page… 421

Chapter 46: Friday Early Morning, February 14th, 2025

Life Is but A Dream Page… 433

Chapter 47: Friday Morning, February 14th, 2025

The Aftermath of Abuse Page… 441

Chapter 48: Saturday Evening, March 1st, 2025

Camp David with the Children Page… 445

Chapter 49: Tuesday Afternoon, March 18th, 2025

Welcome Back, Madam President Page…453

Chapter 50: Monday Afternoon, March 24th, 2025

The Second Interview Page… 461

Chapter 51: Tuesday Afternoon, April 1st, 2025

Madam President Page… 475

Acknowledgments

About the Author

I dedicate this book to all of the strong, courageous, brave, and remarkable women in the world, of all ages, who may have lived through and miraculously survived a story such as the one you are about to read. To those women of the world, you are not alone, and there is always a way out.

Author's Notes

Hello, welcome to another installation of my storytelling ventures. I am glad and very grateful that you chose to read this book. This story is my second novel, one of many books that I have published. I must always thank you and show my undying appreciation for your support. If this is the first time you have read my work, I welcome and thank you very much. If you are familiar with my work and have read several other books, I say welcome back and thank *you* most of all for being a loyal reader and supporter. I always start my books with '*Thank you*' and show my appreciation to you, the reader. You could be doing anything else with your time, spend your hard-earned money on other things, but you chose to support my work and read my work, and for that, I cannot tell you how grateful I am to have your support. And I hope that your support will continue as I create other installments to my book catalog.

So, with that said, let me introduce you to my second novel, "*Madam President*." In this novel, you will read about a woman named "Kelissa Morrison." Kelissa is a forty-seven-year-old woman, mother of three children, and married to Ted Morrison. Kelissa is now officially elected as the first woman President in United States history.

The American people love this woman—from the east coast to the west coast *and* Hawaii. Kelissa has won the election by a landslide as her opponent never stood a chance. She is intelligent, beautiful, humbled, and most importantly, she has faith and hope in America.

But Kelissa, unfortunately, has a situation, a *dark* situation, hidden not only from the public but also from her children, her parents, *and* the Secret Service. She has been dealing with this situation up to election night. It is a severe problem, and she does not know how to escape it. And now that she has won the presidential election, she is more trapped than ever before. What is her problem, you may be thinking? Well, that is what you will be reading about shortly.

Now, I take *much* pride and responsibility for my work. I feel that I must give my readers a fair warning on the content of this book. We live in different times, ladies and gentlemen, where you cannot say or do whatever you want to do and not ruffle some feathers, offend people, or have *what* you say taken out of proportion. You cannot say whatever you want, and there be no consequences.

So, with *that* said, I feel that it is my responsibility to inform you that in this thriller novel, there is much profanity, there is graphic violence, and strong, explicit, sexual content. There are moments in this story that may not be suitable or appropriate for some readers. *Please* be advised.

This story is *very* different from my debut novel. I wanted to challenge myself and give you, the reader, an account that has never been created before. At least not to *my* knowledge. Now, this is very important. What you are about to read is something that goes on worldwide. It is hidden, sometimes in plain sight, and no one would even know it is happening. Unfortunately, this happens every single day. May I say this as well? I am in absolutely *no* way making light of this situation. It is not a joke, it is *nothing* to be humorous about, and it is certainly not for the faint of heart.

This book may be triggering for many people. *Please* forgive me if this story is too much for you to handle. But believe it or not, my stories practically write themselves. As I sit there and write, I am a mere vessel. *I*, as the artist, simply get *out* of the way and let the story write itself. Now, of course, I proofread and make changes but overall, I let the story be its own thing. I say that because I do not judge the characters, nor would I want people to take this story literally. Again, I do not see this kind of story as a joking matter. And also, as you begin to read, if you feel that this is *not* a story for you and you must part ways with this book, I understand entirely, and I respect that. As I said, this story may not be suitable for everyone. And it is *not* for anyone *under* the age of 18, to be precise.

Madam President is not a story *specifically* about politics or the presidency, not in its totality. It is a story about the *character*, the *human being* of Kelissa Morrison, and what she goes through *behind* the scenes, dealing with her family and her personal life while she takes on her position as the leader of the free world. She is in a dire, familiar situation—a situation that requires more attention to open the conversation. Now, I cannot say any more about the story's content without spoiling it for you. But you *will* see and may have an inkling about what is going on, right in the beginning.

Also, this is an entirely fictional story. Every single character in this novel is fictitious and has fictitious names. I wrote a story that deals with some politics and the presidency. I had to do extensive research but still ensured that this story was as fictional as possible. There are *no* similarities to actual living people from real life and no names mentioned of any sitting or active politicians. I want to be *very* clear on that.

To be honest with you, there were times I had to close my laptop and just walk away from it. After I finished writing this story, I sat there, thinking to myself, 'I'll never write another book like this again.' I think I covered everything that I needed to before you began to read this "one of a kind" thriller. I did my absolute best, and I hope you do not forget this story. And without further ado, ladies and gentlemen, I present to you, *Madam President*.

Introduction

Friday Early Morning, February 14th, 2025

A Valentine's Day Massacre Occurs

Fresh blood drips from the nose and wounded lips of the President, Kelissa Morrison. Her blood is rapidly dripping onto the faucet of the bathroom sink. President Kelissa Morrison was brutally beaten as she could barely stand herself up. She looks at herself in the mirror, completely mortified at the look of her bloodily defeated face. She has a broken nose with bloody lips, and her right eye is damn near closed shut. Kelissa's face has never looked like this before.

Suddenly, aggressive pounding shakes the bathroom door, and Kelissa is scared shitless. She fears for her life as the knocks grow more and more violent. "*OPEN* THE FUCKING DOOR, KEL!" The person screams. But Kelissa does not budge as her life is in danger.

The pounding and slamming on the bathroom door traumatically continued. Kelissa went to the bathroom corner as she sat and quivered in fear. She covered her ears and closed her eyes as the person shouted and yelled her name—rocking back and forth in a fetal position as the wicked flashbacks of her violent past began to dance in her mind, one after the other. The person continued to scream as the banging on the bathroom door was causing Kelissa a high level of anxiety and chilling panic. The panic button has been pushed. Now, Kelissa picks up her Blackberry and calls Secret Service agent Carl.

Finally, Carl and the other Secret Service agents came barging in with their guns drawn. BANG! BANG! BANG! BANG! BANG! Kelissa's body jumped five times at the sound of their gunfire. "*Jesus Christ*, notify the pilots, *right now*!" Carl projected. Kelissa continued to sit in a cradled position in her bloody white pajamas, barefooted on the cold bathroom floor. Again, she heard knocks at the door. But *this* time, it was Carl.

"Madam President!" Carl shouted. "Madam President, are you in there?"

"Carl?" Kelissa cried. "Oh, dear God, *Carl*, is that you?"

"Yes, Madam President, it's me!"

Kelissa painfully got up from the floor and slowly walked towards the door. Her limping walk caused a great deal of pain at every step. As she finally opened the door, Carl stood there in absolute disbelief. He looked at Kelissa as if he could not believe his eyes. He saw the President's face, beaten to a pulp.

"H—He was going to kill me, thi—this *time,*" Kelissa said, slipping in and out of consciousness.

"Madam President, what do you mean *this* time?" Carl responded in devastation.

"*Please,* Carl, I—I can't talk anymore. Can you please ta—take *me* to th—the hos—hospital, *please*?"

"We're taking you right now."

President Kelissa Morrison began to slip in and out of consciousness as Secret Service agents rushed in the bathroom to assist Carl. They immediately carried her down to the State floor and headed out to the South Portico where Marine One had landed. It was entirely out of their traditional routine as Carl and the other agents boarded Marine One with President Kelissa Morrison. "Notify Mr. Vice President and the Chief of staff, *right now*! We're taking *Wyrd* to Walter Reed Medical Center," Carl projected to the other agents. Marine One then took off from the White House.

All President Kelissa Morrison could hear was the sound of Carl's voice. "Hang in there, Madam President. You're going to be alright. Just *stay with me*!" Carl said. A hazy vision as

President Kelissa Morrison looks up at Carl, seeing two of him out of one eye.

"Carl," Kelissa softly spoke. "Is h—is he—*dead*?"

"Yes, Madam President, he's dead," Carl responded.

"Te—Tell my kids I—I *love* them, Carl. Because I'm not going to make it."

"Yes, you will! Just *hold on*, Madam President! We're almost at the hospital."

President Kelissa Morrison is now in the fight for her life. But before we go any further, we must go back a year earlier to a brighter and better day—the *special* day of her Inauguration. History is about to be made as President-elect Kelissa Morrison is sworn in as the *first* woman President of the United States of America.

Chapter 1

Saturday Morning, January 20th, 2024

Inauguration Day Celebration: History Has Been Made

Finally! The first-ever woman President in the history of the United States of America has happened. President-elect Kelissa Morrison is about to be sworn in as the forty-seventh President of the United States of America. This monumental achievement has been a pipedream come true—a *woman* who is soon to be the head of the Oval Office. Kelissa is sitting in the backseat of her limo on her way to the ceremony. Both of her palms are growing damped and clammy as she is overwhelmed with nervousness and excitement.

Inside the limousine with her are her three beautiful children. Her eldest son, Ted, Jr., is seventeen, her daughter Madeline, fifteen, and her youngest son, eleven-year-old Bryan. Riding in the limousine behind them is Kelissa's husband, "The First Gentleman," Theodore "Teddy" Morrison Sr. Kelissa, however, always calls him Ted. Ted had an important phone call and did not want to make any distractions.

Kelissa was on her Blackberry, talking with her mother, Suzanne, telling her mother that she wished she was attending the Inauguration. But unfortunately, Suzanne had to undergo a surgical procedure, and Kelissa's father stayed behind to care for his wife. As Kelissa was on her Blackberry, listening, her mother said to her, "Kelly, my words cannot *reach* a comprehension of how proud I am of you. You worked incredibly hard for this extraordinary and historical moment in your life. You *did it*, my love. You made history as the first woman President of the United States of America. As my daughter, you make your mother and father *over* the moon proud of you. We can't wait to see you on T.V. as you take the oath and are officially sworn in. I love you dearly, Kelly." Kelissa began to wave her hand in front of her eyes as they grew misty and watery. Her mother's words touched her deeply and sincerely.

Kelissa responded to her mother, saying, "Oh, *Mom*, I am so glad to make you and dad proud. I hope I continue to do so as I lead my country. I love you too, and tell Dad I love him." Kelissa then put her Blackberry away. She began to go over the rules with all three of her children on conducting themselves during the Inauguration.

"Guys, listen up," Said Kelissa, "Okay, so, when we arrive, be sure to *smile*, be polite, and be on your very best behavior. Remember, we are going to be on national television. Cameras will be rolling all over the place."

"Aww, come on, mom," Ted, Jr. responded. "I think you raised us right. We know how to behave."

"Oh, you *do*? What about the time I was looking for you and your sister at the rally in Connecticut, and you guys wandered off?"

"Oh, mom, that was *so* different," Madeline responded.

"Are you *kidding* me? You two snuck off and took a cab to a college campus."

"It was so *boring* there in Connecticut; we just wanted to have some fun."

"Yeah, mom, we were coming right back," Ted, Jr. added.

"Yeah, well, I hope you both got that out of your system. Because once we move into the White House, there won't be any more of that '*sneaking out*.' Have I made myself clear?"

"Yeah, loud and clear," said T.J.

"*Maddy*? Do we *understand* each other?"

"Yes, ma'am. Whatever you say."

"Oh, we're *definitely* going to have a conversation about that sassy attitude of yours."

"Mom, really—"

"No, no, no… That's for later. Right now, I need *smiles*! All I want from the three of you are smiles. We're about to stop."

The limousine makes its way to the U.S. Capitol. There are tens of thousands of people all over the place, millions even. Kelissa just could not believe her eyes. So many people from all over the country came to honor their nation's first woman President. Kelissa became so emotional as she had to fight off shedding tears. But quite a few began to fall.

"*Mother*," Madeline said with sass. "No one's around to fix your makeup. *Enough* with the tears."

"You're right, baby; I'll stop," Kelissa chuckled.

"Are we *there* yet?" Bryan whined.

"In a minute, sweetie. We're about to get out."

There were signs, *hundreds* of them. Signs saying,

"**KELISSA MORRISON MADE HISTORY**,"

"**MORRISON IS HERE 2024**,"

"**KELISSA MORRISON IS MY *HER*-**O."

There were also red hats. Not the red hats you're thinking about; these are new red hats. Since Kelissa is the head of the "G.O.P.," people were wearing red caps with her slogan,

"**KELISSA MAKES *HER*STORY**."

"Guys, are you seeing this right now? *Look* at all of these people," Kelissa projected with excitement. She continued to look around, seeing people shout and cheer her name. Kelissa knew, in that exact moment, that she represented something special. She gave millions of women much inspiration for generations to come—not just women in America but women worldwide. She showed women *and* young girls that *anything* is possible and that being a woman does *not* come with jurisdiction for their success.

Chapter 2

Saturday Afternoon, January 20th, 2024

Inauguration Day Celebration: The Arrival to The Capitol

The back door of the limousine has opened. The first to come out was Teddy, Jr. He was wearing a navy-blue peacoat with a navy-blue suit and a red tie. He stood pretty tall at six feet two inches. And not to mention, *very* handsome features. The second to come out of the limo was Madeline. She had a midnight purple coat with a matching hat covering her long brunette hair. She carries her father's looks, but she has some of Kelissa's fiery personality. Then came out Bryan, also wearing a navy-blue suit with a powder-blue tie. And lastly, the woman of the hour, President-elect Kelissa Morrison.

The second Kelissa's foot stepped onto the concrete—*thousands* of people began to scream at the top of their lungs. The energy in the atmosphere was at an all-time high. She was standing in a mauve-colored coat with a matching suit, designed by her favorite French designer, Dori McPhonzè (Mick-Fon-Zhey). Kelissa stood five feet seven inches tall with a short, curly, dirty-blonde hairstyle and immaculate features. If she weren't a politician, she would have certainly been an A-list movie star—just drop-dead gorgeous. Not bad for a woman who is forty-seven years old, which is coincidently the same number she holds as the forty-seventh President of the United States of America.

Kelissa waves to the crowd as she makes her way into the Capitol building with her children. Her husband, Ted, was not too far behind. "Hold on, you, guys. Let's wait for your father," Kelissa projected. Ted, with his head down, gazing at his Blackberry, Kelissa called Ted to get his attention.

"Ted," said Kelissa. "Ted, we're *waiting*."

"Just walk in without me. I'll be just a minute," Ted responded.

"*No*, we have to walk inside together. *Please*?"

"Okay… Okay. I'm off the phone now."

"Thank you."

As the soon-to-be 'First Family' makes their way inside the Capitol building, waiting to make their grand entrance outside, Kelissa looked around inside the Capitol building, witnessing one of the most incredible views she's ever seen. She walked through the Capitol building with her family, looking at all the history surrounding her. Many people were already in attendance; former U.S. presidents, vice presidents, first ladies, staff representatives, and members of Congress were all waiting outside, sitting in their reserved seating. Kelissa and her husband Ted stayed inside the Capitol building as the current Vice President and President took their seats.

The children had already made their grand entrance and took their seats. President-elect Kelissa Morrison was next in line, along with her husband, the First Gentlemen, Ted Morrison, Sr., who stood as tall as Ted, Jr., and was even more handsome. Now standing in the hallway waiting for their queue, Kelissa and Ted began a quiet conversation. Ted said, "On a scale of 1-10, how nervous are you?" Kelissa looked at Ted, giving him a look that said, 'Are you kidding me?' She didn't say a word to him. Instead, Kelissa squeezed his hand as tightly as she could.

"Kel, my love," Ted whispered. "If you squeeze my hand any tighter, you'll be able to tell my blood pressure."

"Sorry," Kelissa said as she let go, "I just didn't think I would be this nervous."

"Well, hey, there's no going back now. You asked for it, and you got it."

"Well, jeez, thanks a lot. You're helping tremendously right now."

"Listen, you need to be tough," Ted said with sincerity. "Now's not the time to show any weakness or fear. You are the President-elect.

You're about to be sworn in as the *first* woman President. So, act like it."

"Alright, Fine... I'll relax."

The time came for President-elect and the First Gentleman, Kelissa and Ted Morrison, to make their grand entrance. Kelissa and Ted walked down the hall, then down the stairs as Marine sentries stood like statues, saluting the couple. As they stood before the golden double doors, Kelissa's heart was racing, but she was ready. The announcement was made, and Kelissa put on her trillion-dollar smile as they called her name. The doors opened, a standing ovation as President-elect and the First Gentlemen made their way outside. People held up their phones as they captured the moment. The screams and cheers grew louder and louder as Kelissa waved to the American People. Dozens of women surrounded her with teary eyes as they felt that they were part of history, *witnessing* history and seeing this impeccable woman about to take the oath.

As Kelissa took her seat, people continued to stand, giving her an incredible round of applause. She was so touched by this unforgettable moment that she stood up and waved in much gratitude. Women from all different cultures, African American, Caucasian, Latina, Asian, crying at the mere sight of her face. For these women, Kelissa means *everything* to them. There was no telling of how many people were in attendance. But analysts were predicting that it would be record-breaking, being that Kelissa is the first woman President in U.S. history.

President-elect Kelissa Morrison has now taken the oath; she is officially the forty-seventh President of the United States of America. It was now time for Kelissa to give her historical presidential speech. U.S. Senator, Sandra McPhee-Sutton, was the one who officially introduced President Kelissa Morrison to the podium to make her speech. As Kelissa was about to stand up, her husband Ted whispered something in her ear. "Don't forget to mention what I told you about."

Kelissa looked at Ted with an expressionless face and responded, "Thanks, Ted, but I think I'm okay." As Kelissa got up and made her way to the podium, she turned to look at her family. Ted, Jr., Madeline, and Bryan were all smiles as they saw their mother shining bright. Ted, Sr., however, was not. Ted gave Kelissa a very bedeviled look. She was too familiar with that look, but she had no time to feed into it as she was ready to speak.

About five minutes into Kelissa's speech, she talked about her vision of creating a better America, policies, and her mission as President. In the middle of her speech, Kelissa said this:

"As this country's first woman President, I will make it my mission to ensure that I won't be the last or the only. I will do my absolute best to inspire women of all different ages to strive and excel in whatever they choose to do in their lives. Along with my administration, I will do my diligence to create a better America for a better tomorrow. Even though tomorrow is not promised to any of us, I promise to maintain our nation's economic wellbeing. Our government has suffered tremendously during the last several years from the tragic event of the Covid-19 pandemic. However, I tend to boost our nation's economy, create more jobs, and *decrease* the unemployment rate, as it has trickled back up to seven percent within the last several months. But it's never too late for progress. It is *never* too late to rebuild our nation's economic structure. As we move forward as a nation, businesses will continue to grow, and so will our hope—hope that we can and will overcome the obstacles that our country faces day by day. I hope that we can make a better society that will prepare the next generation for life's obstacles.

As your first woman President, I understand that this is a dream come true for *many* women. Some of you may have never thought this moment would be possible. A little over a hundred and four years ago, on June 4th, Congress passed the ninetieth Amendment and then ratified the 19th Amendment on August 18th, 1920, allowing women the right to vote. It took over a hundred years of fighting for our rights. You, women, *and* men have taken your right to vote, and you've voted me into the highest chair in the office. This milestone was a very long time coming, but you've made this possible, and I do not take any of this for granted. I know my worth to you all, and I will do my absolute best as your leader to continue granting women more rights and equality, higher positioned jobs with equal or even higher pay. And most importantly, to finally present you the rights of what *you* choose to do with your bodies."

After Kelissa spoke, the colossal crowd of people began to cheer uncontrollably. Kelissa had to pause her speech until the applause simmered down. There was a standing ovation behind her and in *America's front lawn*, which they call the front lawn of the Capitol Building. Hundreds of thousands of mini-American flags were waving back and forth in people's hands. It was a patriotic moment as

Kelissa raised her hand, waving it to the American people. As the crowd began to silence themselves, Kelissa wrapped up her speech by saying this:

"There is a lot of work to be done, new policies to be enforced, a better nation to build, with quality and class. Thank you all for joining us today; my family and I are forever grateful to you for your trust in my administration and me. God bless you, and may God bless America."

Chapter 3

Saturday Evening, January 20th, 2024

The Morrison Family Moves into The White House

The new "First Family" has finally moved into the White House. The *previous* First Family's personal belongings had already been moved out during the Inauguration. Because Kelissa is such a history buff, she was fascinated by the painted portraits hanging on the walls. Her favorite room on the State floor was the Vermeil room, which is the room in honor of America's 'First Ladies.' Kelissa was in awe seeing portraits of those women. It is a fact that Kelissa is in the opposite position of what they once were in, but Kelissa honestly believes she would not have made it there without the inspiration of the *First Ladies* of the past. There was a moment when Kelissa was standing alone in the Vermeil room, looking at the portraits of the First Ladies. "I won't let you women down," Kelissa softly said, looking at the paintings.

It was a long, exhausting, yet monumental day for President Kelissa Morrison. She met and greeted six hundred and twelve of her staff members in one day. After touring the entirety of her new place of residence, the White House, Kelissa was ready to take a shower and hit the sack, as she had a hectic day and will have an even more challenging day ahead of her the following morning.

Before Kelissa took a shower, she went into the west bedroom, which is now Madeline's room. A gentle knock Kelissa gave to Madeline's bedroom door.

"Yeah?" Said Madeline.

"It's mom, Maddy," Kelissa spoke. "Can I come in?"

"Yes."

"Hey—*oh, wow*. You've really made yourself at home, I see."

"Yeah, I just finished putting up all of my posters."

"Great! And what poster are you going to put on that empty spot?"

"I'm putting up a picture of you."

"Of *me*?"

"Yes, *you*. I mean, it's not every day that a teenage girl can say her *mother* is President of the United States. Excuse my language, mom, but you're that *bitch*."

"*Maddy*," Kelissa said with shock. "I'm glad you *excused* yourself. But I guess I can take that as a compliment."

"Well, what I'm really trying to say is that *mom*… I'm just so proud of you, and I am *so* honored to be your daughter."

"Oh, *baby girl*… That means so *much* to me. I love you, sweetie."

"I love you too."

A warm and intimate moment between them as Kelissa hugged and kissed Madeline and said goodnight. After leaving Madeline's room, Kelissa went next door to check on her youngest son, Bryan, who stayed in the east bedroom. Kelissa then gives an encore knock on Bryan's bedroom door. "Bry?" Kelissa spoke, "Bry, it's mommy. Can I come in?" After there was no response from Bryan, Kelissa opened the door to find that Bryan was not in his room. At first, Kelissa grew worried. Even though this is their new residence, it is still a strange place that Bryan is unfamiliar with and has 'off-limits' areas. Kelissa then walked back over to Madeline's room, knocked, and opened the door, asking Madeline her brother's whereabouts.

"Have you seen your brother?" Kelissa asked.

"Bry?" Madeline responded.

"Yes."

"Two words, mom: *ice—cream*."

"Ah, say no more, say no more."

Kelissa and Madeline both shared a duet of laughter. Kelissa knew *exactly* where Bryan was as she walked down the center hall, making her way to the kitchen. As she walked into the kitchen, Bryan was sitting on the kitchen floor with a spoonful of his favorite, blue raspberry ice cream. Bryan could eat a whole container of blue raspberry ice cream, which he was trying to do.

"Bry," Kelissa projected. "You keep eating ice cream like *that*, and you will *turn* into a blue raspberry. Now hand over the spoon, and head to bed."

"Oh, *mom*," Bryan whined. "Can't I just have one more bite?"

"*No*, sweetie, give me the spoon and go to bed. I mean it."

"Fine—here."

"Thank you… Uh, you're not going to *hug* me—no kiss *goodnight*?"

"Oh, sorry, mommy."

Bryan walked over to Kelissa and gave her the biggest hug a mother could ever receive from her child. "Oh, this is a *great* hug. Thank you, baby, I needed that," Kelissa said to Bryan. She then picked up the blue raspberry ice cream bucket and placed it back into the freezer. After that, Kelissa walked back to Bryan's room and tucked him in bed.

"Mommy?" Bryan said.

"Yes, sweetie?" Kelissa responded.

"Now that you're the President, does this mean that you're not going to be around as often?"

"Well, baby, mommy *will* be busy—*very* busy. So, yes, there will be times when I may have to travel to different places, different *countries*, and I *won't* be around."

"Oh, I see," Bryan said with disappointment.

"But listen, daddy will be around while I work."

"I understand."

Kelissa knew this moment would come—when her youngest son would be the most affected by her absence. As Kelissa rubbed on Bryan's head, she said to him, "Sweetie, listen, mommy has to run a country now. *Millions* of American citizens are expecting me to provide them with a stable economy, with stabled jobs so that they can take care of *their* families and live their best lives. And I *know* these last two years have been tough for you and Maddy *and* TJ. They've been tough for *me*. But just because I'm the President, that doesn't mean I'm not going to be your mother anymore. Okay?"

As Bryan turned around to face Kelissa, he said, "You promise that no matter what, we'll still be close?" Kelissa, now looking in his eyes as she said to him, "We'll be closer than we've ever been before. I *promise*, baby. *Nothing* will come between the bond of my children." That put a genuine smile on Bryan's face. Kelissa then kissed him goodnight, and right before she left the room, she said, "By the way, go to the bathroom and give your teeth a good brush—your mouth is all blue." Bryan then got out of his bed and did as his mother said.

As Bryan walked, he mentioned something to Kelissa about what Ted, Jr. said to him. Bryan said, "Mommy, can you check upstairs to make sure the old Presidents' ghosts aren't up there? TJ said that there are Presidents' ghosts up there." Kelissa, now irritated, told Bryan that there is no ghost *anywhere* in the White House and for him not to be afraid. "Don't let your brother scare you, honey. I'm going to have a talk with him right now," said Kelissa.

After Kelissa left Bryan's bedroom, she headed up to the residence's second floor to Ted, Jr's bedroom. There were several guest rooms on the second floor, a game room, and a music room. Making her way up the stairs, she heard the loud sounds of drums coming from the music room. Kelissa began walking down the center hall as she covered her ears as the pounding of the drums grew more piercing. She walked into the music room, seeing Ted, Jr. banging on the drums like Ringo Starr, hypnotically in the zone. "TJ! TJ! *TJ!*" Kelissa shouted.

"Oh, I'm sorry, Mom," said Ted, Jr. "Was I making too much noise?"

"Are you *kidding* me?" Kelissa sarcastically responded. "Any louder, you would have woken the *dead*."

"Sorry, Mom."

"*Speaking* of the dead, *why* would you tell your brother that ghosts live up here?"

"Oh, I *knew* he was going to squill on me. I only said that so he wouldn't come in my room."

"You *know* how he gets about that stuff."

"I was just *playing* with him, Mom. He's gotta grow up eventually."

"Yeah, and so do *you*."

"Alright, *fine*. I'll talk to him tomorrow and tell him it was just a joke."

"Good… And enough with the drums tonight, *please*? Get some rest; we all have a very long day tomorrow. Well, *I* do."

"I'll go to bed in a little bit, Mom. I was just getting started."

"It's 11:11 at night, go—to—*bed*."

"Whatever you say—*Mrs*. President."

"That's *Madam* President," Kelissa said as she pinched Ted, Jr.

"*Ouch*, mom!"

"President or not, I can still slap you upside your head, *smarty*."

"Goodnight, Mom."

"Goodnight, TJ."

As Kelissa made her way back down to the residence's first floor, she was ready to take that quick shower. She walked into her bedroom, where Ted, Sr. was already in bed, fast asleep. He has been sleeping for a little over an hour now. Kelissa didn't want to wake him, so she carefully grabbed her bathrobe and pajamas and tip-toed into the bathroom. She then placed her robe and pajamas on the hook of the bathroom door, leaving the door wide open. She was happy to see that her favorite soap, shampoo, and conditioner were placed in the shower as she requested.

Kelissa then turned the showerhead on as she began to undress. The shower is running as she looks at herself in the mirror. Carefully removing her shirt, then her underpants. She continues to stare at herself in the mirror, now in the nude. Kelissa looked at her body as she began to touch the spots—spots that were *stained* with bruises—bruises that were not accidental but were intentionally placed there through physical altercations. Kelissa was brutally decorated with *three* bruises: one on the left side of her rib cage, one on her left shoulder, and the other on her right thigh. These bruises have been there for the last several days. Yet no one besides herself knows when, where, or *who* is responsible for these bruises, not even her children.

Kelissa goes into the shower, rubbing the soap between her hands, lathering a foamy cloud to cover her bruises. As she washes her body, she begins to have these horrid flashbacks of when the bruises occurred. Every time she thought about it, she would cringe. Then, she put the shampoo in her hair and stood under thc rain shower head to rinse it. She closed her eyes, preventing the suds from getting into them. With her back turned to the shower door, Kelissa opened her eyes. She had a hazy vision, couldn't see as clearly until she turned around and saw a dark fuzzy figure outside the shower door.

"AHH!" Kelissa screamed.

"Would you like some company, baby?" Ted calmly asked.

"I—I was just about to get out."

"Okay, I'll see you in bed."

Kelissa was so startled at the sight of her husband standing outside of the shower. Her heart was beating so fast she had to take a few minutes to calm herself down. She then turned off the showerhead, slowly breathing to calm her nerves. After getting out of the shower, Kelissa dried herself off and put on her silky blue pajamas. She opened the bathroom door and walked through her dressing room to find Ted in bed, with his back to her. Kelissa just looked at him, still a bit shaken from that moment in the bathroom. Finally, she gets in the bed, with *her* back towards him. Since the bruise on her left shoulder still delivered pain, Kelissa could only sleep on her right side.

As a few minutes went by, there was no sound, no movement, and Kelissa began to close her eyes. Then suddenly, she hears Ted's voice. "How are the bruises?" Ted softly asked. Kelissa's eyes opened wide as she heard him. She turned her head towards him briefly, looking at him with disgust. She then turned around and responded, "They're still there, where *you* put them." After Kelissa said that, a back and forth discussion occurred.

"I lost my temper," said Ted. "It won't happen again."

"You keep saying that, *over* and *over* again, Ted—*saying* that it won't happen again," Kelissa emotionally responded.

"Believe me; it won't."

"This has to *stop*. I can't keep going through this. You keep putting your hands on me."

"Don't do this now, Kel—not tonight."

"I can't keep hiding this from our children—hiding the bruises."

"Maybe if you just *listen* to me when I give you advice, I won't get so *angry* with you."

"You have *no* right to keep putting your hands on me. I am the President now. I have a reputation and an image that I have to live up to."

"Go to sleep, Kel. And I don't want to hear any *more* of your *bitchin*."

Kelissa lays there in silence as she does not know what else to say at that moment. So, she said nothing. A few days ago, her husband, Ted, the First Gentleman, physically abused her. He has been doing so since the very beginning of her presidential run. Kelissa did not want to ruin her opportunity to run for the presidency. So, she hides this abuse from her children, parents, Secret Service, and the world. But now, Kelissa is faced with a traumatizing dilemma. She is the first woman President in United States history. But her secret is causing significant pain, mentally, physically, and emotionally. In the eyes of millions of American people, she is a hero. But in her *husband's* eyes, she is nothing more than a worthless punching bag that he purposely beats at his pleasure.

Chapter 4

Monday Morning, February 5th, 2024

Air Force One

Two weeks after being sworn in, President Kelissa Morrison has never been this busy before in her entire life. Meetings after meetings, documents to read, letters to write, it is just the beginning of her presidency. She is on her way to San Francisco to sit down with middle school students, who will be performing a musical recital in her honor. This middle school is one of the nation's top leading schools in performing arts, and Kelissa cannot wait to attend.

Before heading to her flight on Air Force One, Kelissa sits in the Oval Office while reading letters from the American people. The smile on her face is priceless—the gratitude in her soul for such kind and heartwarming words. The White House receives *thousands* of letters and emails addressing the President per day. Kelissa, depending on her schedule, reads at least seven letters a day. And she has responded with a written letter to every single person. One of the letters Kelissa received was from a seven-year-old girl. It was short but oh so sweet. In the written letter, the little girl said:

Dear President Morrison,

I am happy that you are the winner of the presidential race. When I grow up to be a woman like you, I want to be a hero for all future women, just like you are a hero to me. Seeing you on T.V. was magical, like a Disney movie. My favorite Disney movie is Finding Nemo. What's yours? I hope you read this letter so that you know how much you mean to me. I didn't know that girls could be leaders too. But you showed me that it's possible. Thank you.

I love you,
Amanda ☺

Kelissa was incredibly touched by this little girl's letter. Written in such very elementary handwriting, and the smiling face in the letter was made with an orange crayon. Kelissa immediately hand-wrote a letter to send to Amanda. In *Kelissa's* letter, she wrote:

Dearest Amanda,

Your kind words were very magical and heartwarming. I am so pleased to know that I am a hero of yours. I can tell that what you said came straight from the purity of your heart. It was honest and sincere. As you get older, promise me that you will never lose your honesty and purity. Even when life gets rough for you, never lose that honesty. Be brave, sweetheart, study hard, and blossom beyond your wildest dreams.

Most importantly, as you become a young woman, protect yourself and embrace your independence. By the way, my favorite Disney movie is *Snow White and the Seven Dwarfs*. But I also like *Cinderella*, maybe a bit more than Snow White.

God Bless you, Amanda.

P.S. I Love you too.

President Kelissa Morrison

Kelissa then signed the letter, big and bold, with the date on it as well. For some reason, Kelissa felt it was imperative to write in the letter that Amanda must protect herself and embrace her independence as she becomes a young woman. Because of the conflicted and abusive situation with her husband, Ted, Kelissa believes that a woman's independence is the armor that protects a woman's sanity. Kelissa then placed the letter in an envelope, ready to hand it over to her personal secretary, Joan Gamble.

There were a couple of knocks at the concealed door of the Oval Office. "Yes?" Kelissa projected. Secret Service agent, Carl McDaniel, informed Kelissa that everyone was ready to leave.

"We're ready to go, Madam President," said Carl.

"Great—*oh*, is Joan sitting at her desk right now?"

"She is."

"Can you give her this letter, please? I want to make sure it goes out as soon as possible."

"Yes, ma'am."

As Kelissa left the Oval Office, she ran into the White House photographer, Georgette Wilson, who came highly recommended by her favorite fashion designer, Dori McPhonzè. Georgette was a fashion photographer who switched to photographing political icons and public figures. Kelissa hired Georgette to be the White House photographer for the duration of her first term.

"Ah, Georgette," Kelissa smiled. "Just in time, we were on our way out."

"Good morning, Madam President. Thank you so much for bringing me on board. I've actually never been to San Francisco."

"*Really*? Well, I haven't been to Saint Fran since the beginning of my campaigning."

"Well, my cameras are ready, and I'm ready to get some snaps."

"Wonderful, you can ride in the back seat with me. That way, you can get some shots in now."

"Oh, great! That'll be fabulous."

As Kelissa puts on her coat and gloves, she walks towards the exit on the West Wing of the White House. The Marine Sentry was given three buzzer sounds as a signal to open the door and salute the President. Kelissa is still not used to the complete stillness and emotionless stance of the Marine Sentries. She finds their statue-like position genuinely fascinating. Carl, who is the head Secret Service agent and protects Kelissa at all times, is escorting Kelissa out to one of the black-armored Cadillac limousines known as "The Beast." For security reasons, the specs on the Beast are highly confidential, and whenever the motorcade is on the road, there is *always* two: Beast one and Beast two. As President, Kelissa must *always* enter the limousine from the door facing the exit and *never* walk *around* the car to enter from the other side.

"Madam President," Carl spoke.

"Yes, Carl?" Kelissa responded.

"Mr. Morrison will be joining you in Beast one instead of riding in Beast two.

"Oh, did he say why?"

"He said he wanted to discuss something with you in private."

"Well, *I'm* ready to go."

"Yes, ma'am, he's coming out now."

Five minutes later, Ted finally exits out of the White House with his detail leader. Secret Service always has a detailed leader for *each* 'protectee.' That also goes for the children. As Ted came into the Beast one, Kelissa said to him, "You're *late*, Ted. We're already behind schedule." Ted gave her a very distraught look as if he was saying something through his eyes—something with anger. Kelissa saw the aggressive expression on his face and said not another word to him.

They then took off in a motorcade of at least forty vehicles. For Kelissa, this is a whole new ball game, now that she is President of the United States of America. Her travels have to be orchestrated and planned out *weeks* ahead of time. *Everything* has to be precisely designed to run smoothly without any hiccups from point A to point B. Carl, as always, is positioned in the passenger seat of Beast one while Kelissa and Ted are together in the back seat, alone.

"Kel," said Ted. "I don't like it when you do that."

"When I do *what,* Ted?" Kelissa asked.

"When you talk *down* to me."

"How do I talk down to you?"

"You just said to me, 'Ted, you're *late.*' As if it was my *fault.*"

"We have a very tight schedule that we *must* follow, Ted."

"But you always make it seem like it's *my* fault all the time. *Don't* do that."

"My God, you're *such* a child."

"See? You do it again!"

"Ted, keep your *fucking* voice down."

"Kel… I'm *warning* you."

In Ted's eyes was the look of a profoundly troubled man—an *insanely* jealous man whose wife is now the leader of the free world. Kelissa knows that when it comes to her husband, Ted, who has a *very* short fuse, she must tread the waters extra carefully and not push any of his buttons. Even though she has the highest power in office and is the leader of the free world, it is a far cry from what she can control with her husband behind closed doors.

The motorcade has finally arrived at the heavily secured airbase. This moment is the first time Kelissa will take flight on Air Force One, a colossal, customized Boeing 747. As Beast one came to a complete stop, Kelissa's eyes lit up like a child with a sweet tooth at a candy store. She was looking at the beautiful blue and powder blue colors, seeing the words "UNITED STATES OF AMERICA" on the top side of the plane, the seal of the President of the United States on the side, and the American flag on the tail of the aircraft. "That is the most beautiful sight I've ever seen," Kelissa said to herself. Ted, however, did not say a word. He sat there in silence, a disturbing silence. Kelissa looked at him as if she wanted to tell him, "What is your fucking problem?" But she knew that if she added fuel to his fire, she would eventually get burned.

As Carl opened the back door to let Kelissa out, the Press pool was already outside, *freezing*, ready to greet their new President with dozens of clicking cameras. "Good morning, Madam President," was all that Kelissa heard. She waved her burgundy leather-gloved hand around as she walked alongside Ted as they were surrounded by Carl and over a dozen other Secret Service agents.

Security checks were tight and very professional. They have to be when the President is about to board the plane. Kelissa was really on cloud nine as she climbed up the stairs to board Air Force One. The

President is always the last to board the plane after everyone else has gone through security checks and has come on board. As Kelissa reached the top of the stairs, she turned around and began to wave her hand high. Ironically, she was waving to no one. The only people standing on the ground were the press as they were still snapping pictures, capturing the moment of her entering Air Force One. The motorcade was then boarded onto the C7 Galaxy Air Force cargo plane, holding the two armored Beast limousines. In case of emergency, the Beast one has to remain open until President Morrison has safely reached her destination.

As Kelissa and Ted entered Air Force One, they were greeted by the chief flight attendant, Sam Schumacher, and the chief presidential pilot, Mark Webster.

"Good morning, Madam President," said Mark.

"Good morning," Kelissa said. "You're Mark, I take it?"

"Yes, ma'am."

"Great! And you must be Sam?"

"Yes, Madam President," said Sam.

"Pleasure," Kelissa said with a smile.

"We'll be taking off right away, Madam President."

"Sounds great, Mark. Oh my God, excuse my manners. Sam, Mark, this is my hus—"

"Ted, nice to meet you two," Ted swiftly spoke as he cut off Kelissa. "Can someone escort me to the restroom?"

"Yes, sir, it's right this way," said Carl.

A little embarrassed by Ted's rudeness, Kelissa wanted to go straight to her office. Allison, the second flight attendant, escorted Kelissa to her office. As the door opened to the Oval Office in the sky, Kelissa walked in at a complete loss for words. She could not believe that she had made it—she was on board Air Force One. She looked around at the office, admiring the design, the couch, the large television, and her desk. It was all becoming authentic.

"Would you like something to drink after we takeoff, Madam President?" Allison asked.

"Yes, I would *love* some tea, please," Kelissa smiled. "Oh, with honey and sugar."

"Yes, ma'am."

Air Force One was already moving, about to taxi down the runway for takeoff. And that is how it works. Once the President has boarded Air Force One, the plane immediately gets ready for takeoff. Those accompanying President Kelissa Morrison on Air Force One is the Secret Service agents, senior advisors, and traveling press. There is also a permanent doctor on board. Kelissa wanted to make sure there would be press on board to get her first looks in the Oval Office in the sky.

Everyone's seatbelts were securely fastened, and Air Force One picked up speed down the runway. Kelissa is soaking deeply in this particular moment, hearing the sounds of the engine roar as she takes flight and makes history.

Chapter 5

Monday Morning, February 5th, 2024

Air Force One-Press Play

Three hours have gone by, nothing but smooth, turbulence-free flying on Air Force One. President Kelissa Morrison sits at her desk in her office, wearing a navy-blue suit, white blouse, and the famous American flag pin on her left lapel. Dozens of snapshots a second as the press click away on their cameras, capturing every angle of the President. As Kelissa sips on her tea, the press begins with their questions.

"Madam President," said the reporter. "How does it feel to fly on Air Force One for the first time?"

"This is a true honor and a privilege," Kelissa spoke. "To be flying on such a historical, iconic aircraft. I'm practically speechless."

"Madam President," said the second reporter. "Now that you're in office, what are some of your priorities when it comes to policy?"

"Well, definitely one of my *top* priorities is decreasing unemployment. Ever since the pandemic, the unemployment rates have been unpredictable. My administration has been working countless hours to find the best solution for our country to get back on its feet."

"Uh, Mr. Presi—" the reporter accidentally said. "Oh my God, I'm *so* sorry—*Madam* President."

"It's a *whole new ball game*," Kelissa laughed. "That's okay—continue, please.

The press had a good laugh on that one. Even Carl, the head Secret Service agent, had half of a smirk on his face. Everyone in the office smiled, except for Ted—standing behind the press. Kelissa saw his emotionless face. She tried her best to ignore it and paid him no mind. But he was undoubtedly the elephant in the room.

After the press finished their barrage of loaded questions, Kelissa toured Air Force One. She explored the Situation Room, the medical room, and other confidential locations where she may have to be transferred if any emergencies occurred. Kelissa loved every bit of Air Force One. She loved the designs of the rooms, the delicious entrees, and the luxurious bathroom.

The plane was soon to land in San Francisco. So, Kelissa decided to spend the rest of her time in her office. As she sat at her desk, she read essential documents—signing confidential papers as she sips on more tea. As she continued to look over other documents, there was a knock at the door.

"Come in," said Kelissa. "Yes, Carl?"

"Madam President, is it a good time to go over the rope line procedure?"

"Uh, yes, sure, we can do that."

"Okay, so, *basically*, people will be behind the barricade, waving their hands and so forth. When you reach out to shake people's hands, it is best that you *don't* overextend yourself. Maintain your distance."

"Understood. And you'll be by my side?"

"*Of course*, I will. As well as several other agents."

"Carl, can I ask you something?"

"Yes, Madam President."

"Why do you do this?"

"It's my job."

"Yes, I *know* that. But *why*? Why risk your life for one person day in, day out?"

"It's what I choose to do—*somebody* has to do it, right? It might as well be me. Besides, I've been protecting presidents and politicians for over thirty years, and I'm still standing."

"Yeah, well, I'm *glad* that I have you to protect me. I appreciate you."

"It's my duty and my pleasure, Madam President."

Kelissa always wanted to ask that question. Why would someone want not only to dedicate their lives but *risk* their lives, protecting a stranger? Kelissa connected with Carl to remedy that, and they began to know more about each other. Another knock at the door, Carl walks over to open it. It was Ted, holding a bowl of fresh fruit in one hand and a bottle of Perrier sparkling water.

"Carl," said Ted. "You mind if I have a word with my wife in private?"

"Sure, Mr. Morrison," Carl responded.

"But wait," Kelissa spoke. "Ted—*Carl* and I were going over the rope line procedure."

"It'll only take a second," Ted reassured.

"Not a problem," Carl said. "I can wait outside."

"Thank you, Carl," Ted responded.

Ted sat on the beige suede couch across from Kelissa's desk as Carl left the office. Ted sat there, taking huge bites out of his large, juicy strawberries. Kelissa was expecting Ted to speak as he said he wanted to talk with her privately but said not a word. He sat on the couch, staring at her while she read documents. As Kelissa looked up from the papers, she saw Ted staring at her with a very familiar look on his face. It was the look of a troubled man. "What did you have to say, Ted?" Kelissa asked. But Ted did not respond immediately. Instead, he stood up from the couch with his bowl of fruit and walked over to Kelissa. Kelissa is very familiar with Ted's violent tendencies and grew nervous as he approached her.

Ted stood behind Kelissa and placed his bowl of fruit on the desk. She had no idea of what he was planning to do. She did not know whether or not he was going to slap her upside her head or possibly put her in a chokehold. But Ted picked up a strawberry, dangling it in front of Kelissa's mouth. "Take a bite—they're *delicious*," Ted sarcastically said. Kelissa swiftly jerked her head away from the strawberry. She looked up at him with a face of agitation and said, "Ted, you *know* I'm allergic to strawberries." Kelissa is, in fact, allergic to several things: strawberries, dogs, cats, as well as the chemicals in specific food coloring. So, unfortunately, there will be no dogs for the First family.

"I just thought I would set the mood for us," Ted said seductively.

"What mood?" Kelissa asked.

"Well, I always wanted to join the mile-high club. And what better plane to do it on than *Air Force One*?"

"You're joking, right?"

"Does it look like I'm joking?"

"Your timing could not be any worse, Ted. Not to mention, you picked the *worst* fruit to try to seduce me with."

"*Why* do you *always* have to ruin the *fucking* moment?"

"Ted, you're trying to seduce me with *literally* a forbidden fruit, right before we land? No, let's *not* do this right now."

"I swear, this President shit has gotten *so deep* into your head. I told you before, Kel—*I'm* still the man of the house. We may live in the *White House*, but *I'm* the man of the house."

"Ted, *please* leave my office."

Ted just stared at Kelissa, smiling at her with a menacing demeanor. He took his bowl of fruit—slowly shook his head, and left her office. As Ted left, Carl then entered the office. "Carl, I'm sorry, could I just have a few minutes alone, please?" Kelissa asked. Carl obliged and told her that they would be landing in fifteen minutes.

Kelissa, sitting there at her desk, tried to make sense of what just happened with her husband, Ted. He was always romantic with Kelissa throughout their marriage. He knew how to turn her on. But that romance was tainted by Ted's sexual aggressiveness. When it came to the bedroom, Ted no longer made love to Kelissa; he made pain. But now, it was time for Kelissa to take that nonsensical scene out of her mind as she prepared herself for landing and walking the rope line.

Chapter 6

Monday Afternoon, February 5th, 2024

The Eagle Has Landed

Air Force One has touched down. The C7 Galaxy Air Force cargo plane landed a few minutes before Air Force One, making sure President Morrison's motorcade was aligned and ready to go. Kelissa, looking out the window to a large crowd. Some people had signs of her name with her slogan, while others were waving miniature American flags around in their hands. As the stairs made their way up against the plane, Ted was missing in action for the grand exit.

"Carl," said Kelissa, "Where is Ted?"

"We're looking for him now, Madam President," Carl responded.

"Why does he *always* have to be *fucking* late? *Always*."

Kelissa wanted to exit out of the plane with Ted by her side. She wanted that perfect photo opportunity of the first woman President and the First Gentleman making their grand exit. But Ted once again was the cause of the delay. Kelissa was beginning to get very vocal on the plane. "*Jesus*, he's holding everything up—it's only but *so* many places he could be on this plane. Can someone please locate him and tell him to get here *now*?" Kelissa projected.

Finally, Ted came from the back of the plane. He said he was stuck in the bathroom and could not get out. Kelissa, however, already aggravated, told him off. "Ted, it would be *great* if you could get with the program and stop holding everyone *up*! We are *all* on a strict schedule—do you *think* you could get on the same page?" Kelissa's stern voice caused a sudden silence on the plane. Ted began to look around at the group, embarrassed at Kelissa calling him out in front of everyone. As Ted looked at Kelissa, he said, "My apologies, everyone. Won't happen again."

Finally, the airplane door has opened. Before stepping out, Kelissa locked hands with Ted. Ted looked down at their locked hands and then looked up to Kelissa as *she* looked at him. He then smiled while he began to squeeze the life out of her hand viciously. He wanted Kelissa to feel every ounce of anger coursing through his veins. Ted was starting to cut the blood circulation in her hand. Kelissa knew that her rage and frustrations had gotten the best of her and that she would have to pay for it later.

As Kelissa and Ted stepped out of Air Force One, the crowd went wild. People cheering, screaming, waving their signs and flags around. Kelissa has the biggest smile on her face right now. She waves back at the crowd as they go down the stairs. Secret Service agents were already in position as Kelissa began to work the rope line.

"Ted," said Kelissa. "Please, *please*, let go of my hand?"

"I'll be riding in the other limousine," Ted spoke.

"Fine."

Ted was holding Kelissa's left hand so excessively tight that she lost feeling for a solid minute. But the distraction of her gorgeous smile blinded the crowd from acknowledging the tension between her and Ted. That was the thing about Kelissa. She is walking around in pain, her bruises are covered, yet no one knows. That contagious smile of hers—no one, absolutely *no one*, could see through it. No one could see the torment she faces from her husband.

Kelissa carried along for a few more moments, shaking the hands of American citizens, but was ready to wrap things up. "Okay, Carl, I'm ready to move out when you guys are," Kelissa said. White House photographer, Georgette Wilson, was allowed to sit in the back seat of the Beast one with Kelissa to take some snapshots. As Georgette was capturing the image of President Morrison, Kelissa began to stare out of the window. She was in deep thought about what would come later on once she was alone with Ted. Kelissa regretted how she lost her cool, telling him off in front of everyone after he warned her not to. Starting to gain feeling in her left hand, Kelissa removed her glove, revealing the redness after Ted squeezed it. But because Georgette was taking pictures, she immediately put her glove back on. Kelissa then attempted to make conversation with Georgette.

"If only I could roll down this window and get some fresh air," Kelissa sighed.

"Oh, I'll do that for you, Madam President," Georgette responded.

"NO! You can't roll the windows down," Kelissa chuckled. "For security reasons, they have to remain up."

"Oh, I'm sorry, I didn't know that."

"It's okay; I was just saying I wish I *could* roll down a window and get some fresh air."

"Do you want me to stop with the pictures?"

"Oh no, *please*, continue. Click away."

The motorcade followed a very orchestrated route to the middle school. Kelissa was busy in the back seat reading documents as she regained all the feeling in her left hand. Ted must have squeezed it like he was trying to squeeze the last drop of water out of a sponge.

Georgette Wilson was clicking away with her camera. Being that they were sitting in the back of the Beast one, Georgette only had so many angles she could take pictures of Kelissa. At one moment, Kelissa began to look out the window, looking at the San Francisco skyline. The last time she was there was during her campaign run two years previous to her presidential election. Kelissa, however, is a native of San Francisco.

In the Financial District, she was born and raised by Gregory and Suzanne, Kelissa's father and mother. But Kelissa's parents had their sights set higher and moved to Pacific Heights. The cost of living in San Francisco has always been set at an exorbitant standard. Gregory and Suzanne, however, were not intimidated by the high price neighborhood, being that they were both making a substantial six-figure salary.

Kelissa's father, Gregory, is a retired child psychiatrist. He specialized in children between the ages of 5-14 years old. In his forty-five-year career, he saw over 15,000 patients. Many of the children he helped, but some kids were too far removed from reality, and there was no coming back for them.

Kelissa's mother, Suzanne, retired from interior designing. She worked for a company based in San Francisco and became a senior partner. Suzanne's vision was unique and original, which put her in a league of her own. She even gave Kelissa some pointers on decorating certain rooms in the White House. Their lifestyle was a sophisticated one. But being that her parents had such high demanding careers, Kelissa barely spent time with them. Not to mention, she is an only child.

But Kelissa did not take that as a weakness. She gained a strong base of independence and an interest in helping others. After Kelissa graduated from high school, she decided to go into the military and became a nurse, caring for wounded soldiers. She also became a mentor to the veterans who had post-traumatic stress disorder. That was always Kelissa's passion; to help people.

The motorcade had arrived at the middle school right on time. Kelissa was looking forward to listening to the music the middle schoolers had prepared for them. The *San Francisco Middle School of the Arts*, where Kelissa attended *herself*, in the seventh and eighth grades. As Carl opened the back seat door, Kelissa stepped out, looking up to the building. She began to look around, reminiscing about when she was that young child with her lunch box in her hand, escorted by either her nanny or one of her grandparents.

People were on the other side of the street, barricaded off. Secret Service is always ten steps ahead of the curve, protecting the President's every waking move. There were snipers on multiple rooftops, dozens of San Francisco police officers on the grounds, all prepared for the President's visit. Ted made his way towards Kelissa as they began to walk up the stairs of the middle school, surrounded by Secret Service agents. The middle school principal, Mrs. Walker, and some staff and faculty waited inside. As Kelissa entered, she was greeted with praise.

"Madam President," said Mrs. Walker. "It is so *great* to have you here. To have you here is *truly* an honor and a pleasure."

"Oh, the pleasure's all *mine*," said Kelissa. "Thank you for having me. Now, where are these *talented* musicians? I'm *dying* to hear them play."

"Oh, right this way. The seating arrangements are set."

Carl began to orchestrate and position the other Secret Service agents around the area. The agents were at their designated locations of every exit in the middle school. In case of any emergencies, they know where and how to escort the President out safely.

As Kelissa made her way through the halls, her reminiscing thoughts continued. She remembered the time when she would run the hallways with her friends, and the security guard would catch them and send them to the office. In the seventh grade, she remembered that one of her classmates, Jessica, was bullied by some older kids in gym class. But Jessica could not take the bullying any longer. She balled up her fist and swung with all her might, but Jessica missed. The older kids then ganged up on Jessica and beat her to a pulp. Jessica could barely move. The ambulance had to be called, and Jessica was rushed to the hospital. Kelissa never saw or heard anything else about Jessica again. She always wondered what had happened to her. But Kelissa learned something that day in the gym. She learned to face her fears and stand up for herself, and even if she missed, just keep on swinging.

Before President Kelissa entered the auditorium, where the concert was taking place, the school principal, Mrs. Walker, gave a brief speech to the hand-selected classes in attendance and then introduced their guest of honor. "Ladies and gents, it is with *great* pleasure to welcome our nation's *first* woman President of the United States of

America. Could you *please* give a round of applause for President Kelissa Morrison?" Mrs. Walker proudly projected.

The auditorium doors opened, loud noise and clapping little hands from the dozens of students in the first four rows began to roar. Kelissa waved her hand to the crowd of rambunctious little ones. The kids were not allowed to bring their cellphones to the concert, for security purposes, of course. Georgette Wilson, White House photographer, was snapping away from different angles, practically making herself invisible as she captured some fantastic shots. Before the concert began, Kelissa wanted to greet some of the students. Kelissa shook the students' hands and asked for their names. She adored their ambition and energy.

After a few minutes went by, the concert was ready to begin. Kelissa's seating arrangements were set centered to the far back of the auditorium. Kelissa and Ted must be seated in seats closer to the nearest exit for security reasons. There were two exits: one to the right and one to the left. Kelissa and Ted were placed in between the two entries, with Secret Service guarding the doors, the main interest, the exits in the back of the stage, *and* standing guard of The Beast one and two.

As Kelissa and Ted took their seats, the music instructor began the concert. The music starts by playing a very familiar tune. A tune that Kelissa has been *deeply* in love with since she was a teenager. Of course, the students were playing '*Eleanor Rigby*,' by The Beatles. Kelissa could not be any happier to hear them playing The Beatles.

She is overly obsessed with The Beatles music catalog, songs like '*Michelle, Girl, Yellow Submarine, And I Love Her, I Want to Hold Your Hand, Strawberry Fields Forever, A Taste of Honey, Help,*' you name it, she's heard it and *loved* it. Kelissa hopes to meet Paul McCartney and Ringo Starr during her presidency.

As the concert is going, Kelissa enjoys every minute of it—tapping her bare feet on the floor after she removed her heels, in sync with the cadence of the music. She briefly looks at Ted, sitting right next to her. She notices his unamused face. But she refused to let him take away her joy in this exciting moment. Kelissa was having such a great time listening to these highly gifted young children.

"I'm going to the restroom," Ted whispered.

"*Now*?" Kelissa responded.

"*No*, how about two years ago? Yes, *now*."

Ted's sarcastic remark almost took the joy away. But Kelissa immediately refocused her attention on the concert. Several Secret Service agents escorted Ted to the restroom while Kelissa continued to sit and enjoy the musical magic.

There was one song left in the show—a song that was written so long ago by French composer Erik Satie; Gymnopédie No. 1. There was pure silence in that auditorium—you could hear the fading echo of a pin drop. Kelissa never listened to this song in a live performance. It was perfect; she could not *believe* the musical genius of these young kids. As she listened to the music, she reminisced again. She thought about her disturbing situation with her husband, Ted. In her mind, she knew that it was getting worse. Ted's violent tendencies began to grow, and his punches left darker marks on her body. And yet, Kelissa has been keeping this away from the public for the past two years. Her parents know nothing of her situation with Ted, not even Carl or her children.

As that beautifully melancholy song ended, the young children in the audience began to give a round of applause. The clapping hands awoke Kelissa as she was still daydreaming about her abusive secret. She then wiped the few tears from her right eye as the combination of emotions from the music and the reminiscing got to her. Kelissa then stood up with *her* clapping hands and a smile, blowing kisses to the students on stage. She was so pleased by their incredibly extravagant performance.

After the performance, Mrs. Walker asked Kelissa if she could come up to the podium to accept a gift that she would find warmly useful. Carl and several other Secret Service agents walked down the aisle with Kelissa and stood up on stage to receive the gift. The gift was placed in a patriotic bag, wrapped in sheet paper. As Kelissa removed the gift from the bag and unwrapped it, it was a thick-knitted scarf with the colors of red, white, and blue. Kelissa was so touched that she had this to say, "This is such a wonderful gift. Thank you all *so* much for this sensational performance. I am *so* proud of this *talented* group of young scholars. Your music touched the very core of my soul. You've made my day, and I thank you for this scarf. And I will definitely *use* it because it is *freezing* now in Washington D.C."

As the middle school students, faculty, and staff continued to clap and cheer, Kelissa saw Ted standing in the far back of the auditorium near the exit. The same stoneface look he had before he used the restroom is what Kelissa saw. She stayed for a few more minutes, taking pictures with the students. Georgette was still snapping away with her camera, capturing a plethora of shots. Kelissa also took a group photo with the students who performed on stage, with Carl standing a few feet away. Carl and the other Secret Service agents; they *have* to keep their hands free at all times and could *not* carry the gift bag. But the gift was *thoroughly* inspected to make sure there were no suspicious objects *hidden* inside the bag.

Overall, Kelissa could not ask for a better day to spend her time. But now, it was time to go. Carl then spoke into his earpiece, preparing the Secret Service agents for Kelissa's exit from the school and into The Beast one.

"Madam President," said Carl. "We're ready to exit."

"Okay, great!" Kelissa responded.

"Mr. Morrison said he will ride in Beast two again."

"Okay then… Well, shall we?"

Kelissa was escorted out of the middle school. It was surprisingly cold outside at forty-nine degrees, yet there were hundreds of people cheering on the President, screaming, and hollering voices coming from across the street. But there was no time for meet and greets. The motorcade departure had to be on schedule. As Kelissa made her way into The Beast one, she took a deep breath and exhaled. As the limousine drives off, she prepares herself for a long flight back home at 1600 Pennsylvania Avenue. She *also* mentally prepares herself for the possible argument with Ted.

Chapter 7

Monday Evening, February 5th, 2024

This Has to Stop

A tired President now sits in her office after having a meeting in the conference room of Air Force One. Kelissa cannot wait to be home in the White House, under her blue, silky smooth bed sheets. The rest of the staff are seated, counting sheep while they have a chance. As Kelissa sat at her desk, she made a call to her youngest son, Bryan.

"Hi, sweetie," said Kelissa. "How was school today?"

"It was okay. But mommy, I'm having a hard time."

"A hard time with what, honey—with school?"

"No, with this whole life change. Living in this big White House, surrounded by these strange guys in black suits. It's hard."

As they continue to talk on the phone, Kelissa says to Bryan, "Listen, sweetie, we talked about this the night we first moved in the White House. I *know* this is very difficult for you right now—changing homes, transferring into a new school, making new friends. It's hard for all of you guys. It'll be a struggle for the first year, but as time goes on, everything will be okay."

As Kelissa continued talking on the phone, there was a knock at the door. "Come in!" Kelissa projected. It was Ted, peeking his head through the opening of the door. Kelissa, giving Ted a very umbrageous look, said to Bryan on the phone, "Sweetie, your father just walked into my office. I'll see you soon. Get some sleep, okay?" Kelissa kept her eye on Ted as she gently placed the phone back on the base.

"*Your* office?" Ted sarcastically said.

"Yes, *my* office, Ted. Is that a problem?"

"No, no—*no* problem at all. But what I *do* have a problem with is how you disrespected me in front of *everyone* this morning."

"Ted, listen. I'm only trying to set a good example."

"A good *example*?"

"*Yes*, I don't want people staggering around, showing up late, and that includes *you*!"

Kelissa stood up from her desk as the argument continued, making her way to the presidential bathroom. Ted was still standing at the desk with a very dark, troubled look. It was as if you could see the *fury* rippling throughout his skin. As Kelissa stood in the bathroom, she began to remove her makeup while looking at herself in the mirror.

As Kelissa looks in the mirror, she sees Ted's reflection as he walks in the bathroom, gently closing the door behind him. She turned around, saying, "Ted, what are you *do*—" Ted aggressively wrapped his hands around her neck as he began to choke her. Kelissa, now gasping for air, desperately trying to stop Ted by slapping his arms repeatedly.

"Te—*Ted*!" Kelissa pantingly said.

"*Shut up*!" Ted said with a silent, savage tone.

"*Please—Ted—*STOP!"

Ted was choking Kelissa so viciously tight; she was on the path of unconsciousness. Her legs were starting to give way. As Ted saw her face turning red, he suddenly let her go as she fell straight to the bathroom floor—gasping for every ounce of air her lungs could absorb. "You continue to disrespect me, and *this* will be the repercussions," Ted softly spoke. Kelissa—lying helplessly on the bathroom floor as Ted made his way out of the bathroom.

Five minutes go by, Kelissa is crying her eyes out in the bathroom. Her tears left a clear trail on the marble floor: the heavy breathing, the fear, the trauma, and the sudden shock running chaotically through her veins. Kelissa held on to the edge of the sink to slowly pull herself up—barely able to stand on her own two feet. She burst into tears, observing her defeated, mortified reflection in the mirror. Her face was red, with some of her makeup still intact. Ted choked her so aggressively that his handprints were still visible. Then suddenly, there was *another* knock at the office door.

"Madam President, It's Carl. May I come in?"

"No," Kelissa swiftly responded. "Don—don't come in, Carl. Just one moment, please."

Kelissa could not let Carl see the aftermath of her compellingly enduring, abusive situation. Still coughing, now trying to clear her sore throat. But she had to think quickly and move swiftly. She needed something to cover her bruised neck. "Madam President?" Carl said. Kelissa, panicking as she says, "Yes, Carl, one minute, *please."* Then Kelissa looked over to the couch and saw the gift bag. The same gift bag she received from the middle school. She remembered they gave her the red, white, and blue scarf. Kelissa immediately reached for the bag, ripped out the scarf, and quickly wrapped it around her neck. Carl knocked once again, and Kelissa finally opened the office door.

"Hi Carl," said Kelissa. "*Sorry* to keep you waiting. Is there a problem?"

"I should be asking *you* that question, Madam President," Carl responded. "Is everything alright?"

"Oh... *Yes*, I was just in the bathroom. Had some stomach cramps."

"Would you like for me to get Dr. Dickinson?"

"Oh no, no, I'm—I'm *fine*. It's just a woman thing. But I would *love* some more tea, please—with honey and lemon."

"Yes, ma'am, I'll notify the flight attendant. I see that scarf came in handy."

"Oh, Carl… You have *no idea*."

"Oh, and I was just coming to let you know that we'll be landing in 45 minutes."

"45 minutes—got it, thank you, Carl."

"My pleasure, Madam President. I'll have them bring the tea for you right away."

"Sounds good, than—" Kelissa groans. "*Excuse* me, *thanks*, Carl."

"By the way, a reminder that Bryan and Madeline's school have a delayed opening tomorrow."

"Delayed opening, okay. Thank you for all the info, Carl."

As Kelissa closed the door to her office, she took a deep breath and sighed with her back against the door—slowly sliding down, collapsing to the floor. The look on her face was like never before; she was devastated. Ted never choked her before—this was the closest he had ever come to harming her face. The insanity of his evil abuse is so strategic. To avoid being found out, Ted *never* hits Kelissa in her face, only her body, which she can cover with clothing. And being that it is the winter season, Kelissa will be fully clothed and covered up for quite some time.

Still sitting on the carpet floor, a softly crying Kelissa repositioned her body, now on her knees in a praying position. "Father, who art in heaven, I pray for your protection. I am so lost, so trapped. Please give me the strength, the wisdom, and show me the way out of this brutal insanity. Give me the courage, and I beg of you, father—If *anything* happens to me, I *beg* of you, please protect my children. Amen."

Kelissa now realizes that she is in serious trouble. Ted could have killed her, and there is no one she could tell. If Kelissa were to say something to anyone, everything she's worked hard for—*everything* she has become, an icon in this country, it all would come tumbling down. It would all be over. And Kelissa's pride is not ready to let all of this go. She can't let it go—she is the leader of the free world, and she refuses to have it all come crashing down. But *this* has never happened before. Even though it was the first time Ted had choked Kelissa, she feared it would not be the last.

Chapter 8

Monday Evening, February 5th, 2024

A Pain in the Neck

It is 11:11 p.m. The motorcade reached its destination over an hour ago, and President Kelissa Morrison is at home on 1600 Pennsylvania Avenue. Both her and Ted are on the residential level of the White House. Ted is in their bedroom, sleeping like an innocent baby as if nothing even happened tonight. Kelissa is in her private office, sitting at her desk as the tears run down her face. Because the residence level has no cameras, the First family has all the privacy they need. Kelissa does *not* allow Secret Service on the residence level unless there is an emergency. Ironically, that works in Ted's favor.

Ted left his mark on Kelissa's neck. The bruising around her neck had a darkened red color, and the pain went into full effect. Kelissa told a lie to Dr. Dickinson, the doctor on duty on Air Force One—telling him that her allergies were becoming a burden due to the winter chills, and she was given two tablets of ibuprofen. As Kelissa was getting herself together in her private office, she called one of the kitchen staffers to bring her some tea. As she waited for the tea, Kelissa watched a movie called '*The Shawshank Redemption*,' starring Tim Robbins and Morgan Freeman. It was towards the end of the film where the character of Andy was crawling through the dreadful sewage tunnel, escaping prison to have his freedom.

As Kelissa watched, she could not help but shed more tears, realizing how much she could relate to being in prison. The fact that she *is* in a prison of constant abuse, and no one, not *no one,* can help her but herself. But how? *How* could the most powerful woman in the world reveal such a dark, abusive truth and *still* keep her position of power? How can she break free of the torment her abusive husband bitterly bestows upon her? Only two months into her presidency, how will she be able to survive? Heaven only knows.

Chapter 9

Tuesday Morning, February 6th, 2024

Midnight with a knife

There is a delay with the tea. Kelissa called the kitchen staffers and asked them to bring up two slices of pecan pie topped with whipped cream. When it comes to foods and drinks for President Kelissa Morrison, the kitchen staffers thoroughly screen everything before the President consumes any foods and beverages. Midnight was approaching, and after what happened to her, Kelissa was restless. Then came a knock at her office door. As Kelissa wiped her teary eyes, she responded.

"Yes?" Kelissa projected.

"Madam President," said the butler. "I have your pie and tea."

"Oh, yes, please come in."

"Hi, Madam President, sorry for the delay. Is there anything else you need?"

"No, that'll be all... Um, can you tell me your name again, please?"

"My name is Vanessa, Diaz."

"Thank you, Vanessa. I'm sort of a midnight snack kind of woman."

"Oh, it is my pleasure, ma'am."

"I appreciate it. Have a good night, Vanessa."

"You as well, Madam President."

Kelissa still had a scarf over her neck to cover the bruises. But *this* time, she had a black scarf covering her neck. After Vanessa left the office, Kelissa poured the piping hot tea into the cup. She then removed the silver cover, revealing two large slices of pecan pie, topped with a swirly batch of whipped cream. On the side of the tray were a spoon, a fork, and a butter knife. But there was another knife on the tray, a much *sharper* knife, sharper to easily cut through the unsliced lemon. Kelissa picked up the knife and began to stare at it. As the knife's glary reflection was diagonally cast across her face, Kelissa had a sudden thought dancing in her mind.

Kelissa opened the door to her private office, slowly peeking her head out, making sure none of her kids saw her. She steps out of her office, gently walking down the center hall towards her bedroom. As she makes it to the bedroom door, she reaches for the doorknob with her right hand, and what is she holding in her left? The knife.

Kelissa carefully opened her bedroom door and walked in. The lights were off; it was quiet, still, and Ted was fast asleep. She began to walk her way towards him slowly. Kelissa stood there, looking down at him with that knife firmly gripped in her hand. She began to think about the day when his violent tendencies would become too much for her, and she would have to defend herself. But Kelissa knows she could not possibly handle Ted physically. But with a *knife*, she would perhaps have a chance.

"GO TO HELL!" Ted suddenly shouted in his sleep. Kelissa was so startled that she jumped in place and dropped the knife on the floor. Her fast-paced breathing made her a nervous wreck. She picked up the knife and carefully went to *her* side of the bed, quietly placing the knife in the drawer of her nightstand, and hurried out of the bedroom. As Kelissa's back was turned coming out of the room, there was a swift touch to her right shoulder.

"AHH!" Kelissa screamed. "Maddy, are you *trying* to give me a heart attack?"

"I'm *sorry,* Mom… I heard some noise, so I figured you were still up."

"Jesus, Maddy, *yes*, I'm still up. But what are *you* still doing up? It's a school night."

"I know, Mom. I couldn't really fall asleep. Still getting used to living in the White House, you know?"

"Yeah, I know, honey. You guys have been trying to adapt to this *whole new* living arrangement."

"Yeah, it's just *strange* to have people in black suits follow you around everywhere you go."

"I know it's a lot to deal with, sweetie. But things will get better. *Hey*, how about we continue our girl-talk in my office? I have two slices of pecan pie."

"Oh, *awesome*, okay. Oh, and can we watch a movie too?"

"For a little while, it's still a school night."

Kelissa and Madeline sat on the comfy brown suede couch in her office. They devoured the pecan pie, now binge-watching *Seinfeld*. Madeline never laughed so hard, but Kelissa had to be careful with her laughter. She was still in pain from almost being choked to death by Ted. But to make sure her daughter did not grow suspicious of anything, Kelissa gave off a few chuckles. Every time Kelissa took a bite of the pecan pie, it caused a sudden pain to her throat when she swallowed. As the binge-watching continued, Kelissa took a look at the clock on the wall and saw that it was five minutes past two o'clock in the morning.

"Maddy, sweetie," said Kelissa. "I think we *both* should get some sleep."

"Okay, Mom. By the way, why are you wearing that scarf? Isn't that making your neck hot?"

"The *scarf*?" Kelissa said while touching the scarf. "Oh, I've been wearing it since I got off the plane, and I just never took it off."

"Oh, well, you have on your *pajamas*, so I was wondering why you would still have on your *scarf*."

"I just had a little chill, Maddy. That's all."

"*Okay*, it's just a little awkward to me."

"You know what, we should *really* get some sleep—*hectic* day tomorrow," Kelissa said as she kissed Madeline. "Good night, sweetie. I love you."

"I love you too, Mom."

Kelissa was not going to beat around the bush with Madeline. The bruises on her neck were hidden—right underneath that black scarf. Kelissa felt incredibly terrible to keep this a secret from her daughter, *knowing* that she would die if *Madeline* kept any abusive secrets hidden from *her*. As Madeline went back to her bedroom, Kelissa made a quick stop to the room of her youngest son, Bryan. As she opened the door, Bryan was wrapped up in his blanket like a burrito, comatose. She quietly walked over to kiss him on the back of his head.

Kelissa stared at Bryan for a solid minute. After what happened that evening on Air Force One, she knew that this violent dilemma could no longer go on and had to stop. But she understands that something as ugly as this will not just disappear on its own. Kelissa is so lost, trapped between power and abuse.

As Kelissa made her way back to her bedroom, Ted was still asleep, with a snore or two; she then walked into the bathroom and closed the door. She looked at her reflection in the mirror—gently removed her scarf, and saw the aftermath of what Ted did to her. Kelissa began to touch her neck, utterly disgusted with herself for tolerating such abuse.

She then closed her eyes, shaking her head at her bruised image as it *burned* through the good memories they shared before the campaign run. Ted was not always like this.

When Kelissa opened her eyes, a single teardrop streamed down her face. But at that moment, she realized that she had to pull herself together to prepare for that busy morning. But the one thing Kelissa was *not* going to do was sleep in the same bed with Ted. So, she grabbed her pillow, one of the extra sheets from the bed, and decided to sleep in one of the guest bedrooms on the second-floor residence. As Kelissa made her way out of her bedroom, heading up the stairs, she realized that she had forgotten her scarf in her bathroom. Leaving the pillow and bed sheet on the stairs, Kelissa headed back to her bedroom, as she would try her best not to wake up Ted. But as she walked into her bedroom, Ted was no longer in bed.

As soon as Kelissa saw the image of the empty bed, a slight chill went up to her spine. And before she could even inhale, Ted came from behind the door, wrapped his arms around Kelissa, with his hand covering her mouth, preventing her from screaming.

"AH—" Kelissa screamed before Ted covered her mouth.

"Shhhhhh…" Ted softly spoke. "It's just *me*, my love."

"Mmm," Kelissa mumbled.

"Shh, shhh… There's no need to talk. Let's just go to bed."

Ted viciously pushed Kelissa forward as she fell on top of the bed. Her body began to tremble in fear like never before. Her hands could not stop shaking, her breathing sped up, and all she could do was look up at Ted's unapologetic face. As Kelissa looked in his eyes, she saw no remorse, no hope for change, no love at all. Ted began to crawl himself on top of her. With his big hands, he began to caress her badly bruised neck.

"Hmm… I sure did leave a mark, didn't I?" Ted grinned.

"Ted," said Kelissa. "Ted, you *have* to stop this. Carl and the others will find out."

"Oh, yea? Are you going to tell them? Huh? You and I *both know* that if you say a *word* about this, the press, the media, will eat you *alive*, and your legacy will be *over*."

"You don't know that."

"Oh, but I *do*. *I* know you want this power more than *anything* in the world. And what would you do if you lose it all?"

"Ted, get off of me. *Please*, just get off me."

"Remember this; you may be the leader of the *free* world. But this will *always* be a man's world. Do you hear me? A *man's* world."

Kelissa just looked at him while he was still on top of her. His eyes were not the look of a loving husband but a jealous, devilish force of violence. The physical abuse was not enough for him. Ted wanted to *torture* Kelissa emotionally and mentally—simply kill her spirit. But the one thing about Kelissa, she is a *strong* woman. She learned how to be strong and courageous from her years in the service, caring for all those wounded soldiers.

As Ted finally got off of Kelissa, he gave her an order. An order so low, so degrading, an order *no* man should *ever* give to his wife. As he looked down at her while she lay in bed, he said, "You're going to sleep on the bathroom floor tonight, no pillows, no sheets." Kelissa could not believe what her ears just pulled in. Ted said it with solid conviction, and he was not going to take no for an answer. She got up from the bed, standing next to Ted as she begged him to stop this.

"Ted, *please*," Kelissa cried. "*Please,* don't do this."

"Okay, Kel… You're *right*. This *is* crazy," Ted responded.

Ted then walked towards Kelissa, kissing her frontal lobe with a sinister smirk on his face. Kelissa sighed with relief that he would not make her sleep on the bathroom floor. Then all of a sudden, "BOOM!" Ted punched her with all his might, right to her abdomen area. Kelissa collapsed straight to the floor. She coughed, coughed, and coughed as that punch took the air out of her lungs. Then the worst happened; Ted grabbed Kelissa by her hair, dragged her out of her slippers, and into the bathroom. Kelissa could barely catch her breath as she had no oxygen even to let out a scream. Ted stood over a defenseless Kelissa with such malice, and all he said to her was, "Sleep tight, sweetheart." Ted then closed the bathroom door as he walked out.

Kelissa could do absolutely nothing but lay there on the floor, sobbing her eyes out. The pain was not even dismissed from her neck, and now she has excruciating pain in her abdomen area. She cried, cried, and cried. But then, the bathroom door quickly opened; it was Ted, once again, with even more rage in his eyes. Kelissa was so terrified that she promptly moved to the bathroom corner as she thought he would attack her again. But Ted made his way to her and grabbed her by her hair again. "Sweetheart, you better stop this crying *right now*. Stop it! *STOP IT*!" Ted said in such a menacing tone of voice.

Kelissa held back her tears and sniffled emotions. The fear in her eyes was like never before. As Ted turned around, making his way out of the bathroom, Kelissa barely had the energy to move. She felt helpless, hopeless, and also powerless. When Kelissa thought about the reality of who she is and what she represents to America, to the world, to women, and most importantly, to her daughter, she could not help but cry some more. Here she is, leader of the free world, lying on her bathroom floor, suffering the pain caused by the hands of her husband. Kelissa does not feel like a leader but a worthless peasant in Ted's prison.

The aching pain in her neck was slowly beginning to fade. But the pain from the punch was beginning to grow. Kelissa was still lying on the bathroom floor as her tears were falling horizontally down the side of her face. Lying on the floor, she repeatedly said, "Oh *Jesus*, oh God, oh God, *oh, my God*." Her situation is destined to be doomed. As her teary eyes grow heavy, Kelissa begins to fall asleep on the cold tiled floor.

Chapter 10

Tuesday Morning, February 6th, 2024

An American Dream

Dreaming the night away, Kelissa sleeps on her bathroom floor, where Ted dragged and left her. Her slight jerks and movements changed her sleeping position as she dreamed. In the dream, Kelissa and Ted were dancing naked in a garden. It was a desire, a *fantasy* Ted always had, but Kelissa was never willing to do something like that in real life. As they danced naked in the dream, Kelissa was hit with arrows all over her body. She was bleeding—crying, and Ted just stood there with an evil grin as he said nothing. He had the same demonic smile when he put his hands on her. As the '*dream turned nightmare'* carried on, Kelissa continued to fidget and move in her sleep on the bathroom floor.

Kelissa met Ted a little over twenty-one years ago when she was a mentor for veterans who had PTSD (Post Traumatic Stress Disorder). Ted was in the military as well, but very briefly. He was wounded after being hit by fragments of bullets while stationed in Afghanistan. Then after his time in Afghanistan, he was transferred to Baghdad, Iraq. It was there that Ted saw the worst happen—seeing his fellow soldiers lose their lives to bombings, friendly fires, and stepping on land mines. Ted's military career was short-lived after being diagnosed with PTSD. He was sent back to America—San Francisco, where he had initially been stationed and was obliged to join a program that brings veterans together who suffer from PTSD. Kelissa was part of that program as one of the mentors, and after they met, the rest was history.

It started with an innocent ice cream date on a lovely summer evening. Ted was charming in his unique way. Incredibly handsome features with a tall and lean physique. Ted could have become a model without question. And from that night on, they were inseparable.

Ted did not come from a wealthy family. He grew up in a small Iowa town called Spirit Lake. His father was a military veteran as well, who fought in Vietnam. But when his father came back from the Vietnam War, he did not come back as a father but as a monster. A drunken fiend, constantly beating on Ted's mother. Sometimes he would hit Ted on occasions. Until one day, Ted's father skipped town, which gave him and his mother the opportunity to leave.

But what Ted's mother *did* was go out of her way to track down his father so that they could be a family again. She found him in San Francisco, had two more children, and then his father skipped town again. But *that* time, they never saw him again. The psychological wounds, however, never healed in Ted's mind. The abusive fuse was lit, and it never was put out.

The abuse triggered something within Ted, poisoned him even. After seeing his parents' violent relationship, Ted honestly believed that even if he abused his lover, she would *always* forgive, forget, and take him back. As Ted got older, he told his mother that he would also join the military and become a better soldier than his father ever was. His mother hated the idea. But Ted was over 18 and could make his own decisions. So, he joined the military, left the military, met Kelissa, got married, and started a family.

Their first-born son, Ted, Jr., was born on June 11th, 2006, Madeline was born on December 14th, 2008, and Bryan, their youngest, was born on September 3rd, 2012. They indeed were the perfect family. As Kelissa got older and more caring, she made her focus to help people and to help communities build and grow. Then one day, Kelissa had a vision. A *vision* of power and purpose. Kelissa wanted to *be* more and *do* more. She wanted to be an *icon*. She decided to run for mayor of San Francisco and was elected. She did very well during her term, but she was not satisfied with just being a mayor. She wanted to climb up that ladder. At first, people felt that Kelissa was biting off more than she could chew when she announced that she was running for President. But Kelissa believed that this was her mission—*this* was her dream. To be the first woman President in United States history. She had a dream, a *vision*, and she was determined to see it through.

Kelissa had the support of her parents and children. Ted, however, was not on board. He once told Kelissa that the presidency might be too much for *any* woman to handle. Kelissa felt that it was very misogynistic and sexist of him to make such a degrading comment. But she did not allow Ted's disapproval to stop her from running for President.

It was one late night; Kelissa was finishing up with meetings with her campaign to prepare for debates between the other candidates. She came home exhausted, the children were asleep, and Ted came to her with a pack of questions, questioning why she was coming home late every night. Kelissa snapped at him, cursing up a storm, telling him how much stress she was under daily. And then, suddenly, Ted threw her to the ground as he began to kick her on her backside and her upper left thigh area repeatedly. Kelissa was in immediate shock. After all those years, she could not believe that Ted would put his hands *or* feet on her.

But Kelissa was in too deep. She was in it to win it. She wanted to go all the way and become President-elect. But to do that, she had to keep this squeaky-clean image intact. She kept the abuse away from the public, her parents, and her children. And the main reason Ted has never been *caught*, he never aims for the head. All of his vicious attacks on Kelissa are only landed between her chest and upper thigh. And he has been doing so ever since that night.

For over two years, Kelissa has been suffering from domestic violence. While the world is infatuated with her, she lives in fear behind that perfect image. If *one* bruise is *ever* revealed, Kelissa's perfect image goes down the drain, and her presidential legacy is tainted forever. Her power would be tarnished, and her American dream would die. And *that* is why Kelissa refuses to tell *anyone* this dark secret. But how, *how* much more abuse can this woman, this *human being*, physically and emotionally handle? This American dream of hers has become a dauntingly violent nightmare.

Chapter 11

Tuesday Morning, February 6th, 2024

Bad Morning to You

A quick splash of water hits Kelissa directly in her face. “Rise and shine,” Ted said to her, holding an empty glass. As Kelissa looked, she realized that Ted filled that glass with water and then tossed it on her face to wake her up. Before leaving the bathroom, Ted did the cruelest and most heartless thing. He held the glass in front of him and purposely dropped it on the floor. Glass shattered into tiny, sharp pieces. “Watch your step,” Ted sarcastically said as he left.

Kelissa could not believe the night she had. Here she is, the President of the United States of America, lying on her bathroom floor, surrounded by broken glass fragments. To avoid stepping on the glass,

Kelissa began to carefully slide the pieces of glass with her hand and placed them into one pile. She spent five minutes crawling around the bathroom floor, getting every tiny bit of glass she could.

As Kelissa stood up, she still had to walk with caution as she was barefoot. Looking at her reflection in the mirror as her face and hair were still wet. But underneath the wetness was a dry look of pain and suffering. As Kelissa touched her abdomen area, where Ted punched her, there was still a soreness. Still looking at herself in the mirror, Kelissa slowly lifted her pajama shirt and gave off a deep gasp. She could not believe the size of the bruise on her abdomen area. This bruise was by far one of the worst she has ever had. The bruise had the colors of black, blue, red, and purple. Not to mention, the bruises on her neck were like the red ring of death.

Kelissa was beginning to get emotional, but she knew she had to restrain herself from releasing those awaited tears. She has to control her emotions, as she has a possibly hectic day ahead of her. Kelissa then went over to turn on the showerhead. It was a rainfall showerhead, a request she had before moving in. She then removed her pajamas and underwear and carefully went into the shower. The lukewarm water began to rinse through her hair and down her body. She then grabbed the soap bar and began to rub a white sudsy cloud all over her body. But the bruise was so dark and visible that she could not help but look down and be reminded of what happened late last night. As the water fell from the showerhead, Kelissa pressed her forehead against the wall as tears fell down her face. She could no longer control her emotions as she cried uncontrollably in the shower. Through the sounds of the running water and her sobbing, Kelissa prayed again, asking God for protection, strength, and serenity. She had to find a way to calm herself down before stepping out of her bedroom, facing her children and her staff.

It is close to 8 a.m. this Tuesday. Kelissa is now thoroughly dried and fully dressed. She was just about ready to exit her bedroom. But first, she made her way back into her bathroom to put on her makeup. She put an extra coating of foundation all over her neck to cover the bruising and then made her way up to her face. As Kelissa looked at herself in the mirror again, she thought in her mind, saying to herself, "I have to do something. I can't keep this bottled in—it'll kill me."

Kelissa, now wearing a wine-red scarf to cover her neck, came out of her bedroom, standing quietly in the center hall. She walked over to Madeline and Bryan's room, but they were not there. As she walked down the hall, Martha the butler came out of the dining room. "Good morning, Madam President. I've prepared your breakfast in the dining room as you requested," said Martha. Kelissa thanked Martha and made her way to the President's Dining Room.

"Thank you, Martha," Kelissa said.

"You're welcome, Madam President. Oh, Mr. Morrison is already in the dining room. He said he wanted to join you."

Kelissa paused in her tracks. After all that had happened, she did not want to be *anywhere* near Ted at this time. "Darling, get it while it's hot," Ted projected as he saw Kelissa in the hall. Since Ted had already spotted her, Kelissa walked into the dining room and sat down. She sat on one end of the dining room table while Ted sat at the other end. Martha and two other butlers had prepared breakfast. Turkey bacon, turkey sausage, roasted potatoes, and scrambled eggs were prepared with fresh fruit, toast, *and* coffee. Kelissa made the kitchen staff fully aware of her food request and allergies. But somehow, strawberries were still on the table.

"Is there anything else you need, Madam President?" Martha asked.

"I think I have everything I need for now. Thank you, Martha," Kelissa responded.

"Martha, you did a *wonderful* job. *Everything* is perfect. Thank you," Ted said with his handsome smile.

"Oh, and I may not have mentioned this, but I'm allergic to strawberries—"

"Those are for me, Kel," Ted interjected. "Martha, I'll take those strawberries."

"Martha?" Kelissa said with a concerned look.

"Yes, Madam President?"

"Uh… You know what, I was *just* going to ask for some tea and avocado. But I don't want to trouble you to go all—"

"Oh, *no*, Madam President, not a problem. It is my *pleasure*."

Ted was grilling Kelissa at that very moment, seeing if she would spill the beans and reveal the dark secret. But Kelissa did not fold. As Martha and the other butlers leave the dining room, Ted turns his head to ensure they would not hear what he was about to say. He took a sip of his coffee and then got up from his chair as he said, "Go ahead, *tell* them. Tell them how your husband is attacking you. *Punching*, *kicking,* and *dragging* you all over the bedroom. Tell them about *all* the disrespectful things I've said to you. Tell Carl. They won't believe you. Or maybe they *will*. I'll go to jail; you'll *lose* your power and be voted out. *Hell*, they'll probably impeach you by summertime, and *all* the hard work will go straight down the *fucking* toilet. They'll see you as a complete *fraud* and will have you removed from office. Is *that* what you want, Kel? Do you want them to take me away from *my* kids? Who *loves* and *adores* me? And then you become that *bitch* of a mother? I don't think so, sweetheart. You may have power over the *world*, Kel. But *I* have power over *you*. Enjoy your breakfast."

Ted kissed Kelissa on the top of her head, and right before he left the dining room, he said, "I love you, Kel. I *do*." Kelissa lifted her head, looking at him in disbelief. She could not believe that he would have the audacity to say those words to her after last night. Mind manipulation is what Ted is a mastermind at; it *is* his specialty. Ted would always say sweet, apologetic things to make Kelissa feel loved and wanted. He would always tell her how *much* he loved her and the kids. Even though the physical wounds would eventually heal, Ted knew he had to heal the *emotional* wounds, giving her compliments and making condescending comments—easing her mind to make her feel that he would "change."

As Kelissa continued to sit there at the dining room table, she took a few bites of eggs and toast, but her appetite had already left the table five minutes ago. Martha had returned with the tea and a neatly sliced avocado.

"Martha, you know what?" said Kelissa. "I have to head down to the Oval Office. I have a *lot* of work to do today."

"Oh, would you like for me to bring some tea down to your office?" Martha asked.

"Yes, please. That'll be *great*."

As Kelissa left the President's Dining Room, she headed to Madeline and Bryan's bedroom. Once again, as she knocked on Madeline's door, there was no answer. Kelissa then went to *Bryan's* bedroom and knocked on his door. But again, there was no response. Kelissa, confused as to where the kids are, makes her way up to Ted, Jr's bedroom. But surprisingly, he was not there either. "Where the *hell* are the kids?" Kelissa said to herself.

Kelissa then made her way down the center hall and began to hear the sound of video games and shouting. She realized Bryan and Ted, Jr. was in the game room. As Kelissa walked into the game room, she saw Ted, Jr., and Bryan sitting in their game-chairs, playing a soccer video game.

"Uh, *Bryan*, sweetie?" Kelissa spoke. "What are you doing here? Shouldn't you be at school already?"

"Didn't they tell you, mom? There's a delayed opening today," Bryan responded.

"Oh, of course—must have slipped my mind. Um, where's your sister?"

"She's down in the library, reading her *Harry Potter* books. She's *obsessed* with books," Bryan said.

"Well, *hey*, I rather she spends her time reading *books* than sitting down, playing these life-sucking video games."

"Aw, *come on*, mom," Bryan whines. "Video games are *relaxing*."

"They're also *addictive*. In *fact*, I'm putting a time limit on how long *you two* can be on these games."

"*Both* of us?" Ted, Jr. asked. "Wait, why do *I* have to cut back?"

"Because you're the *oldest*, TJ, *and* you have to set a good example for your sister and brother. Besides, *you're* heading off to college in the fall. Have you been filling out those applications?"

"Some of them. Dad really wants me to go to an Ivy League. But what do you think, mom?"

"Well, I think you should go to whatever college *you* choose. It's not *my* decision or your *father's* decision. It's *your* decision."

"Thanks, mom."

"You're welcome, sweetie. Now, enough with these video games. You guys go and have some breakfast."

Kelissa tried her best to take her mind off what happened last night. She also makes it her mission, day by day, to keep the children entirely oblivious to their father's violent behavior. As she left the game room, she headed down the stairs to the State floor, where Carl and several other Secret Service agents wait for her.

Kelissa fought hard with the PPD (Presidential Protection Division) to have her privacy on the residence level. The one thing she would not stand for was walking out of her bedroom and having two Secret Service agents guarding the door. Kelissa made it mandatory to have privacy on the residence level as she wanted her children to feel that they lived in a *natural* home, not prison. Kelissa was very adamant about having her privacy.

Secret Service compromised; however, a panic button was installed in the President's room—in case of an emergency. But the *real* reason for privacy was the reality that Kelissa did not wish for Carl or *any* of the Secret Service to find out that she was being abused by the *one* person they could *not* touch, her husband. And to Ted's benefit, this gave him much freedom to attack Kelissa during the late nights in the bedroom. Now on the State floor, Kelissa is greeted by Carl.

"Good morning, Madam President," said Carl.

"Good morning, Carl. You know, I *completely* forgot that you told me on the plane that there will be a delayed opening."

"Yes, ma'am. The school will be opening at 10:45 a.m."

"You're the *best*, Carl. Um, I feel a little embarrassed to ask this, but *where* is the library again?"

"It's on the ground level. I'll take you to it."

"Oh, um, I just need to speak with Maddy *privately*."

"I *understand*, Madam President. But unfortunately, I can't leave you unsupervised. I'm afraid we will have to escort you down there."

"Yeah... Privacy is the *one* thing I miss."

Even though Kelissa truly appreciates Carl and the Secret Service, her limits to her privacy and where she could go have become a personal burden to her. Being escorted around the White House was *not* her forte. They made their way down the stairs to the ground level.

"Carl," Kelissa spoke. "I will also be making a phone call to my mother this afternoon."

"Copy that."

Kelissa cannot make personal phone calls without Secret Service being informed. She tries her best to reach out to her parents at her earliest convenience. The phone calls have to be on a secured phone line. Since her mother went through a surgical procedure in January, Kelissa likes to check in on her whenever she has the time during her heavily occupied schedule.

Kelissa, Carl, and the other agent walked towards the library. "We'll stand out in the hall, Madam President," said Carl. As Kelissa walks into the library, she sees Madeline lying on the rose-red couch with her head buried in a book. Kelissa loves seeing Madeline putting knowledge in her mind. When Madeline was three years old, Kelissa would read to her every night at bedtime until she read to herself. Madeline would read book after book. And when she got her hands on the *Harry Potter* collection, she was never the same again. As Kelissa stood there, she spoke to Madeline.

"Maddy?" Kelissa said.

"Yes, Mom?" Madeline responded.

"Good morning."

"Oh, good morning, mom."

"Did you have breakfast?"

"Um… *No*, I woke up early and came down here."

"You should eat something before you head to school."

"I'm really not that hungry."

"Well, at least have some *toast* and some *orange juice,* perhaps?"

"Okay, mom. I'll snack on something before I leave."

"Good. *So*, I'm going to be very busy today. And I may not see you until later on this evening. A lot of meetings, a lot of phone calls."

"Well, to be honest, I'm starting to get used to not seeing you around that much."

"Hey… Listen, no matter *what*, I'm still your mother, and you're still my daughter. That will never change. And I am still here for you. *All* of you."

"I know, mom… I know."

"Okay… BREAKFAST! Now, *please*? Thank you."

As Madeline was heading out of the library, Kelissa noticed a book on the table; it was a notebook. On the front of the notebook, it said, '*Maddy's Journal.*' Kelissa then picked up the notebook and said to Madeline, "Sweetie, is this yours?" Madeline walked back over and took it from her mother.

"Is that for school or something personal?" Kelissa asked.

"Well, my teacher recommended that we keep a journal."

"*We*?"

"Us *students*, mom."

"Oh, I see."

"She recommended that we *students* write down our feelings every day. She said we could write down anything we want."

"Well, whatever you write, shouldn't leave this house. Nor should you share it with anyone. That should be for your eyes only. Alright?"

"Of course."

"Okay, have a good day, honey. Love you."

"I love you, mom. Have a good day as well."

Kelissa then kissed Madeline on her cheek and smiled at her. After Madeline left the library, Kelissa thought about that journal. She thought about having a diary of her own to write down the violent dilemma between her and Ted. The truth is the President cannot have any type of documents hidden or private; every email and letter is kept on file for security purposes.

Kelissa, however, decided to keep a journal for the sake of expressing herself and what she goes through in secret. She realized keeping the domestic abuse trapped in her mind was beginning to affect her mental health, and the only way she would be able to cope with the pain was to write it down. And by writing it down, Kelissa knows she could always trust the pieces of paper. The paper will not judge her or expose her to the public. But she also knew that everything she wrote on those pieces of paper, she would have to guard it with her life. Guard it with the same intensity that Secret Service uses to protect her.

As they came back to the State floor, Kelissa made her way to the Oval Office, located on the West Wing. Her staff members formally greet her, saying, "Good morning, Madam President," and Kelissa returning the morning greetings as she has grown somewhat used to it. Martha, the butler, had the freshly brewed tea waiting for Kelissa near the Oval Office.

"Oh, *God*, Martha, I'm *so* sorry to keep you waiting. I was having a chat with my daughter," Kelissa said apologetically.

Martha made a fresh batch of hot tea as the tea from upstairs was already lukewarm. As Kelissa heads inside the Oval Office, she is greeted by her personal secretary, Joan Gamble, who hands her a stack of open letters to read. Carl and another Secret Service agent, Sam, were standing guard of the office door.

"Joan," said Kelissa. "Is there a spare stack of paper lying around here somewhere?"

"Uh, yes, ma'am. There's a *lot* of paper, actually," Joan responded.

"Great, I would like some. Just to write some ideas down."

"Oh, well, if you want, we just ordered some journal booklets with a black leather cover."

"*Really*? That will work."

"Okay, here you go, Madam President."

"This is *perfect*, Joan. Thank you."

Carl then opens one of the concealed doors of the Oval Office for Kelissa to enter. She walks in with her letters and her new black leather journal. Martha came right behind her with the silver tray of tea. The honey for the tea comes straight from the beehive, on the location of the White House.

"Thank you so much, Martha," said Kelissa.

"My pleasure, Madam President."

In the Oval Office, Kelissa added a few things at her request. She wanted a bust of Hedy Lamarr, who was not only an actress but an innovator who had breakthrough inventions. Kelissa felt that Lamarr's legacy was a perfect example that women have their beauty *and* can also be intellectually gifted. Kelissa had a painting of the late Jackie Kennedy hanging on the wall, facing her desk. She *loved* Jackie Kennedy's style, her looks, as well as her *strength*, especially when she lost her husband, the late John F. Kennedy. Most of the furniture in the Oval Office was left as is. Except for the carpet and the window curtains. Kelissa wanted a brand-new powder blue oval carpet and powder blue tapestry for the curtains—several American flags, including the presidential seal flag, were surrounding the office. For Kelissa, every time she entered the Oval Office, she felt that sense of empowerment. She could even taste it. Still, she had to pinch herself and realize that she was the President of the United States of America, the most powerful person in the world.

But now, the most powerful woman in the world has a hectic schedule to get through. Letters to read, essential phone calls to make, and an aching feeling in her abdomen area that she is ignoring for the rest of the day.

Chapter 12

Tuesday Evening, February 6th, 2024

Dear Journal

It is a quarter to eleven in the evening. A very long and stressful day as President Kelissa Morrison is just finishing up in the Oval Office. Carl and the other Secret Service agent, Sam, had switch swifts for the evening, and most of the staff and administration left hours ago. Kelissa knew that many late nights would come with this job. But now, there is no going back.

As Kelissa left the Oval Office for the evening, she asked one of the kitchen staffers to bring some tea and chocolate chip cookies to her *private* office, located on the residence level. As she said good night to the few staff still working, Kelissa was escorted by Secret

Service to the State floor and made her way up to the residence level. But she was not heading upstairs empty-handed. The new black leather journal she received from Joan was in her right hand.

As Kelissa got to the residence level, there was complete silence in the center hall. Kelissa was so busy in the Oval Office. She did not have time to see her children after school or even have dinner with them, and this was not the first time of her absence. But Kelissa thoroughly explained to Ted, Jr., Madeline, and Bryan that she might be missing in action from the dinner table some nights.

Kelissa wanted to make sure she did at least kiss her children goodnight before going into her private office to work on some things. She walked to Bryan's room, softly knocking as she opened it. "Bryan, sweetie, are you awake?" Kelissa said. But Bryan was fast asleep. His left leg and arm were dangling off the side of the bed. Kelissa placed her journal on Bryan's table and walked over to him. She gently put his arm and leg under the covers and kissed him good night. "Sleep tight, darling boy," Kelissa whispered.

Now, it was time to check on Madeline. Kelissa walked over and knocked on Madeline's door. But again, there was no answer. So, Kelissa opened the door and saw something that was utterly prohibited. Madeline's window was wide open. Kelissa immediately walked over and shut the window. While living in the White House, the President and the First family *cannot* open the windows under *any* circumstances (except fire emergencies). "Maddy? Maddy?" Kelissa shouted. She looked in Madeline's bathroom to see if she was there, but there was no sight of her. Kelissa then called Madeline on her Blackberry, but she noticed that Madeline's phone was ringing right there on the bed. So now, Kelissa has to go on a scavenger hunt to find her daughter— living in a house that consists of 132 rooms.

Kelissa went up to Ted, Jr's room, speed walking down the center hall. As she came to the front door of his room, she heard laughter. It was then that Kelissa knew that Madeline was with Ted, Jr, in his bedroom. Kelissa quickly knocked and opened the door, and surprisingly, Ted, Jr. *also* had his window open. Kelissa, without hesitation, went straight to the window and slammed it shut.

"*Jesus*, mom," said Ted, Jr. "What was *that* all about?"

"What part of 'You *cannot* open the windows' did *you two not* understand?" Kelissa shouted.

"Oh," Madeline uttered. "I'm sorry, mom. It just gets hot sometimes in my room."

"Yea, mom, it does get a little toasty in he—"

"I *don't care*, rules are rules, and this is a rule you *will* follow. Have I made myself clear? HELLO?!"

"Yes, ma'am," Ted, Jr. responded.

"Yes, we're sorry, Mom," Madeline said.

"Both of you get to bed. It's a school night, Maddy. You should have *been* in bed."

"Yes, ma'am."

"Oh, and by the way," said Kelissa. "The *windows*? I don't want to have this conversation again. They are to remain *shut* at all times. Do you two understand?"

"Yes, we're *sorry*, mom. It won't happen again," Madeline said.

"Listen, I don't mean to make you guys feel bad, okay? And I'm sorry for not making it to dinner this evening. I was swamped today. But I'll try my best to sit down and have dinner with you all tomorrow night."

"Okay, mom," Ted, Jr. said.

"Alright, Maddy, say good night to your brother."

"Good night, TJ," said Madeline.

"Sweet dreams, sis," Ted, Jr. responded.

"*Good night*, TJ."

"Good night, mom."

Kelissa and Madeline both walked down the stairs to the second floor. Martha, the butler, was waiting in the center hall with the silver tray of tea and chocolate chip cookies, just as she was waiting for Kelissa earlier in front of the Oval Office. When Kelissa saw Martha waiting, she placed her hand on her forehead, disgusted with herself for keeping Martha waiting once again. "Oh, Martha, *please* forgive me. I'm *so* sorry for having you waiting for me again. You can just place the tray in my office. The door is open; thank you so much," Kelissa said with sorrow. Kelissa still had a few things to say as they stood there in the center hall.

"Well, mom," said Madeline. "I'm going to head to my room. Good night."

"Wait a minute," Kelissa spoke. "What were you and brother talking about up there?"

"Oh, nothing much. Just shooting the shit."

"Excuse me?"

"Oh, sorry. I mean—just *talking*."

"*About*?"

"Nothing, mom, *really*. It was just teenage talk."

"Okay, sweetie, listen to me. You guys know that *mom* will be very, *very* busy these next couple of months. There are a lot of events and a lot of meetings I must attend. A lot of traveling. I'm not going to see you guys as often as I would like."

"I *know* that, Mom—"

"*And* I *also* need you to know that there are rules that *must* be followed for the duration of this term. So, there will be *no* sneaking out, nor will there be any more opened windows."

"Okay, *okay—jeez*."

"This is for our own safety, Maddy. And we all have to be on the same page."

"Can I go inside my room now?"

"Yes, we'll talk about this at a more convenient time. Good night."

"Good night."

Before Madeline went into her room, Kelissa quickly said, "Hey... Where's my kiss?" Madeline then walked over to Kelissa, hugged her, and kissed her cheek. "That's very important to me, okay?" Kelissa spoke, "Us showing affection. And I'll need that from you guys a lot more as I'm running this country." Kelissa then watched Madeline go into her room and shut the door. In the center hall, Kelissa heard a round of gentle applause from her bedroom door opening. It was Ted, clapping his hands as he looked at Kelissa. She turned around and looked at him with confusion, surprised that he was even standing there. "I gotta hand it to you, Kel," Ted said, walking towards Kelissa, "To balance your presidency *and* being a mother to my kids, you truly are a *master* of your priorities. It's just too bad that you can't do the same for me."

After a long night, Kelissa was in no mood to look or even speak to her husband. But Ted was adamant that the two of them have a conversation. Kelissa then shook her head and began to walk to her private office. Ted followed behind her and waited until they were inside the office before saying anything else.

"Still angry with me, I see?" Ted sarcastically said.

"What do you think, Ted?" said Kelissa. "You almost choked me to death. Punched me, grabbed me by my hair, and *dragged* me into the bathroom. You made me sleep on the floor, and *then* you smashed a *glass* on the floor, with *every* intention of me leaving bloody footprints. Am I *angry* with you? What the *fuck* do you think?"

Ted said nothing; all he did was smile as he took one of the chocolate chip cookies from the tray on the desk. As he took a bite of the cookie, he humorously said, "You know, *that* is why I love you,

Kel. The more and more I throw at you, you just take it and keep coming back for *more*. You don't know when to *stop*. You keep pushing my buttons, and your *sassy* attitude has created *much* trouble for you. I'm not tolerating any more disrespect from you, Kel. You are *never* to belittle me in front of the staff again. You do not undermine what I say to the kids, and most importantly, don't you *ever* forget that *I* wear the pants in this family."

Kelissa's eyes—*filled* with instant rage. As she looked at Ted, all she could say was, "Get the *fuck* out of my office, Ted." Ted gave another smile as he took one more cookie and headed out of Kelissa's office. Before he left, he said to her, "I'll let that stomach of yours heal for now. But I owe you one. Good night."

Kelissa sat down in her office chair; her heart was beating at such a rapid pace. Her hands began to shake as she poured herself a cup of tea. That last comment by Ted did not sit well in her mind. As Kelissa gave herself a few minutes to calm down, she remembered that she had left her black leather journal in Bryan's bedroom. Kelissa got up from her chair and walked out of her office. As she made her way to Bryan's bedroom, she quietly opened his door. Bryan was still fast asleep, but his arm and leg came out of the bedsheet again. So, once again, Kelissa carefully put his arm and leg under the sheets, grabbed her journal, and left his room.

Even though Kelissa did not have time to eat dinner with her children that evening and Ted ruined her appetite, she knew she had to get some food in her system to keep her strength. As she went back into her office, she made a phone call to one of the kitchen staffers. She asked them for a particular dish of cheese and spinach ravioli, with a side of asparagus and roasted potatoes. That is the luxury and *privilege* of being President of the United States of America. Even at the wee hours of the night, you can request a fresh home-cooked meal. And even though it is a terrible time to have a full meal, Kelissa understands the necessity of her nutrition.

While Kelissa waited for her meal, she began to stare at the black journal on her desk with the tip of her thumb pressed between her bottom lip. Kelissa thought very hard about what she wanted to say and how much she *would* say about her situation. That is when she remembered one thing her high school English teacher, Ms. Carmichael, said to her, "*Don't think about it, just write.*" So, that is what Kelissa did. She picked up her pen, opened the journal to the first blank page, and began to write. And my God, Kelissa held *nothing* back. In the journal, she wrote:

Tuesday Evening-February 6th, 2024, 11:47 p.m.

Ladies and gentlemen, I'm in serious trouble. I believe that my life is in ocean-deep waters of great jeopardy. I have bruises the size of Texas on my body. The pain, at times, is unbearable. And yet, the world doesn't know anything, not even my children. But here is my truth. My husband, Ted, is abusing me; emotionally, verbally, sexually, and also physically. Ted has been beating me ever since the beginning of my presidential campaign. At the beginning of our marriage, he would never even think to lay a finger on me. Ted never even put his hands on our children. But why, why does he hit me? Is he perhaps jealous of me? Jealous that a woman, his wife, actually became President of the United States of America and became the most powerful person on the planet?

It is getting worse, ladies and gentlemen. Just last night, for the very first time, he choked me on Air Force One. I almost slipped into unconsciousness; that is how intense it was. I now have a dark red ring around my neck that I have to cover with makeup, turtlenecks, and scarves. Thank God it is wintertime. It gives me a great excuse to always have a scarf around my neck. And then, after returning home, he punched me with all his might, right in the gut. I fell to the ground immediately. I had never felt that amount of pain before. I thought I was going to have to be admitted to the hospital. But Ted was not finished with me. He then pulled me by my hair and dragged me into the bathroom, where he made me sleep for the night.

As I write this journal entry, I am in pain. My neck is still a bit sore, my mid-section still hurts, and no one knows anything. I haven't told a soul about what is happening to me. But how can I? I'm the President of the United States of America. The first woman in U.S. history to be the leader of the free world. If I tell anyone, all of the glory, power, and my legacy will cease to exist. My team and I have worked so unbelievably hard to make it to the promised land. How would my children react? To be honest with you, ladies and gentlemen, I'm scared to death. I'm afraid of what will happen to me. Ted will not stop attacking me. I know he won't. He wants me to suffer, to beg for his mercy. He wants to show me that he is the head of this family. I just don't know what to do. But for me to not go batshit insane, I just thought I'd share my story with you, ladies and gentlemen. Good night, until next time…

This moment gave Kelissa a sudden sense of relief. For the first time, she released some of the agony and mental stress by simply writing it down. Kelissa knew the pages would never reveal her secret. And as long as she kept this private and hidden from everyone, her secret would be safe. As much as Kelissa wants to do something about her domestic violence situation, she is too afraid to lose *everything* her campaign and administration worked incredibly hard for these past few years. She is fully aware of what is at stake if she discloses any of this to Carl, her children, parents, *anyone*.

Another knock at the door. It was Martha, the butler, with Kelissa's meal. She thanked Martha again for another late-night request and thoroughly enjoyed her delicious entrée. The kitchen staffers also included some pecan pie with ice cream; Kelissa appreciated it very much.

After finishing her scrumptious meal, Kelissa called it a night and headed to bed. But under the circumstances, she was not planning on sleeping in the same bed with Ted. Kelissa planned on sleeping in one of the guest rooms on the residence's second-floor level. As she left her private office, Kelissa thought of the perfect place to hide her journal—a place where Ted would not think to look. Kelissa will hide it in one of her shoeboxes in the dressing room. At first, she thought it would be too obvious and that she should hide it in storage. But Kelissa then thought to herself, "What are the odds he'll find it?"

Kelissa quietly entered her bedroom with her journal and tip-toed her way to the dressing room. As she undressed and put on her navy-blue pajamas, she had to find a shoebox to hide her diary. With so many shoes to choose from, Kelissa did not know which box to put the journal inside. "Kel, what are you doing?" Ted shouted from the bed. Kelissa, now in panic mode, hurried and placed the journal in a random shoe box and came out from the dressing room.

"What did you say, Ted?" Kelissa said with an anxious tone.

"W*hat* are you *doing*?" Ted responded.

"I was just using the bathroom, Ted."

"Get in the bed. It's late."

"Um… I'm going to spend a little more time in my office."

"Kel, *get* in the *bed*."

"I'm not tired, Ted."

"Kel, we can do this the easy way, or we can do this the hard way. I am your husband, and *I'm* telling you to get your stubborn ass in the *fucking* bed, *NOW*! Or would you like to spend another night on the bathroom floor?"

Kelissa did not want to be anywhere near Ted. But at that moment, her choice was either being in bed with Ted or sleeping on the bathroom floor. And Kelissa knew she was *not* spending another night on that floor. So, she walked over to her side of the bed and got in, with her back turned to Ted. But Ted was not going to accept that.

"Kel," said Ted, "Turn around."

"What?" Kelissa responded.

"Turn around and look at me. I want to see your face."

Kelissa took a second to think about it, but she did as he said to avoid any brutal conflict. She turned around, now facing Ted in the bed. Ted stared at her for a solid minute while Kelissa wondered her eyes elsewhere. "*Look* at me, Kel," Ted imploded. With a brief hesitation, Kelissa finally looked Ted in his eyes. It was difficult for her to look at the man abusing her whenever he had a chance. But Ted had another frame of mind. With audacity, Ted asked Kelissa this.

"Don't you love me, Kel?" Ted asked.

"*Love*?" Kelissa responded with confusion.

"Yeah, I *love* you very much. Don't you love *me*?"

"How could you *possibly* expect me to love someone who *beats* me?"

"I beat you out of love, Kel. I would *never* hurt you."

"You're crazy, Ted… You're *crazy*."

"I'm crazy about *you*."

Kelissa had just about enough as she turned her back to Ted again, adjusting herself under the bedsheets. Ted, however, was not done with her. He began to get closer to Kelissa, caressing her body and kissing her back. He kissed her the way he used to when they first fell in love. Kelissa rejected it initially, but Ted's seduction was too powerful for her rejection. He continued to caress, touching her, kissing her, making her feel alive again. In her mind, at that moment, Kelissa could not understand how a man's hands could be *so violent* but *also* pure and compassionate—romantically comforting and protective.

Ted then turned Kelissa around to have her lying on her back. He looked at her as she looked at him. "I love you, Kel," Ted uttered while on top of her. But Kelissa refused to return those words to him. Ted, however, pleaded with Kelissa to say it.

"Tell me," Ted cried. "*Tell* me that you love me."

"Ted… *please*," Kelissa also cried.

"Tell me, Kel—*Tell* me you love me."

"Please, Ted, stop, *please*."

"Tell me, *TELL ME*!"

"No, Ted! *Please,* stop, get *off*!"

"Tell me that you love me the way I love *you*!"

"NO!"

Ted then ripped Kelissa's pajama shirt—buttons flew all over the bed. Kelissa, now with her bare breast exposed and tears in her eyes, could not move as Ted pinned her arms above her head. Then, he began to shed tears of deranged emotion as he said, "I *love you*, Kel. Please, *please* tell me that you still love me. I would *kill* for you; I'll *die* for you. Tell me—Tell *me*! Oh, *God*, Kel, *please*, *please* tell me."

Kelissa knew, from that point on, that the man she once loved was gone. This man on top of her was *nothing* but a demon. A demon disguised as the man she was in love with a long time ago. *That* is what made Kelissa cry the most.

After that crazed moment, Kelissa was no longer sleeping in the bed with Ted. She had been better off sleeping on the bathroom floor. She changed her pajamas and went up to the residence second-floor level, where the guest rooms were. Ted was lying there with his face buried in the pillow, crying uncontrollably. Kelissa was in absolute disgust as she could not bear the sight of him.

As Kelissa went into one of the guest rooms, she closed the door behind her—*slowly* sliding down the door as she began to sob. It was as if she had lost her best friend in the whole world—her loving partner in crime has become her worst enemy, a *villain* looking to destroy an American superhero. Ted's sexual aggression worsened. Kelissa knew where that was heading and got away before Ted took it to the darkest way.

Still crying on the floor, Kelissa began to stand up and made her way onto the bed. She crawled on top—crying fresh tears on the fresh pillow. As she was crying herself to sleep, Kelissa knew that she could not go on like this for much longer. She felt trapped as if she was in an hourglass, and the sand was quickly pouring down, *suffocating* her by the second. One way or another, Kelissa would have to escape from Ted.

But still, in her mind, Kelissa, unfortunately, believed that if she lost her husband, if she lost the perfect image of the '*First family*,' she would lose the love and respect of the American people, and she would also lose her power. And that was the very last thing she wanted to lose.

Chapter 13

Wednesday Evening, February 14th, 2024

Spitting Image

Snowflakes are beginning to lightly sprinkle all across Washington D.C. It is Valentine's Day, a special day for many lovers but a challenging day for President Morrison. Kelissa spent most of her day in the Oval Office. Phone calls and documents were galore. Kelissa's administration discussed policies and attended press briefings that Kelissa was too preoccupied with participating in as her schedule was insane. However, her interview with award-winning journalist Catherine Chang is approaching. A month from now, America's first woman President will hold her first televised interview. As Kelissa is in her private office, sipping away at her tea, she pulls out her journal and begins to write down what she was feeling that day.

Wednesday Evening-February 14th, 2024, 10:05 p.m.

Ladies and Gentlemen, forgive me for missing out and not documenting the last three days. I've had a rough day and a rough week—meetings after meetings. I've must have read over five hundred pages of documents this past week. Not to mention, I have my first cabinet meeting coming up and my first televised interview with Catherine Chang. I heard this woman delivers a callous questionnaire. But I have to remind myself that I am the President of the United States of America.

I'm also a mother of three children. Good God, I've seriously got my work cut out every day. And just about every single day, Ted has been attacking me, whether it is verbally, emotionally, or physically. Two days ago, I was standing in my dressing room, rearranging some dresses and business suits. Ted walked in, looking very angry with me. I missed dinner with the family again. I was swamped that day. I'll admit, my priorities are very disorganized right now. But being the President is severe; it's a serious job. I understand that family comes first, but sometimes, the nation comes first when you're the leader of the free world. God, that sounds terrible. But the world has no idea what I have to go through every single day. But this is what I signed up for, right? I took the oath, and now I must endure.

But anyway, back to Ted. Literally seconds after I hid this journal in my shoebox, Ted came into the dressing room, shouting at me about missing dinner. But honestly, I really don't want to sit across from a man who is abusing me on a daily basis. The fact that I hide this from my own children, my parents, and for God's sake, Carl. Jesus, if Carl ever found out about this, it's all over.

I told Ted that I was so busy with phone calls and meetings. There was no way I could squeeze in dinner. I was speaking with prime ministers from other countries. I told him that he has to be the one who has dinner with the kids. I have to work. But I guess he didn't like how I delivered that message because the next thing I knew, he ripped one of my thick metal clothes hangers from the rail and began to strike me across my left leg. He hit me with the hanger five times, as hard as possible.

Here's the thing, ladies and gentlemen, Ted is very strategic in how he physically abuses me. He only hits me on areas that I can cover up. Ted never hits me on the face, only on my body. And he hits me just enough, to where I don't have to go to the hospital. Because if or when that happens, it'll all be over, he would be found out. That's why when he hit me with the metal hanger, he only struck me on my upper left thigh. But unfortunately, the bruise metastasized down, right above my knee. So now, I have to wear pants to cover my legs. Or if I wear a skirt, I have to wear jet black stockings so no one can see the bruising.

This is ridiculous, isn't it? I'm the President of the United States of America, and my husband, the "First gentleman," is beating me. How did this happen? How did I put myself in such an inhumane predicament? That same night Ted hit me with the metal hanger; he repeatedly called me a bitch. Yep, after he hit me with that metal hanger, he called me a bitch and walked out of the dressing room. And also, the other night when Ted was on top of me? I actually thought he was going to rape me. He never did that to me before—ripping off my pajamas, trying to compel me to tell him that I love him. But I can't love an abuser. This is no way for any woman to live.

I was so scared yesterday. I thought Carl would find out about this disturbing situation because my leg was still hurting, and I was walking with a slight limp. Carl asked me if I was okay; I just lied and told him that I accidentally hit my knee on the nightstand, but I was okay. I was so disgusted with myself, lying to a man whose job is to protect me. Carl puts his life on the line every single day for me. This is so fucking bad, ladies and gentlemen. And this may sound bizarrely ironic, but I don't feel like a victim at all. I feel like I've caused this upon myself. I blame myself for all the abuse Ted has badly bestowed upon me. I feel like an enabler to this demon. I may be wrong, or I may be right. But dear God, I am so lost.

Kelissa, now in her pajamas, closes her journal and calls it a night. She has been retiring for the evening, upstairs in the guest room for the past four nights. But before heading up, Kelissa had to hide her journal back in the dressing room. As she walked into her bedroom, Kelissa looked around the room to see if Ted was there. She then checked the dressing room, as well as the bathroom. But there was no sign of him.

After Kelissa hid her journal, she went to use the restroom. Since it was not too late, Kelissa decided to take a quick shower before bed. She turned on the showerhead and began to undress. As she turned around and saw herself in the mirror, she was mortified by the large bruise on her left thigh caused by the beating. She was looking forward to running some cool water on her leg to ease the pain.

Kelissa stepped into the enclosed shower. As the water was a little *too* cold for her comfort, Kelissa turned the knob to increase the heat. The water grew hotter, and the bathroom became steamier. The shower's glass door was beginning to fog up from the mist. Then all of a scary sudden, the was a loud sound. BAM! The bathroom door slammed open. Kelissa jumped and turned around, facing the misty shower door. An eerie dark figure was walking its way towards her. Her heart was racing as she knew it was Ted. But Kelissa did *not* know whether or not he was there to be civilized or violent.

The hot water is still running, steam is still rising, and Kelissa's eyes are locked on Ted. She sees Ted's dark and blurry figure behind the foggy shower door. The eeriness of his presence is that he said not a word—a haunting silence. Instead, he took his left index finger and slowly rubbed it against the misty shower door. His finger made a squeaky sound like a windshield wiper as he created the shape of a heart. Inside the heart, Ted rubbed these words:

"I LOVE YOU"

Ted wrote it backward as Kelissa saw it from her point of view. After that, Ted finally spoke.

"Happy Valentine's Day, Kel," said Ted. "I have something for you in the bedroom."

"I—I'll be out in a minute, Ted," Kelissa fearfully responded.

"Don't keep me waiting for too long."

Kelissa, now standing there as the water poured down on her head, had no idea what Ted had in store for her out in the bedroom. All she could do was hope for the best—hoping his behavior would not be conflicted.

Kelissa then turned the showerhead off and stepped out of the shower. She grabbed her robe hanging on the hook of the bathroom door. As she put on her robe, Kelissa stepped out of the bathroom, through the dressing room, and saw something that she would not have expected. Ted stood there with a bouquet of white roses and a heart-shaped box of chocolates. She stood there as Ted walked forward and gave her the flowers and candy, with a kiss to the side of her wet head.

"Ted... *Why*?" Kelissa asked.

"I wanted to," Ted responded. "I wanted to show how sorry I am. You don't deserve this, Kel. You deserve better."

Kelissa was not impressed, nor did she accept the Valentine's Day flowers and chocolates. She placed the chocolates on the bed and looked at the bouquet of white roses. Kelissa knew Ted picked these up from the flower shop down on the ground level of the White House. When it came to Ted being romantic, Kelissa was so far removed from it at this point.

Kelissa looked at Ted as if he had lost his entire mind. After taking a deep breath, she said to him, "Did you honestly think this would *work* for you? Did you really *think* that I would just accept these roses and forgive you for whipping me with a *fucking* hanger? How dare you? *Look* at my leg, Ted! I had to *lie* to Carl, tell him that I hit my leg on my *goddamn* nightstand! All because of you. And you just come here with flowers and candy and pretend that everything is *okay*? No, this is *not* okay. This shit has to stop; it *has* to stop, Ted!"

Kelissa picked up the heart-shaped box of chocolates and threw them straight to the ground. Some of the chocolates went all over the floor. Ted looked around at the floor, not saying a word but smiling—the same sadistic smile he often gives to Kelissa. Looking at

Kelissa, he squatted down to pick up a piece of the remaining chocolate from the box—picking it up with his thumb and index finger. Ted held the chocolate up to Kelissa as he was on one knee, looking as if he was proposing. "Have one," Ted said with that sadistic smile. Kelissa looked at him with disgust as she shook her head. "NO! *fuck you*!" Kelissa projected.

Ted did not say anything; he grinned and placed the chocolate in his mouth. As Ted chewed, he chuckled, and then began to look at Kelissa's face as if he was analyzing it. He said, "Kel, you have something on your face." Kelissa, with a look of confusion on her face, had no idea what he was talking about. And just like that, "Ptui!" Ted spit the chocolate debris in Kelissa's face—the most disgusting, dehumanizing, disrespectful thing a husband could do to his wife.

Kelissa stood there as she was now in traumatic shock. She dropped the bouquet of white roses, standing there with her eyes closed. Kelissa could feel Ted's saliva running down her face. She tried to contain her heavy breathing and process what had just happened. As she tried to open her eyes, the chocolate remains were close to seeping in. Kelissa slowly took her fingers and rubbed off the remaining spit from her face. She then looked at her fingertips as they were covered in the mixture of chocolate and Ted's saliva. She looked up at Ted as he was smiling with chocolate dripping down his chin. Kelissa once again wiped her hand across her face to get the remaining spit off, picked up the bouquet of white roses, and began to swing away at Ted.

"You BASTARD!" Kelissa screamed. "How *dare* you spit in my face?"

"*That's* it, baby! *Show* me that rage!" Ted sadistically said.

"I *HATE* you, Ted! You *fucking* burn in hell!"

"Aw, I'm sad you feel that way. Because I *love* you!"

Kelissa continued to swing the bouquet of white roses, hitting Ted as a shower of white rose petals fell all over the floor. Ted parried it as she took another swing, grabbed her arm, and slung Kelissa across the bedroom—making a sudden impact against the wall. Kelissa immediately fell backward, landing on the floor. Now, her defenseless body cannot move. She laid there on the floor with her bathrobe halfway off her body. All Kelissa could do was breathe. Her eyes were closed, only focusing on her breathing and the sound of Ted's wicked laughter. She knew he was walking towards her. And then, he asked her a question. "Where does it hurt, babe? *Tell me* where it hurts?"

Ted stepped over Kelissa, now facing her as she was still laying on the floor in a cradled position. If only you could see the painful look on her face. And if only you could see the *monstrous* look on *his* face. Even though Kelissa's vision was dazed, she noticed Ted's eyes. His eyes were *filled* with this immeasurable sense of satisfaction. But *Kelissa's* eyes were filled with nothing but fear and heartbreaking tears. Ted, however, was not finished with her.

Ted was still fully dressed and still wearing his dress shoes. Wearing a size thirteen shoe, he began to lift his leg as he had every intention of stomping on Kelissa. "T-Ted… *don't*," Kelissa said with a weakened voice. Right before Ted was about to press his foot down onto Kelissa, there was a knock at the door. Ted looked up at the door and quickly put his foot down. Kelissa was in so much pain that she could not move, speak, or even *think* about calling for help. Ted hesitantly walked over to the door—scared that Carl was on the other side.

"Wh—who is it?" Ted fearfully asked.

"Daddy, it's me, Bryan," Bryan responded.

"Oh, *Bry*… Um, one second, okay, buddy?"

Ted quickly walked over to Kelissa and pulled her arms as he swiftly dragged her over to the bed. As he pulled her arms, the pain grew all over her body. Kelissa gasped and gasped, trying not to scream. Ted then picked her up from the floor and plopped her on the bed. He then covered her up with her bathrobe and wrapped the bedsheets around her to give Bryan the illusion that she was sleeping. Then, Ted went over to open the door.

"Hey, Bry," said Ted. "What's wrong, buddy?"

"Daddy, I had a really bad dream. Can I please stay with you and mommy?"

"Oh, Bry… You know, you're a little too old to be sleeping in the same bed with us, bud."

"Please, daddy? I really don't want to be alone tonight. *Please*?"

"Umm… Okay, I'm going to take a shower. But be careful and don't wake up your mother. She's had a tough day."

"Okay… Daddy, why are there *flowers* on the floor? And *chocolate*?"

"Oh, well… I don't know. I guess your mother didn't appreciate them. She hasn't been very nice to me."

"Why, daddy?"

"She's just been really moody lately. But it's okay. I love your mother regardless. And don't worry, I'll protect her. I'll protect all of you guys."

Kelissa was lying in bed; even though she pretended to be asleep, there was no acting about the pain. Kelissa heard *everything*, and after hearing what Ted just said to Bryan, she realized how sick he truly is, hearing the evil sarcasm within the lines. Ted then walked into the bathroom and turned on the showerhead, leaving Bryan and Kelissa in the bedroom.

Bryan then got into bed with Kelissa as she had her back turned to him. Because Bryan was still scared after his nightmare, he wrapped his arm around his mother and *squeezed* oh so tightly around her aching body. Kelissa did *everything* in her power not to scream in pain. She buried her face in the pillow as the tears began to *bleed* out of her eyes. But then, Bryan made the sweetest gesture and said this to Kelissa, "Good night, mommy. I love you." And then he kissed her on her left shoulder. That was all Kelissa needed to ease that pain. She then took her hand and wrapped it around Bryan's arm as they both fell asleep.

The following morning, Kelissa is still sleeping, still dreaming. But it was not a *pleasant* dream, tossing and turning as if she was being slapped around. Then finally, she receives a shake on her right shoulder. "Mommy, mommy," said Bryan. Kelissa quickly woke up as she saw Bryan standing there by her bedside.

"Mommy," said Bryan. "Mommy, are you okay?"

"Yes," Kelissa said with a startled face. "Yes, baby. I'm okay. I hope I didn't scare you, sweetie."

"It's okay, mommy. But you have something on your face. Is that chocolate?"

"Oh, no, sweetie. That's just my makeup. I fell asleep and forgot to wipe it off."

"Did you have a bad dream like I did?"

"Yes, baby," Kelissa said emotionally. "I had a very, *very* bad dream."

"Don't cry, mommy. Daddy will *always* protect us."

It haunts Kelissa how *massive* the naivety of her children is. They have absolutely no idea what is going on. But unfortunately, Kelissa has to keep it that way. Bryan then hugged Kelissa and asked her if she was coming to breakfast. "I will be there in ten minutes," Kelissa said to Bryan. Bryan then left the bedroom, leaving Kelissa there by herself. She slowly got herself up from the bed and walked into the bathroom. Looking at herself in the mirror as she disrobed, Kelissa looked at her naked anatomy and quickly began to weep. She saw the bruising on her arm, ribs, and thigh, and she could not hold it in. Kelissa placed her hands over her face and cried like a newborn baby.

Last night was a nightmare Kelissa could not prepare for at all. The abuse was getting worse and worse, and as for the stress that came with being the President of the United States of America, it was just the beginning.

Chapter 14

Thursday Afternoon, March 14th, 2024

The Conversation She Feared

Today is the day for President Kelissa Morrison. Her first televised interview as President of the United States of America is happening in two hours. Journalist Catherine Chang has gone through security screening and is preparing as the film crew sets up the cameras and lighting equipment. Kelissa is up on the second floor of the residence level as the hair and makeup team begins to doll her up. As requested, Kelissa had a full-size beauty salon installed in the White house. She can have her nails and hair done right there in the White House. The salon had an all-white theme, which is not surprising, being that her current residence *is* the White House. The salon also has a full-size rectangular Hollywood vanity mirror with multiple lights. As Kelissa is in the chair getting ready, she gets a surprising visit from Ted.

"Hello ladies," said Ted. "If it's not too much trouble, could I have a word alone with my wife?"

"Ted, I'm about to have my interview; it's not *really* a good time," Kelissa responded, hiding her nervousness.

"It won't take long. Ladies, if you please?"

The hair and makeup team stepped out, leaving Kelissa in the salon with Ted. Since Kelissa was in the salon with two uncommon guests, two Secret Service agents had to stand guard outside the salon door. The usual routine would be a Secret Service agent standing *inside* the room with the President, fully armed, in case of emergency. But Kelissa only wanted them to stand guard of the door, and the door had to be opened at all times.

Ted, however, had to come correctly and casually while in the room with Kelissa, being that Secret Service was right outside the door. Kelissa, with the black barber cape wrapped around her neck, sits there as Ted stands behind her. But she was in no mood for him. She stared directly in the mirror, not looking at his reflection. "Ted, *what* do you want?" Kelissa said very sternly.

Ted did not look directly at Kelissa. He sat on the edge of the vanity table with his hands folded on his leg—staring at her reflection. As Ted continued to look, he whispered, "You are the most *beautiful* woman I've ever laid eyes on. Did you know that? That is why I never, *ever* touched your face. Your smile could make me *drool* like a hungry hound dog—on the hottest summer day. From the first day I met you, I just *knew* I would marry you someday. I knew that *one day*, I was going to get down on one knee and ask yo—"

Kelissa stopped Ted in mid-sentence as she had to quietly respond, saying, "Ted, I'm only going to say this one time, so hear me well. It could never, *ever*, go back to the way it was. Have you *seen* the bruises? *You* did that to me. I have to *fucking* hide these bruises from *everyone.* Do you really think that you could just beat the hell out of me, over and over, and think that *we* can still be a loving, happily married couple? Did you forget how you ultimately disrespected me by *spitting* right in my face? And you think you can sweet talk me and make me feel good? What we had, that's dead, Ted. And *you* killed it. I've put myself in a terrible position that I just *can't* get myself out of right now. So, here's what's happening, I will be *incredibly* busy running this country. Just play your position and *pretend* to be a good husband and a good father to my kids. And after this first term is over, I am *through* with your abusive ass. Do you hear me? And you will *never* see my kids again."

Ted's face grew incredibly red after Kelissa quietly told him off. But then Ted said something to *Kelissa* that restored the irreversible fear right back in her heart. Ted looked over to the door to ensure Secret Service would not see or hear him. He then pointed his finger at Kelissa and quietly said, "You *sassy, stupid bitch.* You better pray that you even *survive* the first fucking *year* of this term. You threaten me, telling me that you'll take away *my* kids? Telling me to play my *position*? Let me tell *you* something, *Madam President*… I have no problem slicing your *fucking* throat, right in this very house. I have *no* problem having the kids wake up and find their mother lying *dead* on the bathroom floor with a Columbian bowtie sliced throat. If I were you—I would sleep with one eye open. You never know; I may come after you in the dark and *kill you* in your sleep."

Kelissa's legs could not stop shaking. Her body was trembling in fear of this man. Not because of what he said, but because she knew he meant every word. Kelissa knew that Ted would kill her. As Ted was about to take his leave, he stood behind the salon chair, leaning on Kelissa as she sat there.

"Who are you?" said Kelissa. "Why do you want to kill me, Ted?"

"I don't *want* to kill you, Kel. I only want to *control* you. You—belong—to *me*."

"Get out, Ted. And don't say it. *Please* don't."

"I love you, Kel."

Kelissa could not bear to hear those words coming out of Ted's mouth any longer. She closed her eyes and covered her ears instantly while he said those three words. He then kissed Kelissa on the back of her head and said, "Knock em' dead." Ted began walking out of the salon, whistling the theme song from the old T.V. show, '*Happy Days*.' As if Kelissa needed any more pressure before this interview.

The hair and makeup team came back into the salon. Stella, who is in charge of doing Kelissa's hair, humorously said, "Good lord, Madam

President, I thought your husband was *never* going to leave." Beatrice, the makeup artist, added to that, saying, "Yea, *I* thought he was in here beating your face." Kelissa, however, did not find Beatrice's comment humorous at all and responded aggressively, saying, "*Beating* my face? And just what are you trying to say?" Stella looked at Beatrice with a startled look, as if they both were in trouble. Even the Secret Service agent had to peek his head into the room to see if anything was wrong.

"I am *so* sorry, Madam President," said Beatrice. "I meant beating your face, as in '*beat face*?' With makeup? It was a bad joke. I'm *terribly* sorry, ma'am."

"Forgive me, please," Kelissa responded. "I wasn't thinking clearly. I'm just a little nervous right now about this whole interview."

"Oh, we *understand*, Madam President," Stella said. "But uh, not to worry because *we* are going to turn you into the *Belle of the Ball*. Just show that gorgeous smile of yours, and you *win*."

A woman suffering from domestic violence can always affect her sanity. Kelissa could see Stella and Beatrice's reflection in the mirror as they awkwardly looked at each other. Kelissa never felt so embarrassed, sitting there with the five-hundred-pound gorilla in the room. And the fact that Kelissa is in the highest position of power, she fears for her life, as no other President has ever feared before. Fresh bruises on her body, covered up and *hidden* from the world.

As Beatrice was putting the makeup on Kelissa's face, she told Kelissa to close her eyes so that she could powder her eyelids. As she kept her eyes shut, Kelissa began to think about what questions journalist Catherine Chang would ask her. She wanted to take her mind off of her alarming conversation with Ted. Catherine Chang has had a nineteen-year career, and she has interviewed *thousands* of people, including several U.S. presidents. Kelissa will be Catherine's third U.S. president to be interviewed.

Kelissa's hair and makeup were complete, and she most definitely looked like the *Belle of the Ball*. The interview was in ten minutes, and Kelissa was ready to get the show on the road. As she exits the salon, Carl and two other Secret Service agents proceeded to walk her down to the East room, where the interview was being held. As they walked, Carl presented something to Kelissa that she was delighted to possess. "Madam President," said Carl, "I have something for you." It was a new and highly secured Blackberry device.

"Oh, Carl, thank you so much," Kelissa said joyfully.

"Absolutely," Carl responded. "Obviously, we cannot provide you with a smartphone for security reasons. But the Blackberry has been modified."

"Yes, it's better than nothing. But I'm surprised that we can still use them since the Blackberry was discontinued."

"Well, because you can't use phones with cameras or microphones, our tech team provided some for you and the staff."

"I see; well, this is great. Thank you, Carl."

"My pleasure, Madam President. And we are still working on providing a new Blackberry device for the children."

"Great! Well, for Bryan, I don't think it would be necessary. But then again, he hates being left out from things. So, he can have one too."

"Yes, ma'am. And we have already provided Mr. Morrison with *his* Blackberry."

"Oh, *did* you?"

"Yes, but unfortunately, we still have to monitor *your* phone conversations for security purposes."

"I understand. Thank you, Carl."

Ever since Kelissa was sworn in as President, she requested a device to communicate with and contact her children. But being that this was a unique Blackberry, with a specific contact list, Kelissa can only communicate with her kids, Ted and Carl. The cool thing about the Blackberry is the code names in the contact list. Every First family that comes into the White House has code names, beginning with the same initial. In their case, the Morrison family's code names start with "W." Ted is called "Wolf," Ted, Jr. is "*White Snake*." Being that Ted, Jr. is a huge fan of the rock band, '*White Snake*,' he could not resist and followed that code name. As for Madeline, her code name is "*Whisper*," and Bryan's code name is "*White Tiger*," as the *Power Ranger.*

As Kelissa and her entourage of Secret Service agents made it down to the State floor, the camera crew still had a few more things to set up. As she waited, Kelissa thought this would be the perfect time to talk with Catherine Chang before the cameras rolled.

As Kelissa walked into the East Room, Catherine Chang was sitting in the chair that she would be sitting in for the interview duration. She walked over to Catherine to introduce herself. Catherine was beyond honored to meet President Kelissa Morrison finally. "Oh my, Madam President, this is *truly* an honor to finally meet you," Catherine said enthusiastically. Kelissa was all smiles, filled with gratitude that so many women are in awe of her. It is a feeling that she does not, for one day, take for granted. After shaking hands and casual greetings, Kelissa began to ask Catherine a few questions of her own.

"*So*, about this interview," said Kelissa, "What *exactly* will you ask of me?"

"Oh, well, Madam President, it usually depends on how the conversation goes. I don't go by cue cards."

"Oh, so it's just random, '*Rabbit out of the hat'* questions?"

"You could see it that way, *yes*. I'll try to be fair, Madam President."

"Well then, I guess we can get this all started, yes?"

As the film crew finished tidying up the camera equipment, Beatrice and Stella did last looks on Catherine Chang and President Kelissa Morrison. Kelissa's nerves were not as bad as they were before at that very moment. Even though she had no idea what Catherine would throw at her, Kelissa thought, "Just breathe and keep swinging away."

Chapter 15

Thursday Afternoon, March 14th, 2024

The Interview

The cameras were rolling, the last looks were done, and the interview began. Being that it is televised, President Kelissa Morrison had to walk into the East Room to make a grand entrance as she shook hands with Catherine Chang and took her seat. For COVID-19 safety protocols, Kelissa and Catherine maintained social distance and initially wore a Kn95 face mask. As Kelissa and Catherine got comfortable, they removed their mask, and the interview began.

"I hope you're not *too* nervous, Madam President," Catherine said.

"Oh, I think I'll be okay; you'll be fair, right?" Kelissa responded.

"Well, I have some rather complex questions, but I'm sure you'll be fine."

"Okay, well, ask away."

"Okay… Well, *first*, before asking *any* questions. May I just say how deeply honored I am to be sitting across from you, the very first woman President in United States history."

"*Aww*, you're so kind, Catherine. Thank you."

"Yes, you are an *icon* to generations of women all over the world. So many little girls who look up to you and love you."

"And I love *them* as well—*dearly*. I am *honored* that people trusted in me to be their 47th President."

"As do *I*… But I do have a confession to make, Madam President."

"Oh?"

"Yes, I'm open about my political views. I'm actually a *Democrat*. But I put my political bias to the side because I really *believed* that it was time *this* country had a woman President."

"*Wow*!" Kelissa said with gratitude. "Well, you've made a political sacrifice. Thank you so much for believing in me, Catherine. *I must say,* this is a very *positive* way of beginning an interview."

"It *is*," Catherine laughed.

So far, so good in President Morrison's first interview. Kelissa appreciated Catherine's positive engagement. All the praise and flattering compliments were helping Kelissa be more opened to Catherine and her questionnaire. But the brownnosing was all part of Catherine's plan. As the interview continued, the questions became very loaded.

"*So*, the country is still suffering, *financially*, from the aftermath of Covid-19. What is the next step to help rebuild our country's economic system?" Catherine asked.

"Well, our next step is to create more jobs and aid for businesses. In *fact*, I will be attending my first Cabinet Room meeting with my advisors in a few weeks, and I will be making the employment deficiency my *top* priority in that room," Kelissa responded.

"Are you pleased by how the country has bounced back from this pandemic?"

"I *am*... However, we still have very much to do. The work is not finished. And I feel that the American people should *continue* taking the necessary precautions when traveling. We are not exactly cleared from discovering new variants."

"So, you would still recommend people wear a mask?"

"Oh, *absolutely*. As you saw, I still wear *mine*. But it is not mandatory *now*, and the majority of the American people have been fully vaccinated *and* received their booster shots. I believe that we are as prepared as we *can* be—*if* or *when* we are faced with another variant or if Covid cases were to re-emerge."

"That's understandable."

"Well, the thing *is*, there is no such thing as an *extinct* virus or disease. Once it's here, it's here for good. And all we can ever do is prepare ourselves for whatever or *whenever* there's a reoccurrence."

"Very well said, Madam President. I never thought of it that way... Changing subjects, are we still at war with the Taliban?"

"Well, we're not at *war* with them, not *anymore*. However, we have to bring our remaining troops back home."

"Will that be an easy task?"

"With this job, *nothing* comes easy."

As the interview carries along, Kelissa has been holding her own. She was answering Catherine's questions to the best of her ability. However, Kelissa found herself having an epiphany. Before the interview began, Catherine mentioned that she does not use cue cards or write down her questions. But now, Kelissa is well aware that Catherine had her questions memorized prior to this interview. Because Catherine Chang is a nineteen-year veteran journalist, she knows how to conduct an interview professionally well. As the questions continued, Catherine took the direction of the discussion to a more personal lane.

"So, not only are you the leader of the free world, but you're also a mother of three children," said Catherine.

"Yes, two sons and a daughter," Kelissa responded.

"How do you *juggle* those responsibilities? Being a mother, a wife, *and* President of the United States? That's not easy."

"No, you're absolutely correct. As I said, it's *not* an easy job. It's the ultimate challenge for me. To run a country and be there for my children. I have to work many late nights, and I try to spend some quality time with them. I think Bryan is having the hardest time because he is the youngest. So, I try to keep most of my attention towards him."

"And your husband, the First Gentleman?"

"Yes, what about him?"

"How is he handling such a role switch?"

"*Role switch…* That's an interesting way to put it. *Well*, my husband has *plenty* to keep himself occupied. He's never really showed me that he has any issues with the "Role *switch*," as *you* call it. He helps me by spending time with our children."

"Do you get much rest at night?"

"Honestly, I have some good nights, where I sleep very well. And then *some* nights I am up working. I guess it depends on the workload."

"Of course, well, you've only been in office for about fifty-five days now. There is still much time left in your first term. What are some of the policies you hope to execute for women?"

That question right there was the question that Kelissa needed a moment to think on. She had an answer, but her response was so complex and full of detail. As Kelissa got her thoughts together, she looked at Catherine and said, "What I strive to do is create equal opportunities for women of all different backgrounds—women with different political views, religious beliefs, and cultural backgrounds. I believe that the time *has come* for women to receive equal salaries, and I'll make that one of my missions. I also want women's voices to be heard and *not* to be ignored. And being that I *am* a woman, I am fully aware, and I have prepared myself for the harsh reality that I *will* face sexism, possibly some degradation, and world leaders not taking me seriously."

The interview was then cut as the film crew took a ten-minute break. The next shot of the discussion will be taking place outside in front of the Kennedy Garden. Kelissa quickly went to the nearest restroom with Carl escorting her. She looked to him and asked, "How am I doing so far, Carl?" Carl gave Kelissa much praise in a very settled and professional way.

With Carl standing outside, guarding the restroom door, Kelissa walked in. She took a deep breath and slowly sighed as one-fourth of the interview was complete. But Catherine has been hitting Kelissa hard with the questions. Crazy thoughts were racing through Kelissa's mind: the questions and horrible things Ted said to her before the interview. It was a struggle for her indeed.

There was a part of Kelissa that was beginning to grow very sad. To step into such a demanding position, she has all the support she needs from her staff. And yet, she does not have that *personal* support system behind the scenes. Instead, Ted is the exact opposite of any support. She longs for the personal comfort of a man, to have a loving husband by her side. But what she has is a jealous monster who wants to see her crumble and fail as the President.

But Kelissa was not willing to give up. All the extremes she went through to be where she is today. There is a drive within her that keeps her going no matter what. But with Ted consistently causing severe harm to her, Kelissa is stuck between a rock and a hard place—a dark secret dimming darker and darker by the day.

Catherine Chang and President Morrison just finished the second part of their interview in the Kennedy Garden, located on the West Wing of the White House. Kelissa welcomed Catherine into the Oval Office as White House photographer, Georgette Wilson, took many photos of them while Kelissa sat at the *Resolute* desk. Several recent Presidents used the *Resolute* desk. It is also known as the 'Hayes desk' because it was a gift to President Rutherford B. Hayes from Queen Victoria in the late 1800s. Kelissa wanted to continue that presidential tradition, and she truly loved the desk.

As the film crew began to set up back in the East Room for the remaining of the interview, Catherine and Kelissa were still in the Oval Office, having a brief conversation off-camera.

"*So*, how do you feel about the interview? Not so bad, right?" Catherine asked.

"No, not bad at all. I think you've been great," Kelissa responded.

"Thank you… Madam President, I know that you've only been in office for a couple of months now. I don't think anyone should expect you to turn things upside down any time soon. So, you're in good shape."

"I appreciate that, Catherine. Thank you."

"You're welcome, Madam President."

"Uh, Catherine?"

"Yes, Madam President?"

"Um…. Never mind," Kelissa said, chuckling. "I was just thinking how much I admire your outfit."

"Oh, thank you, Madam President. I had this one in my closet for a while. I was waiting for the right interview to bring this baby out. And here it is."

"I love it. It looks great on you."

Kelissa was willing to risk it all—standing there with Catherine, just the two of them in the Oval Office. She wanted to tell her secret so severely. But Kelissa was afraid, *afraid* that her secret would not be kept behind that oval wall. So, she switched gears in her mind and did not *dare* to utter a word about Ted's abusive history.

The interview was soon to reach its conclusion. It was only meant to go for an hour, and the footage was already past fifty-two minutes. As Catherine carried on in the East Room, she and Kelissa were surprised by an unexpected guest. Ted came to crash the interview. Kelissa looked at him with a smile on her face, but in her mind, she thought, "What the *fuck* are you doing here, Ted?" Catherine, however, was willing to roll with the punches. The production assistant brought in another chair, and Ted joined the interview. The façade of laughter and smiles were coming from Kelissa's face. But the cameras were rolling, and Kelissa did not want to make that kind of scene. So, she continued to smile and began to pretend.

Ted sat down beside Kelissa, locked hands, and kissed her cheek. "Oh, I hope I didn't ruin your makeup," Ted said humorously. Now, Catherine's attention was focused on Ted as she wanted to get *his* point of view as the country's "First Gentleman."

"So, Ted," said Catherine. "What is it like to be married to the *first* woman President in U.S. history?"

"Oh, wow!" Ted sighed. "You know, it gives me goosebumps just when you *say* that. I am *proud* of this phenomenal woman—*over the moon* proud. It's just so *surreal* that she actually *did* it."

"You definitely sound like a proud husband."

"Why *yes*, I'm a *very* proud husband. I've *never* seen a woman who works so hard for other people, the way she works."

Kelissa could not believe her eyes *or* ears as Ted was going on and on with immense praise—talking about how *proud* he was of her. It was as if she was looking at a completely different Ted. A man who would *never* lay a finger on her, nor would he harm a hair on her head. This man sitting next to her is *not* the monster she faces in the dark. Kelissa continued to smile and put on a performance, as was Ted. But then, Catherine went for the kill when she asked Ted this question. "Ted, being that the roles have switched, your wife is now President of the United States of America—the most *powerful* woman in the world. Would you say that her position of power has given you some "envy" towards her? Even if it's just a *little* envy?"

Ted took a few seconds to think about that loaded question. Kelissa was eager to hear Ted's answer to this question, especially since this is all televised. Ted turned and looked directly at Kelissa as these words came out of his mouth. "You know Catherine; I'll be honest with you. I *do* grow jealous at times. But not for the reasons you may be thinking. I grow jealous because my wife has become *so* busy, and there are just *not* enough hours in the day. There are late nights when she's up, exhausted and stressed, and I feel that we don't get the quality time we need anymore. But I understand the circumstances, and I know that what we signed up for would be a very demanding job. I worry for her a lot. But since I'm here talking, and this is on camera, I'll just say this. There is no woman in the *world* who I would rather go through this with than Kelissa Morrison. She is the ultimate wife, an *incredibly* loving mother, and overall, just a *great* human being. A *brilliant*, *beautiful* woman that can *still* melt my heart by the mere sight of her presence. I even look at *myself* and ask if I've done enough—if I have *supported* her enough. And she *needs* that support every single day. I love this woman to *death*, Catherine. I've loved her since the very first day I laid my eyes on her. Every morning, her smile takes my breath away. I'm a very blessed man, Catherine."

After hearing what Ted said, Kelissa began to weep with absolutely no control. This man literally looked in her eyes earlier that afternoon and said he would kill her. And now, he looks her in the eyes *again* and says the most beautiful thing she has ever heard him speak about her. This manipulation messed with Kelissa's mind so much that she had to break free of Ted's hand and excuse herself from the interview. "Please excuse me for a second, Catherine," Kelissa emotionally said as she speed-walked into the restroom.

Kelissa went into the restroom, shut, and locked the door. Her mind did not know how to handle what had just taken place. She could not believe anything Ted was saying. But still, it got into her head. And that was always Ted's specialty; he knew exactly how to get into Kelissa's head. One minute, he is the devil she knows, and the next, he is the man she fell in love with so many pale moons ago. His enriched conviction of what he says never fails him.

Kelissa then looked at herself in the mirror. The makeup under her eyes created black tears, and a sad, confused face was presented in the reflection. As Kelissa stood there, still looking in the mirror, she asked herself a frightening question, "*Why* do I still love this man?" Ted has beaten Kelissa on numerous occasions, *threatened* her, *spit* on her, yet ironically, her heart still has a place for evil disguised as love. As Kelissa ran water from the golden faucet, wiping her eyes and blotting her cheeks with a tissue, there was a knock on the bathroom door.

"Yes?" Kelissa projected.

"Madam President," said Carl. "They are waiting for you in the East Room."

"Oka—okay… I'll be right out, Carl. Thank you."

With her eyes closed, Kelissa took a few deep breaths to collect herself before going back to the interview. After a few seconds went by, she opened her eyes and looked at herself in the mirror. She came very close, wanting to pull Carl into the bathroom and tell him *nothing* but the truth about what was going on behind the scenes with Ted. But her solid stubbornness would always prevent her from moving forward with that thought. So, instead, Kelissa cleaned her face, said a prayer, and opened that bathroom door.

As Kelissa came back to her seat, the interview continued. Stella and Beatrice, Kelissa's hair and makeup team, quickly put on some finishing touches. While Kelissa was getting pampered, she said to Catherine, "Um, Catherine? I want to have that emotional part removed from the interview. I want this to look as professional as possible, okay? No tears." Catherine agreed and continued with her questions. "Okay… So, we're *back*. Madam President, how do *you* feel about your husband?" Catherine asked.

This question was the most complex out of Catherine's questionnaire. Kelissa desperately wished she could bypass answering this question. As she sat there, Ted was standing off to the side, watching her like a hawk. In her mind, Kelissa just wanted to *scream* in the East Room—scream out and say, "HELP! SAVE ME!" She wanted to scream the truth out, revealing to everyone that Ted was abusing her. Her body was trembling just at the *thought* of doing so. But Kelissa knew that it would all come crashing down if she made such a spectacle or told the truth. No more presidency, no more power, and her legacy would be destroyed. So, Kelissa did what she hates the most; she lied, right on camera. In a very slick and sarcastic way, she subliminally revealed what was going on behind the scenes.

As Kelissa answers Catherine's question, she says this about her husband, "*Ted* is… Well, there's so much I could say about this man. He's someone who just *whips* me into shape. He shows me tough love and also warm love. Just this past Valentine's Day, he gave me chocolates in bed. He's someone very unique indeed." Catherine found that so touching and continued asking more questions about Ted.

"Aww, that is wonderful," said Catherine. "It almost sounds like you still get butterflies in your stomach."

"Oh, I get more than *butterflies* in my stomach," Kelissa laughed.

"Well, it sounds like you guys have each other's backs through all of this, and there is much love and support, which is great."

As Kelissa looked over to Ted, he smiled and then walked out of the East Room. Catherine was finished with all her questions, and the interview was wrapped. Kelissa then said her goodbyes to Catherine.

"Thank you so much, Madam President. This is definitely one for the books," Catherine said.

"The pleasure is all mine, Catherine," Kelissa responded.

Kelissa then told Carl to wait for her at the bottom of the stairs as she headed up to the residence level to change her outfit. She went up to the residence level and into the dressing room to change her clothes. She stripped down to her bra and panties with her back turned to the doorway. Out of nowhere, sneakily in walks Ted. Her back was turned, and she had no idea that he was behind her. And then, BAM! Ted gave her a heavy hit, right to her lower back. He swiftly covered Kelissa's mouth so that no one could hear her scream. She slowly fell to her knees, *crying* in pain. Still covering her mouth with his hand, Ted quietly said this to her, "You want to play *games*? Huh? *Do you* want to play *games*? I *heard* what you said—I *read* through your subliminal *fucking* comments. I am *warning* you, *bitch*. Do you hear me? *DO YOU*?"

Kelissa was in so much pain. All she could do was slowly move her head up and down, compromising with Ted. He then let her go, leaving her lying there in the dressing room, bawling her eyes out. "Oh my God, oh my God, oh my God… Oh *dear* God, I *can't*." Kelissa said as she cried on the floor.

The back and forth, the threats, the sweet talk, and now this happens. Kelissa was in an ocean of insanity, all alone and slowly drowning. Her mind was nomadic, going from one train of thought to another. To go through all of this just to hold on to a position of power.

Since Carl was downstairs, Kelissa did not want to keep him waiting and draw any suspicion. In much pain, she got up from the dressing room floor and put on another outfit. Still hiding some bruising on her thigh, she had to find an outfit that would cover her legs. So, Kelissa chose an olive-green suit with a white turtleneck. As she put on her turtleneck and suit jacket, she walked into the bathroom and looked at herself in the mirror. Her face was stained with coagulated makeup. She quickly rinsed it off, splashing handfuls of water on her face, one after the other. Her hair was now wet, her face was red, and she did not have time to apply a fresh makeup mug. Kelissa grew rather angry with herself as she then realized she should have wiped her makeup off first *before* getting dressed as the inside of her white turtleneck was now stained. But with all that just happened, Kelissa could barely think with sanity.

In her quick way of thinking, Kelissa decided to put on her face mask to cover at least half of her face. She then used her hairdryer to blow out the dampness in her hair. With no more time to waste, she walked out of the bathroom, fully dressed in her new outfit. As Kelissa walked out of her bedroom, Bryan greeted her with a big hug. He wrapped his arms around Kelissa's waist, applying pressure to her now aching back. She had no choice but to play off the excruciating pain throbbing in her back. "OH! That's such a big hug, baby!" Kelissa projected. Bryan then looked at his mother, confused with her face being covered.

"Mommy," said Bryan. "Why are you wearing a mask inside?"

"Well, I just wanted to set an example for the staff, honey," Kelissa responded.

"Do I have to wear my mask too?"

"No, not in your *room*."

"Okay."

"How was your day, baby?"

"Oh, it was good. I'm making a lot of new friends."

"Well, that's *great*, honey. Maybe we can invite your friends here to the White House for your birthday."

"Yeah, sure."

"Listen, sweetie. I have some work to do in the Oval Office. I'll see you guys at dinner, okay? And make sure you finish all of your homework. I'll check it later."

"Okay, mommy."

As Bryan walked into his room, Kelissa closed her eyes as she tilted her head down, exhaling in disgust. The one thing she hates the most about lying is lying to her children, especially to Bryan. As Kelissa hurried down to the State floor, Carl was standing right there at the bottom of the stairs.

"Carl, I am *so* sorry to keep you waiting," Kelissa said apologetically.

"No apologies *necessary*, Madam President," Carl responded. "It's my job."

"I'm just wearing this mask because I don't have no makeup on, and I look like shit right now. Again, it's a woman thing."

"Whatever you want, ma'am. You're the President," Carl lightly chuckled.

Carl is not one to show much emotion or humor, only because he is focused on protecting the President. And Kelissa hates that he does not know anything about her domestic abuse situation. And yet, her self-forbiddance keeps her secret *safe* but brutal.

Chapter 16

Thursday evening, March 14th, 2024

A Letter from A Soldier-less Mother

Kelissa was escorted to the Oval Office by Carl. Her personal secretary, Joan, handed her more letters to read from the American people. “Madam President, I think there’s one letter that you will find *very* touching,” Joan said with a smile. Carl and another Secret Service agent stood guard of the Oval Office door while Kelissa entered. Inside the office, Kelissa stood there in complete silence and pain. She then removed her mask, exposing her red, distraught face. Her face was so far from a Mona Lisa smile. Kelissa then took off her shoes and began to walk around the office—walking back and forth for five minutes before she laid on the couch, face-first in the cushion. At that moment, all Kelissa could think of was taking a warm bath to ease the pain from her aching body.

The sun was soon to take its leave for the winter evening. After lying on the couch for fifteen minutes, Kelissa slowly got up from the sofa and headed towards her desk. Looking out the window, she saw multiple Secret Service agents walking around with their canine (K-9) dogs outside in front of the office. She then carefully sat down at the *Resolute* desk as she began to read the letters from the American people. Kelissa had several letters for the day: three from kids and two from older men inquiring about social security. But there was one letter that caught Kelissa's attention.

A letter from a woman named Robin Vassallo. Robin was a mother of three children. Like Kelissa, she had two sons and a daughter. All three of Robin's children went into the military, and Robin wanted to share her story. In the letter, Robin Vassallo wrote:

Dear President Kelissa Morrison,

How are you, ma'am? I hope all is well and that this letter finds you well. My name is Robin Vassallo. I'm a college professor who teaches philosophy at Yale University. I've been teaching at Yale for over thirty-two years. I am soon to be retired at the end of the spring semester.

I am writing this letter because I wanted to share my story with you. My children: my oldest son, Matthew, my middle child, Jessica, and my youngest, Perry. All three of my children are in the pictures I sent taped to this letter. Matthew is the one who is the most decorated. Aren't they beautiful? Well, they were beautiful. Matthew was killed in Iraq back in 2010. Jessica was killed a year later in Afghanistan, two weeks before deportation. And my youngest son, Perry, well, Perry survived Iraq and was deported on medical leave. But mentally, I knew that I would never have my son back. He eventually took his own life. He just couldn't handle it. My husband, William, their father, made his departure twenty years ago, losing his battle to cancer.

I'm all alone now. But I try my best to live my life day by day, the best way I possibly can. Not having them in my life has been extremely rough for me this past decade. I miss them terribly; sometimes, the pain is too great. But anytime I feel upset, I'm reminded of this quote, "The pain will win some battles, but love will always win the war." I do not want to come off as a victim or for you to pity me in any way. My children served their country and sacrificed their lives for the liberation of our nation. I understand that the powers that be have made some decisions that have cost the lives of many soldiers. I just pray that no other mother or father will lose all their children in one lifetime. There's a lot of evil in this world, and I believe that you, Madam President, will change things for the better. That's why I voted for you. I thank you for reading my letter. May God continue to bless you, and God bless America.

Sincerely,

Robin Vassallo.

Kelissa was *instantly* moved to tears—tears not caused by the pain in her back but the pain of Robin. Kelissa sat at her desk with her curled index finger pressed against her mouth. She felt deeply for Robin. Kelissa could not imagine what that must feel like for a woman to lose her whole family. But what also crossed Kelissa's mind was the thought of *Ted* killing her one day, and *her* children would be motherless. That scared her even more. Without hesitation, Kelissa grabbed a pen and a blank sheet of paper with the White House letterhead and began a rough draft of her letter to Robin. In the letter, Kelissa wrote:

Dearest Robin,

Your words, your story, your pain, and your strength, I felt all of it coming off the paper. I cannot begin to express the colossal sympathy I have for you. Your three courageous, beautiful, heroic children have made the ultimate sacrifice to serve their country and combat those who bring forth mass destruction and pure evil to this world. It is never easy to send our youth into situations that do not guarantee a safe return home.

But what I can guarantee is that I will award all three of your children: Matthew, Jessica, and Perry, the Congressional Medal of Honor. And I would be more than honored to have you visit the White House and accept these honorary medals on their behalf. Also, I will see to it that I remedy the unacknowledged mental health crisis of our soldiers and the mental health of the American people. I was in the service. I was a nurse who took care of the wounded veterans. I understand what war does to our soldiers. It is time to bring attention to this tragic phenomenon and address it thoroughly. I am with great gratitude for receiving your letter, Robin. I thank you for the service of your children, and I look forward to meeting you in person.

Please continue to stay safe during these trying times.
God bless you, Robin.
President Kelissa Morrison.

After a few crossed-out words and sentences, Kelissa finally had a rough draft letter. As she walked around the Oval Office, reading the letter to herself, she heard a knock on the door. "Come in!" Kelissa projected. It was Carl, stepping into the office. He notified Kelissa about dinner and that her children were waiting at the Family Dining Room. Kelissa promised them that she would have a sit-down dinner with the family this evening and that it was a mandatory family dinner. "Okay, thank you, Carl. I will be right there."

Kelissa read through the letter a few more times, made changes, and a few minutes later, the letter was ready. She then rewrote the final letter on a new sheet of paper. She proofread it once more, now prepared to be signed, sealed, and delivered. Kelissa then put her shoes back on and made her exit.

Joan was still sitting at her desk, typing away, sending emails. Kelissa handed Joan the final letter for Robin Vassallo.

"Joan," said Kelissa. "You were right; that letter was *very* touching. I would like you to send this letter to her as soon as possible."

"Right away, Madam President," Joan responded.

"Thank you, Joan… Oh, and make note that I will also be inviting this woman to the White House to award her three late children the Congressional Medal of Honor."

"Wow, Madam President, that is very generous of you."

"No, they've earned it. Robin's been through a lot, Joan. That's the *least* I can do for her. Well, I'm off—have a great night."

"You too, Madam President."

Kelissa, with the escort of Carl, was making her way to the Family Dining Room, where her children were waiting. But before attending, Kelissa wanted to change her outfit once more. She asked Carl to remain in the same position near the stairs that he had stood earlier. She quickly went up the stairs to the residential level and into her dressing room. Because the pain in her back was still affecting her, she had to undress carefully, trying not to provoke any more pain. Curious to see the aftermath of her back, Kelissa took a small circular mirror into the bathroom with her. In order to see the reflection of her back, Kelissa turned her back to the bathroom mirror while *holding* the circular mirror in front of her. She closed her eyes for a moment, took a deep breath, and then opened them to take a look.

As Kelissa held the circular mirror up, she almost dropped it. She could not believe the size of the bruise on her back. It was another bruise to her brutal collection. The mere sight of the violent decoration of bruises on Kelissa's body had killed her spirit and ruined her appetite. Kelissa decided that she was going to take a rain check on dinner. She gave Carl a call on her highly secured Blackberry and told him that she would no longer be attending dinner and would remain upstairs. Instead of dinner, Kelissa did what she planned and drew herself a nice hot bath.

Kelissa then went to the bathtub and turned on the faucet. As the water was beginning to fill up the tub, she sent a text message to Madeline, Bryan, and Ted, Jr. In the text, she said:

Hey guys, I really hate to disappoint you, but I've had a very rough day today, and I still have work to do. I know that this was supposed to be a mandatory dinner. I'm so sorry for this. But I promise that I will make this up to all of you. I love you guys very much. Enjoy your dinner.

Once again, Kelissa told a lie she did not want to tell. She did not want to see Ted sitting across from her at the dining room table. She could not stand his sight after what he had done to her earlier that day. All she wanted to do was dip her naked body into that hot bath and soak out the misery, the pain, and escape from this harsh reality she is suffering from at the hands of her abusive husband.

Chapter 17

Thursday evening, March 14th, 2024

Don't Drown Me

The bath has been drawn, and Kelissa has been soaking her body for the last twenty minutes. Pure silence, no music, no outside noise, and no Ted. The pain in her back was slowly fading away, but the memory of the attack was going nowhere. Kelissa sat in the tub with her eyes closed. She began to think about her children and how she would make it up to them for flaking on them.

As Kelissa opened her eyes, she reached over to the far end of the tub to grab the soap bar. Since she is the President, all of her bathing products had to be carefully screened and tested before use, just to ensure there were no toxic chemicals that would cause harm or damage to her body. Unfortunately, her toxic and abusive *husband* is the one who brings injury and damage to her body.

Kelissa attempted to rub the soap on her body, but it was too soon and painful to touch. All she wanted at that moment was escapism—to escape from her harsh reality. Kelissa closed her eyes again, took a good deep breath, and slowly sunk her head underwater. Kelissa, now completely submerged underwater, with her eyes still closed. She saw nothing and heard nothing—completely escaping from the world.

Then all of a sudden, as Kelissa opened her eyes, a swirly image was standing right above her; it was Ted. Before Kelissa could even scream, Ted reached down for her neck, briefly choking her while she was still submerged underwater. Kelissa panicked; water splashed all over the floor as she kicked her legs and grabbed Ted's arm, trying to remove his hand from around her neck. At that very moment, Kelissa thought this was it—this was going to be the end.

Those six seconds of panic felt like a lifetime of hell. But finally, Ted let her go. Kelissa immediately emerged from out of the water and let out a scream. But her scream was short-lived as she was still trying to catch her breath. Some water got into her windpipes, making her cough and gasp for oxygen. Her naked body was exposed as she climbed out of the bathtub, lying wet and helpless on the floor. Kelissa cried every tear she possibly could. But her tears did nothing except contribute to the wet puddle on the floor. Ted stood there; with the most despicable smile you could ever see on a person's face.

At that moment, Ted was no longer a person in Kelissa's eyes. Perhaps, Kelissa was no longer a person through *his* eyes. As she lays on the floor, wet and exposed, Ted squatted down and disturbingly said this with an innocent tone, "Aww, *honey*... Did you honestly think that I was going to *drown* you? I was only *kidding* with you. I would *never* do something like that to you. To be honest, *drowning* someone is too easy. I rather beat someone to death. *That* way, they could feel *every* ounce of pain that I could give them. You know, when I was in Iraq, I beat someone almost *to death*. It made me feel *so* powerful. You'll just *never* understand what it's like to have power over the weak. Remember, Kel, if you *tell* anyone, it's all over for you. You'll lose everything. This shit will all come crashing down, and you'll be *nothing*—nothing but an absolute failure."

Kelissa, still on the bathroom floor with her temple laid against the wet tile, completely naked and defenseless. She had no way of wrapping her brain around this monster who stood over her. As she continued to cough and cry on the wet floor, Ted turned around to make his exit. Right before he left the bathroom, Ted pointed at Kelissa and said, "The next time you make a promise to *my* kids, you better *damn* well keep it. Don't miss any more family dinners. You hear me?"

The bathroom grew quiet, minus Kelissa's sobbing. Her body *quivered* in fear, shaking, trembling, afraid that Ted would return. But he did not, which gave Kelissa time to recover. Still, on the wet bathroom floor, she saw her bathrobe. She crawled over to the sink to carefully pull herself up. Cautious of the slippery floor, Kelissa then took towels and placed them down on the floor to dry.

A trembling walk as Kelissa grabbed her bathrobe off the door and made her exit out into the dressing room. Still a bit shocked after what happened, she sat down on the chair in the center of her dressing room. Kelissa begins to look around the dressing room, sitting there in silence. Her emotions began to rise as she placed her hands over her face and wept uncontrollably. She believed that Ted was going to go all the way this time. She felt that he was going to drown her. Kelissa just curled up on that chair and cried for a half-hour.

At this moment, Kelissa did not know what to do. She did not know whether she should tell Carl or remain silent. She knew in the back of her mind that if she said a word about *any* of the abuse, her entire legacy would crumble. And what she feared the most was the thought of letting down the American people who voted her in office. The millions of little girls and women who look up to her, Kelissa feared they would consider her a fraud, which was the last resort she wanted to face.

A good twenty-five minutes went by; Kelissa was still sitting there, wiping her now red eyes as there were no more tears to shed. She took off her bathrobe and put on her pajamas. She then put on her walk-around robe, placed her feet in her furry slippers, and walked out of the dressing room.

At that moment, all Kelissa wanted to do was go into her private office and sip on some tea. As she walked into the bedroom, Kelissa grabbed her pillow and an extra blanket as she planned on staying in her private office for the night. She walked out of her bedroom with the pillow and blanket and was surprised by someone's voice from behind.

"Mom?" Madeline said.

"Huh? Yes! What?" Kelissa projected.

"What are you doing with that pillow and blanket?"

"Oh, I just had some work to do in my office, and I'll probably be working late tonight. Sometimes I fall asleep on the couch."

"Weird… But anyway, you missed a wonderful dinner tonight, mom. Thanks for standing us up, *again*."

"I'm so sorry, Maddy. I know I promised you guys that I would cut out the work and have dinner with you all. It won't happen again."

"Yeah, well… Goodnight."

"Goodnight, babe… Hey, how about we spend some quality time together *right now*? Just you and me. We'll order up some dessert."

"Uh, sure, why not? I was going to take a quick shower. I'll meet you in your office?"

"It's a date."

As Madeline smiled and walked into her bedroom, Kelissa closed her eyes and painfully sighed as she lied to her daughter once again. Carrying her pillow and blanket, Kelissa walked into her office. As she turned on the light, she saw her black leather journal on her desk. She left it there last night after pulling an all-nighter, writing letters and speeches for upcoming events. But *tonight*, Kelissa had a lot to say.

After tossing the pillow and blanket onto the couch, Kelissa sat down at her desk and opened her journal. Without hesitation, she picked up her pen and let her words bleed onto the paper. In her journal, Kelissa wrote:

Thursday evening, March 14th, 2024

Ladies and gentlemen, my hand is shaking in complete fear as I write to you this evening. I thought this was going to be the end for me. I felt that he was going to drown me in that bathtub. I am so scared. I am terrified of what he will do next. But what am I to do? It's not as if I could just go to the police like any other woman who goes through domestic violence. I'm the fucking President. I don't deserve this shit. I just wish I could kill him myself. But I can't. Maybe I could hire a personal trainer. Someone who could train me, show me ways to throw a punch. But who the hell am I kidding? I can't defend myself. I can't fight him back; he's too strong. Ted will just overpower me and beat me to death.

Carl is the only one who can protect me. But I can't tell him either. I want to tell him everything, but I just can't. I don't know what to do, ladies and gentlemen. It seems as if anything I do wrong, he punishes me behind closed doors. Never—never in a million years would I ever thought that I would be married to a psychopath who tries to kill me. God, I need help. He's a sick bastard, but I'm even worse to let him continue his abusive, gaslighting behavior. Every day, every single day, whether or not he hits me or curses at me in my sleep and wakes me up. I still allow this to happen to me. I'm beginning to process just how crazy I am. But I just don't know what to do; I really don't. Now that I think about it, I am going crazy. Here I am, consistently getting attacked by my husband, yet I'm trying to keep the family's image together, just to have the "perfect" First family. But I don't know how much more of this I can take.

It is only a matter of time before he really snaps, to the point where there is no more Ted, and the only thing that would be left is the demon within him. But I can't tell. I wish I could tell my daughter—I wish I could tell Maddy this secret. But I'm so scared for my children. If they lose their father, then it's my fault. But if they lose me, God knows what will happen. Not to mention, I receive death threats every week. But the real death threat is my own fucking husband.

I remember when I was a little girl, I used to believe that ugly monsters were living under my bed. But my father was very grounded. He would always tell me that I just imagined it. But the truth is, there are such things as monsters. I just never imagined the monster being on top of the bed, lying next to me.

To be honest with you, ladies and gentlemen, my body cannot handle any more pain right now. I have to give it time to heal. So, my best alternative right now is to submit myself to him and oblige to his demands so that I don't anger him. I know what you're thinking, ladies and gentlemen, and you're very right. I've totally lost my fucking mind. I am crazy to continue on like this. But the country is depending on me to be their leader. Now is not the time to crack and fail the nation. I must do what I have to do to survive. I have to survive through this abusive situation. I have to survive for my kids and the young women who idolize me. But I still can't believe he was trying to drown me. Please pray for me, ladies and gentlemen. I really could use all the prayers I can get.

A knock came at the door, "Come in!" Kelissa projected. Expecting for it to be Madeline, in came Ted. Kelissa immediately jumped in her seat. Her heart began to race; the fear in her eyes said it all to him. Ted knew that he had Kelissa right where he wanted her, under his command.

"Please, Ted, don't," Kelissa begged. "I can't handle any—"

"Stop," Ted interjected. "Don't say another word. I just want to talk with you."

"Ted, Maddy is coming to spend time with me, I wan—"

"Kel, I said, '*stop.*' I need you to listen, not talk."

"Okay, I'll listen."

Ted closed and locked the door and slowly walked towards Kelissa. Kelissa, realizing that she still had her journal opened, immediately shut it to prevent Ted from looking at what she wrote down. As Ted stood near Kelissa's desk, he stared at her, and she stared right back at him. Ted had that same despicable smile on his face. He then sat on the edge of the desk and said this to her. "Kel, about what happened earlier in the bathroom? I kind of lost my cool. I was angry that you didn't attend dinner this evening. I don't like for our children to be disappointed with us—well, with *you.* You know you should have been there, having dinner with your family. I may have gone too far tonight. But, since we're being honest here, it really is *your* fault that this happened. If you had just shown up to dinner, none of this would have happened. But we make mistakes, and I think not only do you owe my *children* an apology, but you also owe *me* an apology."

Almost instantly, Kelissa's fear turned to furious anger. She could not believe how narcissistic and sociopathic Ted was. His gaslighting mentality was his poison to her open wounds. But Kelissa *knew* she could not handle any more attacks. And she knew Ted would attack her if she got out of line with him. So, instead of Kelissa being defensive, she decided to be submissive. As she looked at Ted, Kelissa said to him, "Ted, I am *so* sorry. You are absolutely right. I should have been there, having dinner with my loving family. I am truly *sorry* for my self-involved behavior. That is unacceptable, and I am *grateful* to have a husband like you to put me in check."

As those words put an enormous smile on *Ted's* face, they gave Kelissa the most bitter, *dreadful* taste she ever had in her mouth. But Kelissa knew what she had to do. She knew, however, that apologizing to him was utterly ridiculous. But she *also* knew of the danger she would be in if she did not compromise and agree to his terms. Another knock at the door came. Kelissa knew that it was Madeline.

"Goodnight, Ted," Kelissa said with a phony smile.

"I want you to join me for bed tonight. And I hope you have some energy left. Because you're going to need it," Ted said as he winked his eye.

"Ted… I—I don't think I have the ener—"

"That's an *order*, Kel."

"I—I'll be there shortly."

"Good girl."

Ted kissed Kelissa on her forehead and took his leave. Madeline was there as he opened the door, ready to spend quality time with her mother. Ted kissed her and said goodnight. As Madeline came into the office, Kelissa had to give her some more disappointing news.

"Maddy," Kelissa softly said. "I—I'm afraid I'm going to have to take another rain check on our midnight snack rendezvous. I'm sorry, sweetie."

"Are you *serious*, mom?" Madeline said with anger.

"I'm so sorry, Maddy. Some more work came up that I have to finish. I *promise* I will make it up to you, baby."

"Whatever," Madeline said as she stormed out of the office.

"Ha—have a goodnight, sweetie," Kelissa projected.

Kelissa, once again, closed her eyes and sighed as she stood there in her office. She was disappointed in herself for leading Madeline on and flaking on her again. But she knew that Ted was waiting on her, and she did *not* want to keep him waiting. Kelissa then took her black leather journal and placed it in the top drawer of her desk, securely locked. She then walked out of her office, closing the door behind her. Before taking another step, Kelissa took a deep breath and exhaled, as she did not know what she was about to walk into.

As Kelissa got to her bedroom door, she stood in front of it for a few seconds. Her shaking right hand reached for the doorknob. Opening the door, she saw Ted standing in his robe with his back turned, facing the draped-covered window. He then turned his head, looking straight at her. "Close the door, Kel," Ted softly said. Kelissa closed the door and began to make her way onto the bed. "No, no. Come *here*," Ted said. Kelissa looked at Ted, confused at why he wanted her to come to him. She then stood in the center of the bedroom. An eerie moment of silence as Ted began to stare at her.

Kelissa continued to stand there, looking at everything in the room besides Ted. "*Look* at me, Kel!" Ted projected. Kelissa immediately focused her eyes on him. He then began to walk towards her. She was terrified; Kelissa had no idea if he would grab her, punch her, or kick her to the floor. Ted was now standing right in front of her, gazing at her with the eyes of evil seduction. Kelissa looked up to his six-foot-three-inch frame with eyes of vulnerability and fear. Ted then took his hand and gently, oh so gently, caressed her face. He brushed his thumb back and forth across her left cheek while he leaned in to kiss her right cheek. He kissed, and kissed, and kissed.

Kelissa did nothing, standing there like a statue with her eyes closed. She refused to see his face, but she felt his lips all over hers. Ted slowly began to take off Kelissa's robe and then her pajamas. She stood there, now in the nude. Ted then removed *his* robe, as he was already naked underneath. She knew now that this was about submitting herself sexually to him. Then suddenly, Ted took both hands and aggressively grabbed Kelissa's shoulders. Startled at Ted's physical gesture, Kelissa began to backpedal towards the bed. Ted then tossed Kelissa onto the bed as he pounced on top of her. Her heart was pounding like a fist pounding on a closed door. In her mind, this was not fornicating, and this was not lovemaking. *This* was Ted having his way with her.

Ted continued to kiss her, but *this* time, he only kissed on her bruises. Ted kissed her bruises as if they were first place trophies he won. He kissed the bruise on her ribs, on her thighs and quickly turned Kelissa around on her stomach and began to kiss the large bruise on her back. Kelissa was disgusted that he would do such a thing. But for her, this was mind over matter. Kelissa went to another place in time while Ted was on top of her.

Kelissa went back to when the two of them were just married, and they were on their honeymoon in Jamaica. She remembered that very first night when they made love. As she remembers that night, Kelissa tries to pretend, at that very moment, that *this* night is just like the first night of their honeymoon. But it did not take long for Kelissa to realize that those days were gone.

Now, here comes the penetration. Ted began to excessively kiss Kelissa—*kissing* her all over her face, her neck, leaving teeth marks on her shoulders. Aggressive strokes and thrusting as Ted comes close to reaching climax. Kelissa just kept her eyes closed as tears began to leak down the side of her face. Ted's heavy grunting noises overpowered her cries as she felt that she was being maltreated. But to add salt to the wound, Ted begins to say to her repeatedly, '*I love you; I love you; I love you.*' His voice grew louder and louder until finally, "Oh, *FUCK*!" Ted shouted as he climaxed, "*Jesus*… Kel, that felt *so* goddamn good."

Kelissa was lost in the thousands of thoughts cycling through her mind. She opened her eyes and began to look up at the ceiling—now hearing a heavy-breathing Ted as he was still on top of her. He then kisses her damp face, saying how great it felt. But ironically, through all of that, Kelissa demanded that Ted try again.

"Now, make love to me," Kelissa whispered as she gazed at the ceiling.

"W—*What*?" Ted responded.

"I said make *love* to me. Make love to me the way you did on our honeymoon."

"Whatever you say, Madam President."

Ted smiled as he was still on top of Kelissa. He remembered that night precisely and began to proceed. Kelissa knew what she wanted to feel, and she would not settle for anything less. Ted switched gears as his fornicating tempo changed drastically. He knew what Kelissa wanted, and he gave that to her. Even though the bruises were still painful, the multiple orgasms created sexual healing to the point where Kelissa felt no pain.

For the rest of the night, Ted gave Kelissa the lovemaking she requested. Kelissa was able to dismiss the abuse to the side, *just* to have that feeling again—that feeling of being loved, wanted and pleasured—to be treated as a woman, a human being, and that was all

Kelissa wanted. With all the stress of being the leader of the free world, this feeling could not have come at a perfect time for Kelissa.

As Ted retired for the night, Kelissa's eyes were still opened. The digital alarm clock just changed to "3:00 a.m." She carefully removed the covers and got up from her bed. Kelissa looked over at Ted as she placed on her pajamas and nightrobe, making sure not to wake him. As she came out of the bedroom, Kelissa began to walk around to clear her head. The residence level was tranquil; not a sound was made, minus her footsteps. With everything that happened: the interview, the punch in the back, Ted trying to drown her in the bathtub, and the unpredictable "lovemaking." Kelissa was more confused than she had ever been. Ted's influence began to take control over her mind. She did not know how or what to feel anymore. She did not know if she hated him or if she needed him. All that was for sure was that Kelissa needed time to heal. She did not want another bruise *anywhere* on her body. And if this was the scenario she had to endure for Ted to stop his attacks, then so be it.

Chapter 18

Sunday Evening, March 31st, 2024

A Daughter's Secrets

Alone in her private office, Kelissa is in her journal, writing down whatever she feels is necessary to be documented. She has been somewhat consistent with writing in recent days. The words have bled through her pen—line after line, page after page, there was no stopping her. In one of her paragraphs, she wrote about how Ted has become extremely sexual with her ever since the interview with journalist Catherine Chang.

In her journal, Kelissa wrote this specifically:

Wednesday-Evening-March 31st, 2024

Ladies and gentlemen, I have a disturbing confession to make about Ted. But before I tell you, all I ask is that you don't judge me. Sex with Ted has never been better. I don't know what has gotten into him. But I know what has come into me, if you know what I mean. Ted has been pleasuring me like there's no tomorrow. Multiple orgasmic nights, over and over. I've never moaned as much as I have these past few weeks. But I don't know if that's a good thing or a bad thing. But it feels so damn great in bed. However, I know I can't let sex dismiss the abuse. At the same time, the sex has become my drug, my physical "painkillers" to all the abuse Ted has put me through. And ladies and gentlemen, I am here to give my testimonial and say that I am addicted to the "painkillers." Sex with Ted is the only thing that takes the pain away.

But what scares me is the fact that I am now under his control, completely—right where he wanted me to be, under his control. I let him sweet talk me in the interview, and I fell for it passionately. What the hell is wrong with me? Am I so desperate for love that I am willing to settle for this? Mind you, I still have a country to run. Millions of American people who are depending on me. And yet, I am getting beaten and fucked by my husband on the same goddamn day.

Ladies and gentlemen, I think I've really lost my fucking mind over this man. I've become his personal ragdoll, his toy, and I'm afraid. I'm worried that if I rebel against him, he will continue to put his hands on me, and I don't know how much more my body could withstand. I don't know how many more punches I can take. I'm holding on to this dark secret, ladies and gentlemen. But eventually, this dark secret will have to come to light.

As Kelissa closed her journal for the evening, she decided to call it a night and head off to bed. But before she went, Kelissa headed up to the second floor of the residence level to talk with Ted, Jr. about his plans for the future. Ted, Jr. has begun to look at brochures of colleges he plans to visit for the upcoming fall semester.

As Kelissa got to Ted, Jr's room, she heard his drum banging in the music room. Surprisingly, Kelissa enjoyed the catchy cadence he created on the drums. Walking down to the music room, Kelissa intervened. "That sounds pretty good, TJ," Kelissa smiled. Ted, Jr. smiled right back, appreciative of his mother's compliment.

"Thanks, mom," said Ted, Jr, "I've been practicing a lot. I wish I could show this on social media."

"Yeah, that *would* be nice, huh?" Kelissa agreed. "But unfortunately, I can't have you guys on those things. For security reasons."

"But I'll be able to have a smartphone and use social media when I go off to college, right?"

"I'll think about it, TJ."

"Oh, mom, *come on*. I *need* those things."

"No, you *don't*."

"Literally *everyone* at college will have a smartphone and social media. There's *no* way I can survive without it."

"I'll get back to you on the smartphone. As for social media, I'll see what I can do. But I *don't* want you guys on those platforms. They're extremely addictive."

"Yeah, but it's the way of the world now."

"You know, I should just make a policy and ban *all* that *crap*."

"MOM, DON'T!"

"I'm just *kidding*; go to bed."

"Alright, good. Goodnight—oh, by the way, dad thinks that I should apply to Georgetown University."

"Oh? Well, where would *you* like to go?"

"I mean, I think that makes sense to go apply for *there* since it's right here in D.C."

"Well, it's still *your* decision, sweetie. So, choose wisely."

"I will. Thanks, mom. Goodnight."

"Goodnight. Love you," Kelissa said with a hug and kiss.

"Oh, *mom*!"

"What?"

"Always have to *kiss* me."

"Uh, *yes*, you're my son. My *firstborn*—get over it. Now hit the sack."

They both shared a laugh. Kelissa thought about what Ted, Jr. said about applying to Georgetown. Even though she wants Ted, Jr. to apply to whatever college of his choice, she liked the idea of him being close by because she may need him to come home right away if anything ever happened to her.

As Kelissa went down the stairs of the residence level, she went to check on Madeline. She walked to Madeline's door and gave it a few knocks. A few more knocks were given, but there was no answer. "Maddy, sweetie? It's me," Kelissa said. But still, there was no answer. Kelissa then grabbed the doorknob and gave it a turn. Surprisingly, Madeline was there, lying in her bed. As Kelissa looked at Madeline's shiny face and glary eyes, she realized that Madeline had been crying. Kelissa immediately went over to sit on Madeline's bed to comfort her.

"Maddy, sweetie," said Kelissa. "What's wrong?"

"Nothing," Madeline responded as she shook her head.

"No, talk to me. Why are you crying?"

"Why should I tell *you*? You wouldn't care anyway. You're always so busy in your *stupid* Oval Office."

"Oh, *Maddy*… Baby, I'm very *sorry*. I know this whole presidency lifestyle has been *rough* on you kids. But I *do* care. I'm your mother; I care about *all* of you."

"Whatever."

"Are you going to tell me what's really bothering you?"

"I just want to be left alone, *please*."

"Okay… I love you, Maddy. I *truly* do. Goodnight."

Kelissa gave Madeline a goodnight kiss to the side of her head and exited her bedroom. As Kelissa closed the door, she could hear the emotional echo of Madeline's sobbing in her bedroom. It even brought Kelissa to tears. Now leaned up against Madeline's bedroom door, crying, Kelissa began to think about her relationship with her daughter. She felt the strong bond between her and Madeline was rotting and weakening, right under their feet. Her only daughter has grown distant—a disconnect has been created, and Kelissa does not know how to rekindle their relationship.

Suddenly, Kelissa's bedroom door had opened. Ted stuck his head out as he looked down the center hall. Already in his pajamas, he stood there as he waited for Kelissa to join him for bed. Still upset from Madeline giving her the cold shoulder, Kelissa did not want to join Ted for bed. But Ted being *Ted*, stood there with an emotionless face and continued to wait for Kelissa to enter their bedroom.

After a good thirty seconds, Kelissa finally began to walk down the center hall, making her way to her bedroom. As she stood there in front of Ted, he looked down at her and said, "The bed is nice and warm for us, baby." Kelissa just looked at him as if he was a senseless stranger. But to avoid any problems, she looked away and made her way into the bedroom. And Kelissa endured another late night, filled with Ted's sexual hunger.

There was a part of Kelissa that was beginning to feel numb. Her emotions were not intact, and her heart was in a different place. The relationship with her children was starting to fade, particularly with Madeline. Eventually, sex with Ted would become more and more of a one-sided pleasure routine. Everything going on behind the scenes in Kelissa's personal life was taking its toll on her. But the presidency was beginning to put her mind through more stress than ever before.

Chapter 19

Thursday Afternoon, April 4th, 2024

The Stone of Hope

It is an essential moment today—a busy day. Today is the day that President Kelissa Morrison visits the Martin Luther King, Jr. Memorial site. Being that today marks the fifty-sixth anniversary of his death, Kelissa wanted to take time to pay her respect and visit the thirty-foot statue of Dr. King, which is called the '*Stone of Hope*.' Kelissa, along with Bryan, Madeline, and White House photographer Georgette Wilson, were all riding in the Beast one. Ted, Jr. went along with his father to look around the campus of Georgetown University.

Riding in the Beast two was Vice President Harry Griffin and his wife, Jessica Griffin, and their detail leader. As the motorcade pulled up to the Martin Luther King, Jr. Memorial site, Kelissa was completely in awe. To see such a colossal statue of a man who broke barriers, focused on bringing peace to this country, and African Americans having freedom and equality across the board. Kelissa was almost brought to tears by the mere sight of the statue.

Carl made his way to the back of the limousine to open the back door. Before getting out, Kelissa told both Bryan and Madeline to mind their manners and give off some smiles. Madeline, however, was still moody after last week. As they exited the Beast one, dozens of Secret Service agents were scattered around the premises of the memorial site—several of which were surrounding Kelissa and her children.

"It is divinely magnificent, isn't it?" Kelissa said as they walked toward the '*Stone of Hope*.' The cherry blossom trees were fully bloomed all across the memorial site. A sight for sore eyes indeed. As Kelissa made her way to the statue, dozens of cameras clicked away. The press got every shot of the President standing next to such a monumental American treasure. Kelissa and Vice President Harry Griffin stood next to each other for a photo opportunity. While standing side by side, they began a quiet conversation.

"This is nice," said Harry, "Didn't realize how enormous it is."

"Isn't it?" Kelissa responded. "I'm glad I brought my children with me. To see history."

"Madam President, the first Cabinet Room meeting is coming up."

"Yes, six days, to be exact."

"Are you nervous?"

"*Nervous*? Why would I be nervous, Mr. Vice President?"

"Oh, I don't know. Maybe you shouldn't be. It's just a meeting, right?"

"I'll be *fine*, Mr. Vice President. I'm not worried *or* nervous."

As President Kelissa Morrison and Vice President Harry Griffin were finished with the photographs, Kelissa called it a day and told Carl that it was time to head home. Carl spoke into the microphone hidden under his shirt sleeve and gave the call to move out. The press continued to click away at their cameras, asking the most outlandish questions that Kelissa ignored entirely.

Right before leaving, Kelissa took one last look at the statue of Dr. King. An engraved quote on the right side of the sculpture says, '*OUT OF THE MOUNTAIN OF DESPAIR, A STONE OF HOPE.*' Kelissa had much despair in her personal life—without any natural way of finding hope that she could escape this situation that she is in with Ted. But Kelissa now realizes that she has to hold on to the one thing that will genuinely get her through it all: her faith.

Chapter 20

Thursday Evening, April 4th, 2024

Table For Two

After a long, productive, busy day, Kelissa made time to have dinner with her family. But unfortunately, her family did not make time for her. Ted, however, decided to have a meal with Kelissa and have a private conversation in the Family Dining Room. Ted was enjoying his chicken marsala with sauteed mushrooms and asparagus. As the kitchen staffers and butlers left the dining room, Kelissa began to speak.

"Where are the kids?" Kelissa asked.

"I told them they could order something of their choice and eat it in their rooms," Ted responded.

"*Why?*"

"Well, this is a special *occasion*, of course. I wanted you and *me* to celebrate your first cabinet meeting, taking place next week, yes? I gave you some great advice on foreign policy. You're going to knock em' dead."

"Ted… There's something that I need to tell you."

"*Please* don't tell me you're pregnant?" Ted humorously responded.

"That's not funny. And no, it's about the advice you gave me with foreign policy."

"Oh? What about it?"

"Well, I really do appreciate your input. But after careful consideration with my advisors, I think it's best that we go with *my* plans on foreign policy."

"Oh, I *see*… You're just full of surprises, aren't you?"

"I was going to tell you at the Easter egg roll, but I didn't want to ruin the fun."

"Well, you *definitely* ruined this delicious meal for me," Ted said as he wiped his mouth with his napkin.

"I'm sorry."

Kelissa knew that disagreeing with Ted could mean that she would suffer potential consequences and repercussions later. But she had to tell him the truth. Ted took a few more bites out of his meal, a few more sips of wine, and then stood up from the table. Kelissa was still sitting there as she sipped her glass of ginger ale—nervous about what Ted was going to say next. He walked over to the end of the table where Kelissa was seated. He stood there next to her, staring down at her with a piercing look. Then, he gave her a slow kiss on her lips. "See you upstairs?" Ted asked with a sinister smile. Kelissa nodded her head up and down, giving him a disingenuous smirk on her face. Ted landed another kiss on her cheek and walked out of the dining room.

All Kelissa could hear were the clicking sounds of his shoes as he walked off. As she remained seated, she closed her eyes and took a deep breath, slowly blowing out the air of fear and anxiety. She knew Ted all too well; she knew that an attack was bound to happen, and all she could do was prepare herself.

Kelissa continued to sit there at the dining room table and looked down at her dinner plate. Her appetite left the room right along with Ted. She could not pick up another forkful. As Kelissa closed her eyes again, she began to zone out and contemplate which part of her body Ted might abuse. Suddenly, an innocent voice came into the dining room, saying, "Mommy?" It was Bryan, but Kelissa was too zoned out to hear him. Bryan repeatedly said, "Mommy, mommy," but no one was home. He then touched Kelissa's shoulder; immediately, she jumped in her seat, scaring Bryan. Kelissa thought it was Ted grabbing her shoulder, getting ready to attack her. Once she realized it was Bryan, she swiftly hugged him and said, "Oh, sweetie, I'm sorry. I wasn't even paying attention. Mommy is *so* tired."

Kelissa held on to Bryan for what seemed to be two minutes. She didn't want to let him go. The paranoia within her has been snowballing because of Ted's unpredictable attacks—not knowing when or where he will strike next. To stall from going into her bedroom, Kelissa came up with the idea of reading Bryan a bedtime story.

Before heading upstairs, she and Bryan took a brief tour of some of the rooms on the State Floor. After leaving the Family Dining Room, Kelissa asked Bryan which room he wanted to look at first. "The Blue Room, blue is my favorite color," Bryan said with excitement. As they entered the Blue Room, Kelissa began to explain to Bryan the history of this particular room and how it received its name. The Blue Room is the oval-shaped room located in the center of the White House. Rooms with an oval-shaped were very popular during the late 1700s. It received its name, "Blue Room," in 1837 when President Martin Van Buren redecorated with blue textiles.

To the left of the Blue Room is the Green Room, which President Thomas Jefferson used as a dining room. It was once known as the "Green Drawing Room" by John Quincy Adams in 1825 for the color of the fabrics. It was also the room where President James Madison signed America's first declaration of war, which was the war of 1812 against Great Britain. Lastly, Kelissa concluded the brief tour by visiting the Red Room. The Red Room was initially decorated with red color fabrics in 1845. First ladies have often used it for interviews and guests who visit.

There were so many pictures and paintings, antique furniture—a lot to take in for the young Bryan. And even though Bryan is still too young to understand the history behind it, Kelissa wanted him to know how important it is to learn American history and understand how fortunate they are to reside in the most historical landmark in the country. While walking through the rooms, Bryan made a special request.

"Mommy," said Bryan. "Even though I had dinner with Maddy, is it okay if I can have some ice cream?"

"Sure, sweetie," Kelissa said as she smiled at Bryan.

Kelissa and Bryan made their way up to the residence level and into the kitchen. She had a variety of flavors of ice cream in the freezer. As Bryan sat at the kitchen counter table, Kelissa asked him what kind of ice cream he wanted.

"Sweetie," said Kelissa. "What flavor would you like?"

"Blue raspberry, mom, *duh*! That's my *favorite*," Bryan responded.

"You ate it all, sweetie."

"I *did*?"

"Yep."

"Um… Well, what other flavors *are* there?"

"Let's see… There's strawberry, vanilla, chocolate, rocky road, butter pecan, *and—oh*, cookies and cream."

"Um, can I have strawberry, vanilla, *and* rocky road?"

"You can have *one scoop* of each."

Bryan was so excited as he rubbed his tiny hands together, looking forward to devouring that bowl of ice cream. Kelissa was getting the ice cream prepared as she pulled out the silver ice cream scooper from the kitchen drawer and gave it a hot rinse. Scooping out of one container at a time, Kelissa almost forgot to add toppings. "Sweetie, would you like some toppings?" Kelissa asked. But Bryan shook his head "no," as he harpoons a spoonful of ice cream, one after the other.

"Bryan, sweetie, slow *down*," Kelissa laughed.

"Oh, it's *so* good, mommy," Bryan smiled. "Aren't you going to have some?"

"Oh, not right now, honey."

"Well, I don't want to eat ice cream *alone*."

Kelissa felt a bit guilty watching Bryan sit there, enjoying the ice cream by himself. But her appetite was nowhere in the kitchen. Then Bryan looked at her with his sad puppy dog eyes, which Kelissa could never resist. "Well, I guess I could have a scoop or two," Kelissa said as she grinned at Bryan.

It was a special table for two as Kelissa and Bryan sat at the kitchen island, enjoying their scoops of delight and having a wonderful mother and son conversation.

"Mommy," said Bryan. "Do you like being President?"

"Yes, baby… For the most part, I do," Kelissa responded.

"Are you *happy* to be the President?"

"Um… Sure, I'm pretty happy, *yeah*. Are *you* happy?"

"I am *now,* now that I have this *ice cream*."

"Ha, ice cream always can put a smile on your face—unless you're lactose intolerant."

"What's *lactoes* intolerant?"

"Lac-*tose* intolerant… It's when your body has difficulty digesting dairy food, such as milk, ice cream, cheese, yogurts."

"Oh… Mommy, can I ask you another question?"

"Of course, baby."

"Why were you crying in your room the other night?"

"*Crying*?" Kelissa confusingly said. "I wasn't crying, baby."

"Yeah, you were. I heard you outside the door. You were crying."

"What were you doing outside my bedroom door?"

"I had another bad dream, and I wanted to stay with you and daddy. But I heard you crying, so I went back to *my* room. I didn't want to bother you. That's why I asked if you're happy being the President."

Kelissa was so touched that Bryan knew to give her some space. But she was also mortified by the thought that her son had to witness her pain. As Kelissa rubbed on Bryan's back, she said to him, "Bryan, sweetie. It's true; I *was* crying that night. But that doesn't mean that… Well, *yes,* it's true, I wasn't so happy at that moment. There are days when mommy lets her job get in the way of her happiness. It can be *very* stressful. And *sometimes*, letting out a few tears *releases* the stress. Being President is extremely demanding. So much work to be done and not enough hours in the day. I keep missing dinner with you guys. But I don't want you to think that I'm not happy. I'm taking care of myself. You don't have to worry about me, okay?"

As Bryan looked at Kelissa, he put his little hand on her right cheek, and with his innocent voice, he said, "Daddy will protect you, mommy. Daddy protects all of us." Kelissa's eyes were growing teary as she heard Bryan say that. She looked at him, and in her mind, she thought, "If only you knew, baby… If only you knew." Kelissa rubbed her hand over his brown curly hair, saying, "You're such a good boy. You have a great heart, baby. Don't ever lose that."

Bryan did not leave a drop of ice cream in that bowl as he scrapped it clean. But Kelissa made sure that he washed his dishes. Even though butlers and maids serve the First family, Kelissa refuses to allow the kids to take advantage of that. She makes *all* of them make their bed, clean their rooms, and wash their clothes *and* dishes.

As Bryan and Kelissa rinsed and dried their dishes, she walked with him to his bedroom. Once they came to Bryan's bedroom door, he said, "Mommy, it's okay, you don't have to read me a bedtime story." Kelissa did not know what to say at that moment. She just wanted to avoid going into her bedroom for as long as possible.

"Well, sweetie, you know you have a hard time falling asleep sometimes. One story won't hurt," Kelissa spoke.

"It's okay; I feel like I'm too old now for you to read me bedtime stories," Bryan said.

"Oh… Well, if *that's* the case, don't you think you're a little too old to be sleeping in *my* bed?

Bryan looked at Kelissa in silence. He did not appreciate that last comment, and Kelissa saw that when she looked into those sad puppy dog eyes. Bryan quickly turned around and stormed into his bedroom. "Bryan, sweetie, I'm so sor—*Bryan*!" Kelissa said as Bryan slammed the door shut. She began to knock and plead with Bryan, apologizing for what she said.

Now, *Kelissa* is the one who is hearing Bryan cry outside his bedroom door. She stood there as she tilted her head back, looking up, and began to sigh. Now, gently banging her forehead up against the door with her eyes closed as she can hear Bryan's sobbing voice. Kelissa wanted to go in and hug an apology onto him. But like Bryan did the other night, she decided to give him some space. Before leaving his front door, Kelissa said under her breath, "Goodnight, darling boy. I love you."

As Kelissa walked to the front of her bedroom door, she looked at it and kept walking. She went into the kitchen to grab a glass of water and walked to her private office. She sat down at her desk with her hand pressed against her forehead, rubbing it repeatedly to ease the stress. But that was not enough to ease it down. So, Kelissa picked up her black leather journal, opened it, and began to write. In her journal, she wrote:

Thursday Evening, April 4th, 2024

Ladies and gentlemen, I'm losing. I've won the election, I am the President, but I am losing my children. I'm losing their trust, their faith in me, and what I fear the most; I believe I am losing their love. I didn't mean to hurt Bryan. I know he's a momma's boy and loves being under me whenever he can. But he's eleven years old. He's not an infant or a toddler anymore. And yes, I partake in spoiling him. He's my baby boy. But he's growing up, certain habits and traditions that we've established have to remedy. I should have stopped letting him stay in my bed when he was eight. That was my fault. But I didn't mean to hurt his feelings. I want to go back over to his room and talk with him. But I'll let him sleep it off.

The cabinet meeting is coming up next week—all of my advisors will be in the same room. We have so much to cover: jobs, budgets, policies, military cutbacks, the environment, American culture, gun violence, everything that keeps me up at the wee hours of the night. Paperwork on top of paperwork. To be honest with you, ladies and gentlemen, I am so busy that the only thing that reminds me that I am in an abusive relationship is the very pain that I feel from Ted's attacks. The bruises and the pain that I cover up every day—that is what reminds me. Otherwise, the workload takes my mind off of him.

But look at me, here I am, stalling, avoiding being in my own bedroom, staying away from him. And after I rejected his proposal about foreign policy, I don't know what I'm about to walk myself into when I go in the bedroom. Ted has been making me sleep with him every night. Just the other night, I was asleep on the couch in my office. I was so tired from the busy day that I just crashed on my couch. I already had a pillow and blanket stashed away from before. So, when Ted came into my office and saw me asleep with the pillow and blanket, he assumed that I was avoiding him and that I deliberately disobeyed him.

From what I remember about that night, I remember him removing the blanket, picking me up from the couch, and carrying me into the bedroom. But then, he did something that I would've never imagined him doing to me. At first, I thought he would carefully place me on the bed, wrap the covers around me and kiss me goodnight. I guess my naivety caught me off guard. Do you know what he did, ladies and gentlemen? He tossed me in mid-air and watched me land sideways on the floor. The sudden impact woke me up instantly, and the pain was unbearable. I was in so much pain that night. But I'm still in distress; my right elbow has a large bruise. It's springtime now, and I can't even wear spring attire because the bruises are so large and would be too revealing. I'm fortunate that I didn't suffer any broken bones.

But as I said about that night, I couldn't even move from off the floor. For a second, Ted stepped out of the bedroom. I had no idea where he was going, and I didn't know if he would get something to hit me with; I couldn't move. I was scared to death. But then he came back with the same pillow and blanket from my office. He dropped them on top of me and said, "Sweet dreams, bitch. And you better stop with that fucking crying before I suffocate you with that pillow." He made me sleep on the floor that night.

Ladies and gentlemen, I am living in an entirely unimaginable nightmare. The level of emotions, mood swings, and the mind control that Ted has bestowed upon me is affecting my work as the President, it's affecting the relationship with my children, and I miss my mother and father terribly. On top of all of that, I don't have any friends. No girlfriends that I could sit down and talk with anymore. No one to tell my secret to... I am so lonely, ladies and gentlemen. So lonely.

It was close to midnight, and Kelissa was not even in her pajamas. She did not want to go into that bedroom with Ted. But Kelissa knew that he would come looking for her if she did not show up sooner or later. Kelissa got up from her chair and took the empty glass to the kitchen.

Kelissa made it to the kitchen to rinse the glass and place it back in the cabinet. She then decided to hide in one of the guest rooms on the second floor of the residence level. But first, Kelissa had to change out of her casual clothing and into her pajamas. Knowing, however, that Ted would be waiting for her, she decided to skip the pajamas and just head up to the guest room.

As Kelissa reached the top of the stairs, she peeked her head down the center hall, ensuring that Ted, Jr. would not spot her. Tip-toeing her way down the hall into the guest room, she closed the door—a sigh of relief as she felt safe for the night. Kelissa then removed her clothes and shoes, leaving only her bra and panties on as she lay in bed.

It was pure silence in the guest room. As Kelissa lay there, she stared at the painted portrait of the first President, George Washington. The more Kelissa stared at the painting of George Washington, the eerier it began to look. It appeared as if he was looking directly into her soul—*looking* at her situation and telling her that she had to find a way out before it was too late. It became too scary for Kelissa's sight. She turned her back to the painting and looked the other way, facing a white wall.

Kelissa wanted nothing more but a good night's rest. She didn't want to hear, see, or even *think* about Ted. All she wanted was a few hours of undisturbed sleep. As she closed her eyes and retired for the night, she did minimal movement in her sleep, and she *would* have had a peaceful good night's sleep. But unfortunately, there was a mistake. Kelissa left the door unlocked.

Chapter 21

Friday Early Morning, April 5th, 2024

Nightmare Husband

It is four in the morning, Kelissa is fast asleep, far away in her dream world. The hallways are silent, and the children are in their rooms, counting sheep. The blue light from the moon-lit sky, coming through the window, casts upon Kelissa's sleeping face.

But suddenly, that blue light was eclipsed by a hand; it was Ted, aggressively pressing his hand over Kelissa's mouth. Kelissa instantly woke up in a panic with her eyes widely opened. Ted's tight grip prevented her from making a peep. She saw the look in his eyes; it was as if there was no one home—no soul, no Ted. She saw Ted's right hand balled up into a fist, and just like that, BOOM! BOOM! BOOM! He punched her three times in her abdomen area.

But Ted's abusive attacks were not complete. He then took his balled-up fist and began to slam it down on Kelissa's left thigh as if he was a judge slamming down his gavel. Kelissa could not stop him; every impact was more brutal than the last blow. She could barely see anything clearly as the tears poured out of her eyes. To avoid being heard, Ted quietly said to Kelissa, "Did you *think* I would not find you? *Huh*? You thought you could *hide* from me? You *can't* hide from me, Kel. Everywhere you go, every corner, I will be there. You keep disobeying me, and you pay the price."

Kelissa was defenseless as Ted was on top of her. With her mouth still covered and her eyes still shedding rapid tears, Ted said, "I should just *strangle* you to death. But I'm going to spare you, Kel. I'm going to let you *live*. But I am warning you, don't you *ever* disobey me again. Don't do it. I'm going to remove my hand from your mouth now. If you scream or make any sound, so help me, *God*, I will break your neck."

Ted finally removed his hand from Kelissa's mouth. His hand was pressed down so hard that it left her lip print on his palm. But still, Ted was not finished with her. He then took his thumb and gently rubbed it across her bottom lip, giving her a glaring look as if he wanted to kiss her. And that is what Ted did. He kissed her repeatedly, over and over again. Kelissa was not only in pain, but she was in absolute shock at the sudden change of action. Ted kissed her all over her face and neck and then made his way down her body. He then ripped off her bra and began to worship her breast.

Ted's sick and demented behavior was overpowering Kelissa as she lay there and let him do whatever. She was too afraid to resist his advances as she thought he would attack her again. Every time he kissed her on her navel, it was a kiss of pain. And then, as Ted ripped off Kelissa's panties, she quickly said, "NO! TED! *PLEASE*! I HAVE MY PERIOD!... I have my period. *Please* don't." As Ted looked down, he saw the proof of Kelissa's menstrual cycle. And he did not proceed any further with his sexually aggressive desires.

Now, a scary moment of silence in the guest room, as Ted was still on top of Kelissa. With her bra and panties ripped apart, Kelissa, now in the nude, said this to Ted in her broken voice, "Ted, I beg of you, *please* stop hitting me. My body cannot handle it anymore. My heart cannot take it anymore. I can't go on like this—*anymore*!"

Ted is still on top of Kelissa as he gives off his sinister smile. "Oh, how I just *love* it when you beg for mercy. You're not a *fucking* President. You're just a weak, scared little *bitch* of a woman who got lucky. Just like you got lucky having your period," Ted said with enriched satisfaction.

That comment struck sharp through Kelissa's mind as if a knife stabbed her right through her brain. Ted was trying everything he could to break her mentally. He wanted her to suffer in ways she would never imagine. Finally, Ted got off Kelissa and looked down at her. He was still clothed in his pajamas while Kelissa lay on the bed, naked with only her arms to cover herself. She had never been more mortified and humiliated than she has right now. But what was even worse was that Ted took *all* of her clothes with him as he left the guest room. He even took her ripped bra and panties. "Since you're so *lucky*," Ted said while holding Kelissa's clothes. "Good luck getting back to the bedroom with no clothes on."

As Ted shut the door, Kelissa broke down and cried—planting her face deep into the pillow as she screamed. Kelissa's pain, suffering, humiliation, the beatings, and the stress of her job as the President—*everything* stacked on top of her, and she was close to the breaking point.

After about ten minutes of tears, screams in the pillows, and an aching body, Kelissa finally got up. Since she was in the guest room, she had no other clothes in her possession. And even though she was all alone in the room, her mortified mentality made her think to cover herself with her arms. But she had to think quickly about how she would be able to come out of the guest room.

Then, it hit her; Kelissa realized that her best chances were to grab the bed sheet from the bed, use *that* to cover herself and make it down to her bedroom. She then grabbed the olive-green bed sheet and wrapped it around her body like a toga. Kelissa now had to walk out of the guest room with caution, as she knew that Ted, Jr's bedroom was right across the center hall. Kelissa went to grab the doorknob, slowly turning it to open the door carefully. As the door opened, she tilted her head to the side of the opening, making sure there was no one in sight.

Luckily enough, it was still the early morning, and no one was awake—so she *thought*. Without any more hesitation, Kelissa moved swiftly to the staircase and went down the stairs. But right at the very bottom of the stairs, as Kelissa stepped her bare foot onto the floor, she heard a loud cough. Kelissa stopped immediately and leaned her back against the staircase wall—as if she was taking cover. She realized that Madeline had just come out of her bedroom. Kelissa slowly peeked her head out from the stairs to see where Madeline was standing. She saw Madeline standing in front of *her* bedroom door, giving it a few knocks. At that moment, Kelissa had no idea why Madeline would be at her bedroom door so early in the morning.

As Madeline knocked again, the door opened. But obviously, it was Ted who opened the door. Kelissa, still peeking her head out, looks down the center hall as she sees Madeline talking to her father. Barely able to hear the conversation between Ted and Madeline, Kelissa decided that now was the time to make her move. She moved as quickly as possible and made it inside her private office. Kelissa gently closed the door, then closed her eyes and sighed relief. But still, wrapped in the bedsheet, Kelissa was in dire need of some clothes. Just as if things could not possibly become any worse, they did.

A round of knocks came to Kelissa's office door. Kelissa went into a straight panic mode. All she could think of at that moment was to lay on the couch and pretend to be asleep. "Mom, are you in there?" Madeline said after knocking once more. But Kelissa did not say a word. Instead, she hurried to the couch and laid there with the bedsheet now blanketed over her naked body.

"Mom, if you're in there, I'm coming in," Madeline said as she opened the door.

Kelissa quickly closed her eyes and went into acting mode. She could hear Madeline's slippers scrapping onto the carpet as she walked towards the couch. Madeline then gave Kelissa a gentle shake on her left shoulder. "Mom? Mom, wake up," Madeline said, still shaking Kelissa.

"Hmm?" Kelissa mumbled, pretending she just woke up, "Oh, Maddy. It's so *early*, sweetie. What are you doing up?"

"Well, I *want* to ask you the same thing. Dad said you might be in the office still working."

"Oh, I was working late last night, and I just fell asleep on the couch again. But why are you up so early?"

"I'm not feeling so good. And I wanted to know if I could stay home from school."

"Oh, um… Well, *why*, what's wrong?"

"Well, I think it's just stomachache or cramps."

"Cramps? Did you get your period?"

"No, that ended four days ago. I think it was the dinner from last night."

"Oh, I see. Well, we'll have Dr. Deric-John take a look at you, okay."

"Alright… Are you okay, mom?"

"Yes, of course… Why do you ask?"

"I don't know; you seem a little… Off."

"Well, what do you *expect*? Waking me up at 5:05 in the morning," Kelissa said as she chuckled.

"You're right; I'm sorry, mom. But *can* I? Take the day off from school?"

"Yes, as long as Dr. Deric-John takes a look at you. We'll take you to see him, eight o'clock sharp."

"Okay. Thanks, mom."

As Madeline headed for the office door, Kelissa said, "Maddy, are you going *straight* to your bedroom?" Madeline looked at Kelissa as she thought that was a weird question. "Uh, *yeah*, mom. I'm going back to bed for a few hours. Maybe *you* should let Dr. Deric-John take a look at you too," Madeline responded.

Madeline walked out of the office and closed the door. Kelissa got up from the couch, wrapping the bedsheet around her body once again. She then opened the door and peeked her head out into the center hall, making sure that Madeline went directly to her room, and she did. The *second* Madeline walked into her room and closed the door, Kelissa speed-walked as fast as possible into *her* bedroom. As she came into the bedroom, Ted was lying in bed, sleeping like a baby—completely unbothered.

Kelissa could not believe it. It was as if abusing her had become so natural for him. In her mind, she thought, "How can he attack me, over and over, and just sleep on it, as if nothing has happened?" She quietly walked into her dressing room. Her clothes and her ripped bra and panties were piled up on the floor. Kelissa hurried and as she grabbed a new pair of everything and made her way into the bathroom—locking the door behind her.

After placing her clothes on the bathtub edge, she turned around and looked at herself in the mirror. The bruises were fresh and painful. The red marking on the side of her belly was huge, and the bruise on her left thigh had already turned purple. Kelissa could no longer look at herself in the mirror anymore. She hated her reflection. And from that point on, she ensured that she would not look at her body in the mirror again.

As Kelissa took care of her business, wiping herself down and changing her tampon, she got dressed and stepped out of the bathroom. Walking back into the dressing room, she grabbed her ripped bra and panties, went to the kitchen, and dumped them in the garbage. But the paranoia started dancing in her mind. Kelissa believed that since she is the President, someone may look through the trash, find her ripped bra and panties, and become suspicious. And Kelissa did *not* want anyone to find out. So, she immediately took her bra and panties out of the garbage and went back to the dressing room.

As Kelissa entered the dressing room, she grabbed one of her shoeboxes and hid the bra and panties underneath her shoes. "No one will find them in here," Kelissa whispered to herself. She then placed the shoebox back on the shelf and hung up her remaining clothes. Unfortunately, the pain kept coming through every time she squatted down to pick up the clothes.

After hanging up her clothes, Kelissa slowly walked back into the bedroom. Ted did not move an inch as he was still sound asleep. But Kelissa refused to lay in bed with him. That was the last thing she wanted to do. Instead, she collected the outfit she wanted to wear for the day and took that to her private office. She also took some extra clothes, bra, and panties and placed them in hidden places in her office, just in case Ted ever pulled a stunt such as he did, again, upstairs in the guest room.

Now, with the office door locked, Kelissa thought of the one thing that could help her release all the stress, pain, and anger within herself. She pulled out her black leather journal and began to document. In her journal, she wrote:

Friday Early Morning, April 5th, 2024 5:45 a.m.

Ladies and gentlemen, it is a quarter to six in the morning, and I am up writing to you all. I cannot even comprehend what just happened to me. How evil could this man get? How insane could one person be? And what the fuck is wrong with me? Why am I still hiding this abuse? If only you could see the size of these bruises. And thank God that I have my period. Because I did not want him inside of me at all. In fact, I don't ever want him touching me again. I don't care how good the sex feels. I'm so tired of him beating me and then thinking that he could make me feel better with a few fucks.

Well, ladies and gentlemen, I have no more fucks left to give. If he keeps hitting me regardless, I think it's time that I start to defend myself. Ted, Jr. begged to have some workout equipment upstairs in the workout room. And there is a punching bag up there as well. It is time that I take a few swings at that punching bag.

Jesus… I can't believe he took all of my clothes and was going to make me walk completely naked in the center hall of the fucking White House. What if TJ or Bryan saw me walking with only a bedsheet covering me? It's as if he strategically calculates his evil behavior. It's like he knows how to humiliate me from every angle. What kind of woman am I to allow all of this? I feel ashamed and disappointed in myself. This is not the way any woman should be living. To be tormented by a man I thought loved me, who I thought would love me forever. But this is not love. I don't know what the fuck this is, but it sure as hell is not love. Hell, I don't even think I know what love is anymore.

But you know what, ladies and gentlemen, the American people won't give a damn. They want to see results. They want me to prove why they made the right choice in voting for me. I now have that enormous responsibility. But I am so lost—my mind is so screwed up. I can barely think straight at times. Part of me wants to stand in the middle of the cross hall, in front of all the staff, fall to my knees, and scream as loud as I possibly can. I want the entire universe to hear my pain.

But I'm so trapped. And I'm terrified. Even if I learned to punch and fight back, he would overpower me and eventually kill me. Maybe I made a mistake. Perhaps Ted is right about me. Maybe I'm not a real President, and I just got lucky and won the election. You see, ladies and gentlemen? Do you see what's happening to me? He's breaking me down. He's destroying me, stripping me of my confidence and character, just as he orchestrated.

I know; I know that I have to remain strong. In time, my bruises will heal, the pain will go away, and I will be alright. I know that now, more than ever. But I have to keep praying.

Kelissa's mind was beginning to shift gears as her survival tactics began to shape. As she finished writing in her journal, Kelissa, now in her pajamas, went back upstairs to the second floor of the residence level and walked into the workout room. As she walked over to the punching bag, she imagined that the bag was Ted. Her body began to quiver and shake, not filled with fear but anger and rage. Kelissa's hands began to ball up into two fists of iron.

The last time she threw a punch was when a girl bullied her in fifth grade. Kelissa threw a right hook to the girl's chin and knocked the girl on her ass. It made Kelissa feel good until she was suspended from school for two weeks, and on top of that, her parents grounded her for a month.

But as Kelissa put her fist up, she slowly brought her arm back and swung with all her might. BAM! Kelissa became addicted to the sounds of the heavy chains holding up the punching bag. The more punches she threw, the better she began to feel. As the punches were rolling, Kelissa realized that she should have been doing this since day one of moving into the White House. Now, she had two outlets to keep her sanity. The black leather journal would be for her to cope with her emotions and pain, while the punching bag would be her physical outlet.

As Kelissa built up a mild sweat, she called it quits and began to have a breather. Her pajamas were pretty damped, but she was indeed a happy woman. She went back downstairs with a smile on her face as she headed to take a shower. Kelissa's logic was simple, whenever she gets into it with Ted, or even if he places his hands on her, she will go to the workout room and have a go with the heavy bag. And to make it even better, she gave the heavy bag a name... That's right; she named it '*Ted.*'

Chapter 22

Thursday Afternoon, April 11th, 2024

The Cabinet Room

The day has finally come; President Kelissa Morrison soon participates in her first Cabinet Room meeting. Advisors, generals, the Chief of Staff, and Vice President Harry Griffin will attend, including the heads of fifteen executive departments.

The heads of the executive departments are now standing outside the Cabinet Room. But before they enter the Cabinet Room, everyone must place their phone in a basket. To avoid any misplacements, Cabinet secretary, Brenda Bittner, puts a sticky note with their names on their phones.

Kelissa is in the Oval Office, finishing up on some reading. The meeting begins in precisely seven minutes. But she wanted some time to herself to prepare. After reading and signing some documents, a knock hits her door.

"Madam President?" Carl spoke. "Everyone has arrived."

"Great! Thank you, Carl. I just need one minute."

"Yes, ma'am."

As Kelissa sat behind her desk, she turned around and began to look at her family photos. There were photos on her second desk next to the three south-facing windows. One of the photos was of her parents at their 40th-anniversary party. There was a picture of Ted, Jr. when he graduated from high school and another picture of Madeline and Bryan sitting next to each other on a boat from when they took a vacation. And lastly, a family photo of the five of them, including a family dog.

Interestingly, the dog in the picture is not part of the family but is just a stand-in. Kelissa is highly allergic to dogs and cats, so there are *no* pets in the White House. But because of the Presidential tradition of having a family pet, the dog was included just for the photo.

As Kelissa continued to look at the family photo, she looked explicitly at Ted. In the picture, he was smiling, with his right arm wrapped over Kelissa's shoulders. She could not help but reminisce about a happier time in their lives. A time when she was in *love* with him, and *he* was deeply in love with her. But her nostalgic desire of going back to a time when Ted was so loving was short-lived. The Ted

Kelissa knew way back when—he would slice his *wrist* before laying a *finger* on her. But that time has vanished, and so did her love for him.

Kelissa was ready; she made her way out of the Oval Office with a look of focus. A *casual* look, but still, a face of preparation. Carl and another Secret Service agent escorted Kelissa to the Cabinet Room. Waiting in front of the Cabinet Room was Kelissa's Cabinet secretary, Brenda Bittner.

"Good afternoon, Madam President," Brenda said.

"Good afternoon, good afternoon," Kelissa responded. "Are we ready?"

"Yes, ma'am, everyone is inside."

"Great, and is everything in order with the press?"

"Yes, Madam President. The press is aware of the time they will be permitted to come in."

"Excellent. *Okay*, let's get this show on the road."

As Brenda opened the Cabinet Room door, everyone rose from their chairs, honoring their leader of the free world, President Kelissa Morrison. Everyone in the room was instructed to wear their facemask, as President Kelissa Morrison requested. "Good afternoon, Madam President," the ensemble of staff projected.

Over two dozen cups and several pots of coffee and tea were on the table, and a large bowl of gummy bears and M&M minis at Kelissa's special request. Kelissa walked over to her chair in the center of the table. Since this was her first meeting, Kelissa was filled with joy and humbleness as she rubbed her thumb across the small plaque on the back of her chair. On the plaque, it said:

"THE PRESIDENT, JANUARY 20TH, 2024."

With Vice President Harry Griffin sitting right across from her, Kelissa was ready to begin. Kelissa, with a smile on her face, spoke to her administration, "Good afternoon, everyone. *Please*, take your seats. You can remove your mask; I think we're all okay now. It's nice to see you all here at the same time. Since this is our first meeting, could you all say your names and which department you are the head of? And I do want to hear from *everyone*, just to get an idea of the progress of each department. So, my priorities are employment, health, education, and budget. Now, of *course*, Covid-19 has run its course for the *most* part. But we are not guaranteed that the marathon is over. As I said before, there's no such thing as an extinct virus or disease. *So*, you all have my undivided attention. I'm all ears, and I would like to begin with the Secretary of Labor."

The Secretary of Labor, Jonah Adams, introduced himself to Kelissa. Jonah was a mid-age man with thin glasses and a clean-shaven face. The funny thing about him was he had a puzzling birthmark on the left side of his neck—shaped like the state of Texas. As Jonah began speaking, he said, "Thank you, Madam President—Jonah Adams, Secretary of Labor. So, our staff has started the process of a new re-employment service. But to help *motivate* people, we propose increasing the federal minimum wage to $9.25 per hour for nonexempt hourly workers. We still would like to take the necessary precautions in keeping work environments healthy and safe for workers. As you mentioned, Madam President, the marathon is not over. So, we would like to recommend that workers *continue* to wear their face masks until we know for *sure* that we will not face another variant." Kelissa thanked Jonah for the information. But she had some questions for him.

"As for the $9.25 per hour, will that cause risk for inflation?" Kelissa asked.

"No, Madam President," said Jonah. "Businesses have been doing very well since last quarter, and the economy has been strong enough to raise our minimum wage."

"*Wonderful*… That's *great* to know. *Speaking* of wages, I'm putting this on the table right now. I'm proposing equal salary standards—for *women*—in whatever work field they're occupied in."

The *second* President Kelissa Morrison finished saying what she just said, the entire Cabinet Room grew eerily silent. Since most of the people in the Cabinet Room were *men*, the feedback was nonexistent. As Kelissa looked around the room, she saw the look on the men's faces. She could *smell* the stenchful aroma of male chauvinism *seeping* through their pores. Kelissa then went to the Secretary of Health and Human Services, Allison McKnight, quickly changing the subject.

As Allison had the floor, she said, "Good afternoon, Madam President. Thank you. I'm Allison McKnight. So, as of today, Covid cases have barely been showing up. The last recorded cases of a higher rate were back in early January of *last* year. And approximately ninety-five percent of the American population are fully vaccinated and have received booster shots. So, we truly don't believe that it is necessary to create any mandates. Although we *should* continue to leave it optional if people choose to wear a mask in public places and workplaces, just to take the necessary precautions."

"And what about education? How are we doing in that area?" Kelissa asked Allison. Allison took a look at some documents as she said, "So, with *education*, funding is low, and so is the overall attendance of students. A lot of schools going with '*virtual learning*' ever since the pandemic, students have taken advantage of that, and now they are very behind in their classes."

Kelissa continued listening, one by one, to every department. While grabbing small handfuls of gummies, Kelissa was attentive to hearing everyone out—paying attention to what progress has been made and the issues that need to be addressed. Kelissa's wise thinking pulled many departments out of the rabbit hole. Vice President Harry Griffin was so impressed by Kelissa's knowledge. Kelissa is sharp as a tack when she is focused on her work. For the first time in weeks, Kelissa cleared her mind of all the havoc she goes through behind the scenes in her personal life.

As Kelissa carried on, she spoke to the Secretary of Defense, Blake Talley. Talley is a fifty-five-year-old man, retired from the United States Army as a four-star general. He knows all the ins and outs of the armed forces.

"Mr. Secretary," said Kelissa. "I was informed by Chief of Staff of the Army about the situation over in Afghanistan."

"Yes, Madam President," Blake responded. "The situation with the Taliban is becoming more uncontrollable, specifically in Kabul."

"I see… Nothing will change with those people—unless *we* make a change. How many of our soldiers are stationed in Afghanistan now?"

"1,100 as of today, Madam President."

"Okay, let's have another thousand deployed, Mr. Secretary."

"Uh, Madam President… I don't think that would be necessary."

"Why not?"

"Well, we are actually looking to get our troops *out* of Afghanistan right now. Plus, we would need congressional approval to deplo—"

"Mr. Secretary, I'm looking to declare *war* here. But some women and children are being beaten, starved to death, and are under the *Taliban's* control—God *knows* what is happening to them behind closed doors. We need more troops to go in for a rescue mission. Make that *happen*, Mr. Secretary."

"Yes, Madam President."

Kelissa had a change of plans as far as bringing the troops home. She decided that she wanted to send *more* troops overseas to execute her agenda as she plans to rescue Afghan women and children from the control of the Taliban. While doing so, she wants to create opportunities for Afghan women, give them work in America, and provide them a better life with equality, security, and be set free of the imprisonment bestowed upon them. Kelissa is well aware of the challenges that will come of it. But her willpower and the fight within will help her prevail.

The meeting has now gone on for an hour and a half. Kelissa had discussed with each head of the executive departments the progression and improvement of the country. A lot she has learned and much to unwind. The heads shared *their* proposals, and Kelissa shared hers. But after Kelissa proposed equal pay for women, the thousand-pound elephant appeared in the room and never left.

Kelissa was now ready for the press. The Cabinet Room became a media circus. As soon as the press entered the Cabinet Room, they clicked away at their cameras—faster and louder than the sound of crickets chirping in the night. Kelissa took a few sips of her tea before making a statement about her first Cabinet Room meeting.

As the cameras rolled, Kelissa cleared her throat and said, "Thank you, everyone, for joining me on this special occasion. As you all know, this was my *first* Cabinet Room meeting. I must say that it went well. My advisors and the head of each department are doing *very* well at their job. We've exchanged some proposals, and we'll see if we can reach a common ground and receive some *progressive* results. I want the American people to know that we are working on increasing the minimum wage. Covid cases *have* plummeted to record-low numbers. And even though cases may *remain* at low rates, we still would like to keep people safe and recommend that they *continue* to wear masks in public locations. It is no longer mandatory;

however, we want people to remain safe and keep the option available. This pandemic is not quite over just yet. As we look into increasing the federal minimum wage, we are also working on creating more jobs, and small businesses are picking back up. And, um, I'm looking *forward* to seeing how much progress we achieve within the next couple of months. *So*, I thank you very much, and I will take some questions, but only a few. I do have some other obligations to tend to after this."

Hands immediately went up in the air. Kelissa did not know who to choose first. She saw a woman journalist and immediately selected her as Kelissa was drawn to her pink suit jacket.

"Yes, over there, in the pink jacket," Kelissa pointed.

"Thank you, Madam President," said the journalist. "Rebecca Madison, reporting from SMH-DC News. I just wanted to know what your plan is for abortion laws?"

"Yes, thank you. *So*, as we all know, each state has different laws on abortion. Some are stricter than *others*, so it is still a *battle*. We haven't *lost* the battle; it's just a much longer fight than expected. Unfortunately, we did not reach the topic of abortion in today's discussion. But that'll be on my radar come next meeting."

"And one more if I may," said Rebecca. "*Are* you pro-life?"

"Uh… *Rebecca*, is it?" Kelissa asked with her irritated face.

"Yes, Madam President."

"Okay, Rebecca… I have *always* been pro-life. But as a *woman*, I understand that *life* is *life*. People make certain decisions that they are just not ready for. And I do believe that *women* solely should have *every* right to make whatever decision they need to, that is right for them. *And* women must have the proper resources to help them finalize that decision. But, again, it is a far from over battle."

"Thank you, Madam President."

"Of course… *Okay*, I'll take two more questions."

Hands quickly began to rise again. This time, Kelissa selected the tallest guy in the Cabinet Room. The African American reporter stood about six-foot-eight-inches—you could not miss him.

"You, sir, my gentle giant," Kelissa pointed as everyone had a friendly, honest laugh.

"Thank you, Madam President," said the journalist. "Thomas Penn, reporting from *The Conquest Post*. Even though the country is close to the finish line of the pandemic, *gun* violence has been on an uprise in America. The *Black Lives Matter* movement has grown a louder voice caused by the uproar of police brutality and cops taking advantage—abusing the use of their guns. What is your administration planning to do in order to *change* America's crime rate?"

"Okay, thank you, Thomas, for your question," said Kelissa. "Gun violence is obviously an ongoing issue in our country. *Many* unnecessary shootings take place every single day. But with the gun laws *and* the American people's Second Amendment right, it has become a serious issue to keep our nation safe from one another. There is no walk-in-the-park solution regarding the *regulation* of gun laws.

But that will be another topic to bring up in our next meeting. Thank you."

"Thank you, Madam President," Thomas responded.

"Yes… Okay, *one* more question. You sir, over at the end."

Kelissa saw a short heavyset man standing at the end of the table, holding up his chubby hand. "Hi, thank you, Madam President," said the stocky man. "Tony Lewis, reporting from WLA News. Unfortunately, Covid-19 has now cost the lives of well over *one million* Americans. Health care costs have grown uncontrollably, and hospitals are still understaffed. How prepared is the U.S. government if or *when*, God *forbid*, there's another outbreak?"

Kelissa had to take a brief moment to think about that. As it is true, the virus has changed not only America but the entire world. Kelissa responded, saying, "Thank you, Tony… God *forbid*, I second that. *God forbid* another variant outbreak occurs. But as I said before, we still *strongly* recommend that people wear their masks while living their daily lives, out in public locations, on vacations, and during the holidays. Wear a mask, wear a mask, a*nd* be vaccinated. We *cannot* stress that enough. Five percent of the American population, a little under *seventeen million* of our fellow citizens, are *still* completely unvaccinated. That is a lot of people who are still *very* vulnerable to catching any new variant that comes our way. The only way we can ever *possibly* be fully prepared is by being on the same page with the vaccination. But of course, that is easier said than done." As Kelissa was ready to wrap things up, Tony impulsively continued to speak his mind.

"But Madam President, studies have shown that people still tested positive and *died* even *with* the vaccination. So, there's no guarantee that the vaccination will save *everyone*."

"That is correct, Tony," Kelissa responded. "There *is* no guarantee. But what I *can* guarantee is that if you are *not* vaccinated, this virus will attack, and it *will* cause severe harm to your unprotected body. It is not worth it—to *not* be vaccinated. I understand people want to stand on their *principle*, but enough is enough. It's time people take responsibility for their health."

"Thank you, Madam President… Oh, I'm *so* sorry! I have one final question, please!"

"You're pushing your *luck*, Tony! But go ahead."

"Thank you. Um, do you fault how the last presidency and its administration handled the crisis that this pandemic has caused our country?"

"That is a very loaded *question*, Tony. But I have an answer for you. No, I am not the kind of human being to point the *finger* at my predecessors. I believe they handled this crisis as best as they could, with the *limited* amount of research they *had*, in a *brief* window of time. But today is a new day. And we must move *forward*, not backward, to *prevent* this crisis from worsening. But I hope that I answered your loaded question, Tony."

"You did, Madam President. Thank you *very* much."

As hands of the press continued to go up, begging for President Kelissa Morrison to select them for their questions, she called it a day and politely asked the press to leave the Cabinet Room.

Once the inquisitive crowd took their leave, Kelissa grabbed another handful of gummy bears and got up from her chair. "Ladies and gentlemen, I thank you for your time. *Please* keep up the *great* work, and, uh, until next time," Kelissa spoke. Even though Kelissa wanted to leave the Cabinet Room, she spent an extra fifteen minutes conversating, giving fist bumps to her advisors and heads of departments, as Kelissa refused to have open handshakes with others, preventing germs from spreading.

A wonderful dinner awaits Kelissa and the rest of the First family. Each of them requested their unique entrees. Kelissa only requested a grilled chicken salad and a glass of water, as she will be heading right back to the Oval Office to finish up on some work. But as the Morrison family took their seats at the table in the Family Dining Room, Kelissa was missing in action. Ted told the children to hold off on getting started with their meals, as he wanted to wait until Kelissa had arrived.

Five minutes went by; Bryan, Madeline, and Ted, Jr. all had watery mouths as they could not wait anymore to feast on their delicious-looking entrees. "Dad, can we just *please* get started with dinner?" Madeline begged, "You know how mom is—she may not show up." Ted had a look of frustrated disappointment on his face. In response to Madeline, he said, "You guys go ahead and eat. I'll see what's taking your mother so long."

Ted stood up from the dining room table and made his way to where he *assumed* Kelissa would be. A good four-and-a-half-minute walk from the Family Dining Room to the Oval Office, located in the West Wing. As Ted showed up in front of the Oval Office, Carl and Secret Service agent Sam stood guard of the concealed door.

"Hello, Carl," Ted said.

"Hello, Mr. Morrison," Carl responded. "I'm sorry, sir, but President Morrison is having a private meeting with her advisors and asked not to be disturbed."

"I see… Carl, would you be *kind* enough to inform her that her family is waiting for her in the Family Dining Room?"

"I will deliver the message personally, sir."

"Thank you."

About seven minutes after Ted returned to the Family Dining Room, there was still no sight of Kelissa. Ted began to grow furious at the lingering absence of his busy wife as he barely touched his meal. Then suddenly, out of nowhere, Kelissa shows up with optimistic energy. "Good evening, family!" Kelissa projected with a smile, "And how are we doing today? How's dinner?" Kelissa, one by one, kissed her children, leaving Ted to be the last one kissed. But Kelissa, however, did *not* kiss him. Instead, she kissed her fingertips and placed them on his forehead. After what he did to her in the guest room, there was absolutely *no* way Kelissa would plant her lips *anywhere* on his face.

As Kelissa sat at her end of the table, Ted just gazed at her with a piercing, demonic look. After taking a few forkfuls of her chicken salad, Kelissa began a casual conversation with the children.

"*So*," Kelissa said. "How was everyone's day today?"

"It was okay," Bryan responded.

"Not bad," Ted, Jr. added. "Finished all of my college applications."

"*Wonderful*," Kelissa said with joy. "That's one less thing to worry about."

"Yeah, so *hopefully*, I'll get some acceptance letters."

"Of course, you will, sweetheart, I'm the *President*. I can pull strings and get you *anywhere* you want to go."

"Well, Mom, I'm hoping to get in on my *own*, not just because you're the *President*."

"Oh, no, I didn't mean it like *that*, TJ. Of *course,* you can achieve *anything* on your own. I'm just saying that *wherever* you want to go, we're not taking no for an answer."

"Thanks, mom. You're the best," Ted, Jr. said with a grin.

"You're welcome, sweetie… Maddy, how about you?"

"What?" Madeline asked.

"How was your *day*?" Kelissa responded.

"It was okay. Not much happening in school."

"Okay… Well, I'm sorry for keeping you guys waiting, *again*—"

"How was *your* day, mom?" Madeline interjected.

"Oh, um… It was *terrific*. I had my first Cabinet Room meeting. We achieved a lot of progress today."

"Oh, well, you never told *us* about that, Mom."

"Told you about *what*, Maddy?"

"About your Cabinet Room meeting."

"I didn't?"

"No, Mom. You *didn't*. And to be honest, *I* don't really care."

"*Excuse me*, young lady?"

"Dad, can I please be excused?" Madeline said, about to stand up.

"Of course, baby," Ted spoke.

"Wait a minute, don't you *dare* move from that chair!" Kelissa aggressively projected.

"Kel, keep your voice down," Ted said with a sinister grin.

"Stay out of this, Ted," Kelissa shouted. "Is there something you want to say to me, Maddy?"

"No, mom. I just want to leave the table now."

"Okay, you got it. You can *leave* the table, and you can take *this* with you; you're grounded!"

"*Grounded*? Are you *serious*—

"AS A *HEART* ATTACK! Go to your room, young lady. NOW!"

"Grounded… I've been *grounded* ever since we've moved *into* this *White House*."

Madeline stormed out of the Family Dining Room. Kelissa took another forkful of salad and stuffed it in her mouth, aggressively chewing her food. In frustration, Kelissa begins to speak out loud.

"Unbelievable!" Kelissa projected. "I mean, can you guys *believe* your sister? How *dare* she have an attitude with me? She's *always* been so contumacious towards me."

"Well, Mom, I hate to say this. But I'm kind of in agreeance with Maddy here," Ted, Jr. responded.

"*What*?"

"Well, not exactly with her *attitude*, but you're not always around, mom. You've been missing dinners; we don't see you as much anymore. And we're stuck here in the house. Sometimes it feels like… We don't *have* a mother."

"Okay, maybe the two of *you* should go to rooms as well."

"Are we grounded *too*?" Bryan asked with a worried face.

"*No*, Bry. Just—just head to your room, please?"

As both Bryan and Ted, Jr. left the dining room table, Kelissa continued to eat her grilled chicken salad while Ted sat at the other end of the table. The Family Dining Room grew still and quiet until there was a sudden round of applause. Kelissa looked up from her dinner plate and saw Ted clapping his hands, with a smirk on his face like the Joker. "Ted, *why* are you clapping your hands?" Kelissa asked with an irritated tone of voice.

After Ted did one last clap, he said, "Because *you* are *incredibly* amazing. Your parenting is *superb.* I couldn't have done a better job, Kel. I mean, the *way* you just sent Maddy and the boys to their *rooms*. Maddy's probably crying her eyes out right now, and poor Bryan is probably *so* confused. All of this because *you* can't handle the truth. You *are* an '*M.I.A.*' mom. You're not around, and you're not there for your family. It's all about *you* now, Madam President. It's your way or nothing at all. You should be very proud of yourself."

Kelissa was so angry she could not see straight. She knew exactly what Ted was trying to do. He was trying to turn the children against her—to create a narrative of him being the better parent, a *great* father, and Kelissa being an absentee mother who does not care about her children. But Kelissa was not backing down from Ted.

"I know what you're trying to do, Ted! *What* have you been telling my children?" Kelissa said.

"*Our* children, Kel. *Please* do not forget that."

"What *bullshit* are you putting in their minds?"

"Oh, so now the *truth* is bullshit?"

"You're telling them that I don't care about this family?"

"I'm *telling* them that we've lost our position on *your* list of priorities ever since you've been President."

Kelissa did not want any butlers or kitchen staffers to walk into the Family Dining Room and hear a word about what she would say next. As Kelissa got up from the end of the table, she quietly and *carefully* said to Ted, "Did you also tell them how you're leaving *fucking bruises* all over my body? Huh? Or what about the time you choked me on Air Force One? And how about when you tried to *drown* me in the bathtub? Do those topics ever come up for discussion?"

Ted gave Kelissa a look as if he wanted to lay one on her—not a *kiss*, but a fist. As Ted wiped his mouth with his napkin, he stood up from his chair and quietly said, "You know, Kel, sometimes you *really* ask for it. And every *time*, it is my *pleasure* to give it to you. But to be *honest* with you, I'm a little tired of beating your ass. Even the *abuser* needs a *break*. You've had a *long* day. So, I'll spare you for this evening. Besides, the children are not exactly too fond of you right now. They *hate* you… And as their *mother*, I *know* that's more painful than a fist could *ever* be."

As Ted looked at Kelissa, he kissed her and left the Family Dining Room. Kelissa immediately wiped her face with her napkin as she now hated Ted's kisses. Now standing there by herself, Kelissa felt alone and unloved. She was conflicted with all that was said at the table. But it is true; her demandingly busy schedule has turned her into a ghost when it comes to her children. Ted was obviously of no importance to her personally. And as far as his daily occupations as "The First Gentleman," Ted can be pretty busy himself. But what is happening *now* is what Kelissa feared the most. To have her kids not close to her and them feeling neglected. She hates the thought of that being a reality. Or even worse, that her children no longer love her.

Chapter 23

Friday Early Morning, May 31st, 2024

Time for A Vacation

Diamonds are a girl's best friend. But in Kelissa's current situation, the only rocks she has on *her* body are the cold rocks of ice, wrapped up in a towel. Ted struck yet again. An argument between Kelissa and Ted occurred in the bedroom and then made its way into the dressing room. Ted became so enraged with Kelissa that he grabbed one of her shoes and hit her with the heel, repetitively on her legs. After three punches to the waist area, Ted grabbed Kelissa by her hair and threw her to the ground. The imprint of the heel from Kelissa's shoe was red and painfully engraved in her legs and left arm.

It was very late, way past midnight. The children were in bed, asleep, as their mother was being abused by their father. Kelissa was now in her private office lying on the couch, gently pressing the towel of ice on top of her bruised legs. She just finished shedding the last of her tears. Her face was of absolute misery as she had a tough day in the Oval Office.

Since her presidency had begun, Kelissa had decided to veto three bills from being passed. Veto is when the President has the right—the *power* to reject a bill from being passed by legislation. The President has ten days before deciding to veto the bill. If a decision has not been made after those ten days, the bill will automatically pass and become law.

That is what started the argument between Kelissa and Ted. Ted tried to give Kelissa some input on what she should do. But her decision was already made to veto the bills. Ted, however, *hated* her decision, and he tried to beat it out of her. He hates, more than anything, when Kelissa rejects his advice. But her stubborn ways and her pride sometimes control her more than she thinks. Because she is the first woman President in United States history, she wants to make confident decisions independently, as President, with no exceptions. But sadly, Ted has made her pay for her decision, abusively.

As Kelissa lays on the couch with the towel of ice caressing her legs, she watches a game show on television. A game show called, '**Guess Who's Your Best Friend**?' In the show, there are three contestants; each contestant brings on *three* of their friends. The game show host asks each friend some personal questions about their *friend*, the contestant. Whichever friend out of the three gets the most questions right wins a cash prize *or* a trip to a famous resort.

It became one of Kelissa's favorite shows to watch during her "limited" downtime. The more Kelissa watched the show, the more she wished she had some friends. But Kelissa's political progression and success put a permanent wedge between her and her old friends. On top of that, her old friends are democrats.

As the show went on, the announcer told the contestants that they could win a seven-day trip to Hawaii. Kelissa became intrigued by the images of Hawaii. She always wanted to go but never did. In her mind, Kelissa began to think about going on a getaway—a nice warm vacation. Even though it is not exactly the kind of vacation where she can sit on the beach and be crisp under the sun, Kelissa thought it would be nice to be in a different location. Summer is closely approaching, and Kelissa would love to have some quality time with her children, as they *too*, more than *anyone*, could use a vacation.

Of course, as *President*, Kelissa cannot just book a flight, pack her bags and be in Hawaii for the next two weeks. This kind of trip requires at least two weeks or *more* of careful planning. Hundreds of aides, personnel, and Secret Service agents must also be in attendance with the President. But Kelissa was determined to make this happen.

After the game show ended, Kelissa picked up her journal from the coffee table next to the couch. She had a lot to say about what she had been going through. Not just with Ted but with her children *and* the presidency. In Kelissa's journal, she wrote:

Friday Early Morning, May 31st, 2024

Ladies and gentlemen, I need a vacation. I need to get away from here. My children need a break from being stuck in the White House, as do I. They're not so happy with me, especially Maddy. We had another argument the other night. She told me that I was beginning to feel like a stranger to her. A year before election night, I told Maddy that if I were elected, the first year of the presidency would be my busiest year. And I did not lie to her about that. I have been swamped.

But it's hard for her to understand. It's hard for all of them. I've really put my kids in a complicated position. Bryan needs his mother; he's only eleven years old, soon to be twelve. To be honest, ladies and gentlemen, I am a stranger to my children. I don't know much about them ever since I was on the campaign run. It was just nonstop hard work. But now, I think we could all use a vacation. Well, for me, I'll still be working, but I want them to have a good time when we go to Hawaii. I know that I technically should not be going on a vacation while Covid cases picked up at an alarming rate.

I really need this trip, though. My children need this trip. And I'm going to give it to them. As for Ted, that bastard took one of my favorite shoes and beat me with it. He was walloping me with my shoe so harshly that the heel broke. I can't even get it fixed because I don't want to draw any suspicion. Carl and the other Secret Service agents are very sharp with my attire and presence. If one strain of hair is out of place on me, they will know about it. It's becoming rather hard to hide all of my bruises.

I feel somewhat mortified to say this, ladies and gentlemen, but now, whenever Ted hits me, I have to remind him not to strike me anywhere that I can't cover with clothes. The weather has changed, and I can't wear any warm material.

A few weeks ago, I had a meeting with my advisors and the Chief of Staff in the Oval Office. I was wearing a short-sleeved button-up shirt. I didn't have time to cover the bruise with makeup, so I just put on my suit jacket to keep it hidden. Once I arrived in the Oval Office, I began to take off my suit jacket to get comfortable. But I completely forgot about the bruise on my elbow and quickly turned around and put on my suit jacket before anyone noticed. I almost blew my cover.

I hate myself for this—for putting myself through this craziness. Running a country has been crazy enough for me. The American people have made these despicable judgments of me, telling me that I cannot handle a man's job because I'm a woman. What a sexist comment to make? Sometimes I wish I could just say "Fuck you" to all those shitty people with shitty comments. But I just can't. Those are the same people that I'm representing, unfortunately.

Ladies and Gentlemen, as I said before, I signed up for this. But never did I think that... Wait... I'm sorry, someone's at the door. To be continued...

Some hard knocks came at the door. "Hey, Mom. It's me, TJ," Ted, Jr. projected from outside the office door. Kelissa got up from the couch but had no idea what to do with the towel of ice cubes. But with her sharp and impeccable wit, she looked over at the five empty glasses and placed the ice cubes inside each glass. She then walked over and opened the door; Ted, Jr. was standing there with a handful of letters.

"TJ, it's a quarter to three. What are you still doing up?" Kelissa asked.

"I couldn't sleep," said Ted, Jr., "I was up opening my letters from the colleges, and I have some great news."

"Oh, well, come in, have a seat."

"Okay. *So*, your son has been accepted to GEORGETOWN!"

"*WONDERFUL*, TJ! I am so proud of you, sweetie."

"Thanks, mom. I'm *so* happy they've accepted me."

"Now, is Georgetown where you want to go?"

"Well, my first choice was Stanford, and I got *into* Stanford. But I figured maybe it would be best that I stay close to home."

"Oh, well, just know that it's up to you, babe. Wherever you want to go."

"Yeah, I know. But I *like* Georgetown. I checked the campus out, and I love it. So, I think that'll be my new home. I will be able to live on campus, right?"

"Of *course*, I want you to have that real college experience."

"Will Secret Service be following me?"

"Well, I'll have to think about that. Since you'll be turning 18 next month, *legally*, you'll be an adult."

"Yeah, plus I'll still be here in D.C."

"I'll talk to Carl and Steve about what would be necessary."

"Who's Steve?"

"Steve Packer, he's the Secret Service director. You've *met* him before, remember?"

"We've met *so* many people, Mom. I can't remember *half* of them."

"Ha, I know what you mean… But *hey*, I am *so* proud of you, baby. Come here."

Kelissa opened her arms and gave Ted, Jr. the biggest hug for his great news. But as they hugged, Ted, Jr. could not help but notice something awkward about his mother. "Mom, forgive me for asking, but did you *piss* yourself?" Ted, Jr. asked with a twisted face. Kelissa's navy-blue pajama pants were wet from having the towel of melting ice on her lap. Looking at Ted, Jr., Kelissa tried to throw him off, saying, "*Really*, TJ? You had to ruin the special moment with a question like that? *No*, I didn't *pee* on myself.… *Silly boy*." Ted, Jr. then rolled his eyes and told his mother to have a good night. Right before he left, Kelissa also had some good news to share.

"Oh, by the way," said Kelissa. "Before you head off to college, how about a tan?"

"A *tan*? What are you talking about, mom?"

"I'm *talking* about going on a vacation to *Hawaii*."

"HAWAII! Oh *shit*, really?"

"Hey! Profanity?" I am *still* your mother."

"Oh, sorry, mom. But wow, *really*? We're going to *Hawaii*?"

"Yes, I've put you guys through *a lot* these last several years. I think this will be good for all of us."

"Oh, I am *so* down for this. All this good news, I can't handle it," Ted, Jr. laughed.

Kelissa and Ted, Jr. were all smiles after they exchanged good news. Before Ted, Jr. left Kelissa's office, he said, "Oh, and *whatever* is going on with your pajama pants, you might want to change them. Goodnight." Kelissa then closed the door and sighed with relief. She touched on her pajama pants, definitely wet from the melting ice. But Kelissa kept extra pairs of pajamas and a pillow and blanket hidden in her office. As she removed her damp pajama pants, fresh and day-old bruises were combined all over her legs. She then turned off the lights and made a bed out of the couch. Before she laid back down, she carefully got on her knees, put her hands together, and said a prayer:

"*Father, my Lord, and Savior, Jesus Christ. I pray that you continue to watch over my children and me. I have been trying my very best to make them my priority. But many times, I have fallen short of that. I have fallen far from that. People tell me that I am the most powerful person on the planet. But I know better. I know that you, father, are the only one who has the ultimate power. You, father, are the one who gives me the strength every single day to survive this evil man to whom I married. You give me the strength that I desperately need to run this country. You give me all the tools I need to keep my head above water and handle all the trials and tribulations. Father, I pray that you continue to clothe me with strength, courage, and wisdom. I will continue, father, to keep my faith and my integrity. Please guide me, father, for I am lost. Please heal my bruises, and please heal all my pain, father. Amen...*"

As Kelissa opened her eyes, she got up from her knees and laid on the couch. It was five minutes after four in the morning, and Kelissa had a nine o'clock meeting. But for some reason, she could not get comfortable enough to fall asleep. After all, it *is* a couch and not a bed. Kelissa thought about going upstairs to the guest room, but it became too traumatizing for her to sleep in that room. But then, Kelissa went to the one room she *knew* Ted would not think to look *or* attack her. She took her pillow and blanket and walked over to Bryan's bedroom.

As Kelissa carefully opened Bryan's door, the hallway light pierced through the door opening, shining its way onto Bryan, lying there in his bed. As always, his left arm and leg were hanging off of his bed. And as *always*, Kelissa placed Bryan's arm and leg under his bedsheet and kissed him on the side of his head. After that, she grabbed some of Bryan's pillows that he was not using and made herself a small pallet on the floor. It only took about ten minutes before her eyes closed as she retired in the early morning. It was the *best* three hours of sleep Kelissa had in a long time.

"Mommy? Mommy? Wake up," Bryan said as he shook Kelissa's left shoulder. It did not take long for Kelissa to wake up as she opened her eyes to a rainy Friday morning. Bryan, curious to know why his mother was sleeping on his bedroom floor, began to ask her some questions.

"Mommy," said Bryan. "Did you fall asleep in my room last night?"

"Yes, sweetie, I did," Kelissa responded. "You know, I missed you staying with me. So, I thought I'd stay with you this time."

"*Okay*, I guess," Bryan said with confusion.

"Say, how's about you and me go get some breakfast?"

"Okay. Can I have French toast?"

"You can have *whatever* you like, sweetie."

Another lie told, and Kelissa is far from proud of it. Lying to her children has become the most toxic disability she possesses. Kelissa realized that the more she kept her dark secret hidden and untold, the more it would push her children away from her. And with Ted, Jr. heading off to college, her loneliness was soon to get worse.

Chapter 24

Thursday Evening, June 11th, 2024

For He's a Jolly Good Fellow

And nobody can deny it. It has been a special day for Ted, Jr., as he is celebrating his eighteenth birthday with his family. Kelissa has put up some balloons in the Family Dining Room, and a wonderful dinner was prepared in Ted, Jr.'s honor.

As the family had finished their dinner, one of the kitchen staffers brought out a rectangular-shaped birthday cake, just enough to satisfy the five of them. On top of the cake, there was a drum set with the words that said:

"**HAPPY 18TH BIRTHDAY, TEDSTER**!"

"Okay, let's sing happy birthday!" Kelissa projected.

"Wait," Bryan shouted. "We can't sing until we light a candle."

"That won't be necessary, Bryan. He's not blowing on *any* of this cake—not with Covid still floating around," Madeline spoke.

"Guys, *please*!" Kelissa said. "*And* a one, *and* a two, *and* a three—"

An ensemble of singing is happening as Ted, Jr. sits there with a cheesy grin. As the singing wrapped up, Ted, Jr. did the honors of slicing the first piece of cake. As he picked up the slice of cake, Kelissa's face dramatically changed as she saw the gooey strawberry filling. As mentioned before, Kelissa is allergic to strawberries. Ted stood near the table, smiling at Kelissa as he planned this all along. At his spiteful request, Ted asked the kitchen staffers to prepare a cake with strawberry filling so that Kelissa could not have any.

Kelissa stood up from the table and furiously walked away. "Hey, mom," said Ted, Jr. "Aren't you going to have some cake?" Kelissa stopped in her tracks, turned around, and said, "Uh, actually, *no*, baby, I'm sorry. I guess I overate, and I'm a little full right now. But save me a piece, okay?"

Kelissa did not want to make a scene. She walked up to the residence level, *filled* with anger and rage. As she made her way into her bedroom, she began to pace back and forth, cursing up a storm. 'Ted this and Ted that,' *calling* him a fucking bastard. But unfortunately, that was not enough for Kelissa to cool herself down. And the only thing that she could think of to let off some steam was to head up to the workout room and throw some jabs onto the heavy bag.

Kelissa took off her outfit and placed on her sports bra, workout pants, and sneakers.

As Kelissa got upstairs to the workout room, she headed towards the heavy bag. She looked straight at it—pretending it was Ted. She then put on a pair of Ted, Jr.'s boxing gloves and began to throw some blows. It was working; her anger and fury were starting to come out. Each jab and hook she delivered to the heavy bag were helping her relieve her stress. But as Kelissa was throwing her hands, *another* pair of hands began to clap behind her, loudly.

Kelissa quickly turned around, only to see that it was Ted. He stood in the doorway, clapping his hands as he said nothing. But then he stopped, holding his hands together. Still standing there, he and Kelissa began to throw some words.

"Aren't you going to have some *cake*?" Ted sarcastically asked. "It's *delicious*."

"*Go to Hell*!" Kelissa projected.

"I'm curious, Kel. You seem to be very angry at that punching bag. I *assume* that the bag represents—*me*?"

"Go *away*, Ted," Kelissa said with a lower tone of voice.

"Jesus… *First,* you wanted me to go to *hell*. *Now*, you just want me to go away. Make up your goddamn *mind*."

"Get the *hell* out of here, Ted!"

"No, *no*! *You* want to fight, and *obviously*, I'm the opponent. So, *here I am*! Come on—*hit me*!"

"Go away, Ted."

"Come on, Kel—*take* your best swing!"

"Leave me *alone*!"

"Come on, *hit me*, Kel!"

"Leave me *alone*, Ted!"

"Either you hit *me*, or I'm going to hit *you*."

Ted, unfortunately, was not playing. He balled up his fist, and before Kelissa could make a move, he punched her right to the side of her ribs. He then picked her up and slammed her up against the wall. Kelissa began to kick and swing her arms at him. He pressed his hand over her mouth so she would not scream. "You think you can take me on, *bitch*? Well, you got another *fucking* thing coming to you," Ted maliciously said. But the look in Kelissa's eyes had absolutely no fear. With all her might, Kelissa broke free of Ted's grip, and then suddenly, BAM!

But no, it wasn't Ted throwing the punch; it was Kelissa. For the first time, Kelissa fought back and punched Ted directly on the side of his jaw. Kelissa fell to the floor, as did Ted, grunting as he landed. While Kelissa lay on the floor, she looked over at Ted as he looked directly back at *her*, rubbing on his jaw. He then began to stand up, laughing and chuckling. As Kelissa stood up, she brought her fist up to her face, ready to take another swing. Ted looked at her with shock in his eyes.

"What the fuck is this?" Ted shouted. "You're hitting me now?"

"All of that is over and done now, you *bastard*."

"Oh, so *now* you going to fight back?"

"I'm not going to let you continue to hit me, Ted."

"Sweetheart, I'm a *man*; you could never win."

"A real man doesn't beat on his wife just because she has power."

"*Power*? Oh, *you* think you have *power*?"

"Yes, and you're jealous of me. You've *been* jealous since the beginning of the *fucking* campaign!"

"You're *delusional* to think you have any power. You are *nothing* more than a *goddamn puppet*!"

"I'm going to be the one who goes down in history. *You*—you're going down, asshole."

"Oh, you are *such* a corny bitch, Kel."

Kelissa then took another swing, but *this* time, she missed, and Ted's counter punch to her ribs sent her straight to the ground. Kelissa knew that she was no match for Ted, physically. As he stood there, looking down at Kelissa on the floor, he said to her, "You know what, Kel? I just *have* to give you credit. I mean, here you are, learning how to defend yourself. You finally took a swing at me. But *still*, you failed yourself, just like you're going to fail as President. That's always been your problem, Kel. You just *never* know when to *fucking give up*!"

Ted then pulled Kelissa up from her hair and threw her into the heavy bag. She fell back to the floor but then slowly got herself up, holding the side of her ribs. "You *see*?" Ted laughed, "You see what I'm talking about, Kel? You *NEVER FUCKING GIVE UP*!"

As Kelissa stood there, she balled up her fist again as she planned to take another swing at Ted. "Oh, what? *What*? You want to take *another* swing?" Ted mischievously said. "Go ahead, *hit me*! *Punch* me right in the face. Then *I'll* be the one with a bruise on *my* face. *Imagine* what the press would say? '*President Kelissa Morrison is abusing her husband, the First Gentlemen. She physically attacks him, belittles him, abuses her power onto him. She let all that power get to her head.'* Get the picture? I *won't* cover *my* bruise. I'll go *straight* to the press and tell them how much of a *shitty* person you have become. I'll go straight to them, Kel. You put your hands on me, and you'll have impeachment written all over you. As I said, you *have* no power. You're just a *bitch* who got lucky."

As Ted left the workout room, Kelissa fell straight to the floor, holding her ribs as she screamed and cried uncontrollably. One would think that one of the kids would have come upstairs and seen Ted attacking their mother. But evil *always* finds a way. Ted was ahead of the curve as he sent the kids to the bowling lane, all the way down on the residence ground level. Sadly, the kids will never even know, like many other brutal incidents.

Later that night, a severe thunderstorm came through. Kelissa was sleeping on the couch in her private office. On the coffee table was a wet towel that was once filled with ice cubes as Kelissa, once again, had to ice down her bruised and aching body. Next to the towel were the used tissues of the many tears she shed. Kelissa began to toss and turn on the couch as she was experiencing a nightmare.

In her nightmare, Ted was chasing after her, in the dark, in the cold, in the rain. Kelissa was screaming for help in the stormy back alley, but no one could help her. Then when she turned the corner, Kelissa saw Carl, dressed in his black suit, along with dozens of other Secret Service agents. As Kelissa ran towards Carl, she screamed his name, begging for help. She screamed, "Carl, Carl, *help me*! Ted is chasing after me!"

But Carl said nothing; he just laughed. *All* the Secret Service agents began to laugh. Kelissa, now surrounded by black suits of laughing agents in her nightmare. She looked around with her ears covered. One of the laughing agents said, "You're not a *President*; you're just a *woman*!" Another agent said, "You're a *fucking* fraud!" The laughter continued. Kelissa was in one of the worst nightmares of her life. A nightmare where she is surrounded by men who are supposed to protect her. But they cannot protect her from Ted. In this nightmare, all of the Secret Service agents were men, and the laughter represented their doubts about her ability to run a country.

As the laughter grew louder and louder, Ted came forward. Now facing her, Ted looked at Kelissa with his fist balled up, and then, it happened. Ted punched her right in her face. He punched and slapped as the laughter grew louder and evil—until Kelissa could not take it anymore, and she just *screamed.* She screamed herself awake as she fell off of the couch. Now laying on the floor, in a cold sweat, Kelissa looked over at the window and saw the rain streaming down.

Kelissa was still in pain, grabbing the side of her ribs as she stayed on the floor. The lighting and rumbling sounds of thunder continued to roar while tears fell down Kelissa's face of defeat. But she did not want to be defeated. As she slowly got up from the floor, in pain, Kelissa went to her desk, grabbed a pen and her journal. In her journal, she wrote:

Friday Early Morning, June 12th, 2024

Ladies and gentlemen, I did it. I fought back. I struck him on his face. It felt so liberating to be able to fight him back. As I am writing this, I hear the rain and thunder outside, I see the lightning, and I see a storm coming. I'm not a stupid woman; I know Ted will not stop abusing me. He will end up killing me.

I can't believe I just walked out on TJ's birthday. I know he's upset with me for doing that. I have to make it up to him. But Ted, he's got me trapped now. This vacation can't come soon enough. I told Ted that he would not be welcomed on this vacation. I don't want him anywhere in sight. And do you know what he said to me afterward? Nothing, but he punched me in my stomach in the dressing room. Then he took one of my heavier shoeboxes and threw it on me.

Do you know what is so insane about all of this, ladies and gentlemen? He still climbs on top of me and has sex with me. Please, I beg of you, spare your judgments, please. If you could just put yourself in my shoes, you would understand. I'm a human being just like you. I've been crying, hurting, and I can't escape. I can't leave. I can't just take my kids and leave the White House. Not as the President. Secret Service is around me at all times. I can't drive, and I barely speak to my parents. This life is not living; it's not living at all.

So, please, no judgments. Look in the mirror and ask yourself, "Who the hell are you?" But I don't even know who I am anymore. I can't believe I survived this long with all the beatings, the mind control, and manipulation. I'm coming to a point where I want him just to kill me, or at least beat me half to death so that they can take him away or kill him. But if he kills me, what will happen to my children? They won't ever see their mother again. Jesus, when will this end? How will this end?

Kelissa wrapped her arms around her journal, holding it tight like a teddy bear. She laid back on the couch as she broke down and cried. Kelissa wants this to stop, but she knows that Ted will never stop until she is dead. It's already been six months since she has been in office. And as much as the country loves her, their favorite public figure is in absolute danger, hidden right in plain sight. Through the traffic of her tears and sobbing, Kelissa said to herself, "If you don't take him, Lord, please, just *please*, take me. Take me, and *please* watch over my children."

Chapter 25

Wednesday Afternoon, July 31st, 2024

An Escape to Paradise

Miles high in the sky on Air Force One as the Morrison family is heading to Hawaii for vacation. After weeks of careful planning and *intense* preparation, Kelissa and her children are on their way to Oahu Island. The native home of the 44th President of the United States, Barack Obama.

Kelissa's spirit is better, her mind is in the right place, and Ted is *thousands* of miles away. As Air Force One flies overseas, President Kelissa Morrison is busy in her private office—writing letters and speeches and making a few phone calls to other world leaders discussing confidential manners. Just as she hangs up the phone, she gets a knock at her door.

"Come in," Kelissa projected.

"Mom?" Madeline said. "Are you busy?"

"Hey, sweetie, um, I *am*, but you can come in. I just have to finish reading these documents."

"Okay… *So*, have you ever *been* to Hawaii before?"

"I *haven't*; I always wanted to when I was your age. But your grandparents told me they had a bad experience when they went."

"Oh, really? *What* bad experience?"

"They made me."

"Oh, *Mom*," Madeline laughed. "You're too much."

"See? I have a pretty good sense of humor."

"Uh, mom?"

"Yes, sweetie?"

"That night when I was being mean at the dinner table, and you grounded me, I never did apologize for that."

"Aww, *honey*, it's okay. *I'm* sorry for showing up late for dinner all the time."

"Yeah… I don't *know*; it just feels like ever since you became '*The President,*' we've all become strangers now."

"Well, that is *why* I wanted us to take this vacation. You kids have been *so* supportive with all of this. I know it has not been easy, with the changing of schools and no cell phones with social media. You guys are making a *tremendous* sacrifice for me. And I appreciate all three of you."

"Thanks, Mom. I needed to hear that. But why didn't *Dad* come with us?"

"Your *father*… I asked your father to stay behind to do some work for me at home."

"*Home*, Mom? It's the White House. It's not home."

"Well, the White House *is* our home, sweetie. At least for the next three and a half years."

"Well, Dad said th—"

"Oh, Maddy, *please—enough* about your father!"

"What? All I was going to say was that dad said the White House is not our home, and we're just *guests*."

"Your father is…"

"He's *what*, Mom?"

"Nothing," Kelissa said as she rubbed her forehead. "Can you just do me a favor and look after your little brother? *Please*?"

"Dad was so right."

"About what, Maddy?"

"He said that ever since you've become President, you only care about yourself."

Madeline then slammed the door as she walked out of Kelissa's office. Kelissa sat at her desk with her hand still against her forehead—shaking her head as she softly said, "Your father's killing me, Maddy. He's killing me." The sad thing is Kelissa could not move an inch away from her desk because she was hiding her bruised legs from Madeline.

Kelissa suffered multiple bruises all over her legs from two nights ago. Ted taped her mouth shut, tied her hands behind her back, and brutally whipped her with his belt and a metal hanger in the dressing room. Kelissa was wearing shorts, and she did not want Madeline to see the painful marks caused by her father. But the bitter remarks said by Madeline felt even worse for Kelissa.

Air Force One has landed safely. There is a colossal crowd standing and cheering behind the barricades for President Kelissa Morrison. Being that Kelissa is under the protection of the Secret Service, she and the kids are unable to be traditionally greeted with a fresh flower lei and a warm "Aloha." Instead, they have to get directly into the Beast one and be transported to the rented house where they will be staying for vacation. Even though the taxpayers of America are paying for Kelissa's traveling expenses, she had to come out of *her* pocket to rent the house, buy food, and take care of other necessities.

As Kelissa steps off the stairs of the plane and waves to the cheering people, she spots a small child, *cute* as a button, holding up a sign that says:

"**LET'S TAKE A SELFIE, PRESIDENT MORRISON!**" Kelissa could not resist.

"Carl," said Kelissa. "I want to take a picture with that little girl."

"We really should get going, Madam President."

"It'll only take a second, Carl."

Carl and three other Secret Service agents escorted Kelissa towards the little girl behind the barricade. The mother was holding her as Kelissa greeted them both.

"*Hello*, sweetie pie," Kelissa said as she smiled. "And what is *your* name?"

"My name is Keka," The little girl said in her innocent voice.

"*Keka*, what is the meaning of *that* name?" Kelissa asked.

"It means chosen, selected, or appointed," The mother responded.

"Aww, that's wonderful. It's *very* nice to meet you, Keka. How's about we take that selfie?"

Kelissa picked up Keka, holding her in her arms as the mother took the picture. Carl and the other Secret Service agents had faces of steel as they screened the area, looking for any suspicious activity or potential threats near their protectee. As Kelissa was still holding the little girl, Carl strongly recommended that they keep moving.

Just as Kelissa handed Keka back over to her mother, out of *nowhere*, a Caucasian man, dressed in some jeans, boots, and a retired army jacket, came *through* the crowd and attempted to throw a large glass of icy water at the President. But the man was unsuccessful as two Secret Service agents grabbed him and body-slammed him to the ground. Those agents were on him faster than a starving lion on its prey.

Immediately, agents drew their guns and surrounded President Morrison as if they were forming a body shield around her. Carl gave the order to have the President urgently escorted back on Air Force

One. "CARL, MY *CHILDREN*!" Kelissa screamed. People were screaming—running in different directions. But the main priority was getting the President out of harm's way.

This is why the plane door to Air Force One and the back door to the Beast one remain open at all times in case of an emergency, and the President has to be immediately removed from the area.

As Kelissa went up the airplane stairs with Carl and the other Secret Service agents, she heard, "YOU *BITCH*! YOU *FUCKING* COWARD! HOW *DARE* YOU SEND MORE OF OUR TROOPS BACK INTO THAT *GODDAMN* COUNTRY? YOU *FUCKING* GO TO *HELL*!" The crazy man shouted to Kelissa.

Kelissa, however, was not necessarily in fear for *her* life. Her *only* priority was the safety of her children—and they *were* safe. The other Secret Service agents swiftly and safely escorted them back on Air Force One. The door was shut, and the plane immediately began to taxi down the runway. Madeline and Bryan were holding each other, terrified. Ted, Jr. rushed over to his mother to comfort her.

"Mom, *mom*! You okay? What *happened*?" Ted, Jr. shouted.

"Yes, TJ, I'm fine! Are you guys okay?" Kelissa responded.

"Yeah, yeah; we're good, we're okay!"

"Carl, notify Sam and Mark—tell them to get this plane off the damn ground, NOW!" Kelissa said.

"They're moving the plane down the runway right now, Madam President. *Everyone*, take your seats and strap in!" Carl projected.

Air Force One was heading down the runway about to take off, not even three minutes after that severe altercation. Kelissa's heart was racing as if it was racing the plane down the runway. Her body began to shake as the rumbling of Air Force One grew stronger. As Air Force One was levitating, Kelissa closed her eyes and said a prayer in her mind:

"*Oh father, protect my children… No matter what happens to me, please, always protect my children.*"

Chapter 26

Thursday Early Morning, August 1st, 2024

A Moment of Gratitude

Heading back home to the White House, Kelissa is back in her private office on Air Force One. She is watching the breaking news of the '**Attempted Assassination of the President**,' as the media is now calling it. Channel after channel, Kelissa sees her face in the video footage taken by the people via their smartphones. News anchors and commentators give their two cents of what *they* thought happened. News journalists interviewing people who were not even *there*, saying the crazy man was armed and pointing a gun at the President—many lies and deceitfulness were coming out of their click-baiting mouths. Kelissa had enough as she took the television remote, turned off the T.V., and tossed the remote onto her desk. Now, she sits there with her eyes closed, shaking her head at the disgracefulness. As her office grew quiet, a knock came on the door.

"Come in," Kelissa spoke.

"Madam President," Carl said as he opened the door. "You wanted to speak with me?"

"Yes, Carl. Please, come in and have a seat."

"How are you doing, Madam President?"

"Oh, I'm *doing*; that was a very frightening moment."

"It *was*; that's why we take our job very *seriously*. You just never know when or where danger will come from."

"You're right… And that's why I wanted to talk to you. I am *sincerely* sorry for not listening to you. I should've got in the car."

"Well, Madam President, I've been doing this job for decades. I've seen it *all*. Assassination attempts, and people throwing objects at the President, *just* like today. It's just something we're always prepared for."

"I heard what that man said—screaming about me sending troops back into Afghanistan."

"That man's name is Alexander Williams. He is a U.S. Army vet."

"Wait, you've already *identified* him?"

"Yes, ma'am. *Again*, we take our jobs very seriously."

"Right… Should I have to be worried about him?"

"No."

"Okay… *Oh*, *Carl*, I just feel so *bad* about my *children*. I wanted them to have a great vacation and enjoy themselves. I've really screwed things up for them. And all that tax money for *nothing*."

"Madam President, you shouldn't blame yourself. It just comes with this job. There will be other vacations."

"I know, Carl. Maybe I'll just get some sleep."

"That's a good idea. You need some rest."

As Carl made his way out of the office, Kelissa stopped him.

"Carl?" Kelissa spoke.

"Madam President?" Carl responded.

"I—I wanted to tell you… Something."

Kelissa stood there, awkwardly looking at the floor as she zoned out. "Madam President? *Madam President*?" Carl said to Kelissa. Kelissa heard Carl's voice, but she could not comprehend what he said. She was trying to tell her secret to him. But she could not get the words to pass beyond her teeth.

"MADAM PRESIDENT!" Carl projected.

"Yes, *yes*! Oh, *God*, di—did I just zone *out*?" Kelissa asked.

"I think you *did*, ma'am. And I think you *do* have to get some rest, *please*. We don't land for another six hours."

"Okay, okay. I'll be in my suite."

"*Okay*, Madam President. I'll be sitting right outside the door if you need me."

"Thank you, Carl. And sorry about that."

After Carl left the office, Kelissa just stood there, looking at the door. She was so close to revealing her secret to Carl and telling the truth. But the only outlet Kelissa could tell her truth to was her journal. She brought her journal on the trip just in case she had something to say. Kelissa grabbed her journal and a pen from her desk and made her way into the presidential suite. The suite had a queen size bed with a television and two nightstands. She then undresses from her outfit, removing the jet-black stockings that covered her bruised legs, laid in her bed, and opened her journal. With the pen in her hand, Kelissa began to bleed:

Thursday Early Morning, August 1st, 2024

Ladies and gentlemen, I've had one of the most horrifying days of my entire life. But to be honest with you, I can't say that this was worse than all the insanity I went through with Ted. That crazy man comes nowhere close to the way Ted attacks me. He's nothing more than an amateur compared to Ted. I thank Carl so much, as well as the others. But unfortunately, I'm still in great danger. Ted is going to be waiting for me when I get back. God knows what he's going to say or do to me. I tried to tell Carl; I really did. But I'm just... I'm afraid. I'm so scared of what the aftermath will be. Just look at what the news channels said about the incident from earlier. They chewed it up and created their own narratives. Can you imagine what they would say if I revealed this secret?

The one thing that terrifies me the most about all of this is the danger I put my children through. I am placing an entire team of Secret Service agents on T.J. as soon as he steps foot on campus at Georgetown. I know he will hate me for doing this, but I can't risk my children's safety. I may even have to put Maddy and Bryan through home school. They all will hate me for doing this, but their safety is all that matters to me.

As I'm writing to you, ladies and gentlemen, I'm looking at my legs. If only you could see them. The purplish-black bruises are all over my legs, whelped-up markings from when Ted whipped me with his belt. He taped my mouth shut and tied my hands behind my back as he whipped me with his belt. He must have whipped me at least ten times with his belt. I lost count after he hit me with the metal hanger. My God, it was so fucking bad.

I will have to wear suit pants and black stockings for another two weeks to cover the bruises. I know what you are thinking, ladies and gentlemen. You are thinking about why I won't tell the truth publicly. And I would respond to that by saying this; walk in my shoes for twenty-four hours. For twenty-four hours, I challenge you to walk in my shoes as the President of the United States of America and tell me what you would do. I just can't do it. I wouldn't wish this on my worst enemy. The mental blockage that Ted has put on me is in full form. My mind is just not a mind of my own anymore. I know I have a severe mental problem. I'm reminded of it every day when I look at him.

You know, ladies and gentlemen; today, when that man charged his way through the crowd, I admit to you now that I wish he had a gun on him and would have opened fire and shot me. Then it would all be over—no more secrets, no more abuse, no more pain. But my babies, I just can't leave my babies behind. They need me. See? I've entirely lost my fucking mind. I'm just trying to survive, ladies and gentlemen. Maybe if you were in my shoes, you would understand.

Kelissa's emotions ran wild as she began to cry on the pages of her journal. She then turned off the light on her nightstand and cried some more on her pillow. A short-lived two-million-dollar vacation had come to its end. Kelissa was not looking forward to her sudden return to the White House, where the *real* crazy man was waiting for her. But at the same time, she knew that this was the *perfect* time for her to get some rest. She fell asleep as Air Force One had another five hours before landing in the nation's capital.

Chapter 27

Thursday Morning, August 1st, 2024

What An Actor

The sunrise never looked so beautiful from the sky. After being picked up from a heavily guarded, undisclosed airport, Kelissa and the children are now flying in Marine One as they are five minutes away from landing at 1600 Pennsylvania Avenue.

Kelissa is exhausted, barely able to keep her eyes open. She already knows that the press will be looking for answers but will *not* make any public statements. Instead, Kelissa will briefly discuss with Press Secretary Lesley Richards about making a statement on her behalf. Kelissa could hear the pilots speaking to the snipers on the roof of buildings, scanning the environment to ensure the coast was secured and transparent. Sometimes, even *Kelissa* does not realize how heavily protected she is under the Secret Service.

As Marine One begins to descend to the south lawn of the White House, Kelissa wakes up the children. She shook Madeline's shoulder to wake her up, but Madeline shrugged off Kelissa's hand, not wanting her mother to touch her. Her attitude towards her mother was becoming more distasteful. But Kelissa was too tired to react.

As Marine One landed, two of the Marine Sentries stood near the helicopter to salute the President. Two Secret Service agents exited Marine One first, then the children, two other agents along with Carl, and *then* Kelissa. As Kelissa left Marine One, she almost forgot to salute the Marine Sentries. She turned around and walked towards them as she lifted her diagonal hand and gave the two of them a salute.

Press and news crew were distantly standing on the lawn as they recorded the President heading into the White House. As Kelissa walked closer to the south portico of the White House, she saw Ted standing there in his pajamas as he hugged Bryan, Madeline, and Ted, Jr.

Kelissa could hear Ted say, "Dear *God*, I was *so* terrified. I'm so glad you guys are okay." As Kelissa made her way towards the door, Ted began to put on a show. "Oh my *God*, Kel. Are you okay?" Ted said as he passionately hugged Kelissa. He began to kiss her as if there was no tomorrow. She could not believe the performance Ted was putting on right now, mainly because she still had bruises on her legs caused by him. As Kelissa, Ted, and Carl walked inside the White House, they began to conversate.

"Oh my God, I was so scared. I heard some crazy man had a gun?" Ted asked.

"No, Mr. Morrison," said Carl. "There was no gun."

"You can't believe everything you see on the news, Ted. You know that," Kelissa spoke.

"Yeah, of course, but I had no idea. You never called."

"I know, that's why I had Carl call to inform you that I was okay. I didn't want to talk to *anyone*. My mind was not in the right place. I was in *shock,* for God's sake."

"Okay, *okay,* I *understand*. I'm just glad that you guys are alright."

"Listen, I have to talk with Lesley. I will see you *upstairs*, *momentarily*."

Kelissa then walked away from Ted, making her way to the Oval Office. Press Secretary, Lesley Richards, waited patiently as Kelissa made her way inside the West Wing.

As she arrived in front of the Oval Office, Kelissa got straight to the point. She squirted and rubbed hand sanitizer between her hands as she began to talk with Lesley Richards.

"Madam Secretary, good morning," Kelissa said.

"Good morning, Madam President. I'm glad you're safe. How are you doing?" Lesley responded.

"I'm *fine*. But let's get started, huh?"

Carl and another Secret Service agent stood guard of the Oval Office. Kelissa and Lesley took a seat and began to go over the statement about what happened in Hawaii. Kelissa wanted to nip this in the bud before the rumors and conspiracy theories rapidly grew. "Okay, Madam Secretary, can you read to me what speech you have prepared for the press briefing?" Kelissa asked. As Lesley opened her brown leather binder, she pulled out the statement about the Hawaii incident.

As Lesley read the statement out loud, it said:

My fellow Americans,

First and foremost, the President would like to thank you for all the heart-warming prayers, concerns, and care that you may have shared. As of now, she is doing very well. The incident that occurred yesterday afternoon was a serious matter but was *drastically* taken out of proportion. The individual who caused the incident did *not* draw a firearm. He *was* apprehended by Secret Service and law enforcement on-site and was taken into custody. As of right now, we have no further information about the suspect to disclose to the public, nor will we. But the President and her children are safe. President Morrison *also* wanted to add that she now holds the record for the *quickest* vacation in presidential history.

Kelissa, even though she was drained, gave a slight chuckle about having the record of the quickest vacation. They added a few other things to the statement, and then Kelissa headed straight for her bedroom as she needed to recharge.

Five minutes later, the sun was up, and the birds were chirping on a beautiful summer day. Before entering her bedroom, Kelissa saw Madeline coming out of Bryan's room. As Madeline looked at her mother, she did not say a word to her. Instead, Madeline shook her head, went into her room, and slammed the door.

Kelissa stood there in silence, upset that she and the children were not on good terms. "I'm sorry, you guys," Kelissa softly said, standing in the center hall. As she turned around to walk into her bedroom, Ted was still awake in bed. As Kelissa closed the door, she looked at him with an emotionless face.

"You're a great actor," Kelissa softly said.

"Not as great as *you*," Ted responded. "How does it feel? To be a victim?"

"I'm too tired for this, Ted."

"You don't *call* me; you don't tell me if *my* kids are okay? You hate me *that much* now?"

"Oh, *cut* the *fucking* act, Ted! You're an abuser! You're a sick, evil, *violent* bastard! Look, look at my fucking legs."

Kelissa took off her shoes and ripped her stockings to reveal the painful decorations of bruises all over her legs. Ted looked for a solid minute. He got up from the bed and stood next to Kelissa. With a sinister look, he said to her, "And would you like to have *more* bruises to go with that? Because I can do that, Kel." Kelissa looked right back at him—shook her head as she responded, "I know you would, you *unimaginable* son of a *bitch*."

Ted heard enough as he grabbed Kelissa by her blouse and threw her to the ground. But Kelissa got right back up. It surprised Ted as he expected her to stay there on the floor. But he saw in her eyes that her fear of him was beginning to fade away.

"Go ahead," said Kelissa. "You wanna hit me again? Go ahead."

"Kel, I'm warning you. You keep pissing me off. I'm fucking *warning* you."

"Go *ahead*, you feel like a *man*? Putting your hands on a woman?"

"You know, Kel, sometimes you are *so fucking* stupid."

Ted grabbed Kelissa once again and brought her down to the floor. Kelissa began to kick and punch Ted as she yelled, "You bastard, you *fucking* coward!" Ted did not know what to do or where to hit her. Instead, he took her two wrists and pinned them to the floor with his strong hands. There was a lot of heavy breathing as Ted was on top of Kelissa, holding her down to the floor. Ted looked lost and confused. He felt that he was losing his power over Kelissa. As she looked at him, Kelissa said, "Can't you see? You keep beating me over and over, but the bruises will eventually heal. And I will still be the President. From now on, I'm going to have Secret Service stand guard of the bedroom door, which I should have done since the first *fucking* day we moved in! Your abusive days are over, you bastard."

As Ted still had Kelissa pinned to the floor, an evil smirk grew on his face. Frustrated that he could not intimidate her, Ted decided to be disgusting. Ptui! Ptui! Ptui! Ptui! *Ptui*! He degradingly spat in Kelissa's face—one after the other. After he hocked his fifth loogie and spat in Kelissa's face, her tears began to mix and fall with the massive saliva and phlegm. Kelissa hated that with a passion—being spitted on, and Ted knew it.

As Ted still had Kelissa on the floor, he said, "You think you're tough, huh? You think you have *power* now? *Yes*, the bruises will heal, but I *will* beat them back on you, *bitch*. You're *nothing* to me; you're just a fucking lifeless *cunt*! And you're *not* going to place *any* fucking agents in front of the bedroom door. You hear me? You *have* no friends, my kids hate your *guts*, and you can *never* get their trust back. And guess what? *I* hate your fucking *guts*. And you know what else? I was *praying* that you were shot. I was praying that the assassination rumors were true. Trust me; if you had died, I would have celebrated your death. Because no one cares about you, bitch. From now on, you better be careful. Because I just may be the one who *fucking buries* you."

Just before Ted got off of Kelissa, "Ptui!" Ted hocked and spit on her yet again. Kelissa was still lying on the floor as she continued to sob and wipe her face from the debris of Ted's saliva. When it came to the physical abuse, Kelissa was growing somewhat used to the pain. But when it came to the *mental* and *emotional* abuse, Ted was *way* too powerful for her. He knew how to break her spirit completely. He made her feel as if she no longer wanted to live. And a piece of her was beginning to feel that way. Kelissa was starting to lose her faith and spirit all over again.

Minutes after Ted left the bedroom, Kelissa slowly got up and went into the bathroom to wash her face off. As she turned on the faucet, tears were still pouring down her face. She took handfuls of water and splashed them on her face, one by one. Kelissa refused to look at herself in the mirror. She kept her head down as she felt disgraceful to her own self. But why? *Why* would she see herself as a disgrace when *she* is the victim?

Ted's powerful manipulation kept an evil reign of terror over Kelissa. His abusive words helped him regain power over her mind to the point where whatever he called her, Kelissa precisely became that. He kept calling her a bitch, and *eventually*, she became one with her staffers and her children. He called her a terrible mother, and she *became* a terrible mother. Ted wanted to destroy her character by any means necessary, and he took sincere pleasure in doing so.

Kelissa was beginning to feel hopeless. Her ambition as President was dying, and she had no passion left. It got to the point where she was becoming nothing more but a puppet. And that is what Kelissa feared more than ever to become, a puppet.

Chapter 28

Sunday Late Evening, August 11th, 2024

Sad Birthday, Kelissa!

"Happy Birthday, President Morrison!" Said by an ensemble of family and staffers. A big extravaganza for Kelissa's 48th birthday celebration. After what happened a few weeks ago in Hawaii, Kelissa was having some fun with her children and some special guests; her parents. Kelissa's parents came from San Francisco to visit her for her birthday. The food, cake, and ice cream were perfect, and for the first time in a while, Kelissa had a genuine smile on her face.

Since Kelissa is the President, her gifts cannot be too expensive; everything has to be below $390. As Kelissa's father talks to his grandchildren, her mother, Suzanne, has a word or two with her.

"Kelissa, sweetheart," said Suzanne. "We haven't talked much since that incident in Hawaii. How are you doing?"

"I'm doing *well*, Mom," Kelissa smiled. "I'm still *breathing*, and that's enough for me."

"Well, that's good, darling. I was just *perturbed* about you. This whole presidency could take its toll on *anyone*. And you're the first woman *ever* to achieve this. That's *great* pressure on you."

"Well, Mom, I can't deny that. It has been very, *very* stressful at times."

"I'm sure it has, my dear. And that's why I wanted to talk to you and make sure you're doing okay. And you're fortunate to have a supportive husband like Ted. He's *such* a great man, isn't he? Your father loves him very much. So do I."

"I'm sure you guys do."

Kelissa was conflicted with the attachment that her parents have with Ted. They love him with all their heart but have no idea of the kind of monster he *truly* has become. "You know what, I'm going to go over there and give my son-in-law a hug and kiss," Suzanne said as she walked away from Kelissa. And Suzanne did just that. She gave Ted the biggest hug and told him how great a man he is for supporting his wife and kids.

Kelissa looked on at the image of her parents and Ted. The taste in her mouth grew so bitter and sour that she had to leave the room. "Everyone, I'll be right back. I left something upstairs," Kelissa said as she headed up to the residence level.

As Kelissa went up the stairs, she began to walk down the center hall, pacing back and forth as she looked at the wall. On the wall were pictures of Kelissa, some of her family, her presidential campaign, and election night. As she looked closely at one of the pictures, Kelissa noticed something alarming. She was wearing a midnight purple suit jacket and a skirt with *no* stockings in that picture. But as Kelissa looked even *closer* at the bottom of the skirt, she saw a bruise on her thigh. That picture was taken at the very beginning of her campaign run. Kelissa was mortified and began to panic.

Kelissa had looked and approved *hundreds* of pictures during her run, but she never spotted that bruise. The strangest thing about that particular photo is the night *before* it was taken. Ted suggested that Kelissa wear the burnt orange outfit, but she wanted to wear the midnight purple outfit, and they got into an argument about that. Ted eventually attacked her and bruised her thigh. Coincidently, people never caught onto the bruise because it camouflaged and blended in with the color of her midnight purple skirt.

But now that Kelissa saw the bruise, she immediately took that picture off the wall. However, the paranoia began to creep in and control Kelissa's brain—believing that other photos on the wall revealed bruises on her body. Without hesitation, Kelissa started to take *all* the pictures off the wall.

One by one, Kelissa unhooked the framed pictures and tossed them to the floor. Anxiety rose as she looked at another photo and saw a dark marking on her arm—thinking it was a bruise. But it was the shadow of Ted's arm waving in the air. Kelissa was falling deep into the abyss of hallucination as she removed thirty pictures off the walls—all piled up on the floor. Then all of a sudden, a voice from behind shouts at Kelissa.

"Mom!" Madeline shouted.

"What?" Kelissa fearfully responded.

"What the *hell* are you doing?"

"I'm… Uh, I'm *just* redecorating."

"*Redecorating*? *Right now*? On *your* birthday?"

"I—I guess it's a bad time?"

"I think you've really gone crazy now, Kelissa."

Kelissa, holding one of the frames in her hand, walked towards Madeline as she said, "Maddy, I know that you and I are not on good *terms* right now. I *know* that we do not see eye to eye with *anything*. But that does not *give you* the right to disrespect me and *call* me by my first name." Madeline began to get very testy with Kelissa. "Well, forgive me, *Madam President*. Because you're *sure* as hell *not* my mom anymore!" Madeline yelled. Kelissa, now enraged, launched the framed picture across the center hall. Glass shattered everywhere as Madeline grew scared of her mother.

"You better get the *fuck* out of my face before I do something that I *won't* regret!" Kelissa shouted to Madeline. Madeline, now with startled, teary eyes, immediately ran out of the center hall and down the stairs.

Kelissa then closed her eyes and fell to her knees, shedding many tears. She could not believe her behavior or what she had just said to her daughter. On the floor were two cracked frames of pictures of herself. Kelissa picked them up and began to look at them. The disturbing reality about all those pictures was that she was suffering behind every smile—*bruises* under every outfit. Kelissa precisely remembered every attack before or after those pictures were taken. She realized that this entire time, from the beginning of her presidential run, up until now, she was not happy—she was *never* truly happy. And what's even worse, her children were becoming unhappy.

Kelissa got herself together and headed back down the stairs. Her father, Gregory, became very vocal to her. "Kelissa, my *God*, how do you disappear on us like that on *your* birthday? We raised you better than that." Kelissa scanned the Family Dining Room. Ted, Jr., and Bryan were chatting with their grandmother while Madeline was standing at the far end of the room, talking to her father. As Kelissa looked at the two of them, Ted kept looking up at Kelissa as Madeline spoke to him. Kelissa knew Madeline was discussing what had recently happened upstairs in the center hall. Madeline started getting emotional, and Ted took her out of the room.

"*Okay*, how about we all go down to the bowling lane?" Kelissa said with enthusiasm. Kelissa's father, Gregory, was thrilled. He has always wanted to see the bowling alley ever since the redesigning of it by Richard Nixon in 1969. But since then, the one-lane bowling alley has been redesigned to a more tech-sophisticated *two*-lane bowling alley. Kelissa's parents took the elevator down to the bowling alley, located on the residence ground level. But as Kelissa was walking down the cross hall towards the stairs, Carl stopped her because of a situation.

"Excuse me, Madam President," said Carl. "I'm sorry to disturb you, but we have a situation on our hands. We need you in the Situation Room."

"But Carl, I'm with my fam—"

"I'm *sorry*, Madam President. We need you in the Situation Room, pronto."

Kelissa, Carl, and two other Secret Service agents then went down to the ground level of the West Wing, where the Situation Room is located (formerly called the *John F. Kennedy* Conference room). As Kelissa entered the Situation Room, staffers swiftly moved around as if America was under attack. She had no idea of what was going on. But Kelissa kept her composure and remained calm. As Carl escorted Kelissa into one of the conference rooms, she was greeted by some of her staff: National Security Advisor, Marcus Van Hamburg, White House Chief of Staff, Andrew Crane, Secretary of Defense, General Blake Talley, the Army Chief of Staff, General Matthew Stokes, and Vice President, Harry Griffin.

"Gentlemen," Kelissa spoke. "What is going on?"

"Madam President," said V.P. Harry Griffin. "There was a deadly bombing that took place in Afghanistan, in the city of Kabul. We've got word that it may have been part of a terrorist group. But we're not exactly sure. And there's something else."

"What else, Mr. Vice President?"

"We've got word that at least twenty-seven of our U.S. troops were killed in that blast. And the numbers are still rising."

"*Jesus*... Oh, dear God. Oh, *God*, no."

Kelissa was devastated at the tragic news. She took a seat as she began to look at the monitors reporting the breaking news. And after deploying another thousand U.S. troops back into Afghanistan, Kelissa felt utterly responsible for the deaths of those sacrificial soldiers.

"Madam President," said General Stokes. "I need you to sign this."

"What is this, General?" Kelissa asked.

"It's an executive order, Madam President."

As Kelissa was reading the executive order, she immediately knew what it was and refused to sign it. "NO, NO! NO! NO! *NO*!" Kelissa shouted as she tore up and threw the order across the desk, "I will *not* sign this and drop *bombs* on their land! We've done *enough* of that for over *twenty fucking years*! Dropping missiles will reactivate the war. And this is *not* the time to go to war with *anyone*!"

The conference room became silent. Kelissa, now focused on the monitors—seeing the corpses of the civilians being dug out of rubble and debris and carried away. Then finally, Kelissa began to speak again.

"General Talley, General Stokes," Kelissa projected. "We *have* to get our troops out of there. We *have* to get them out of that country."

"Madam President, what about the *Savuetage des femmes* Operation?" General Stokes asked.

"*Our* troops come first, General."

"But *Madam Presi*—"

"THAT IS AN *ORDER*, GENERAL! Get them *out* of there!

Dead silence yet again. Kelissa could easily sense the tension in the room. She could tell by their faces that they *hated* the reality of a woman giving them orders. "The operation is a bust. We *have* to remove our troops—*every last one* of them. We're not perpetuating this war with that country. Get our troops out of there as soon as possible. Have I made myself *clear*, gentlemen?" Kelissa spoke with conviction.

The *Savuetage des femmes* Operation was President Morrison's operation. She started this operation right after the first Cabinet Room meeting. "*Savuetage des femmes*," is French for saying, "Women rescue." Kelissa had a goal to rescue as many Afghan women and children as possible and place them in a program to *free* them of the abuse, torment, starvation, and the piss poor treatment they are imprisoned to in Afghanistan. But now, Kelissa felt that she had blood on her hands after deploying another thousand U.S. troops. At that moment, all she could think about was what that crazy man said to her in Hawaii.

About an hour later, President Kelissa Morrison was due to make a public statement in the middle of the cross hall of the State floor. But before making that statement, Kelissa confronted her family, who were all in the bowling alley.

Escorted by Carl, Kelissa made her way down to the bowling alley. There was much laughter and shouting as Kelissa's father, Gregory, scored his tenth strike. But when Kelissa came into the bowling alley, her family turned to look at her and just stood there. Ted, Suzanne, Gregory, Madeline, Bryan, and Ted, Jr. looked at her in silence. "Why are you all looking at me like that?" Kelissa said with a face of defeat. As her father, Gregory, stepped forward, he said to Kelissa, "Well, you just walked out on your family. Didn't say a word, you just disappeared, and we're here for *you.* It's *your* birthday, Kelly."

Kelissa looked at each of them, Madeline had a look of disgust and disappointment, Bryan had an innocent but confused look on his face, and Ted, he loved every minute of it. He *loved* to see the look of defeat on Kelissa's face. Nothing gave him more satisfaction than to see Kelissa feel powerless.

"I had a situation that I needed to tend to," Kelissa responded.

"A situation *more* important than your family? *More* important than celebrating your birthday?"

"Dad, you *don't* understand—"

"*Help* me understand, Kelissa! Help *all* of us understand!"

Kelissa then looked at Ted again. She wanted to tell her family *everything*. It was as if the words of the truth were set right behind her teeth, *waiting* to come out. But as close as Kelissa was to *speak* that truth, all she could get out was this: "*I am* the *President* of the United States of America. I now have to be responsible for *all* American people! You have *no idea* the amount of *pressure*, and *stress,* and *anguish* I am under *every single day*! *None* of you do! *Forgive* me for not being the perfect *wife*, or the perfect *mother*, or the perfect *daughter*! I do the best I *goddamn* can for *everyone*! If you guys continue to judge me and hate me, be my guest. Now, if you all will excuse me, I have to make a speech and address the nation. Enjoy your bowling."

As Kelissa turned around and walked out of the bowling alley, tears began to run down her face. The rest of the family stood there in shock. But Ted, however, had a different state of mind. He obviously knew where Kelissa's pain was rooted from. But the sad thing is, he had something else in store for her that night.

Chapter 29

Monday Early morning, August 12th, 2024

Don't Do It, Kelissa!

The family is fast asleep, all but Kelissa. It is a quarter to two in the morning. Kelissa has been sitting on her single-chair couch in her private office for *hours*, watching news channels as journalists thoroughly criticized her decisions in deploying troops back into Afghanistan. The death toll of the U.S. troops who died in the Kabul bombing had reached thirty-three, and twenty-seven came from the new group of soldiers that Kelissa had deployed.

As Kelissa continued to watch the news, the cruelty of comments that spectators were saying about her made her heavily insecure and less confident as a President. The sexism even got involved as one of the news reporters interviewed an American citizen on the street who said:

"America was just not ready to have a woman as the President."

Ironically, it was a *woman* who said that. After Kelissa heard that woman's comment, she immediately turned the television off and sat there for another ten minutes, deep in her thoughts.

In her thoughts, Kelissa was thinking about what happened down in the bowling alley with her family. Through *Kelissa's* eyes, it looked as if the family was giving her an intervention. But she knows they do not understand what is *truly* happening to her. Down in the bowling alley, Kelissa just wanted to rip off her clothes and reveal the bruises to her family—*showing* them her secret. But her stubbornness has grown like cancer. But now, she knows that cancer has grown too big, and she must cut it out before it is too late.

As Kelissa walked out of her office, she headed to the kitchen to place some orange peels in the garbage and wash off the stickiness from her hands. Already in her pajamas, she was ready to hit the sack. Kelissa's parents were staying in one of the guest rooms upstairs, and being that her parents were visiting, she did not want anything to look out of the ordinary. So, she decided to stay in her bedroom with Ted. But Kelissa is soon to realize that she made a detrimental mistake.

Kelissa entered her bedroom, only to see that the bed was empty. "Ted, are you in here?" Kelissa said. But there was no response. But Kelissa knows Ted well—she knows that he comes with sneaky and evil tactics. Then, suddenly, Kelissa hears the toilet flushing as Ted is in the bathroom. Kelissa was relieved; she then got under the covers and laid her head on the pillow. What she was hoping to be a good night's sleep turned out to be something completely the opposite of such.

Ted made his way back to the bedroom. Kelissa felt the movements of Ted getting into the bed and thought nothing of it. Until she heard a very familiar sound—the sound of duct tape being yanked apart from its wheel. Kelissa's eyes immediately popped open in fear as she turned around and saw Ted ripping the tape with his teeth. She tried to get out of the bed, but Ted's strength was too overpowering as he pulled her next to him—placing three layers of duct tape over her mouth to prevent her from screaming. "*Shhhhhhh*… Quiet, little Lassie," Ted softly said. Kelissa began to mutely cry as Ted yanked off more duct tape from its wheel.

Kelissa tried to fight him off, but it only made him more aggressive. Then came a punch, BAM! Then another, POW! Then once more, BOOM! All three punches landed onto Kelissa's left kidney. But Ted was far from done with his deranged attacks. He then pulled Kelissa out of bed by her left arm as she kicked her legs—knocking things off the nightstand. Ted then aggressively dragged her into the dressing room—her screams could not be heard through the three layers of tape covering her mouth. Kelissa tried to remove the tape from her mouth, but then Ted would punch her somewhere on her body—repeatedly. The hits were so painful that Kelissa could no longer put up a fight. But still, Ted was nowhere near finished with her.

Ted then ripped Kelissa's pajamas off her, leaving her half-naked as she lay there in her underwear. He then pulls her into the bathroom, picks her up, and tapes her hands to the shower curtain rail. Kelissa, now with her arms hanging above her head like a slave or a peasant in a dungeon. "I'll be *back*, sweetie," Ted said with his sadistic smile. Kelissa, with tears rapidly coming down her face, knew instantly that this was going to be the worst catastrophe Ted's ever done to her. And she was right.

As Ted came back into the bathroom, he closed and locked the door. Kelissa's heart was beating tremendously. She thought that Ted was seriously going to kill her. As his back was turned, Kelissa could not see what was in his hands. But when he turned around, Kelissa began to cry and scream uncontrollably. In Ted's hands, he had a belt, a power cord, and a bottle of alcohol. Kelissa was terrified, repeatedly shaking her head horizontally, *begging* Ted not to do whatever he had planned in his dark, evil, twisted mind.

As Ted had the belt in his hand, he said to Kelissa, "You know you deserve what's about to happen to you, right? It was *you* who sent those troops back to that *goddamn* country. And for *what*? So that you could *save* those poor women? Save them from *what*? From *men*? Good Christ, Kel. How *stupid* could you be? Thirty-three of my brothers were killed. *So*, for *that*, I give *you,* thirty-three whips—in their honor."

Through the traffic of her tears and moans, Kelissa *begged* Ted not to whip her. But there was nothing she could do to stop him. Ted began to pour alcohol over the belt and the power cord, and *then*, he started with the first strike.

ONE! TWO! THREE! FOUR! FIVE! Kelissa screamed to the top of her lungs as Ted gave her five quick whippings across her stomach. The red marks appeared instantly. Her hands were so heavily taped above the shower rail that she could not break free. "That's only five, sweetheart… 27 more to go," Ted said as he now used the power cord to whip her. SIX! SEVEN! EIGHT! NINE! TEN! ELEVEN! TWELVE! THIRTEEN! Kelissa's legs were now in terrible shape as red markings were all over her thighs and shins.

"What are you *crying* for, Kel?" Ted shouted, "You brought this on yourself! How do you think those *families* feel right now? It was *your* fucking idea to send them over there to get killed! They'll *never* see their family members again. Huh? YOU HEAR ME!" Ted then raised his arm back and whipped Kelissa yet again. "FOURTEEN! FIFTEEN! SIXTEEN! SEVENTEEN! EIGHTEEN! NINETEEN! TWENTY! TWENTY-ONE!

Kelissa's cries were beginning to grow weaker. Ted put the power cord down and grabbed the belt again as *this* time; he planned to whip Kelissa with the buckle at the end. But Ted realized that Kelissa could not withstand any more of the beating. He was sweating bricks as Kelissa was hanging from the rail, completely drained and defenseless. Her body was as red as a cherry. Then, Ted did something disturbingly foul as he poured some of the alcohol in his mouth and began to spit it all on Kelissa's body. Kelissa screamed *so* loud, but it was as if she was screaming from the moon, where no one could ever hear her.

Ted, now out of breath as he just stopped whipping Kelissa, put the bottle of alcohol down on the sink counter and said to her, "I still owe you another twelve, Kel. That was just twenty-one. But you're just a woman; you obviously cannot handle anymore from a man. Now, I'm going to cut you down. Then after that, I want you to wash up and come to bed. I love you, sweetie."

Ted then cut the tape off of Kelissa's hands. He had to catch her before she collapsed. Her arms were weak and numb as they hung and lingered from the shower rail. Ted had to carry Kelissa as she did not have the strength to stand or walk independently. But then, he began to say the *craziest* of things to her.

As Ted carried her, he said, "You did *so* good, baby. You did so *good* taking such a beating. I'm so *proud* of you. I love you so much, Kel." Kelissa, now in a daze, could not comprehend his sick, wicked, dementedness as he carried her to the bedroom. He then *carefully* placed Kelissa onto the bed and got on top of her. Ted began to kiss all over her face, telling her how much he loved her. Kelissa was so numb to what was happening—as if her mind was in another world, another time. She just closed her eyes as Ted continued his loony fornication.

3:16 in the morning, Ted is now fast asleep as Kelissa lies right next to him, wide awake, reflecting on the aftermath of what Ted had put her through. Kelissa was looking up at the ceiling, restless and emotionless. She did not even feel like a human being anymore. Something came over her—a thought she believed would solve all of this. But before she gave this thought any action, Kelissa got up from her bed and made her way towards her office.

Kelissa slowly walked down the center hall, walking like a brain-dead zombie. She opened the door, walked over to her desk, and took her seat. Her black leather journal and several presidential pens were on the middle of her desk. Kelissa opened her journal, picked up one of her pens, and wrote this:

Monday Early Morning, August 12th, 2024, 3:16 a.m.

Ladies and gentlemen, I regret to inform you that I can no longer be your leader. That's because I'm about to kill myself. I'm going to kill myself, ladies and gentlemen. I'm going in the bathroom with the sharp knife I've kept in my nightstand, and I will slice my wrist and bleed to death. I don't care if it hurts; I don't care about the pain. I pity pain.

I'm sorry that I have failed you, I'm sorry that I've failed our country, and I'm so sorry that I've failed our women. I beg for your forgiveness. If you'd please, ladies and gentlemen, please tell my kids that I love them with all my heart and soul. Tell my parents that I love them. And I love you all too...

God bless you,

And God bless America. Goodbye.

Your President,

Kelissa Jami Morrison

As Kelissa left her office, she walked to Bryan's bedroom and opened the door. Bryan's left arm and leg were hanging off the bed. She went over to place his arm and leg under the bedsheets for one last time. Kelissa just looked at him, gently rubbing his back, then his head. She trembled with sadness and tears, preparing herself to leave him. Kelissa then leaned over, kissed him multiple times, and gently whispered in his ear, "I love you, darling boy." One last kiss to his cheek as Kelissa then backpedaled away from him and quietly left his room.

Kelissa then went next door to Madeline's bedroom. She opened the door and saw Madeline in bed, lying on her stomach. Kelissa, with heavy loads of tears and sniffles, made her way towards Madeline and kissed her on her cheek. "Oh, my baby girl. I love you so much. Take care of your brothers. *Goodbye*, Maddy Dearest." She gave Madeline another kiss and left her bedroom.

Kelissa then made her way up the stairs to Ted, Jr's bedroom. As she made her way in front of Ted, Jr's bedroom door, she turned the doorknob, but unfortunately, the door was locked. Kelissa wanted to knock on his door so badly, just to see her son's face one last time. But she didn't want to wake him. So, she left him be. Kelissa cried tremendously as she gently kissed her fingertips and pressed them on his bedroom door. "*Goodbye*, TJ," Kelissa cried.

Kelissa then made her way down the stairs. She skipped the guest room where her parents were sleeping, as she did not want to make one final visit with them. She then went back into her bedroom. Ted was still in bed, sleeping peacefully as he always does after attacking Kelissa. She then walked over to her side of the bed and carefully opened the nightstand drawer. And there it was. The knife that she has been keeping in that drawer since January. The shiny glare reflected on her teary face. Kelissa then walked around the bed, heading to the dressing room as she did not bother to even look at Ted.

Kelissa then walked into the bathroom—closed and locked the door. It was just her and the knife. She looked at the blade and then at herself in the mirror—Kelissa *hated*, with a passion, her reflection in the mirror. She hated the woman she had become, the *mother* she had become, everything. Tightly holding the knife in her right hand, Kelissa slowly pierced the knife's point into her skin. Her right hand was trembling as she was now puncturing through her skin. Kelissa had never cried more tears before in her life as she was committing suicide.

Then all of a sudden, "BANG! BANG! BANG!" Kelissa dropped the knife and watched it fall to the floor. She then looked at the door as there was another bang. "Opened the door; I have to piss!" Ted shouted as he knocked once more. Kelissa quickly picked up the knife and placed it in the right pocket of her pajama pants. She then wiped her eyes and face to remove the tear stains and hurried to unlock and open the bathroom door. As she swiftly opened the door, Ted stood in front of her, half-sleep. A five-second moment of silence as they both stared at each other.

"I—I'm, I'm not finished using the bathroom," Kelissa spoke with her broken voice.

"You look finished to *me*," Ted responded.

"Well, I—I'm *not*."

"If you don't get the *fuck* out of this bathroom, Kel, I will knock your ass down and *piss* all over you."

Kelissa said nothing else as she exited the bathroom. She then placed the knife back into the drawer of her nightstand and left the bedroom. As she made her way into her private office, Kelissa locked the office door, fell to her knees, and cried until the sun came up. Just two minutes ago, her mind was in a completely different dimension as she was going forward with taking her own life. How ironic is it to have the same man, who was beating her half to death, *save* her life? *Life* is such a twisted trip.

Chapter 30

Monday Late Morning, August 26th, 2024

He's Leaving the White House

It is an essential bittersweet day today as a member of the First Family is leaving the White House. Ted, Jr. is officially a Georgetown University college student. Kelissa was thrilled that her son decided to stay local, as Georgetown is located in the D.C. area. But with Kelissa's hectic schedule and the heavy security needed to join Ted, Jr. on campus, Kelissa decided for the two of them to say their goodbyes in the White House.

As Kelissa was in the Oval Office, she asked Ted, Jr. to come and see her before he left. Kelissa waited as she sipped on some tea—sending emails to her staffers and one to her parents. Kelissa does not like that her phone conversations have to be on a secured line, not knowing who is listening in on the conversation. She decided to send her parents an email, apologizing for her behavior on her birthday a few weeks ago. In that email, Kelissa wrote:

Dear Mom and Dad:

I hope this email finds you well. I just wanted to tell you guys how genuinely sorry I was for my unacceptable behavior a few weeks ago. That was supposed to be a grand birthday celebration for me to cherish. But instead, it ended up becoming a complete disaster. You guys did not deserve that. It was uncalled for, and I am sincerely sorry that you both witnessed my terrible attitude. It was not my intent to ruin it for everyone. Forgive me; I am just going through a lot. There's a lot on my plate, meetings after meetings, press conferences, documents and statements to sign, vetos, NATO summits, and on top of that, TJ is heading off to college. My firstborn is leaving the nest for the first time.

It has been a great challenge for me to be the President and a mother to my three kids. It's a serious job; millions of people depend on my input as their leader. I hope you understand. I try my best; I genuinely do. But I just want you two to know that I love you very much, and you have been the best, most supportive parents I could ever dream of having.

Sincerely,

Your Daughter,

Kelissa Jami Morrison

As Kelissa typed that email, it took everything in her power not to write in her secret about Ted. Her fingers trembled above the keypad, but she could not go through with it. Kelissa is advised not to use specific tech gadgets by her security advisors, but there was no way she was giving up her iPad. However, Kelissa did not want to become a total burden to national security advisors. So, she was willing to compromise, and the security advisors provided her with a very securely modified iPad, *strictly* for sending out emails, nothing more.

Five minutes later, there's a knock at the door. "Madam President, TJ is here," Carl said. Kelissa then invited Ted, Jr. into the Oval Office and had him take a seat on the couch. At first, Kelissa could not take her eyes off of her son. She was happy, proud, and emotional, all simultaneously. Sitting across from each other, they began to have a much-needed 'Mother and son' conversation.

"*So*, my bags are packed, and I'm all set to go," Ted, Jr. said.

"I am so proud of you, sweetie," Kelissa smiled. "You are officially a *college man. My*, have the years sailed through so fast."

"They *have*, especially these last *three* years."

"Baby… I don't want to make any excuses. I put you kids through a lot—I *know* that. And it's not over; I have three more years to get this country in better shape. But it's not going to be easy."

"You see, that's the *thing*, mom. Ever since you've been the 'President,' that's all that's been on your mind."

"That's not true, sweetie. Listen, I'm sorry for how I acted that night on my birthday. I'm sorry for *everything*. I'll admit that I didn't have my priorities intact before we stepped in the White House."

"Listen, mom, I know nobody's perfect. I know your job is hard and stressful. I'm not *really* that mad. I just wished…"

"You wished what, honey?"

"I just wished that things could go back to the way they were—Before you decided to run for President. Back when we went on *all* those vacations together and had *good* times with grandpa and grandma Suzie. You were so *happy*, mom. But now, I feel like I've lost a large piece of my mother to politics."

When Kelissa heard that, it brought a tear to her left eye. She understood where Ted, Jr. was coming from and why he felt that way.

As Kelissa got up from the couch, she sat next to Ted, Jr., held his hand, and said, "TJ, remember when you were seven years old, and we went to that amusement park in Santa Cruz? You wanted me to get on the carrousel with you. I was standing up next to you while you were on the horse. What *I* remembered the most was your laughter. You just laughed and laughed as the horse was going up and down. You were having a ball the whole day. And then I played that water gun game and won that stuffed dog for you. You called it 'Mr. Woofy.' You would run around the house with Mr. Woofy *all day long*, making woof sounds as if it was barking. Then that day when your father accidentally threw Mr. Woofy in the garbage, you were *so* upset. You went to your room and cried the whole day. But I didn't give up. I went to the dump and waited for *hours* to see if they could find him. And when they found Mr. Woofy, he was a little torn up. I took him to the thrift shop, bought some thread and cotton, restuffed him, and sewed him back up. I waited until the next morning to surprise you, and when you saw Mr. Woofy, you jumped up on your bed, *screaming* in joy that I had found him. You gave me the biggest hug and kiss and told me that I was the greatest mom in the world. If I could snap my fingers and go back in time to that happy place, I would. But here we are. You're a young man now, and you're about to head into the real world and face challenges on your own. But that doesn't mean that I won't be there for you. I may be the President, but this is only temporary. I will *always* be your mom. And if it's okay with you, I would like to *keep* that title of being the greatest mom in the world."

Ted, Jr. smiled as he hugged and kissed his mother. He appreciated the nostalgic childhood moment they shared. As Ted, Jr. held his mother, he said, "You'll *always* be the world's greatest mom to me. I love you." Kelissa closed her eyes—letting that sink deep into her heart. But now, it was time for Ted, Jr. to hit the road.

After three buzzers, the Marine Sentries opened the door of the West Wing exit as Kelissa and Ted, Jr. walked out. Madeline, Bryan, and Ted were already standing there, as they will be joining Ted, Jr.—helping him get settled in on campus.

"Okay, mom… So, I guess this is goodbye," said Ted, Jr. "Even though I'll only be fifteen minutes away."

"I'll miss you, sweetie. You take care of yourself, okay? And listen to your detail leaders."

"I *will*, even though I wish they didn't have to tag along, you know? I am eighteen now."

"Well, it's not like they'll be right at your dorm room twenty-four hours, seven days a *week*. It's just to make sure that you're safe."

"Bye mom, I love you."

"I love you more, TJ. I will call you later, okay? Good luck."

Kelissa watched everyone get into the Beast one as the limited motorcade drove off. She stood there briefly, thinking about that night that she was so close to taking her own life. Because if she did, she would not have been there to send her son off to college. It was then that Kelissa realized that her main focus now was to survive.

Later that night, in her private office, Kelissa had a late meal of mashed potatoes and gravy, broccoli, grilled chicken, and sauteed spinach. Kelissa was eating while she watched some of the news coverage on the television. The media continued was the bashing for her decision to send troops back to Afghanistan, as the war was already over. Sometimes, Kelissa would get anxious when they showed her photographs or video footage, afraid that the cameras might have caught an angle that showed some bruises. But miraculously and sadly, Kelissa does wonders when it comes to covering up her bruised body.

As Kelissa finished her delightful meal, she had something to write in her black leather journal. She picked up her pen and began writing. In her journal, she wrote:

Monday Evening, August 26th, 2024

First, I would like to say how incredibly sorry I am for my statements about taking my own life. I was in a completely different state of mind. A mind not my own. I was practically crucified by Ted that night, and the pain was unbearable. I felt the world was turning its back on me, as was my family. And I really felt that I had no other reason to live anymore. It boggles my mind to think that if Ted did not knock on that door, I probably wouldn't be sitting here, writing to you. How crazy is it that the man beating me half to death is the same man who saved my life? I was going to end it all that night. I'm so sorry; I'm sorry that I was going to put my children and my parents through that irreversible agony. I'm so sorry to our country. I realized now how cowardly that is for me to go out like that. And that should never be the way a woman should ever handle domestic violence.

But now, I know what I must do. I must survive this situation that I have been going through. It has been a living hell, but I have to endure this. Not just for the sake of the country but the sake of my children. I have to work on making them my top priority. Maddy is still holding this grudge on me. Now, anytime I walk into a room she's in, she just steps away from me. It's like she can't stand the sight of me. My poor daughter, I just want the best for her. I want the best for all of my kids. For her, for Bryan, and TJ. I have to survive and be the best mother for them. They are the loves of my life.

Some things are coming up, a lot of things. Bryan's birthday is next week. Then I have to fly up to New York City for the 9/11 memorial. God, I can't believe it has been twenty-three years since that tragedy. All of those innocent people. I should have known better than to send those young men and women back into that country. That is one of my biggest regrets as President.

I have other things that I have to do; I have the speech for the State of the Union in January, I have to prepare for the visit of the Prime Minister of France, Ames Rousseau, and his lovely wife, Adele. I'm very busy indeed, ladies and gentlemen. As is Ted, thank God. Lately, these days, with his heavy load of work, he is just too tired to even lay a finger on me. But I still have the bruises on my body that remind me that I have to be careful around him. He is still capable of being a threat. But like I said, I have to survive.

Kelissa closed her journal and called it a night. She then took the tray of empty plates and washed the dishes herself in the family kitchen. Even though Ted has been greatly fatigued from his extra-curricular activities, Kelissa still wants no parts of him. She has made a bed out of the couch in her private office for countless nights since moving into the White House.

Kelissa went back into her office, turned off the lights, grabbed her pillow and bedsheet as she watched a football game. "*God*, I hate football," Kelissa said as she looked. Several months ago, the Super Bowl Championship team visited the White House. Kelissa had no idea of the game or how the game was played as she is not very into sports. And the media let her have it because of her lack of knowledge of the sport of football. But Kelissa wanted to make sure that she was prepared for *next* year by watching and studying the game.

As Kelissa's eyes were getting heavy, she received a text message on her Blackberry. It was a message from Ted, Jr. As Kelissa read his text, it said:

"Hey, I just wanted to let you know that not only are you the greatest mom in the world, but you are going to be one of the greatest Presidents who ever lived. And I am very proud to have you as my mom. I love you."

That message melted Kelissa's heart. She immediately replied, saying:

"Oh, sweetie, you couldn't have said this at a better time for me. I greatly appreciate that. I will try my best to leave behind a great legacy as far as the presidency. I love you more, TJ. Goodnight, sweetie."

Kelissa was happy to know that her relationship with Ted, Jr. was solid with love. But next on the list was fixing her relationship with Madeline.

Chapter 31

Tuesday Afternoon, September 3rd, 2024

Darling Boy, I love you

Another birthday is upon the Morrison family. Bryan has reached the last of his pre-teen years as he is now twelve years old. Kelissa wanted Bryan to have a fun, exciting birthday, so as she promised months ago, she requested to invite several of Bryan's friends from school, where they can enjoy the swimming pool and have cake and ice cream. The weather was beautiful; a sunny, crystal-clear blue sky. As Bryan and his friends were having a ball in the swimming pool, Kelissa stood at the pool's far end. Ted, Jr was unable to attend the party because of his busy Tuesday schedule of classes. Carl and eight other Secret Service agents surrounded the area. Since Secret Service agents are trained in the medical field and know how to give CPR, there was no need for a lifeguard.

"Hey, mommy, come in the pool; the water feels great!" Bryan shouted with much enthusiasm. Kelissa wanted to join Bryan in the pool with his friends. But she would not *dare* put on a bathing suit. Unfortunately, Kelissa's body was not entirely healed from the bruises left by Ted. "Oh, I'm so sorry, sweetie, but I can't get in right now," Kelissa responded with sorrow. Even though Bryan was having such a great time with his friends, he felt slightly disappointed at Kelissa's refusal to join them.

As the kids were splashing around in the pool, Carl escorted Kelissa back to the West Wing and made her way to the Oval Office. She had some documents to look over and sign, a few emails to respond to, and one phone call to make. She promised Bryan that she would not work for the day and give him her full undivided attention. But responding to those emails consumed her time. By the time Kelissa finished responding to the thread of emails, the kids were already dried off and dressed as they prepared to sing happy birthday to Bryan. As Kelissa was sitting in the Oval Office reading papers, there was a knock at the door.

"Madam President," Carl said. "They're about to cut the cake."

"Cut the *cake*?" Kelissa shouted. "How are they cutting the cake without me? I thought they were still in the pool!"

Kelissa then went back to the pool area, escorted by Carl. She got closer to the pool area and heard everyone singing the last verse of *Happy Birthday* to Bryan. The pool area was already set up with cake and ice cream, and the kids were ready to dig in.

Kelissa was heated at the fact that everyone started without her presence. As she got to the pool, she saw Bryan and his friends all sitting at the table as Madeline was cutting slices of cake. "Hold it!" Kelissa shouted, "Before you guys start eating cake, how about we have an encore performance of singing happy birthday? Because I was *not* notified that we were starting *any* of that." As Madeline was cutting the cake, she responded to Kelissa with a sassy attitude, saying, "Well, *maybe* if you didn't sneak off to do work, you would have been here to sing along with the rest of us." Awkward silence as the five-hundred-pound gorilla had arrived. As Ted stood there, he said nothing. But he most definitely had a smile on his face. He loved to see Kelissa being mortified and disrespected.

"Maddy, a *word,* please?" Kelissa said as they walked into the cabana, "I'll be just a minute, Carl." As they stood inside the pool house, Kelissa gave Madeline a piece of her mind.

"Young lady," Kelissa projected. "You are *really* trying my patience! Don't you *ever* disrespect me like that again!"

"Mom, you *promised* Bryan that you would not do any work on his birthday—"

"I *know* I did, Maddy. I know. But I wasn't gone for that long. They were still in the pool, and I just had to respond to some emails and make *one* phone call. That's *it*!"

"But you *promi—*"

"Wait, stop!" Kelissa shouted again. "I do *not* have to stand here and explain myself to you. *You* are the daughter, and *I'm* the parent."

"The *daughter*? Wow, Mom… You know what, to make things easier for you, I don't even *want* to celebrate *my* birthday. *That* way, you can do *all* the work you want to."

"Maddy, just leave. *Please* leave."

Madeline's eyes began to grow teary, and her face turned red. Her frustrations with her mother were at their highest. She immediately turned around and stormed out of the pool house. Even though Kelissa was upset, she did not want to miss out on any more of the party. So, she took a few breathers, fixed her face, and walked out of the pool house with a faux smile. The kids were all sitting as the kitchen staffers served the cake and ice cream.

Kelissa saw the look on Bryan's face. He was not as happy as he was five minutes ago. She knew she had to make it up to him. "You really know how to ruin a party, don't you, Kel?" Ted quietly said with a smile on his face. Kelissa looked at Ted as if she wanted to take a piece of cake and smash it all over his face. But she did not want to make a scene. Kelissa then walked away from Ted and picked up a slice of cake. As she looked closely at the cake, she grew angry as she realized there was strawberry filling in the cake yet *again*, thanks to

Ted's request. Kelissa had been so busy with her work that she forgot to notify the kitchen staff of her allergy to strawberries. As Ted walked inside of the West Wing, Kelissa lingered in fury as she could not even enjoy any of the cake. But still, she did not want to make a scene.

Madeline was nowhere in sight. So, Kelissa went to find her. "Carl, I have to talk with Madeline again," Kelissa said. Since Carl has to accompany the President everywhere she goes, Kelissa had to inform him that she would need some privacy with her daughter once she finds Maddy. As Carl and Kelissa walked into the West Wing, she asked her secretary, Joan, if she saw Madeline walk by. "No, Madam President, I haven't seen Maddy walk by here," Joan responded.

At first, Kelissa was going to check Madeline's bedroom, but she knows her daughter very well. Kelissa knows that whenever Madeline is upset about something, she likes to escape from reality and bury her head in a book.

"Carl, she's down in the library. Can you just wait for me by the stairs?" Kelissa asked Carl.

"I have to be with you at all times, Madam President."

"I *understand* that, Carl. But I *need* to talk to my daughter alone."

"I'll be right at the stairs, Madam President."

So, as Carl stood by the staircase, Kelissa went down to the ground floor to check the library. She wanted to fix the problem with her daughter and rekindle the 'mother and daughter' love they once had for each other. But Kelissa knew that would come with a challenge. Kelissa could hear Madeline's sniffling and crying sounds echo throughout the center hall as she walked towards the library. She slowly walked to the doorway and peeked her head in the library. Kelissa saw Madeline, sobbing her eyes out, in her father's arms. Kelissa quickly pulled her head back, surprised to see the image of Ted comforting Madeline. She did not want to be seen by the two, so Kelissa kept her distance and stayed outside the library but still peeked her head in to see.

As Kelissa listened in, she heard Madeline say to Ted, "I just don't understand her anymore, Dad. She's like a completely different person ever since she became the fucking President. I feel like I don't even have a mom anymore. I *hate* her! I just wish they'd vote her out of office so that I can have my mom back. What's *wrong* with her, Dad? Why does she behave this way?" Kelissa was standing there in the center hall, covering her mouth as she was devastated at what she had just heard. Tears slowly fell from Kelissa's eyes, streaming down her face.

To add insult to injury, Ted made matters worse as he said, "Maddy, I completely *agree* with you, baby. She *is* a completely different person now. Your mother *constantly* undermines me, *telling* me how to be a man and a good father to you guys. She thinks she's in control of everyone. And just the other night, your mother… She—she hit me."

Madeline quickly looked up at her father, saying, "Oh my *God*, Dad! Mom *hit* you?" Ted responded, saying, "Yes, Maddy, she hit me right on the side of my face. But this is between you and me, baby.

Don't tell a *soul*. Don't tell your brothers, don't tell Carl or the agents, don't tell *anyone*. You're my one and only daughter, Maddy—you're my *baby girl*. You're the only one that I can trust. Sometimes I feel like… I feel like she's going to try and *kill* me. I'm *so* scared, Maddy."

Kelissa was gagging in absolute shock as she heard the preposterousness of Ted's psychotic deceit. "But listen, I *don't* want you guys to hate your mother. Just pray for her, sweetheart. She needs prayer, not hatred. And don't you worry. *No matter what*, I will *always* be there for you, Maddy, *and* your brothers. You know daddy loves you, honey. *Promise* me that you will *never* share this information with anyone. *Promise* me," Ted said to Madeline as he hugged her.

"I promise, daddy—I promise—I promise," Madeline said as she cried in her father's arms. As Kelissa peeked her head back in to see the two of them—Madeline's back was turned while Ted hugged her. Kelissa looked in disbelief. Then suddenly, Ted lifted his head and caught Kelissa looking inside. He said nothing but gave Kelissa his sinister smile and blew her a kiss. Kelissa then backpedaled away from the library and walked off as she covered her mouth in devastation. Ted's evil plan of perpetuating the lies to turn Madeline against her mother was fully effective. And now it's even *worse* as he planted in Madeline's mind that *Kelissa* is the abuser.

Kelissa grew weak in her knees as she began to climb the stairs. The fact that Ted had now involved the children, any chance of Kelissa having forgiveness for him just went completely out of the window, forever.

Later that evening, Kelissa still wanted to make it up to Bryan for her brief absences during his birthday party. In her private office, Kelissa was still very upset about the tainted conversation between Ted and Madeline. But she wanted to conclude Bryan's birthday with a cheerful ending. She made her way to Bryan's bedroom and knocked on his opened door.

"Hi, sweetie. Can I come in?" Kelissa asked.

"Sure," Bryan responded.

"How are you feeling?"

"I'm feeling okay. Except for the fact that I may have eaten too much cake."

"Ha," Kelissa laughed. "Well, I just wanted to apologize to you. I know I promised you that I wouldn't work during your birthday. But I sort of did. I know you're pretty upset with me, baby. And I'm sorry."

"It wasn't really *that* promise that bothered me, mommy."

"What do you mean, sweetie?"

"Mommy, when we first moved into the White House, you promised me that nothing will come between our bond. You said that we would always be close, no matter what. But now, you seem like a *stranger*."

Kelissa had no idea of how to respond to that. Her words could not *explain* to Bryan what was *really* going on. Kelissa took a few seconds to think, and then she took Bryan's hand.

Sitting with him on his bed, Kelissa said, "Bryan, sweetheart… I know I haven't been the best mother these last several years. And I *know* that the promise I made to you had gone south. But baby, I—I—I am in a *very* complicated state of mind. I felt that I was strong enough to handle it all—being a wife, a mother, *and* the President. But I've learned something. To gain the power, to *conquer* the *world*, and *lose everything* else that is important to you. To lose sight of that… It wasn't worth it. And you're right; I *have* become a stranger to all of you. I've broken promises as a mother and as a President.

And for now, I have to live with that. But one thing I can always guarantee; I will *always* love you, Bryan. You, and your brother, and your sister, are the most *remarkable* accomplishments that I have on this earth. If I could go back in time to just be a mother to my kids, I would. But I'm going to work it all out, sweetie. I'm going to do better and be a better mother. I just ask that you trust me. And most importantly—that you keep on loving me. Because I *need* your love more than *anything*, baby. Life will continue to get rough for me, and your love is the *only thing* I need that will help me survive this presidency. So, just keep on loving me, baby. That's all I need. Every hug, every kiss, means the absolute *world* to me. Can I count on you to keep loving me, baby?"

Bryan wiped the tears from his mother's eyes as he said, "I never *stopped* loving you, mommy. My love for you can never be broken. And you can *always* count on me." The warm and sacred embrace of a mother and son is beyond words. Kelissa hugged Bryan so tight as she cried. "Oh, my darling *boy*—I love you so, *so* much. We're okay, right? We're, *okay*?" Kelissa cried. Bryan kissed Kelissa on her right cheek as he responded, "Yes, mommy. We're okay now. And I love you too."

After rekindling their bond, Kelissa and Bryan made their way down to the State floor to the White House Family Theater—grabbing popcorn and drinks before heading in for a movie. At Bryan's request, he asked if they could watch a *Harry Potter* film. "You know we're only watching *one, right?* It's still a school night," Kelissa said. Even though Bryan was not into the Harry Potter *books*, he was a fan of the movies.

Bryan chose '*Harry Potter and the Chamber of Secrets.*' Kelissa thought about the movie's title and could not help but relate as she *herself* had a chamber of secrets. As the film played, Kelissa was quite confused about the characters and who was who. But as long as she was spending quality time with her son, she was happy. No distractions, no work, just simply cherishing the moment. Kelissa had even invited White House photographer Georgette Wilson to come in and snap some shots of that particular moment, as she did the photography during Bryan's birthday party.

Even though Kelissa had no idea of the characters in the movie, it did not stop her from sharing a few laughs with Bryan. She loved Bryan's laughter, and she loved sharing this moment with him. And it took Kelissa *everything* in her power not to shed a tear. She thought about the fact that she was so close to ending her life just a few weeks ago—thinking to herself and saying that she would not even be here to share this unforgettable time with her son. But she also thought about where her kids would be if Ted killed her. Kelissa realized that the truth would have to come out. But the one question she had *burning* in her mind was, *when*?

Chapter 32

Wednesday Morning, September 11th, 2024

A Day of Remembrance

The President has arrived in New York City on the twenty-third anniversary of the September 11th terrorist attacks. The Lincoln tunnel has been shut down in both directions as the motorcade goes through. Extensive and careful planning for President Kelissa Morrison's arrival had to be done. The children stayed behind in D.C. as they were in school for the day. As the privacy divider is up in the limousine, Ted attempts to talk with Kelissa.

"You know, you can't ignore me forever," Ted said.

"Ted, I have *nothing* to say to you," Kelissa responded.

"But do you really think this will work? You not speaking to me?"

"After what you said to *Maddy*? You think I'm going to *speak* to you?"

"Well, you're speaking to me *now*."

"Just *don't* talk to me right now."

"You really are *fucking* pathetic."

"I'm fucking pathetic—*I'm* fucking pathetic?"

"I only told my daughter the truth."

"No! You *lied* to her! You made her think that *you're* the victim. As if I'm abusing *you*!"

"I have *no idea* what you're talking about, Kel."

"Okay, I'm *not* playing this game with you."

"Oh, I think you *are*—you have no *choice*. I'm still the one in *charge* here. This is *my* family. You may be a puppet to show off to America, but *I'm* running the show when it comes to *this* family."

"*What* family? You're destroying our family every single day."

"Nonsense—you're *paranoid*, Kel."

"*No*, I'm in *pain* and very *upset*."

"*Aww*... Did I hurt you the other night with that—what was that thing I threw at you?"

"You hit me with... Oh, *God*—you hit me with a *fucking* urn that was carrying my grandmother's ashes."

"*Right*," Ted said as he laughed. "If *only* you could have seen yourself trying to pick up the ashes—looking like a *goddamn groundhog*."

"You unimaginable, *heartless* bastard."

"I take that as a *compliment*, Kel."

"All of this because I ran and became President?"

"I *told* you not to do this. I *told* you *not* to run for President. But do you remember what else I told you? I *told* you that if you *won*, I would make your life a living *hell*. I'm a man of my word."

"You're not a man. You're a *goddamn monster*."

"Well, take a good *goddamn* look, baby. Because this is the *last* time you'll *ever* see a monster like this."

Kelissa looked into Ted's eyes as she saw nothing but pure evil. She knew that this situation was not going to last very much longer. Kelissa had to do something about her current predicament with Ted. But for now, she had to push this discussion out of her mind quickly and get focused as the motorcade was closely approaching the World Trade Center site.

As the motorcade stopped, Carl and over two dozen other Secret Service agents began to take their positions. Snipers were on standby, police, security, the whole nine yards—*everyone* was in position, ready to go. Carl walked to the back door and opened the door closest to the sidewalk. Kelissa was the first to step out.

There were *thousands* of people behind the barricades. People were screaming—waving their hands, taking pictures, and shouting, 'MORRISON! MORRISON! MORRISON!' Kelissa felt the love for sure. But she *also* felt the sudden pain in her abdomen as Ted gave her two quick punches just before the motorcade came to a complete stop.

Kelissa had to take it easy, trying to catch her breath. Not to mention, she was still traumatized by the incident back in Hawaii. It was as if her paranoia and anxiety were walking right next to her—side by side with Secret Service.

Kelissa smiled as best as she could while she was in pain. But it was no time for tears; she had to be focused. She could barely raise her arm to wave at the crowd as any sudden movements would cause excruciating pain.

Thousands of people were walking around to pay their respects to their family members whose lives were stolen from them twenty-three years ago. Even though it was many years ago, the fresh tears from family members made it feel as if it happened just yesterday. As Kelissa took her seat, surrounded by Secret Service and bulletproof panels, the memorial was ready to begin.

Kelissa sat there, listening to the names of all the victims who lost their lives on that tragic day. The violinist was playing so beautifully. But still, there was much sadness in the air. Kelissa gently shook her head as she heard the names, one by one. To this day, she still cannot believe this happened. She could not believe how evil some people could be. But Kelissa is reminded of that evil—every day when she's around Ted.

The time was 8:46 a.m., when the first plane, American Airlines Flight 11, was flown into the North Tower. A moment of silence as the bell was rung by one of the first responders. As Kelissa sat there, her body was still in pain, but she blocked her emotions from pouring out. The names kept going, and the tears kept flowing as it was such a devastating, inhumane moment in history. Since Kelissa was on a very tight schedule, she had to speak to the families in attendance and the American people and leave within the next fifteen minutes.

As Kelissa took a deep breath and slowly stood up, trying to avoid any sudden pain, she walked over to the podium. She did not have any papers with her, as she came prepared to speak from her heart. Even though the bulletproof panels were surrounding her, Kelissa took another deep breath and began her speech:

Twenty-three years ago today, we experienced one of the worst tragedies in United States history. A tragedy that cost the lives of 2,996 innocent victims who did not deserve to die. Evil is a very real and unpredictable force that cycles through the world. Evil comes, it goes, and it conquers the souls of many people in this world. You never know who, what, when, where, or why evil comes. It cannot be explained, nor can it be reasoned with. People commit evil acts with no remorse, leaving families devastated forever.

As life goes on and we continue to live our lives, still, we miss our loved ones. But we continue to cherish their memories for the rest of our lives. We look at their pictures and reminisce; we think about the good times. The nostalgic thoughts of us going back in time and reliving a moment with that family member or friend. Some days are easy, and some days are hard. But we must carry on. We must keep on keeping on.

There is still evil among us today. It is still a battle that we have to fight in life. And as your Commander in Chief, as your President, I make it my everyday mission to see to it that you, the American people, are safe and protected. And that you can live full and happy lives, and also, that we will never endure such pain and anguish, as we have all faced on this day, twenty-three years ago.

As we come here today, we mourn, we remember, but we continue to love. We continue to love our loved ones who are no longer here with us. And we shall continue to carry on their legacies, the memories we have of them, and keep their spirit alive in our hearts forever. One of my favorite quotes I always think of at times like this is, 'The pain will win some battles. But love will always win the war.' But in times like this, I think of the meaning of life. I believe that the meaning of life is finding peace, happiness, beauty, and love within the unfairness of it all.

I would like to thank police commissioner Abraham Goldsmith and Mayor Ian Thomas for their assistance today. I'd like to thank the New York City Police Department for their help and services, and I also would like to thank you, the American people. Thank you for your strength as we commemorate our loved ones on one of the darkest days in our nation's history on American soil. God Bless you, and God Bless America.

Chapter 33

Wednesday Late Evening, September 11th, 2024

Late Night in the Private Office

Pen to paper; Kelissa is at her desk, writing her pain and suffering away. Still exhausted from the travel, Kelissa could barely keep her eyes open as she wrote about her day. She then decided to stop in mid-sentence. In her journal, Kelissa wrote:

Wednesday Late Evening, September 11th, 2024

Ladies and gentlemen, what a day I had. I can't believe he would do that to me. The fact that he dared to attack me right there in the back of the limo. I was in so much pain. He literally punched the air out of me. It took me two minutes to recover in the back seat. I couldn't breathe, I couldn't move, I couldn't escape. When I looked at him, I saw a monster in his eyes—

there was no soul inside them. But then, as we got back on Air Force One, he tried to have sex with me in the presidential suite. He is just so sick and mentally fucking disturbed.

And what he did with my grandmother's ashes—my Gooma, I could never forgive him for that, never. We were arguing in the bedroom, where I had the urn with her ashes on the mantle. He threw the urn right towards my face. I ducked, but the urn cracked as it hit the wall. Gooma's ashes were all over the floor. I tried my best to scoop her up. But I couldn't get all of her ashes together. I sat there on the floor and just cried; I couldn't believe it. How inhumane can one person be?

For me, that was the last straw. 'The straw that broke the camel's back,' as people would say. Everything he has done to me, and how he turned my daughter against me. He brought my kids into his sick scheme, and now, I have to expose him. Soon, I will tell my secret, ladies and gentlemen. I don't care about trying to hold onto the 'perfect image.' He's killing me. And if I carry on with this, he will kill me. I cannot hide this anymore. I refuse to leave my kids in such a violent way. But I'm going to do it. I have to—before it is too late."

As Kelissa closed her journal, she turned off the television and made her way up to the second floor of the residence level. Since Ted, Jr. is now living on campus at Georgetown University, the second floor was completely vacant. Kelissa then made her way into one of the guest rooms for the night.

Ten minutes went by, Kelissa was lying in the guest bed with her eyes closed. But then suddenly, she *opened* her eyes, saying, "Where's my

Blackberry?" Kelissa realized she had left her Blackberry in the office. So, she went back down to get it. On her way down the stairs, into the center hall, she was spotted by Madeline. As they both stood there, Madeline had an inquiring mind that wanted to know.

"What were you doing up there?" Madeline asked.

"I was looking for something," Kelissa responded.

"Looking for *what*?"

"I was looking for…"

"*What*, Mom?"

"*Okay*… I was staying up in one of the guest rooms for the night so that I could get a good night's sleep."

"Well, why can't you rest in *your* bedroom? Oh, *I forgot*, maybe it's because dad kicked you out for being abusive to him."

"*What*? *Oh*, *Maddy*, you just *don't* understand what's going on here."

"No, I know *exactly* what's going on here. You're trying to tear dad down, make him feel *weak—belittle* him."

"NO! Maddy, you're *so wrong*!"

"NO! *I* think I'm *right*! He *told* me that you've been hitting him. *Abusing* him behind closed doors."

"*NO*, Maddy! That is *not* possible!"

"How? *How* is that not possible, Mom?"

"Because I'm not the one abusing your father, your father's abusing *ME*!"

"Wh—*what*?"

"Your father has been attacking *me*, Maddy."

"I don't believe you."

"Oh, you don't *believe me*? Then how did these bruises get on me?"

Kelissa immediately stripped off her pajamas as she stood there in her underwear. "*Now,* do you see what I've been going through? Do you *see* what your father has been *doing to me?*" Kelissa shouted as she cried. Madeline looked up and down at Kelissa. Then suddenly, Madeline looked behind Kelissa and screamed, "AHHH!" Kelissa immediately turned around as Ted was behind her. She had no time to brace herself as Ted swung a broken table leg and hit her across the face—instantly bleeding as Ted stood over her.

Kelissa heard Madeline screaming, saying, "DAD, *STOP*! YOU'RE GONNA *KILL* MOM! YOU'RE GONNA KILL HER DAD! STOP, DAD, *PLEASE*, STOP!"

But Ted was not stopping until she was dead. Kelissa was on the floor, covering her bloody face—seeing Ted swing away through the opening of her fingers. She kicked and screamed, but no one could save her from the violent beating Ted was giving her. Then suddenly, Kelissa closed her eyes and screamed as loud as she could.

BOOM! Kelissa fell to the floor. Her eyes were now opened, and no one was around. She laid there on the floor in a cold sweat while her heavy breathing began to find serenity. Kelissa looked around in the guest room as it was morning. The sun was starting to rise, and the birds were chirping. As Kelissa put two and two together, she realized that she had a nightmare. She did *not* tell her secret to

Madeline; Ted did *not* attack her with a broken table leg. It was all a dream.

As Kelissa sat on the floor with the bedsheet aggressively wrapped around her body, she placed her hand against her forehead and immediately began to sob, saying, "Oh, God, *please*! *Help me, please*."

Chapter 34

Thursday Evening, October 31st, 2024

A Halloween to Never Forget

President Kelissa Morrison is enjoying her candy in the Oval Office. Unfortunately, her love for chocolate was traumatically scarred after what happened last Valentine's Day. But gummy bears and saltwater taffy were her new cravings during this Halloween evening.

In the Oval Office, Kelissa was having a meeting with members of her speechwriting team: Gary Cruise, who is the Deputy Director of Speechwriting. Harvey Davis, the Director of Speechwriting, and the Assistant Speechwriter, Ally Berger. As they all sat on the two couches, they were going over the first draft of

Kelissa's State of the Union speech, scheduled to take place in January.

Kelissa wanted to start preparing her speech, even though it was several months from now. "Madam President," said Gary. "I would like for you to take a look at these two pages and see how you feel about this?" As Gary handed Kelissa a few pages of the first draft of her speech, she took a few minutes and read it.

As Kelissa was reading, she noticed that her Deputy Assistant, Carrie Thompson, was off to the side of the office, holding her hand to her mouth as she was almost in tears, looking at her Blackberry. Kelissa stared at Carrie for a few seconds and walked over to her.

"Carrie, what's wrong?" Kelissa asked.

"Madam President," Carrie emotionally responded. "I just received word that there's been a mass shooting in New Mexico."

"Oh, Jesus." Kelissa sighed in grief. "*Oh, God.* How—how many victims are there?"

"About thirty-seven victims, Madam President. The death toll is now nineteen, and they believe that *sixteen* of the nineteen who were killed—*were* kids—between the ages of six and thirteen."

"Oh *God*, no."

As Kelissa was in shock, Press Secretary Lesley Richards entered the Oval Office to give the President the tragic news.

"Madam President," Lesley spoke. "There's been a—"

"I just heard the news, Madam Secretary," Kelissa responded.

"Madam President, you have to make a statement.

"Okay, okay… Just let me—let me get myself situated. I'll be in my study next door. I just need a *few* minutes."

Kelissa shut down the meeting with her speechwriting team. She then went into her private study *beside* the Oval Office and clicked on the breaking news. Kelissa watched as the Chief of Police made a statement about the mass shooting on television. The shooting took place in Grants, New Mexico, seventy-eight miles from Albuquerque. As Kelissa watched with tears forming in her eyes, she listened to the Chief of Police as he made his statement:

"Hello, everyone. I would say *good evening*, but there is *nothing* good about this evening. I'm Douglas DuPont, Chief of Police here at Grants, New Mexico. About thirty minutes ago, our town suffered the worst massacre in recent history. There was a Halloween festival that took place. It was the fifth annual festival we had. Hundreds of children were at this festival, all dressed in their Halloween costumes. At about 6:05 p.m., *our* time, an unknown shooter, wearing a black hockey mask, began to open fire with an undisclosed assault rifle. The shooter was also armed with two handguns. Um… The shooter opened fire on multiple children. As of right now, seventeen children—between the ages of three and fourteen, have been killed…"

Kelissa could no longer hold her tears as she listened. The Chief of Police, Douglas DuPont, paused as he took a few breathers for himself. As DuPont got himself together, he continued his statement:

"Excuse me, folks. My apologies… As I said, seventeen children between the ages of three and fourteen were tragically killed. We do not have the total number of deceased victims as of yet. But as of right now, there are approximately between fifty to seventy-five victims who were wounded. We expect that many more of the victims are children. We do not know who the victims are. We have been unable to identify who they are because they were… Excuse me… They were *all* wearing Halloween masks. However, we have the suspect in custody as the suspect surrendered himself to the officers. Before officers approached the shooter, he disarmed himself of his firearms and laid face-down on the ground. Police officers immediately placed the suspect under arrest and escorted him to the precinct. As of right now, we cannot make any comments on the suspect, we cannot reveal the *suspect's name*, and there *will* be a full investigation. Again, I've lived in Grant, New Mexico, my *whole* life. I'm fifty-nine years of age. This is by far the most tragic event that has ever happened in our city. I'm completely mortified and devastated, and I ask you all for prayers. We ask for your prayers for those who lost their loved ones. Prayers for those who were wounded, and I *pray* that they survive. Thank you."

Kelissa, holding her hand over her mouth as she shook her head, crying her eyes out. All she could think about was the children who were killed. The one thing Kelissa never understood about America was its infatuation with guns. She never understood why people love to pull those triggers to take a life. But suddenly, Kelissa's sadness quickly transformed into anger.

Now that Kelissa has the highest power, she is prepared to use it. Kelissa then dried her eyes and wiped her face as she stood up from her desk and headed out of her private study. As she stepped out, multiple staffers were standing there in the hallway. Some were in tears, while others had the same angry look on their faces as Kelissa's. As they stared at her, Kelissa looked at everyone and said, "I'm putting an end to this *GODDAMN* circus!

Thirty minutes later, Kelissa was waiting to enter the Press Briefing Room, ready to make a statement about the tragic situation in Grants, New Mexico. Her nerves were in full form while her mind was preoccupied with this situation. The press pool was already inside the briefing room, readying their cameras. Standing next to Kelissa was Press Secretary Lesley Richards. Before heading to the podium, Kelissa and Lesley briefly exchanged some words.

"Babies," Kelissa spoke.

"I'm *sorry*, Madam President?" Lesley confused.

"They were just *babies*. Three to fourteen years old?"

"We're going to fix this problem."

"I am *not* going to be able to sleep tonight."

As Kelissa was ready to make her statement in the briefing room, Press Secretary Lesley Richards and several other of Kelissa's staffers were standing off to the side of the stage. Cameras were clicking rapidly, one snap after the other. Kelissa had no script in hand as she wanted to say *precisely* what was on her mind. Even before she said a word, her face said it all.

As Kelissa stood at the podium, she said, "It has happened *once* again. Another senseless shooting that did not have to happen—

another *tragedy* that could have been prevented. This is one of the *prime examples* of *why* I chose to run for President—to put an *end* to these senseless shootings. I am *distraught* right now, *knowing* that dozens of *children* were harmed and killed. They did not deserve that. *I* have children—*you* have children! *Any* one of those kids could have been one of our own. I just don't get it. Guns are meant to protect families, *not* to *ruin* them! This *has* to *stop*; this *has* to come to an end! What will it take for us to come together and stop *killing* each other for *nothing*? There are *so* many of these shootings—*too* many. And I am *overly* sick and tired of them all. And I know many of you are too. Enough is *enough*! I'm so tired of waking up and seeing another person shot and killed, another African American child losing their life in Chicago, or police brutality—another child finding their parent's gun and then *accidentally* shooting themselves. I'm tired of our country abusing its Second Amendment privilege. Just because you have the right to bear arms does *not* give *anyone* the right to take the lives of innocent people! This will *not* carry on! *Not* on my watch!"

As Kelissa stood there at the podium, the redness in her eyes began to emerge as she was holding back the tears and emotion. As the cameras continued to click away, Kelissa continued talking, "This is *really* affecting me right now… They were—they were *children—babies*. The youngest victim was only *three years old—three*. They did *not* deserve this. My heart goes out to *every* family affected tonight, *especially* those who lost their loved ones. I send my sincerest condolences to the families. I spoke with the Governor of New

Mexico, Governor Emilio Diaz, to let him know that we are keeping them in our hearts and prayers. I also spoke with the FBI director, William Cannon, who will *heavily* investigate this horrific, heinous crime. This is *not* the America I've known to love. And while I am President, I will see to it that I remedy the irresponsibility of gun ownership."

Kelissa stormed out of the Press Briefing Room. The press pool took as many shots with their cameras as possible. "I will speak with everyone tomorrow morning. Thank you for coming in on such short notice. But I *have* to clear my head," Kelissa said to her staffers. She then went into the elevator to head up to the first floor of the residence level. As the elevator door closed, Kelissa began to kick and scream—smacking her hand against the wall, angry at the harsh reality that multiple children tragically lost their lives to gun violence. She cried in that elevator for those kids. Still filled with anger, the only thing Kelissa wanted to do at that moment was to throw a few punches at the heavy bag.

Now breaking a sweat in the workout room, Kelissa was punching and kicking the life out of the heavy bag as she created the clinging cadence of the chains. As Kelissa was jabbing away, she was suddenly distracted by the sound of clapping hands. Ted showed up, clapping his hands as loud as he could. "*Bravo*, Madam President!" Ted shouted with enthusiasm, "All I can say is *who* are *you* and *what* have you done with *my* wife, Kelissa Jami Morrison? I tell you, baby, *that* was some *powerful shit*. I'm just—my *God*, I'm really just at a loss for words. I mean, that *confidence*, that *anger,* and *fury*. Now *that's* my kind of woman! I mean, I *literally* was growing a *hard-on*. If only you could have felt my *dick*; it was as hard as the *goddamn* Washington Monument. I loved every minute of it, Kel."

Kelissa looked at Ted in complete disgust as she said, "You are the most disturbed, sickest *bastard* I ever laid my eyes on. Children are *dead* tonight—*DEAD*! And you find this *humorous*?" Ted looked at Kelissa as he smiled and responded, saying, "Kel, sweetheart, old people, young people, children, babies—they *die* every single day. Some of them die from even *worse* casualties—hell, *parents* kill their own children! You can't deny that. It's the way of the *world*, my darling. And the sooner you wake the fuck up and *realize* that America is *never* going to change, the better you will feel. The house will *never* change the guns laws. You know, for a *Republican*, you *sure as hell* don't act like one, do you?" Kelissa stared right at Ted with these piercing eyes of hatred. She could not believe he would say something as inhumane as that.

Before Ted left the workout room, he turned around, walked towards Kelissa, and said, "By the way, sweetheart, I wasn't lying about that hard-on. I'll be waiting for you in bed. And *don't* make me have to look for you. You know how angry *I* can get." Ted then kissed Kelissa on her lips and walked out of the workout room.

Kelissa then walked over to the bench, removing her gloves as she took a seat. With her two hands covering her face, she began to think about how she would approach the House of Representatives to convince them to change the guns laws. But Kelissa had no clue of how she could make that happen.

Kelissa gave up for the night as she had to reserve her energy for Ted's crazed appetite for sex. Even though the sex is now one hundred percent one-sided when it comes to pleasure, Kelissa tolerates it simply because she would rather him fornicate with her than physically abuse her. But in a way, since Kelissa gives no consent, *nor* does she receive *any* pleasure from the sex—to *her*, it still feels like abuse.

Chapter 35

Thursday Evening, November 7th, 2024

A Night in the Sky

Thousands of miles in the sky, Kelissa is on board Air Force One. She has just departed from Grants, New Mexico, after attending a memorial for the victims of the mass shooting on that tragic Halloween night. Kelissa was sitting in her office, drinking some tea as she had just finished writing in her journal. In her journal, Kelissa wrote:

Thursday Evening, November 7th, 2024

Ladies and gentlemen, I have a heavy heart tonight. I had never seen such sadness and devastation in parents' faces before. This was one of the worst massacres that ever occurred on American soil. As the investigation continued, they reported that there were sixty-three wounded victims, and a total of thirty-one were killed. Twenty-two of them were children, between the ages of two and a half and fifteen. A two-and-a-half-year-old? She was just a baby. Her parents showed me her picture; it took me everything in my soul not to burst into tears. She was so beautiful. She had the biggest, bluest eyes and chubby cheeks. God, you could have just kissed those chubby cheeks of hers all day. But now, her parents will never be able to do that again. They will never see their baby girl ever again. Not in this life. But I will remember her name for the rest of my life. Her name was 'Patty-Mae Judy Peterson.'

You know, ladies and gentlemen, the former Presidents—my predecessors, once told me that there would be days like this during my presidency. I always prayed that there wouldn't be, but sometimes, prayer is not enough. As the President, I must do something about it. I must get the people's attention of the House of Representatives and the senate; I have to get everyone on board to at least try to remedy the outcome. I just have a lot on my plate.

Madeline and I barely talk now. I try to have a conversation with her, but she just walks out of the room. Ever since I had that dream where I told her my secret, I've been waiting for the right time to just come out with it and tell her. But it's as if I don't even exist to her. I wanted to hold her so badly that night when the shooting occurred. But she is just not trying to go there with me. My poor baby girl, I miss her so much. I miss us just having our bond. Maybe if I find some time to get our hair done together and our nails?

Actually, I just had to laugh at myself. I wouldn't want to be clocked with bruises on my arms and legs. Jesus, Ted is the bane of my existence. But I'm going to do it; I'm going to reveal this secret sooner or later. But with all that is happening right now, I'm just taking it one day at a time.

Kelissa then closed her journal as she was done for the evening. Sitting there at her desk, she began to look at the television, seeing the rebroadcast of her speaking at the memorial in Grants, New Mexico. Sadly, Kelissa was more focused on whether or not her bruises were exposed on national television than her actual speech. She stood as stiff as a board at the podium, not making any sudden movements. Since the fall season has arrived, Kelissa is back to wearing more layers of clothing to cover up the bruising. As she took a sip of her tea, there was a knock at her office door.

"Come in," Kelissa projected.

"Madam President, is now a good time?" Lesley asked.

"Yes, Madam Secretary, please, have a seat."

"Madam President," said Georgette Wilson. "Is it okay if I get a few shots?"

"Uh, *sure*, Georgette. That'll be fine," Kelissa responded.

White House photographer, Georgette Wilson, stood in the office corner to capture some shots of Kelissa talking with Press Secretary Lesley Richards. "Madam President, here's the statement I have prepared for the press briefing. I wanted you to take a look at it," Lesley said as she handed Kelissa the statement. Kelissa stood there as she read in silence. As she was reading, Lesley noticed something. "Madam President, I think there's something on your leg," Lesley spotted. Kelissa immediately questioned what Lesley saw.

"What do you mean, Lesley? *What's* on my leg?" Kelissa shouted.

"Madam President, no, no! I meant there's something on the leg of your *pants*," Lesley responded fearfully.

"*Oh*," Kelissa sighed, "I think that's a piece of *tape*?"

"Oh, I'm sorry if I *scared* you."

"Likewise, sorry, ladies. I've just been having one of those *days*, you know?" Kelissa laughed.

"Um, I think I took enough shots for one day, Madam President," Georgette added.

"Yes, um, thank you, Georgette. I would like to have the final approval of those photographs before they are printed, okay?"

"Yes, Madam President," Georgette responded.

As Georgette left the office, Kelissa sat next to Lesley as she felt she owed her a sincere apology. "Madam Secretary, forgive me for raising my voice. I've kind of been out of it with all that's going on. On top of *that*, I still have to meet with the families of the fallen soldiers who lost their lives in Afghanistan. I'm still getting angry flak from all of that, and rightfully so. I should've never deplored those soldiers back over there. Not to mention, I got my fucking period two days ago," Kelissa said as she and Lesley both shared a laugh.

"Oh, *God*, we shouldn't be laughing," Kelissa sighed.

"Yes, we *should*, and yes, we *can*. There's nothing wrong with *laughter*, Madam President. You may be the most powerful woman on the planet, and you may have a lot on your plate with a *lot* of criticism. But you're still a human being. It's *okay* to smile."

"Thanks, Madam Secretary, I needed that. I could *also* use a drink. You know, I haven't had a drink since I took the oath."

"Oh? Is there any reason in particular why you stopped?"

"Well, hell *yes*, I became the President. That's *all* I need, to be standing there at a press briefing, stumbling on my words at the podium, making a complete *fool* of myself because I couldn't handle my drinking. *No,* thank you. I came into this job clean, and that's the way I want to make it out."

"I respect that. But you *are* the President. I think you're entitled to at least *a* drink."

"You know what, Madam Secretary, you're absolutely right. Let's have some wine, huh?"

Ten minutes later, Kelissa and Press Secretary Lesley Richards sat in the office as they enjoyed a bottle of red wine, conversating the flight away.

"Can I pour you another glass, Madam President?" Lesley asked.

"Yes, thank you," said Kelissa. "And *please*, call me Kelissa. Even if it's only until the end of the flight."

"Oh, um, *okay*."

"So, *Lesley*, I never really asked you about your family. Where did you grow up?"

"Well, I grew up in Jersey. Born and raised."

"Which part of New Jersey?"

"Montclair."

"Interesting, I wanted to stop there during my campaign tour, but things got so hectic at that time, so we decided to skip it."

"Yeah, growing up, it was just me and my stepdad. But he was always busy with work, so we never really had the best relationship."

"What about your *real* father?"

"Uh, that's a tough one—to call him my '*real father.*' He was anything *but* that."

"Oh… Lesley, if you don't want to get *into* it, by all means—"

"Oh no, it's fine. Actually, I had to speak about this during the Yankee White security clearance. Um… My *biological* father was an abuser. He used to abuse my mother and me."

"Is that so?"

"Yes… Sometimes he would get drunk, and he'd come home, just ready to attack either one of us. He would just throw me up against the wall and punch my mother in her face. She would have to apply an extra layer of foundation on her face to cover the bruises."

"That's terrible, Lesley."

"It *was*, yes. So, finally, my mother decided to leave him, and we *did*. We left him behind, and she fell in love with my stepdad. We moved in with him, and they got married."

"Well, *that's* a relief. I'm glad you guys got away from him."

"That's not the end of the story, Kelissa."

"It—it's not?"

As Lesley finished her glass of red wine, she began to tell the rest of her story. "My father found out where we lived, so he began to stalk my mother. But she didn't know that he was stalking her. So, one day, my mother was home. My stepdad was away on a business trip, and I was at school. My father was sitting in his car right outside of our house. In his car with him, he had some things. Things that an abductor would have with him. So, he walked up to the front door, and I guess he rang the doorbell, and my mother answered the door. He immediately charged inside the house and began to beat my mother. But my mother was pretty tough; she must have put up a good fight because she left many scratches on him. But to make a long story short, I came home from school, and I saw that the front door was open. As I walked up to the door, there was blood all over the place. There was blood on the living room carpet, the staircase, and the kitchen. It was *everywhere*."

Kelissa was now sitting there with her hand covering her mouth as she listened to Lesley's story. Tears began to run down both of their faces as Lesley continued. "Even though there was blood all over the house, I couldn't find my mom. I screamed for her to answer me. I looked everywhere, but she was nowhere to be found—until I noticed the blood on the string of the attic pull-down ladder. As I pulled it down, I saw that bloody shoe prints were going up the ladder. I was so terrified at what I would see next. I went up the ladder; the attic was dark and eerie. But the blood had a trail, so I followed it. And to this day, I wish I never did. All I remember was *screaming* at the top of my lungs. My mother was there, *hanging* by her neck from one of the beams. There was a paper stuck to her body. My father had used her blood to write on it. I'll never forget what it said:

TIL DEATH DO US PART

It took me *years,* Kelissa, *years* of therapy even to have a "*stabled*" life. It was tough even to get *this* job. I had to prove to them that I was mentally ready. But… *yea*—that was my upbringing."

Kelissa was speechless; it made her think a lot about people and how you just can never judge a book by its cover. All this time, she never knew of Lesley's abusive past. And the way Lesley carries herself, Kelissa would have *never* known. But the one thing Kelissa learned, sitting there with Lesley—when it came to abuse, she was not alone.

"Lesley," Kelissa softly said. "Sweetie, I am *so* sorry that you witnessed something so horrible."

"Thank you, Madam President. That means a lot," Lesley responded.

"You know, the fact that you are still able to smile after what you went through. To me, that is courage."

"Well, I think it's more than courage; it's faith."

"Faith…"

"Yes, faith. It was hard for me to understand that: faith and forgiveness. *Especially* forgiveness."

"Do you ever think you can forgive your father?"

"To be honest with you, Madam President… I believe *any* human being can be forgiven. But my *father*, he wasn't a human being."

Something was beginning to build up inside of Kelissa. She was ready to tell her secret to Lesley. "Lesley, there's something I want to tell you," Kelissa spoke. "Oh, go ahead, Madam President," Lesley responded. As Kelissa was getting ready to open her mouth, there was a knock at the door. "Madam President," Carl said as he knocked and opened the door, "Just wanted to inform you that we'll be landing in twenty-five minutes." Kelissa closed her eyes in complete frustration as she was about to reveal her secret. "Okay, Carl. Thank you very much," Kelissa responded.

"Madam President? *Madam President*?" Lesley said as Kelissa was daydreaming.

"Yes! Oh, I'm sorry, Lesley," Kelissa said as she snapped out of it.

"What was it that you wanted to tell me?" Lesley asked.

"Oh… It was—it was *nothing*," Kelissa chuckled. "Just, *thank you*—for having some wine with me. I really needed the drink."

"Oh, you're welcome. Sorry if my story was too graphic."

"Oh, no, it's—it's *alright*, Madam Secretary. I'm just going to freshen up a bit now."

Right before Lesley left Kelissa's office, Kelissa did something that they both needed more than a glass of wine; Kelissa hugged Lesley.

"You know, there comes a time when we, as women, *really* have to stick together," Kelissa said to Lesley.

"You're such a great woman, Madam President. I'm so honored to be working with you," Lesley smiled.

They embraced once again, and Lesley left the office. All Kelissa could do at that moment was stand there and cry. Even though Kelissa felt that she was crying too much, she could not help herself after hearing the horrific story about Lesley's mother. But what frightened Kelissa the most was the thought of something like that happening to *herself.* But Kelissa quickly wiped her eyes and got herself together before the plane landed and had to step out into the spotlight.

On Kelissa's desk, there was a little wine left in the bottle. she poured the wine in her glass and made a toast alone in her office. "Here's to… Here's to… Here's to *us*, women. May we continue our search and find our purpose, our belonging, and our appreciation as *women* in this man's world." It has been so long since Kelissa has had a drink as the red wine caught up to her. As she sat down at her desk, Kelissa sent a text to Madeline on her Blackberry that said:

"*I love you, Maddy. And nothing will change that, baby girl.*" As Kelissa hoped for a reply from Madeline, her disappointment lingered for the rest of the flight.

Chapter 36

Friday Evening, November 15th, 2024

The Act

Sitting in the Vice President's office, Kelissa, Press Secretary Lesley Richards, and Vice President Harry Griffin were having a conversation. Kelissa, still having a hard time with the Halloween massacre in Grants, New Mexico, had to get something off of her chest.

"I'm just at a loss for words, Mr. Vice President," Kelissa spoke with sadness.

"So am I, Madam President," Harry responded.

"*All* those parents who lost their child. This *has* to stop. It has to stop *immediately*... And I have an idea on how to stop it."

"Oh?"

"Yes, I have a proposal that I'm working on. Something that I feel *will* work as far as getting the House to vote on a bill that will put an end to *some* of these senseless shootings."

"What do you have in mind, Madam President?"

"I'll show it to you. Lesley, give him the rough draft."

Lesley handed a rough draft document to Vice President Harry Griffin. As he was reading it, Kelissa said, "I'm calling this bill the "*Arms Negligence Act*." This bill will require *all* responsible gun owners to *first* and *foremost* be licensed carriers *and* to have *every* firearm they own registered. But here's the thing. *If*, for whatever reason, their firearm is misplaced or stolen, and *that* particular firearm is used in an unlawful shooting, the rightful owner of *that* firearm *will* be held accountable for the crime. *So*, what does this mean? *This* means that every legal and registered gun owner will be held 100% responsible for *their* firearms. Suppose gun owners are careless about where they leave their firearms, and someone else were to use their firearms in an unlawful, illegal manner. In *that* case, they will be held accountable and face mandatory imprisonment, along with the active shooter. *Also*, people will have to go through a mandatory background check and a psychological training course. And I'm making that mandatory, *not* just for American citizens but also for law enforcement officers. There's more to it, but that's what I have so far."

As Vice President Harry Griffin reads through the rough draft of Kelissa's proposal, he slowly looks up to her from the couch and begins to speak.

"Madam President," said Harry. "If we bring this proposal to Congress, they will toss it in the garbage, *laughing* as they do it. They will *never* agree to something like this."

"Mr. Vice President, *Congress* is not the one who has to hug grieving parents who lost their *two*-and-a-half-year-old *baby* to *three fucking bullets*. *Three*. They don't have to show their faces in public. But *I* do, and the American people *will* hold me responsible."

"I *understand* that, Madam President, but the reali—"

"Harry! I will *not* make these mass shootings a norm during *my* presidency! *Something* must be done."

"And you think this is going to be the answer? This bill that you're working on?"

"That shooter in Grants, New Mexico, had stolen his irresponsible father's guns, that were *unsupervised*, and *used* them in that mass shooting. By definition, that is neglect. Gun owners can easily put people in harm's way when they leave their firearms vulnerable."

"But do you really *think* this will *work*?"

"It can't hurt to try, Harry. But I'm *damn* sure going to try."

"Well, Congress is going to be tough on us—"

"And *we* will be tough on *them*!"

"Hey, listen, we're *on* the same team here. *I'm* tired of seeing these kids losing their lives to gun violence *too*. But if we're going to get through to Congress, we'll have to come up with something more reasonable than this."

"I *did* say it's a rough draft."

"Okay," Harry chuckled, "Okay, okay."

"Madam President will also send a Presidential message stating the urgency to enact it into law. But obviously, only Congress can introduce it," Lesley added.

"Well, as I said, Congress *will* give us a hard with this," Harry responded.

"Well, *I* have some work to do. Have a good evening," Lesley said.

"Goodnight, Lesley, thank you," said Kelissa, "Well, now that we got *that* out of the way, how's the wife, Harry?"

"Oh, *Jessica*, yeah, can't complain. She's been a *real* trooper. The kids are living their lives—happily married. And Ted and the kids?"

"The kids are okay. And Ted, *he's*… Busy."

"Well, hey, we're *all* busy. And busy is good. But right now, I'm *tired*. I'm going to head out for the evening myself. Is there anything else we need to discuss?"

"No, I think we've covered enough for the day. Thank you, Harry."

"You're welcome, Madam President. Have a good night."

Kelissa left the Vice President's office, heading upstairs to her bedroom. The time was 10:45 p.m., and she missed dinner once again. As Kelissa made it up to the first floor of the residence level, she noticed dinner trays left out in the center hall, right next to Madeline's bedroom door. Kelissa walked over to where the trays were lying and lifted the silver plate cover. She noticed the half-eaten chicken fingers and French fries on the plate and knew it belonged to Bryan.

Kelissa has been very busy during the last couple of weeks, and she and Madeline still do not see eye to eye. But Kelissa appreciates Madeline taking care of her little brother. Since it was late, Kelissa decided not to disturb them and headed to her private office. She opened the door to her office, clicked on the lights, and sat down on her couch. She then closed her eyes as she took her index finger and thumb, piercing them on the bridge of her nose to ease the stress. Her level of stress has never been higher.

After what happened to the thirty-one soldiers who lost their lives in the explosion and the Halloween massacre, Kelissa could not catch a break. Her sleep patterns have become abnormally chaotic. Then suddenly, with her eyes still closed, the office door slammed. Kelissa jumped in shock. It took her a split second to focus as she saw that it was Ted. "I'm sorry, did I wake you?" Ted said with his sadistic smile. Kelissa was now nervous as Ted locked the office door and headed towards her.

"What do you want, Ted?" Kelissa asked.

"I want my wife—in bed with me, right now," Ted responded.

"Well, I'm really not that tired right now."

"Oh, well, that's *perfect*. Because neither am I. I don't want to go to *sleep*. There are other things that people do in bed, Kel."

"Well, I'm not in the mood for that either."

"I see… *Well*, there are *always* other alternatives."

Kelissa then turned on the television, ignoring Ted as she watched the news. Ted then moved closer to Kelissa as she sat on the couch. At first, Kelissa quickly looked up at him, preparing herself for his potential attack. But what he did next was something Kelissa could have never prepared herself for. Ted unbuckled his belt, undid his jeans' brass button, unzipped his pants, and pulled them down. Kelissa looked at Ted's boxer briefs and quickly looked at his face.

"Ted," Kelissa fearfully said, "What are you doing?"

"I'm not doing *anything*. It's *you* who is about to do something," Ted disturbingly responded.

"Ted—"

"It's been a very long *time* since I had a blowjob. I was going to wait until my birthday. But knowing *you*, I wanted my present early."

"Ted… Please."

As Ted stood there in front of Kelissa, he exposed himself by slowly pulling out his penis, stroking it into an erection. "Now, we can do this the *easy* way, or we can do this the *hard* way. And if I were *you*, Kel, I'd take the easy way out," Ted said as he stroked his penis. Kelissa began to shed tears as she could not believe what was happening. Looking up to Ted with teary eyes, she slowly shook her head horizontally, showing her rejection.

"I'm not leaving here until you blow me, Kel. And neither are you," Ted sternly said.

"No."

"Touch it, Kel. Touch it good."

"Stop, *please*."

"I said *touch it*!" Ted said aggressively.

"No!"

Ted then grabbed Kelissa's arm and pulled her off the couch as she was now on her knees. Kelissa was shaking while Ted kept stroking. "Touch my *dick*, Kel," Ted ordered Kelissa. As much as Ted pressured Kelissa, she would not give in. But Ted was *not* giving up. He then pulled Kelissa by her hair, looked at her, and said, "I guess you want to do this the hard way." Ted then grabbed Kelissa's arm again, pulled her up from the floor, and gave her a gut punch—falling backward on the couch. Kelissa, now holding her abdomen area, crying uncontrollably. Still moving around with his genitals fully exposed, Ted said the most disturbing thing he'd ever said to Kelissa. "If you don't *suck my cock*, *right now*, I will have no other alternative than to *piss* all over your face. And you know I'll do it, Kel."

Kelissa felt helpless; she had no other way to escape this situation. With the heavy sniffles, the tears, the pain, Kelissa decided to do what she had to do. She got back on her knees and held onto Ted's penis. "*Ohh, that's* it, Kel. Now stroke it," Ted said joyously. Kelissa, sobbing her eyes out in utter humiliation. As she stroked his penis, Ted lifted Kelissa's head and said to her, "Now, put it in your mouth." She looked at Ted, pleading with him to stop. "Either you put it in your mouth, or I'll shove it down your *fucking* throat," Ted quietly said. Just as Kelissa opened her mouth, a gentle knock came at the door.

Ted immediately pushed Kelissa off, pulled up his jeans, and buttoned the opening. Kelissa then sat on the couch and wiped her face as much as possible. As Ted opened the door, it was Bryan.

"Hey, buddy," Ted said. "What's wrong? Had another bad dream?"

"No, I went to the kitchen to get some juice, and I heard noises. Is everything okay?"

"Oh, we're sorry, bud. Your mother and I were watching this *crazy* movie, and we had it turned up too loud. Right Kelissa?"

Kelissa looked at Ted as if she was looking at the scum of the earth. But she knew she had to play it cool. Ted looked at Kelissa with a stern face. It was as if he was daring her to say a word. Kelissa then smiled a slight faux grin and said to Bryan, "It was just a crazy movie, sweetie. That's all." Ted told Bryan to go back to his room as he would be there in a couple of minutes.

"Goodnight, mommy," Bryan said. "Dad, your *zipper* is down!"

"*Oh*, I didn't even notice, bud. Thanks. I'll be right there."

As Bryan left the office, Ted closed the door, turned around—looking directly at Kelissa. As he walked towards her, he said, "You still owe me that blowjob. So, either we finish it here or do it in the bedroom. Take your pick." Ted then kissed Kelissa on her forehead as he made his way out the door. "Better yet, we'll finish this in the shower," Ted said as he gave Kelissa a wink.

Kelissa's whole body was trembling in fear. As soon as Ted closed the door, she broke down and collapsed on the floor. With the humiliation and degrading she just endured, Kelissa felt as if she was not even a woman to him but a badly bruised piece of meat. She was not a wife, not a woman, not even a human being to him. The pain was so heavy that Kelissa could not even pray. But she knew that when Ted wanted something from her, he would get it one way or another.

Several minutes went by; Kelissa then got up from her office floor and headed to the bedroom. She slowly walked down the center hall as she held her midsection—still hurting from the gut punch. As Kelissa walked into the bedroom, she could hear the shower running, which meant that Ted was already inside. She walked through the dressing room, making her way into the bathroom. There he was—naked and wet, waiting for Kelissa to join him. As Ted opened the shower door, he looked her up and down but did not say anything.

Kelissa was still sniffling as tears kept running down her face. She then slowly undressed, taking off her suit jacket and pants. Ted watched every second of her undressing until Kelissa was fully nude. And yet, she was still clothed with the painful decorations of bruises and marks all over her body. As Ted looked on at Kelissa, he said the most disturbing thing. "You look *so* beautiful, baby," Ted soothingly said, "Those marks on your body—are *my* creation. Come—*join me*. The water feels great." Kelissa slowly walked towards the shower as her *eyes* were the showerheads to her tears.

As Kelissa stepped in, her brown curly hair began to flatten by the wetness of water—*pouring* down on her fatigued body. Ted looked at her as he began to rub his fingers over her face. Kelissa, still trembling, closed her eyes, crying as she just wanted to escape this living nightmare. Ted then said with a soft, aggressive voice, "Look at me, Kel. This is the best night of my life. It feels *so goddamn good* to have control over someone. But there is *nothing* like having control—over the *President* of the United *fucking* States of America. I feel like a *God* right now. And *now*, *God* says get on your *fucking* knees." A trembling Kelissa as she closes her teary eyes, gently getting on her knees as she mortifyingly finishes what was started in her private office. And the shower of suffering still runs.

Chapter 37

Sunday Evening, December 1st, 2024

Ted's Got Her Back

The motorcade has departed from the Pentagon, the headquarters building of the United States Department of Defense. Kelissa is sitting in the back seat of the Beast one, also known as *Cadillac 1*, alone, with Carl in the passenger seat. It is precisely a ten-minute drive; Kelissa wanted some peace and to be with her thoughts. In her hands was her black leather journal. She brought it with her just in case she had something to write about while riding. As *Cadillac 1* was heading back to the White House, Kelissa began to write:

Sunday Evening, December 1st, 2024

Ladies and gentlemen, I just left the Pentagon. It was my third visit to the grounds. Finally, I received some great news. The last 1,500 U.S. Troops have been deployed from Afghanistan. Our troops are coming home, and they are staying home. I will be greeting all of them when they arrive and thank them personally for their service. Just last week, I met with the last group of families who lost their loved ones during that blast. A few of the families were rather not happy with me. And I understand, for it was my request to send another thousand troops back to Afghanistan. I just really wanted to help those poor women and children. But I'm not giving up. America has a healthy relationship with Pakistan, and we will continue to work with them to help set those women and children free. I admit to you, ladies and gentlemen, this operation was a failure. It was my mistake, and it cost the lives of thirty-one of our troops.

As for the "Arms Negligence Act," Vice President Harry Griffin and my advisors spent countless hours editing this proposal before we could even present this to the House. But we got it done, we then presented this legislation to the U.S. House of Representatives, and by the grace of God, the House has gone through with introducing the bill. As of now, the bill is in the hands of the committee members, and if they approve it to the House floor, the bill is then debated and voted on. 'Dear God, I pray that this bill is passed.'

Also, ladies and gentlemen, Ted has reached the lowest form of humanity over the last few weeks. I never thought he would make me get down on my knees and give him oral sex. Never in my life has a man ever made me feel so low. I didn't even feel like a person. I didn't feel like a woman, and I certainly did not feel like the President. It felt like he took all the power I had and used it against me. To feel so powerless and helpless, I just could have died right there in that shower that night.

But that wasn't even the most degrading thing. When he was finished, he made me swallow his semen. Forgive me for being too graphic, ladies and gentlemen. But this is the truth. As painful as it is for me, this is the truth. But soon—very soon, the secret will be out. I cannot continue with this. I have to get rid of him, once and for all. The time is coming soon. I don't know when, but I know it's soon. But I just know my kids will be so confused. And Ted has already brainwashed Madeline, making her think that I'm the abuser. And she still will not talk to me. I just hope she will be polite next week when the Prime minister of France comes to visit the White House.

Well, ladies and gentlemen, I just pulled up to the West Wing entrance. I shall continue at another time. I must say, I still find it fascinating how the four Marine Sentries are so professional and committed to their duty here. I make sure always to salute them.

Carl opened the back seat door of *Cadillac 1* that faces the West Wing entrance to let Kelissa out. Kelissa stepped out with her journal in her left hand and saluted the four Marine Sentries with her right hand as she walked inside. Before heading up to her private office on the residence level, Kelissa asked one of the staffers to prepare some tea with lemon slices and honey as the cold air was getting to her throat.

As Kelissa made her way up to the residence's first floor, she paid a visit to Bryan's bedroom. She gave a few knocks to his door and opened it. "Hey, sweetie, can I come in?" Kelissa asked. "Hi, mommy. Sure," Bryan responded. As Kelissa looked around Bryan's bedroom, she noticed his new poster on the wall.

"Bry, sweetie," said Kelissa. "Who's that?"

"A poster," Bryan responded.

"I *know* it's a poster, but who is he?"

"It's a Marvel character, Dr. Strange?"

"Oh, well, he *looks* strange, so I guess that's a good name for him," Kelissa said as she chuckled.

As Kelissa stood there, Bryan paid no attention to her. He was still upset with her for canceling the last two movie nights with him. Kelissa, feeling the self-disappointment, took a seat on his bed as she had something to say to him. "So, I guess you're still upset with me for canceling our movie nights. And you have every right to be upset with me. I'm the flaky one. I'm not really good at keeping promises, huh?"

Bryan turned around as he sat at his desk, shaking his head as he said, "No, mommy, you're *not* good with promises! But that's okay. Because dad *always* keeps *his* promises! He *watched* movies with *me*. So, it's okay." Kelissa did not like the tone of voice delivered by Bryan. Looking at him, she then raised *her* voice.

"Hey!" Kelissa shouted. "Don't talk to me like that! I am *still* your mother!"

"I-I'm sorry, mommy," Bryan said with a broken voice.

"Baby, I *know* I broke promises, and I'm *sorry*. I'm *so sorry* for breaking our movie nights."

"But why, *why* is being President more important than *us*?"

"It's *not* more important than you guys, Bryan! It's *not*! For God's *sake*, I am *TRYING*!"

"Well, *try harder*!"

"*What* did you say to me?"

"*Try harder*!" Bryan cried. "Dad doesn't let work get in the way of us. *Why* can't you be more like *dad*? You don't deserve him!"

Kelissa was so close to taking her journal and smacking it across Bryan's face. But she contained her emotions and anger as much as she could. She discovered a wicked epiphany that her darling boy is now "team Ted." A large knot was beginning to grow inside Kelissa's throat as she felt that Ted had now turned Bryan against her. She slowly stood up and made her way out his bedroom door. Before she left Bryan's room, Kelissa said, "You're absolutely right, baby. I *don't* deserve your father… Good night."

Kelissa left Bryan's room, heartbroken and devastated. As she closed his door behind her, Kelissa made her way to her private office. "Madam President, your tea," said Steven, the butler, holding the tea tray. Kelissa thanked Steven and asked if he could place it in her office. As Steven placed the tray on her desk, he then asked Kelissa if there was anything else she may need. "That'll be all, Steven. Thank you, and good night," Kelissa said with a smile.

As Steven left the office, Kelissa walked over to lock the door, preventing Ted from barging in as he did two weeks ago. Too exhausted to cry, she took a seat at her desk and had some tea. Kelissa turned on the television, only to see the media talking about her like a dog. Even though the American people love her, the press, the news, and the media saw her as a dizzy dirty blonde chick with no business in the highest chair in office. Kelissa, however, tries her best not to feed into the media. She would not dare to use social media and see the negative comments from random people. But even if Kelissa wanted to use social media, Ted would not allow it. She then turned off the television and sat there in complete silence. Then, at that moment, Kelissa thought about Ted, Jr., and decided to give him a call on her Blackberry. The phone rang several times, then finally, there was an answer.

"*Hello*, mother," said Ted, Jr.

"*TJ*! Hi, honey. Oh, it's so good to hear your voice, baby."

"It's great to hear your voice *too*. How's life as the President?"

"Oh, it is what it is, sweetie. Lots of busy days and lots of disappointment."

"What do you mean, disappointment?"

"Well, the workload is insane, and I've been making promises to Bryan that I can't keep. And your *sister*, well, she's not really talking to me."

"Oh, well, maybe I should talk with her."

"NO! No, baby, That's okay. *I'll* speak with your sister. I'm just giving her some space for now."

"*Okay*, so, how are *you* doing, Mom? Is dad taking care of you?"

"Well, *I'm* taking care of me, son. Your father is taking care of other things while I'm working."

"I see… *Well*, I'm glad you're taking care of yourself, Mom. It must be hard being President, a wife, *and* a momma bear all simultaneously."

"You have *no idea*, sweetie."

"Yeah… Oh, by the way, I got an A on my mid-term."

"You *did*? *Excellent*, TJ! Which course?"

"Philosophy. The professor's pretty decent as well."

"I'm so proud of you, baby. You're setting a *great* example for your sister and brother."

"Thanks, Mom. I appreciate it."

"You're welcome, sweetie. Made any new friends?"

"Uh, a few. But It's kind of hard to build that social life with Secret Service still around."

"Oh, well, baby, I know you're 18 now, legally an adult. But you're still my kid. And I want to do everything in my power to protect you. There are so many lunatics out there who mean us harm. And since I'm a sitting President, I'm just not willing to have you without proper protection."

"That *sucks*, Mom."

"*Terribly*, it sucks *terribly*, I know. But that's the world we live in, baby. Unfortunately."

"Yeah, well, for *you*, I'll cooperate… Mom?"

"Yes, sweetie?"

"I'm not sure if I said this to you already, but I'm very proud of you."

"I think you have, but I always appreciate it, sweetie. I really need the positive energy."

"Well, I also want to say that I love you. I may not say that to you enough."

"*Aww*, I love you more, TJ. I'm so lucky to have you in my life."

"Likewise, Mom. Good night."

"Good night, darling boy."

As Kelissa ended her call with Ted, Jr, she pressed the edge of her Blackberry up against her grinning lips, thinking about the brief yet *wonderful* conversation she just had with her oldest son. Kelissa was glad that she and Ted, Jr. were still on good terms.

As Kelissa finished her cup of tea, she was ready to call it a night and go to bed. She took the tea tray and walked over to the kitchen. As she turned on the hot water to rinse out the tea tray, Kelissa thought about the Prime Minister of France coming to visit the White House next week. She then pulled out her Blackberry from her pocket and texted Ted, Jr.:

Hey, sweetie. I completely forgot to tell you that the Prime Minister of France will be visiting the White House next weekend. So, I'll need you to be here on Saturday, December 7th. Save the date, okay?

Kelissa then headed to her bedroom. As she slowly opened the door, she saw Ted, who was asleep. Because she was still dressed in her outfit, Kelissa went into the dressing room to change into her pajamas. It was calm, quiet, and dark in the bedroom. But the bathroom light was on, giving the dressing room enough light for Kelissa to see but not wake up Ted.

After Kelissa changed into her pajamas, she put her Blackberry in her pocket and went into the bathroom, leaving the bathroom door wide open. Still unable to look at herself in the mirror, Kelissa turned on both sink faucets to create lukewarm water. As the water ran, she felt a vibration on her thigh. Her Blackberry vibrated, which meant that Ted, Jr. replied to her text.

Kelissa pulled out her Blackberry and looked at the text:

"Copy that, Madam President LOL! I'll be there. Goodnight."

Kelissa smiled as she read the text. She then placed the Blackberry on the sink counter and leaned down to splash her face, over and over with hand-puddles of warm water. With her eyes closed, Kelissa grabbed the washcloth on the sink counter and began to dry her face. She then stood straight up, with the washcloth still covering her face. And then, the unthinkable happened.

"AHHH!" Kelissa screamed as Ted crept up behind her. He covered Kelissa's mouth with his right hand as he placed a sharp knife to her throat. Kelissa was frozen in fear—could not move or speak. As she looked at Ted's reflection in the mirror, he looked the same as when he tried to drown her, soulless with no remorse.

Ted brought his lips to her ear and softly said, "Look what *I* found in your nightstand? Now, just *what* were you planning to do with this knife? Huh? Were you planning on *stabbing* me to death in my sleep? You were going to *kill* me, Kel? You don't have it in you.

But I do, and I *will*. You really fucked yourself now, baby. I *should* slice your *fucking throat* right now! Yeah, maybe I should do that."

Kelissa was scared to death, shaking, quivering in nothing but fear. Ted was dead serious as he took the sharp knife and began to dig into Kelissa's skin. "I could kill you right now. You know that, right? I could *kill* you! I *should* kill you!" Ted shouted. He was piercing Kelissa's neck so hard that blood was beginning to show on her neck. Kelissa's mouth was still covered—preventing her from making a sound.

Ted finally calmed himself down but still had the knife to Kelissa's throat. "You thought about killing me, didn't you?" Ted said, "You were going to stab me, in my sleep, and take me away from *my* children, the *only* people in this world who love me! Well, guess what? *They* don't love you. They only love *me*, and *I* made that happen. They *hate* you! *I* hate you!"

Kelissa's tears were falling and flowing. Then, as Ted slowly removed the knife away from her throat, he devilishly said, "Take two of these and *die* in the morning." BAM! BAM! Kelissa shouted at the top of her lungs as she thought Ted stabbed her twice in the back. But fortunately, he only *punched* her in her back twice. It knocked the wind out of her as she fell straight to the floor. Kelissa coughed and coughed, gasping for oxygen. Ted then crawls on top of Kelissa, gently scraping the surface of her face with the knife. "Your time is coming, bitch. Your *time* is coming. Be prepared to meet your maker. *Pray* to that son of bitch. I don't care if I go down with you. But you will *never*, *ever* kill me before I kill you," Ted said with evil conviction.

Kelissa looked into Ted's eyes and saw nothing but pure evil and darkness. She knew that if she held onto this secret long enough, her days were numbered. Ted then got off of Kelissa, now standing over her. As she turned her body to the side, Ted saw another opportunity to inflict excruciating pain onto her. Without warning, Ted *kicked* Kelissa in the same area of her back where he punched her. She screamed, cried, but Ted just stood there, looking down at her on the ground.

Ted could never be happier with the level of pleasure he was receiving from just seeing Kelissa suffer. As Ted stood there in the bathroom, he said, "You have no *idea* how much I'm enjoying this, Kel. Your *suffering* is my salvation. The fact that I'm getting away with all of this, and nobody knows. Nobody knows. I just feel *so fucking* invincible. Soon—soon, you will take your last breath. But since I'm *still* your husband, I will *allow* you to *choose* your sudden, unfortunate death. How would you like to die, Kel? *How* would you like to *die*? Strangulation? Stabbed to death? How about I set you on fire? No? Okay, *I got it*, you want to be *drowned*, don't you? What about poisoning your food? *Jesus*, the possibilities are *endless*!"

Kelissa is so defenseless as she lays there on the bathroom floor, hearing the death wish Ted is planning for her. "I—I'll… I'll," Kelissa tried to speak. "What's that, sweetie?" Ted disturbingly responded. Kelissa tried to speak as clearly as she could, saying in a broken voice, "I'll do whatever you want. Just please, don't kill me." Ted looked at Kelissa and began to laugh.

"Oh, it's too late for that, baby," Ted spoke, "I told you *not* to run for President. I told you *not* to disobey me, but you *didn't fucking listen*. You wanted the *power*. You wanted to make *history*. And *soon*, you'll *be* history." As Ted began to walk out of the bathroom, he turned off the light, leaving Kelissa in the darkness. Just before he left, he said, "If you're thinking about telling anyone, and I find out, I'll kill you right where you stand. Good night, Kel. I love you." Ted's sick and twisted mind—the insanity of telling Kelissa that he *loves* her after abusing her.

Kelissa was in so much pain, *too* much. As she lays there in the dark, she hallucinates, seeing things come at her in the darkness. The tears kept pouring out of her eyes, and the pain in her back was overwhelmingly unbearable.

A few minutes went by, Kelissa slowly began to crawl out of the bathroom, moving forward with her forearms. She made her way out to the dressing room and attempted to stand up. With the help of the chair, sitting in the middle of the dressing room, Kelissa carefully got to one knee, struggling through the pain as she finally stood up. Her balance was a bit off, but she got to her feet. Her mind could not begin to comprehend everything she had just gone through. As Kelissa walked into the bedroom, Ted was in bed, fast asleep. She could not believe how he could even sleep at night. But more than ever, she knew this had to end as soon as possible.

Kelissa walked out of the bedroom, down a quiet center hall. She walked in painful devastation, unable to turn her body in any direction. Kelissa made her way to the front door of her private office, but she decided not to go in. Instead, she looked to her left and walked over to the next room, The Lincoln Bedroom. Kelissa visited The Lincoln Bedroom many times since living in the White House. Sometimes, to hide from Ted, she would go in there to sit and read the '*Letter of Gettysburg*.' She would also go into The Lincoln Bedroom to think, pray, and find peace.

As Kelissa entered The Lincoln Bedroom, she clicked on the lights and went straight onto the bed. She never laid on the bed before, but tonight, she made an exception, as it was the one place Ted would not bother to look. Kelissa was now lying on her stomach as her mind just went blank. She laid there, in too much pain to cry any more tears. Instead of weeping, Kelissa began to softly sing these lyrics, "*I look at the world, and I notice it's turning, while my guitar gently weeps. Every mistake... We must surely be learning... Still my guitar gently weeps.*" Kelissa was singing the lyrics of a song by The Beatles called, '*While My Guitar Gently Weeps*.' She quietly sang that song—over and over as she wept herself to sleep.

The morning had arrived, and Kelissa was due to be up as she had a full schedule ahead of her. As the sun's light broke through the windows, Kelissa began to awaken. Her back was still very sore, and she still had to be careful how she moved. But as she lifted her head from the pillow, she noticed a stain on the gold pillowcase. It was a bloodstain. Kelissa was so out of it that she forgot her neck was bleeding from last night. She immediately ripped off the pillowcase and got out of the bed—instant moans as she moved too fast, causing pain in her back. She carefully stood up with the pillowcase and made her way out of The Lincoln Bedroom.

Kelissa stuck her head out of the doorway, ensuring no one was there. She walked down the center hall with the pillowcase balled up in her hands. She then went to the kitchen sink and turned on the hot water faucet—squirting dishwasher soap on the pillowcase in an attempt to remove the bloodstain. Kelissa removed as much bloodstain she could get off the pillowcase, but the remains were still evident. She then took one of the kitchen knives, cut out the bloodstain from the pillowcase, and threw what was left in the garbage. As Kelissa stands there, she drifts off in her mind. Then suddenly, she heard a voice.

"Good morning," said Ted. "And how are *you* feeling?"

"I'm *alive*—and as far as I'm concerned, that's good enough for me," Kelissa responded with attitude.

"That's good, Kel. It feels *good* to be alive, doesn't it? *Enjoy* it! Just remember this. *Tomorrow* is not promised. Make sure you cover up that neck of yours."

As Ted walked away, Kelissa's body was trembling. She did not know what to think, what to feel, or what to believe in anymore. But she *knew*, more than ever, that she had to tell her secret before the day came that Ted would kill her. As Kelissa looked at the clock on the wall, the time was 7:05 a.m. She is due to meet with her advisors at 8:30 a.m. in the Oval Office. Before getting dressed, her main priority was to cover her wounded neck with a lot of makeup and a scarf. But first, Kelissa cleaned off the minor cut on her neck at the kitchen sink. To avoid Bryan or Madeline seeing the cut on her neck, Kelissa embarrassingly wrapped a kitchen towel around her neck. Even though she looked utterly awkward, no one would see that cut.

Kelissa then took the cut-up piece of the bloodstained pillowcase with her and left the kitchen. Walking in the center hall, she saw Madeline come out of her bedroom. "Good morning, Maddy," Kelissa smiled. Unfortunately, Madeline had nothing to say to her mother, not even a 'good morning.' Madeline walked back into her room and closed her door. Kelissa just stood there, upset, exhausted, in pain, and *highly* paranoid. All she could say at that very moment was, "I'm going to die, baby. Your father's going to kill me." There was a part of Kelissa that wanted to stick around and fight. But there was another side of her that was beginning to give up.

Kelissa then walked over to Bryan's bedroom door and gave it a few knocks. "Good morning, sweetie. I just wanted to make sure you're up and getting ready for school. I have to get dressed too. Have a great day, baby… I—Mommy loves you," Kelissa projected in front of Bryan's door. She then walked down the center hall to her bedroom. As Kelissa went into the dressing room, she took the bloodstained piece of the pillowcase and placed it in one of her shoe boxes. In the dressing room, she took a minute to herself to just breathe. All Kelissa could think of doing at that moment was to close her eyes and pray. As she closed her eyes, she said, "Father, who art in heaven... I understand that my life is in shambles. My family has fallen apart, and I'm in *so* much pain and so much trouble. I pray that whatever happens to me that you protect my children. And I *beg* of you, father, for your forgiveness for when I was going to take my own life. Father, I beg of you, please—*please* forgive me, my lord. Protect my children, and please, have mercy on me."

Chapter 38

Saturday Evening, December 7th, 2024

Hell of a Party

The party is soon to begin. In honor of The Prime Minister of France, Ames Rousseau and his wife, Adele, will soon arrive at the White House for the State Dinner. This is the first State Dinner for President Kelissa Morrison, and she wants to make a *great* first impression.

Kelissa just stepped out of the shower, drying herself off as she makes her way to the dressing room in her bathrobe. She will be wearing a custom-made gown by her favorite designer, Dori McPhonzè. The dress is all-black and strapless with a high slit and a long trail. But before Kelissa placed on her dress, she had to head upstairs to the second floor of the residence level for hair and makeup.

But Kelissa had to be extra careful before stepping out as she still had bruises on her legs and a massive bruise on her back. Since over a hundred guests will attend the State Dinner, Carl and Sam are standing guard of her bedroom door for the evening. She had to think quickly about what she could wear upstairs that would not reveal any bruises. So, Kelissa went in one of the dressers where she kept her exercise attire. She pulled out black leggings and a black shirt. After putting on her bra and panties, she put on the shirt and leggings, then her bathrobe, and looked at herself in her brand-new six-foot body mirror in the dressing room. Kelissa knew how ridiculous she looked. But she could not take any chances of being clocked, not on this night.

As Kelissa walked out of her bedroom, she said to Carl, "Hey Carl, can you send for Stella and Beatrice? I'll be waiting in the salon." About three minutes later, Kelissa was sitting in her chair, thinking about the evening ahead. She grew nervous about the whole event. The Prime Minister and his wife were not due at the White House for another two-and-a-half hours. And being that this was her first meeting with Prime Minister Ames Rousseau, Kelissa wanted to make a solid impression by looking her best. Then, there was a knock on the door.

"Madam President," Carl said as he opened the door, "Stella and Beatrice are here. Should I send them in?"

"Oh, yes, of course. I'm ready," Kelissa responded.

"Hi, Madam President. It's great to see you again," Stella spoke.

"Hi ladies, it's great to see you too. Oh, *Beatrice*, I *love* what you have on."

"Oh, thank you, Madam President," Beatrice responded.

"So, I wanted to have the usual. But I *kind* of want to change my look a little bit. But I don't really have a *clue* of what would look good for me," Kelissa spoke.

"*Okay*... Hmm... Well, Beatrice has a great vision when it comes to hair," said Stella.

"And I have *just* the style," said Beatrice. "We're going to take these curls and make you look like a *princess*. No, a *queen*."

"Oh, that makes me feel great already. I'm excited," Kelissa said with a smile.

Stella and Beatrice got to work on Kelissa's hair. There was no need to wash it as Kelissa had already washed and conditioned her hair in the shower. All she needed was the style that Beatrice had in mind. As far as makeup, Kelissa already had a head start as she had to put on foundation to cover the cut she suffered from the knife. Kelissa was very focused and committed to covering her bruises and marks. She could be at events, meetings, press conferences, wherever she had to go—no matter *what*, she came prepared.

"Hair, *check*—makeup, *check*," Stella said. Stella and Beatrice were finished with Kelissa but now had to doll up Madeline. Kelissa then headed back downstairs to get dressed. Dori McPhonzè was also invited to help Kelissa with her gown. Kelissa asked Carl to send for Dori as she waited in her bedroom. As she went to the bathroom, Kelissa looked at herself in the mirror. For the first time in a very *long* time, Kelissa was able to see just how beautiful and worthy she was. She *loved* who she was looking at in the mirror. Beatrice did wonders on her hair, making the curls of her hair pop with style. The exquisiteness of her contoured jawline and features—it was as if Stella and Beatrice worked magic on her. Kelissa had a hard time looking at herself in the mirror, as she felt the shame of who she was becoming at the hands of Ted's abusive behavior. She did not feel loved or beautiful until now.

Not really paying attention, Kelissa heard Carl's voice as he opened the door and projected, "Madam President, Ms. Dori McPhonzè is here!" Kelissa, still looking at herself in awe, said, "Yes, okay." Kelissa then took off her robe, t-shirt, and black leggings as she was now standing in her bra and panties. As she walked out of the bathroom, she was instantly shocked when she saw Dori standing there in the dressing room. "*OH*, GOD!" Kelissa shouted. Kelissa quickly turned around as she covered herself and ran back into the bathroom. *Dori* was also in shock. Not because Kelissa was half-naked but shocked at the brutal image of bruises and marks on Kelissa's body. "Madam President, are you okay?" Carl said with concern as he heard Kelissa shout. To prevent Carl from coming into the dressing room, Dori responded to Carl, saying, "*Oh*, *Carl*, President Morrison is in her underwear; she's putting on her dress right now, she's okay." But that was not good enough for Carl. He needed to hear Kelissa's voice and make sure she was okay.

"Madam President," Carl spoke. "Are you okay in there?"

"Yes, Carl. I'm just in my underwear. I need you to leave the dressing room," Kelissa responded inside the bathroom.

"Yes, ma'am. I'll be right outside your door."

As Carl closed the bedroom door, Dori stood in the dressing room as she stared at the bathroom door. She heard Kelissa in there, *crying* her eyes out. Dori said to her, "Madam President, I saw what I saw. Please, come out." Through her tears, Kelissa responded, "I *can't*, I can't come out. Just tell them to cancel the party—*please*."

Dori stood next to the door, trying to get Kelissa to come out of the bathroom. She knew she had to get Kelissa out of there, one way or another. So, Dori had to give tough love and convince Kelissa to see reason.

"Madam President," said Dori. "There's no way you can stay in this bathroom forever. I promise you I won't tell a soul."

"I *hate* promises! they're always broken!" Kelissa shouted.

"Okay-*okay*… You have my *word* that this stays between you and me. How's that?"

"Just step away from the door, please."

"Okay, Madam President. I'm stepping away."

Dori then took a few steps back from the bathroom door. As the bathroom door opened, Kelissa came out, wearing just her bra and panties. Her makeup was ruined. It looked like she cried black rain as her mascara tears stained her face. As Dori looked, she covered her mouth in disbelief as she saw the bruises on Kelissa's body. They go into the bathroom and lock the door to avoid being heard.

"Oh my *God*," Dori cried. "Madam President, who *did* this to you?"

"I can't say," Kelissa cried.

"Madam President, *please. Tell me* who did this to you... Your *husband* did this to you—didn't he?"

"I'm just *so embarrassed*."

"Oh God—Oh *dear* God. Your husband is beating on you?"

"Yes... Yes—he's been attacking me almost every day."

"Jesus... Have you told anybody? Have you told Secret Service?"

"I can't tell *anyone*; my own kids don't even know. I haven't told a soul."

"You *have* to, Madam President. You have to tell *somebody*."

"*No*! Not right now. And neither will you, right?"

"I *promise* you I won't."

"I told you I *hate* promises!"

"My *word*—you have my word."

"Oh, dear *God*, Dori... Please, I *beg* of you, in Christ's name, *don't* tell *anyone*. Oh, Dori, please, *please* don't tell."

"I won't, ma'am. I *swear* to you I won't."

Dori then opened her arms and gave Kelissa a much-needed embrace of comfort. As Dori wrapped her arms around Kelissa's back, Kelissa quickly jerked and moaned as Dori was unaware of Kelissa's back pains. Dori felt so incredibly bad for her. She knew now of Kelissa's very dark secret and that she could not tell a soul. But Dori also knew that Kelissa was in severe danger and had no idea how she could help her. All Dori knew was that she would keep her word.

After twenty minutes of recovery, getting her makeup redone by Dori, and putting on her dress, Kelissa was ready to get the party started. Dori took some last looks at Kelissa, ensuring she was fully covered and not a bruise or mark was visible.

"You look absolutely *stunning*, Madam President," Dori smiled.

"Thank you, Dori—for *everything*," Kelissa responded.

"You're welcome. And for what it's worth, I think you are such a brave and strong woman for going through what you're going through and still being a leader to the American people. I am *honored* to dress you, Madam President."

"If you make me cry *one more time*," Kelissa humorously said.

Dori and Kelissa were able to share a laugh in the dressing room. Kelissa thought they both needed that laughter in the room. She hugged Dori once again before they made their way out of the bedroom. As Kelissa and Dori left the bedroom, Carl and the other Secret Service agent were still standing guard of the door.

"Was everything okay in there, Madam President?" Carl asked.

"Yes, Carl," Kelissa responded, "Sorry if I worried you. Just a little nervous about this whole event."

"I'm sure everything will be fine, ma'am."

"Yeah. Well, let's get this party started, shall we?"

As Kelissa was ready to head down to the East Room where the State Dinner was located, Madeline came out of her bedroom, wearing the most beautiful passion pink gown, *also* designed by Dori

McPhonzè. Her hair and makeup were exquisitely stunning. She took Kelissa's breath away. As they all stood there in the Center Hall, Kelissa approached Madeline with open arms as she went for a hug. "Oh, *sweetie*, you look like a *princess*," Kelissa smiled. But Madeline was not pleased with the compliment. Instead, she responded by saying, "You know, mom, when I was a little girl, you used to say that I *am* a princess. But now, I only *look* like one. I guess people really do change." Madeline then walked away, leaving Kelissa standing there in her thoughts. Kelissa thought complimenting Madeline would ease the tension. But instead, it applied pressure to it.

Guests had arrived, people walking all over the State floor, amazed at the sophisticated decorations and historical furniture. Christmas was just around the corner; the Blue Room was decorated with holiday greetings, including a fourteen-foot tree. Everyone looked incredibly fascinating. The Prime Minister and his wife were due to pull up to the White House within the next ten minutes. So, to kill some time, Kelissa decided to greet the guests who had already arrived.

"Madam President," said Carl, "Prime Minister Ames Rousseau will be arriving in two minutes."

"Okay, let's make our way outside. Can you please locate Ted?" Kelissa asked.

"Yes, ma'am."

Kelissa was then escorted by Carl to the North Portico of the White House, awaiting the Prime Minister and his wife. A chilly night out as Kelissa stands outside waiting. Ted, however, is still missing in action. "Where the *hell* is Ted?" Kelissa shouted. Now talking into the microphone hidden in his sleeve, Carl says, "I need a 20 on Ted." But the other Secret Service agents could not find him in time as the limousine holding the Prime Minister and his wife had arrived. Kelissa, unfortunately, had to meet and greet them by herself.

As the limousine's back seat opened, out came the Prime Minister of France, Ames Rousseau, and his wife, Adele. Kelissa was all smiles, but she was nothing but furious on the inside. As Prime Minister Ames and his wife walked towards Kelissa, they greeted each other.

"Good *evening*, Mr. Prime Minister!" Kelissa spoke. "I'm *so* glad to have you two here this evening."

"Good evening, Madam President," said Prime Minister Ames. "May I introduce my wife, Adele."

"*Very* nice to meet you, Adele; welcome," Kelissa spoke.

"The *pleasure's* all *mine*, Madam President. It is truly an honor to meet you." Adele said with sincere kindness.

"Will your husband be joining us this evening? I would love to meet him."

"Yes," Kelissa responded. "Actually, Ted had to take care of something with our children, on terse notice. That's why he's not here right now with me to greet you two. *Terribly* sorry about that. But he *is* here, so you'll definitely meet him. But *please*, come right in. *So* great to have you guys with us."

As Prime Minister Ames and his wife Adele made their way into the White House, Kelissa was utterly livid. But she had to keep her cool as the cameras were rolling, capturing that moment. As Kelissa walked inside with Carl, she said to him, "I am absolutely *fucking* embarrassed. The first State Dinner, and he's nowhere in goddamn sight. The press is going to have a *field day* on this. *No one* has located him?"

As Kelissa made her way down the cross hall, Bryan, Ted, Jr, and Ted made their way down the stairs. Kelissa immediately walked over to all three of them.

"Where were you guys?" Kelissa asked with an attitude.

"Sorry, Mom," said Ted, Jr. "We were upstairs playing video games."

"*Playing video games*."

"We're sorry, Mom. We lost track of time."

"We'll talk about this later. But right now, I want *you* guys to meet Prime Minister Ames and his wife. And make sure you address him as *Mr. Prime Minister*."

Ted, Jr., and Bryan walked over to the East Room as Kelissa stood next to Ted. "Ted, a word with you, please?" Kelissa said with a stern tone of voice. She had to notify Carl that she was leaving the room to have a word with Ted by the staircase. They made their way down the stairs, standing between the State and the Ground floors. Standing on the stairs, they began a conversation.

"You look *amazing* in this dress, Kel," Ted said with conviction. "You were actually able to cover *everything*. Great job."

"You know what, I'm just going to make this short. You—"

"I'm *sorry* that I was not outside in time for the meet and greet. I *truly* am. And you know what? I've been giving it some thought lately. And I feel that I owe you an apology."

"Wait, *what*?"

"You heard me. I owe you an *apology*. For all the terrible things I said. For all the times I've abused you. I was out of line for *all* of that. And I'm *so* sorry, Kel."

"Why are you doing this to me?"

"Doing *what*, babe?"

"*This*—this *lie* you're telling me. You and I *both know* that after all of this is over, you will put your hands on me once again."

"You're so *beautiful*; you know that?"

"No, this is *not* going to work anymore. I'm *done*!"

"No, *I'm* done! I'll change. I want to be a better man. I never did stop to think about all of what you have achieved. I mean, you are the first woman President in U.S. *fucking* history. That is so amazing, sweetheart. But I was too much of an egotistical maniac who was *jealous* of his *beautiful* wife, who made history. I admit that now."

"What makes you think I believe *any* of what you're saying to me right now?"

"I'm not asking you to. *I* have to believe in what I'm saying. *I* have to believe in myself. I want to be more supportive, Kel. I want to be that *great* husband you fell in love with so many years ago. I pray that you can forgive me."

"You—you're *fucking* insane," Kelissa softly said.

"I'm insane about *you*, Kel," Ted said, crying as he touched Kelissa's cheek. "You have *always* been the love of my life. I just lost my *fucking* mind. Let me make it up to you. I'm still that same man you fell in love with."

"No… I don't believe you. Stop *lying* to me, Ted."

"I'm not lying, baby. I'm sorry. Come on, introduce me to the Prime Minister. I'm *dying* to meet him."

"Stop *fucking* with my *mind*, Ted! I *hate* you for doing this," Kelissa cried.

"Hit me."

"*What*?"

"Hit me, Kel. Just hit me one time; it'll make you feel better."

"I don't want to hit you."

"Come on; I deserve it."

"NO!"

"I love you, Kel. I'm sorry," Ted said as he attempted to hug Kelissa.

"Stop, let *go* of me!"

"I can't help it. I can't help it!"

"*Please*—stop!"

Ted began to caress Kelissa, kissing her all over her face. The more she resisted, the more Ted proceeded. Ted was trying to pull her back into the aggressive current of the sea of forbidden love. But

Kelissa *knew* that if she did not swim her way back to the beach of reality, the current would swiftly pull her in, and she would finally drown. Kelissa then snapped out of the hypnosis of Ted's kisses, pushed him off of her, and slapped him across the face. A moment of silence as the echo of the smack expanded across the staircase. Kelissa looked at Ted as he held his cheek. "It's over," Kelissa said, "I don't love you anymore, and I'm *not* playing this sick game with you *anymore*. How could I love someone who beats me half to death? You think I'm still weak in the knees for you. But you've beat that part out of me. That part of me is dead." As Ted stood there, with his sinister smile, he walked up to Kelissa and said to her, "Well, maybe the rest of you needs to die along with that part of you. I tried to change into the man you once loved. But I guess that part of *me* has died as well. And *you* were the one who killed him."

Ted then walked up the stairs while Kelissa stayed in the staircase. She closed her eyes and leaned up against the staircase wall, breathing in and out to calm herself down. Deep down inside, Kelissa was proud of herself, *very* proud. She broke free of the temptation for the first time and did not give in to Ted's charming yet manipulative seduction. But she knew that she had to prepare for his abusiveness afterward. However, there was one thing Kelissa was no longer willing to do ever again—to live under Ted's lies.

Dinner has now been served. Guests are currently sitting at their assigned tables as they begin to enjoy their delicious entrees. The champagne and wine were flowing, and Kelissa was honoring her guests. As Kelissa was eating, she noticed that Ted was missing from his seat. She looked around the East Room, looking to see where he went. Then she finally spotted him, sitting right next to Madeline. Kelissa saw the two of them having a conversation. She began to study Ted's facial expressions, and he looked as if he was playing the victim. Then, Kelissa looked very sharply and noticed that Ted pointed to his left cheek, where she smacked him. Madeline turned and looked at Kelissa, shaking her head as if she was utterly disgusted with her mother. Madeline got up from the table and stormed out of the East Room. Kelissa then wiped her mouth with her napkin, excused herself from the table she was sitting at, and went after Madeline. Of course, she had to tell Carl not to follow but wait at the stairs.

Madeline went up the stairs to the first floor of the residence level, and Kelissa was right behind her. "Maddy, wait a minute," Kelissa projected. As Madeline stood there in the middle of the center hall, she turned around and looked at her mother.

"I can't believe you," Madeline said to Kelissa.

"What were you and your father talking about? What did he say to you?" Kelissa spoke.

"He *told* me how much of an abusive wife you have been to him. He told me how you just *smacked* him in the staircase. Does that make you feel *good*, Mom? Hitting dad and getting away with it?"

"Maddy, that's not true."

"Oh, it's not true? I *saw* the mark on his face, Mom! I'm not stupid!"

"No, you're not! But your father is trying to break us *apart*, baby. He's *lying* to you. And he's jealous of me!"

"Oh my *God*, Mom. You are un-*fucking*-believable—"

"Don't you *dare* use that language with me!" Kelissa shouted as she walked towards Madeline.

"Oh, so now you're going to hit *me*, Mom?" Madeline cried.

"You *don't* understand your father. You *don't* know who he *is*!"

"NO! I don't know who the hell *you* are! I don't understand *you*! *Who are you*? You're not my mother. *My* mother would *always* be there for me; she loved me. She was my best friend. But you're not *her* anymore. All you are is a *fucking* President and a *BITCH*!"

POW! Kelissa smacked Madeline right across her face as hard as she could. But Kelissa immediately regretted it as she looked at Madeline. Kelissa, now covering her mouth with her hand as tears ran down her face—looking at Madeline's bloody lip.

"Oh, *baby*," Kelissa cried. "Maddy, I'm *so sor*—oh, *please* don't—"

"Get the *fuck* away from me! *I hate you*!" Madeline said as she ran into her room.

Kelissa is still holding her hand over her mouth as she begins to sob uncontrollably in the center hall. Then suddenly, there was a round of applause coming from behind Kelissa. It was Ted, clapping his hands with a colossal smile on his face. "Bravo! *Bravo*! *Fucking* genius!" Ted said as he continued to clap his hands. "*Oh*, *Kel*, you could *not* have choreographed it *any better*. *That* was magnificent. Now, *my* daughter is in her room, *crying* her eyes out, waiting for *me* to come in, to *comfort* her and save the day. Look at you; you *literally* have blood on your hands—typical President," Ted said as he grabbed Kelissa's wrist

Kelissa looked at her right hand, and sure enough, there was blood from Madeline's lips. Tears were dropping from Kelissa's eyes as she looked. Ted then continued as he said, "You did very well, Kel. You make me look like *such* a hero. You know, I was planning on *strangling* you halfway to death for smacking me earlier. I didn't like that at all. But then I thought, 'Hey, tomorrow's my birthday. I *just* might want to fuck you.' So, I'll spare you for the evening. And that was the second time you put your hands on me. There will *not* be a third. Now, if you'll *excuse* me, I have to tend to my daughter; she needs me. She's *heartbroken*, thanks to you… Oh, I *almost* forgot to tell you. I *wasn't* playing video games with the *boys*. *I* was in my office, stalling, *just* to make you look bad in front of the Prime Minister and his *ugly bitch* of a wife. I just *love* this life, don't you?"

Kelissa just stood there in disbelief. She could not believe this was all happening. As Ted walked towards Madeline's door, he said, "You should head back down to the *party*, Madam President. It's very rude of you to neglect your guests." Kelissa, now beginning to feel nauseous, ran as fast as she could to her bathroom as the chucks were regurgitating up her throat. As Kelissa went into her bathroom, she rushed to the toilet, fell to her knees, and vomited.

Ten minutes went by; after Kelissa got herself situation and stabled, she returned to the State floor—having Carl escort her back into the East Room. As many people were walking around, socializing, Kelissa had an eerie epiphany. She realized that no one was looking for her. Everyone was so preoccupied with enjoyment in their political social club; they did not even notice her absence—it was as if they could care less. At that moment, Kelissa realized that being President of the United States of America was just a job. She understood that the love was fake and that the ass-kissing people *feared* her *power* more than they admired her. At that moment, Kelissa discovered the *real* dark secret of politics.

As Kelissa walked around among the hundred and fifty guests in attendance, out of nowhere, Bryan came up to his mother and gave her something that she needed more than anything, an innocent hug. And boy, did he love to squeeze tight. Kelissa held in the scream as Bryan applied pressure to her back, still having pain since Ted punched her twice. "Mommy, I'm having so much fun!" Bryan said with his innocent smile. Kelissa looked down at him and smiled as she said, "I'm so glad you're having fun, sweetie. I love you, darling boy." As Kelissa placed her hand on Bryan's face, he noticed a red stain on her hand out of the corner of his eye. "Mommy, is that *blood* on your hand?" Bryan asked with a worried face. Kelissa forgot to wash her hands upstairs in the bathroom. She immediately responded, saying, "Oh, *no*, sweetie, that's from mommy's red lipstick. I'll be right back; I'm going to wash my hands."

Kelissa then went into the powder room near the East Room. As she went in, Adele, the wife of Prime Minister Ames, was in the bathroom, washing her hands.

"Oh, Madam President," Adele smiled. "How are you doing?"

"Hi, I'm well. Are you enjoying the party?" Kelissa responded.

"Oh, that I *am*. Everyone is so wonderful and friendly. My husband and I are having an *amazing* time. I was talking with *your* husband, uh—Ted? That's his name, yeah?"

"That's his *name*, yes."

"Yes, he's very much a nice man. My husband got along with him quite well. You are fortunate of a woman to be married to him. He's handsome guy, yes?"

"Yes, well, I guess I can say the same for *your* husband."

"Ah, I fell in love with him at seventeen years old. I was young girl when I met him."

"Really? Ted and I met a little *after* our teenage years. I feel like both of us were different people back then."

"I know *just* what you mean. I understand. The older we get, the more we change. But *hey*, as we say in France, 'C'est *la vie*."

"That's *life—exactly*," Kelissa smiled.

"You know, I just want to say that you are *such* an inspiration to many, *many* women and young girls, all over the world. And I can't even *imagine* the *sexism* you must face every day. To be the first woman President of the states, I'm sure men have a problem answering to a woman. What you've accomplished, you've changed the world. I see you as an idol, and I admire you, Madam President."

That put such a heartwarming smile on Kelissa's face. To hear another woman give her such sincere praise and admiration. It reminded Kelissa of her value and that she *does* mean the world to many women worldwide. "Your kind words, Adele, they come at the perfect time. Thank you for believing in me," Kelissa said. Adele then kissed Kelissa on each cheek and headed out of the restroom.

It grew silent as Kelissa took a minute to herself alone in the restroom. She reflected on what happened upstairs between her and Madeline. And the fact that Madeline's birthday was only seven days away, Kelissa had to find a way to rekindle her bond with her daughter. But with Ted's brainwashing tactics, Kelissa knew that was not going to be easy.

As Kelissa took a moment, she leaned up against the glass divider and looked at the ceiling. She thought about all the atrocious nights of violence she had to endure and how all of that would soon come to an end. Kelissa was planning her moment of truth. She did not know when or *who* exactly she was going to reveal her secret to. Kelissa knew that her nightmare would soon be over, and Ted was soon to be history.

Chapter 39

Friday Evening, December 13th, 2024

Camp David

Even though it is not *Hawaii*, Camp David was about as close of a vacation spot as President Morrison could have. But unfortunately, Kelissa is vacationing alone. Madeline decided not to join her, as she was still upset with her mother for slapping her last Saturday at the State Dinner. Ted, Jr. has another six days before the semester ends, and Bryan felt that Camp David would be too boring for him. So, he decided to stay with Madeline and their father at the White House. Kelissa, however, used the space and time to herself to clear her mind.

Kelissa was staying in the Aspen Lodge, which is the presidential cabin. She loved the peacefulness of that area. Even though Secret Service agents with their K-9 partners surrounded the site, they still gave the President space and privacy.

As Kelissa was in the kitchen of the Aspen Lodge, she received a phone call on her Blackberry. It was a call from Bryan."

"Hi, sweetie," said Kelissa. "What are you still doing up? It's late."

"I was playing video games with dad," Bryan responded.

"I don't want you playing too many video games, honey."

"Well, *dad* said it's fine."

"Well, *I* said it's *not*. So, no more games tonight, okay?"

"*Okay...*"

"*So*, what did you call me for?"

"Because I miss you. You've been gone since Tuesday."

"I know, sweetheart," Kelissa said with guilt. "I wanted you guys to come with me. But I will be back home tomorrow for Maddy's birthday."

"But she says she doesn't *want* a party."

"Well, we'll see what happens. But anyway, it's late, so, get some sleep, and I'll see you tomorrow. I love you, sweetie."

"I love you too, mommy."

As Kelissa ended the call, she looked down at her legs and shed tears as Ted did another number on her. As she fixed herself a glass of red wine, Kelissa made her way to the living room couch. The fireplace was burning, and Christmas carols were playing. As she took a sip of her wine, Kelissa picked up her journal and pen and began to write. In her journal, Kelissa wrote:

Friday Evening, December 13th, 2024

Ladies and gentlemen, please don't judge me. I know that I said that I was going to reveal my secret. Well, it's not actually a secret anymore now that Dori McPhonzè knows about it. But I do trust her, and I believe she will not tell anyone. But I will soon have to tell someone before Ted kills me. Can you guess what he did to me, ladies and gentlemen? Well, I will try and get through this without shedding any more tears.

After the State Dinner, I was sleeping in my bed. I was utterly exhausted from my speech, shaking all those people's hands, the argument with Maddy, and then hitting her; I was very fatigued and drained that evening. I wanted to bury myself in that bed. And that is exactly what I did. I didn't even bother to put on any pajamas. I took off my black gown and hung it up in my dressing room. Then I took off my stockings and plopped my body on the Bed. As I was falling asleep, in came Ted.

It was past midnight, which meant that it was his birthday. As he said earlier that evening, he just might want sex. I didn't even want him to touch me anymore. But I was too tired to put up a fight. So, I let him get on top of me and just let him have his pleasure. But I made a terrible, terrible mistake. Ted did not have sex with me. What he did was the absolute final straw. He ripped off my bra and panties, and he told me that he would be right back. I had no idea where he went, nor did I care. I really wanted him to just get on top of me, finish pleasuring himself, and be done with it.

But never would I expect him to do what he did. Ted went into the dressing room and grabbed one of the metal hangers. As he held onto one end of the hanger, he must have taken a lighter to the other end and put the flame underneath it. I was so out of it that I did not even see it coming. But I was soon to feel it. And when Ted came back to bed, He got on top of me as

I lay on my stomach. He took the hot metal hanger and pressed it against my skin. I had never screamed in pain so loud before. But Ted is so strong and quick that I had no control over my screams being heard. He pinned my face to the pillow where no one could hear me scream. He left the metal hanger on my skin for what seemed like forever—long enough to leave a permanent mark on my back. He said that it was payback for my behavior at the State Dinner. I just thank God that I have knowledge and training in nursing from my days in the service and that I know how to treat burns. I feel mortifyingly terrible that I went to the White House Medical Unit in the Eisenhower Executive Office Building and stole some ointment and bandages for burns on my back. I took a handbag with me to hide the medication from Carl. That's why I asked of you, ladies and gentlemen, to please not judge me.

You know, I honestly believe that if he had access to a gun, chances are I wouldn't even be writing to you, ladies and gentlemen. He would have already put the gun straight to my head, pulled the trigger, and killed me. I know that I can't wait much longer. I have to tell someone about this. But with everything coming up; the State of the Union, the House voting next week on the 'Arms Negligence Act,' and a press conference next month, as it will be a year since I've been in office. I can't tell anyone right now. It would just get in the way of everything. But soon... Very soon, my nightmare will be over.

Kelissa then closed her journal and called it a night. She poured herself another glass of wine and laid back on the couch under a cozy olive-green blanket, staying warm next to the fireplace. As she took sips of her wine, Kelissa began to think about her escape. She had a definite date as to when she planned on revealing her secret. And that date was February 17th, 2025. She picked that date because it was the only day she was not swamped in meetings or conference calls. It was a day all to herself. So, Kelissa's date was set. It was established as to when she was going to drop the bomb. But who was she going to tell? Bryan? Madeline? Ted, Jr., or *Carl*, perhaps? Kelissa had no idea. All she knew was that she was tired of being a victim of domestic violence, and all she wanted more than anything was to survive.

Chapter 40

Friday Evening, January 3rd, 2025

The Moment of Truth

Tonight is the night where America may change for the good. The U.S. House is soon to vote for the '*Arms Negligence Act.*'. President Kelissa Morrison is a nervous wreck. Kelissa refuses to show her nervousness publicly in front of her administration. Still, deep down, she knows how important this is for America and how this will make a change in the gun violence that burdens the country.

She was now sitting in the Cabinet Room with her advisors, staffers, Vice President Harry Griffin, and Press Secretary Lesley Richards. White House photographer, Georgette Wilson, was also invited to take some photographs. Sitting at the table, nervous and overwhelmed with emotion, Kelissa watched the large television screen as the House began to tally up the votes.

"What do you think, ladies and gentlemen?" Kelissa projected. "You think the House will pass it?"

"Madam President," said Vice President Harry. "They have no choice. The bill we proposed is very reasonable and realistic."

"Yeah—They would be *insane* not to pass this," Lesley responded.

"Some of them *are* insane. That's what I'm worried about," Kelissa said as the room laughed.

As Dozens of staffers gathered in the Cabinet Room with President Morrison, their eyes were *glued* to the television screen. Kelissa's right leg was shaking the entire time as the votes were due to be revealed at any given moment. The Cabinet Room was so quiet you could hear a cotton ball drop on the floor. As Kelissa watched, all she thought about in her mind was, "218, 218, 218, 218, 218." There must be a simple majority vote of 218 votes for a bill to be passed. There are 435 active House representatives. All Kelissa needs is 218 votes for her legacy to become more significant.

The clock was ticking, and the time was now 10:03 p.m. Kelissa began to sweat underneath her arms as the moment of truth was near. With her hands together, shaped like a ball—*pressed* against her mouth, Kelissa's whole body jerked as the votes finally appeared on the screen. "There they are, folks!" Kelissa projected. The ensemble looked with bulging eyes and sweaty foreheads; they looked at the numbers and *immediately* jumped for joy as they saw the number of "Yea" votes at "222."

	YEA	NAY	PRES	NV
DEMOCRATIC	183	26		
REPUBLICIAN	39	187		
INDEPENDENT				
TOTALS	222	213		

The bill was officially passed. All the votes were in, and the "*Arms Negligence Act*" has become law. A large round of applause came from the Cabinet Room. A bunch of screaming and gestures of celebration. Kelissa was still sitting with her head down and her hands crossed together like praying hands. The moment was too surreal for her.

Vice President Harry Griffin gently placed his hands on Kelissa's shoulders. Kelissa quickly moved, as that was the exact spot of her painful bruises from the previous night. She then smiled at Harry and pretended it did not hurt, even though it hurt like hell. Kelissa stood up from her chair and spoke to Vice President Griffin as the applause continued.

"We *did it*!" Kelissa said as she hugged Harry. "We *did it*!"

"Yes, we *did*, Madam President. This bill will make a difference in our country," Vice President Griffin said.

"And would you *look* at that "*Nay*" vote—*187*—the number that represents *exactly* what we're trying to prevent from happening."

"Madam President," said Lesley. "We'll be making a speech in ten minutes."

"Okay, thank you, Madam Secretary," Kelissa responded.

Kelissa began to walk around, shaking the hands of all of her staff and advisors. The applause was nonstop, nothing but smiles and cheers as everyone congratulated Kelissa, and she *too* congratulated them.

The Press pool was waiting in the East Room of the State floor as President Kelissa Morrison and Vice President Harry Griffin was soon to make a speech. As Kelissa and Harry waited in the Green Room, they had a brief conversation.

"Boy, are we going to party tonight," Harry said with excitement.

"Yeah… But actually, I'll be taking a rain check on the party," Kelissa said with a disappointed face.

"Wait, *what*?" Madam President, we just made *history* tonight. At least stick around for an *hour*."

"Oh *God*, no. I'm already on four hours of sleep in the last forty-eight hours. I need some rest."

"Well, is Ted going to celebrate with us?"

"Ted had some prior obligations to tend to. So, I doubt it. I guess I *should* make an appearance. But just not for long."

"Yeah, that's the spirit."

"Madam President, we're ready for you," Lesley said.

"Thank you, Madam Secretary. Well, let's do this."

As President Kelissa Morrison and Vice President Harry Griffin made their way down the cross hall to the East Room, the cameras clicked a hundred shots every thirty seconds. Kelissa, dressed in her burgundy business suit, with a matching silk scarf around her neck. Vice President Harry Griffin stood to the side, where the rest of Kelissa's administration stood by. As Kelissa took to the podium, she made her speech with much conviction and enthusiasm. As the press clicked away, President Morrison had this to say as the press clicked their fingers away on those cameras:

Good evening, everyone. Thank you all for being here this evening. History was made tonight. The first step in a new direction has been made. Not even thirty minutes ago, the "*Arms Negligence Act*" was passed by Congress. With this act, we are taking America in the direction of great integrity and moral value. With this bill being in effect, we will prevent a lot of senseless murders from happening. School and mass shootings will not occur as easily or as frequently. Unlicensed citizens will no *longer* be able to get their trigger-happy hands on unregistered firearms. To be clear, we are *not* looking to *confiscate* your guns, for those who are already licensed, legal firearm carriers.

But we *are* here to regulate how *and why* you decided to use them destructively. Our country has dealt with far too much violence caused by irresponsible gun owners. I know you've heard that saying, '*Guns don't kill people; people kill people.*' Well, the killings must stop, and they *will* stop. Period! From now on, for *every* legal firearm carrier, *you* are one hundred percent responsible for your *registered* firearms. That means that if someone were to *steal* or *misplace* your gun, and that individual uses it and takes a life *or* disturbs the peace with *your* firearm, you *will* be held responsible and serve an equal punishment as the individual who used *your* firearm. That is where the whole '*Negligence*' comes into place.

Also, suppose you are planning on *becoming* a licensed gun owner. In that case, you will now have to go through psychiatric sessions *and* training to qualify that you are mentally healthy and stable to carry such a deadly weapon. That also goes for law enforcement officers and security guards who can carry firearms for their jobs. I know this may come off as an inconvenience for some of you. But trust me when I tell you, there is *nothing* more *inconvenient*, tragic, *and* conflicting than to see a crying mother and father who just buried their two-and-a-half-year-old child, who was shot three times and died *instantly*. That is *not* the America that I envision. That is *not* a country that is destined for greatness. Yes, you have the right to bear arms, but that does *not* give you the right to take a gun and murder innocent people. The time has come here in America to *value* our humanity. Our humanity is all we have. But if we continue to ignore and *dismiss* that value, there will be nothing left for us to live for."

As Kelissa took a breather, she went ahead and gave thanks to her administration:

I now want to thank my staff, Vice President Harry Griffin, for his contribution to this act and his support. I would like to thank Press Secretary Lesley Richards. And *also,* I would like to thank the *President* of the *National Rifle Association*, Richard James-Mitchell, for his cooperation. We had a brief conversation in which he had expressed his support of the '*Arms Negligence Act.*' And lastly, I thank the press for coming in tonight. As I said, This is a decisive step in a new direction for our country. It's a step *forward* to a safer, less violent, convenient society. A society where parents will not always have to worry about if their child will be the next victim of a school or mass shooting or an African American will be the next victim to another unethical police shooting. We shall, and we *will* become a better America. My fellow Americans, Thank you, God bless you, and God bless these United States of America.

Chapter 41

Thursday Evening, January 16th, 2025

No Ted Thursday

Peace is in the White House for Kelissa as Ted is out of town, giving public speeches for important events and ceremonies on behalf of his wife, the very busy President Kelissa Morrison. Laying in her bed, Kelissa was busy writing in her journal. She had a lot to say as she hadn't written anything since last December. In her journal, Kelissa wrote:

Thursday Evening, January 16th, 2025

A lot has happened since I last talked to you, ladies and gentlemen. And I have much to tell you. I don't even know where to begin. But I'll try my best. I guess I'll just start with Maddy's birthday. Well, she decided not to celebrate her birthday with her family. She didn't even want her friends from school to come to the White House to celebrate with her. She has completely isolated herself from me. I say good morning to her, and she doesn't respond. I walk into a room, she sees me, and then she gets up and leaves. That breaks my heart; my own daughter hates me that much, even after I apologized to her so many times now. But she just won't accept it. Sometimes, I just feel that I've lost her. It feels as if I don't have a daughter anymore. That upsets me, just as I write it. And Ted provokes her behavior and anger towards me. He loves that the kids are more drawn to him than they are to me. Because of my busy schedule, my absence works in his favor.

I'll admit, ladies and gentlemen, I let my priorities fall apart in my first year as the President. What I know now that I didn't back then, I would have made better choices. But I was a fool. A fool to believe the lies that Ted would tell me. He told me he would stop, that he would change his ways, only if I dropped out of the race. But the Leo in me makes me too stubborn. Once I set my mind on something, I just can't let it go. I had to go through with this. But I think that's everybody. Everyone who has a dream will stop at nothing to achieve it. But the price I paid for this, I'm not sure if it was all worth it. No… Maybe I shouldn't say that. My team and I just made history. I believe that we will shape this country into a better decision-making environment regarding guns and the violence associated with them. I still have to remind myself that I made history as the first woman President of the United States of America. In the two hundred and forty-eight years of this country, a woman has never been able to win the presidential election until I stepped in—I did it.

But as I said, ladies and gentlemen, I paid the price for this achievement. Oh, I almost forgot to mention Christmas day. That was the most bizarre, frightening, unimaginable Christmas in my entire life. I invited my parents to come to stay at the White House again for the holidays.

Another big mistake on my behalf. Ted told my parents about the night at the State Dinner, how I smacked him in the face. My mother pulled me to the side and said every word of profanity you could think of to my face. She told me, 'Don't ever put your goddamn hands on your husband. You don't want him putting his hands on you, do you?' I said to my mother, 'No, I don't want that, mom.' But I wish I told her that Ted does put his hands on me. He puts his hands on me all the time. My father couldn't even look at me; he was so disgusted. Ted's been very successful with turning the whole family against me.

But that wasn't even the worst part of Christmas, ladies and gentlemen, not even close. That evening, when everyone was in their rooms, I was lying in bed while Ted was in the bathroom. He must have been in there for an hour or two. I don't recall how long. But while he was in there, he made these crazy grunting sounds. It was so bizarre. Then the room became quiet, and I heard nothing. Then suddenly, Ted called for me to come to the bathroom. At first, I was terrified to go and see what he was about to show me, and I didn't want to go to the bathroom. But then he said, 'I want to show you your Christmas gift.' I wanted to get it over with, so I got up from my bed and went to the bathroom. And ladies and gentlemen, what he showed me, I knew right then and there that I have to get the fuck away from this psychopath as soon as possible.

When I came to the bathroom, he wrapped a towel around his left forearm. He said, 'You ready for your Christmas gift?'

Ladies and gentlemen, do you know what he did? He took a knife and carved my name on his forearm. I could not believe it—I was in utter shock. His arm was bleeding, but he didn't even care. Then he said, 'So, Kel, what do you have to say?' Without hesitation, I told him how sick he was for doing that to himself. I could not even look at him any longer. I just slept in my office that night. February 17th cannot come any faster. That is the day that I tell my secret. I can't live like this. The abuse just gets worse and worse. But I have so much on my plate. I can't have this circulating in the media with everything else going on.

I have a month left, ladies and gentlemen, if I make it. I've been praying. Praying helps me a lot, and it gives me hope—hope that this nightmare that I've been living in for the last three years will soon come to an end. I've prayed that God will forgive me for that night I was going to take my own life. The sad part about all of this is that my children will be the ones who suffer once I tell my secret. They will lose their father once I turn him in to authorities. I'm just scared to death, ladies and gentlemen. I don't know what is going to happen come February 17th. But I'm tired; I'm so tired. All the beatings, all the bruises and marks, and burns, him spitting in my face, oh, and I almost forgot to tell you that last week, he pulled my hair so hard that he pulled out a lock of my hair when he threw me down on the dressing room floor and kicked me repeatedly. It was so bad. I now have a small bald spot on the top of my head.

I'm tired, ladies and gentlemen. Too tired.

Kelissa then closed her journal and placed it in the drawer of her nightstand. As she lay there in her bed, she began to think about Madeline and their conflicted tension. She hated the fact that they were not on good terms. So, Kelissa got out of her bed and made her way to Madeline's room. Even though it was late at night and Madeline was probably sleeping, Kelissa wanted to catch Madeline off guard and talk with her. Surprisingly, she was awake, listening to music. "Hey

Maddy, can I come in and talk to you?" Kelissa asked after gently knocking.

Madeline looked at Kelissa for a few seconds and said, "You're the President, right? You don't need my permission." Kelissa then walked in as Madeline sat on her bed. Kelissa began to step back and forth in the room, thinking about how she could break and ease the tension. As Madeline looked on, Kelissa began to speak. "Maddy, I know you're very angry with me, baby. And you have *every* right to be. Things have been insane, and you may be confused about some things, but I just have to tell you this. I'm going through some things with your father; he and I are just not on good terms. I haven't said this to anyone else. But you're my daughter, and I love you, and I *trust* you. I trust you not to tell this to anyone else. But before I tell you, will you swear to me that you will not tell anyone else and that this will stay between you and me?"

Madeline looked at her mother with nothing but concern and confusion. But she wanted to hear what her mother had to say to her. "I swear, I won't tell," Madeline said with conviction. But as Kelissa was about to tell Madeline her "secret," she thought it would be better to show her. Kelissa then proceeded to take off her pajamas, but Madeline immediately stopped her, saying, "What are you *doing*? I don't want to see you *naked*!" But Kelissa continued as she dropped her pajama pants and *ripped* off her shirt, revealing her bruises and marks to Madeline. Madeline, still sitting on her bed, was devastatingly stunned at the painful image of her mother. Madeline looked as if she had seen a ghost.

As Madeline stared with tears, Kelissa grew emotional as she began to speak. "This is what I've been going through, baby. Your father has been beating me for the last three years. I've been keeping this a secret from everyone. That's why I've been losing my mind. I'm so scared, Maddy. He's been trying to kill me," Kelissa sobbed. Madeline slowly got up from her bed and immediately hugged her mother gently, knowing her mother *had* to be in pain.

"Oh, God, Mom. I'm so *sorry*. I'm so *sorry*," Madeline cried.

"I'm going to fix this, baby. I'm goi—I'm going to fix this, okay?" Kelissa responded.

"How?"

"I'm going to take this to Carl. I'm going to tell him *everything*. But you have to swear to me, baby. Swear to me that you will not tell anyone. Not your brothers, not no one. And don't let your father *think* you know. Just keep it the way it is between you and him, okay?"

"Mom, you should tell somebody *now*."

"I *can't* right now, sweetie. I have too much on my plate. I have to wait until next month."

"Next *month*? Mom, are you *crazy*? He'll *kill* you by then!"

"He's not going to kill me, Maddy. I have a plan, okay? I *have* a plan. But you just have to trust me and *don't* tell a soul."

"Okay… *Jesus*, Mom. Look at your body."

"It looks worse than it feels, baby. But I'll be alright."

"Oh, Mom. I'm so *sorry*."

"*Oh*, no, baby—*I'm* sorry."

Kelissa and Madeline shared a deep and passionate hug as they shed many tears. Madeline then insisted that she stays the night in her mother's bedroom to keep her company. Madeline then grabbed her Blackberry from her nightstand and walked over with Kelissa to her mother's bedroom. As they made it to Kelissa's bedroom, Madeline surprisingly received a phone call. It was her father, Ted.

"Oh, *shit*. Mom, it's dad," Madeline anxiously said.

"Well, answer it! And remember, pretend like you don't know *anything*," Kelissa responded.

"Hey, Dad, how are you?"

As Madeline was on the phone with her father, Kelissa looked on. She noticed the twisted facial expressions on Madeline's face. Kelissa had no idea what Ted was saying to Madeline on the other line. After a minute went by, Madeline hung up the phone. "What? What did he say?" Kelissa asked. Madeline then looked at her mother with a sad face and said, "Dad's mom is dead. She committed suicide."

Chapter 42

Saturday Evening, January 18th, 2025

Kelissa's Sympathy

A long day as Kelissa finishes up a meeting with her speechwriting team in the Oval Office. She had her final meeting with her team: Gary Cruise, Deputy Director of Speechwriting. Harvey Davis, Director of Speechwriting. Carrie Thompson, Deputy Assistant to the President, and Ally Berger, Assistant Speechwriter. The team made time on their Saturday with Kelissa to go over the final draft of her State of the Union speech on Tuesday. Even though Kelissa did most of the writing, she welcomed and *appreciated* her speechwriting team for editing and polishing her delivery.

"*Okay*, ladies and gentlemen, I think we can call it a night. Thank you for coming in during the weekend," Kelissa said.

"Madam President, we *have* the final piece!" Gary spoke with enthusiasm.

"I *second* that—Madam President, you're going to slam dunk this State of the Union speech!" Ally spoke.

"Thank you to all of you," Kelissa said with gratitude. "We've made *so much* progress over the months. I am satisfied with our finished piece. Have a great evening, everyone."

As the speechwriting team packed up for the evening, Carl came into the office and told Kelissa that Ted wanted to see her in his office, located on the East Wing. Ted had just come back from his public speaking ventures earlier that morning. Kelissa has not seen Ted since he's been back.

Carl then escorted Kelissa to the East Wing. Because she no longer trusts Ted, Kelissa asked if Carl could stand guard of the door while she went into Ted's office. Kelissa knocks a few times and then opens the door. She sees Ted sitting at his desk, looking at a picture with his hand brimming over the melancholy look on his face. "Ted, you asked to see me?" Kelissa spoke. Ted looked up and responded, "Yes, please, come in." Kelissa walked over to the beige couch and took a seat. Ted placed the picture on his desk, facing the couch.

As Kelissa looked, she noticed that it was a picture of Ted as a little boy with his mother at the zoo. They were all smiles and happiness that day. Ted then sat down in a chair, now facing Kelissa as he began to speak to her.

"Thank you for coming," said Ted. "It's been a rough two days for me."

"I'm sure it has. My condolences about your mother. I know you haven't seen much of her after joining the military."

"She didn't *want* to see me. One night, we had a big argument, and she said that she never wanted to see me again. So, we *didn't*."

"You know, Ted, I really *want* to sympathize with you. I'm sorry that you lost your mother under those circumstances, but I just don't understand why you keep attacking me. You were the *love of my life*. You *never*… You *never* laid a finger on me when we first met."

"You're right; you're absolutely right. I would never have hurt you. But that's why I asked you to come here. To tell you a secret."

"What secret, Ted?"

Ted took a moment to breathe. He sat there, looking off to the side as his eyes grew watery. Kelissa could see the pain within. As he wipes his eyes, Ted tells Kelissa his secret. "Back when I was a kid, eight years old, I would see my father abuse my mother. He would beat her and beat her, *torment* her daily. He would make her feel worthless any chance he could. He called her the worst of things I ever heard a man call a woman. I would see it all—*every* night, I would hear her screaming in the dark, in *pain*. But my mother would always hide the bruises and the cuts. She would *always* pretend to her friends and family that everything was alright. She was very good at hiding the pain. But the thing I *never* understood was that she would *always* forgive my father and take him back. One day, my father took off and abandoned us, and my mother took me across the country to find him. And when she found him, he abused her even more. I *never* understood why. *Why* would she go back to that monster? I was only eight years old; I didn't understand anything about *anything*. But as I got older, the abuse kept happening. After a while, I thought it was just *normal* for a man to beat on a woman. And I honestly *believed* that a woman would *always* take her man back no matter what. I look back at all those years of seeing my mother abused by my father and being in the military. And that's when I woke up yesterday morning, and I realized that *violence* had become my whole life. I really know nothing else. I'm just a very *violent* man."

Kelissa was speechless as she saw Ted silently sobbing and helpless, mourning the death of his mother. It was as if he was crying the reserved tears he held in ever since he was that eight-year-old child. At that moment, Kelissa finally understood where Ted's abuse came from—it was learned behavior. But Kelissa had some things to say. "Ted, you've been through a lot. I understand that now. But that does *not* justify you putting your hands on me at *all*. You have put me through *hell* these past three years… *Hell*. You don't know this, but *I* was close to committing suicide. So, *sadly*, I'm just like your mom. And I can understand *why* she did what she did."

As conflicting and complex this situation is, Kelissa could not dwell on it any longer. She then stood up from the couch and headed for the door. Before she left, she said, “I won’t be able to attend your mother's funeral, but the children are more than welcomed. But you *do* need counseling, Ted.”

“Kel, wait,” Ted spoke. “Is there any chance in this life of you ever forgiving me?”

“I can’t microwave forgiveness, Ted. It may take a year, five years, maybe my entire life. I don’t have an answer for you.”

“I love you, Kel. And I always will.”

Kelissa looked at him with an absurd expression on her face. The fact that Ted still tells Kelissa that he loves her makes the confusion grow and wickedly blossom. Kelissa is just so far removed from ever loving him again. After three years of abuse, she has had enough; her *body* has had enough. The lies have been told, and the truth is about to unfold. Kelissa is still planning to expose Ted on the 17th of February. It has been a long time coming, and Kelissa is *more than ever* ready to escape the madness haunting her, deeply hidden in the darkness.

Chapter 43

Tuesday Evening, January 21st, 2025

State of The Union Address

The big night has arrived. It has been a year since President Kelissa Morrison was sworn into office. And now, it is time to address the nation in her first State of the Union Address.

Kelissa is dressed to *highly* impress this evening, wearing a navy-blue suit jacket and skirt, a white cowl blouse with a pearl necklace and the matching earrings, and the famous presidential lapel pin. Kelissa looked astonishingly gorgeous and happy.

Her head was held high and mighty as she was soon to take the podium. It was 8:55 p.m., the members of the House had already taken their seats for their joint session, and Kelissa was ready to make her grand entrance inside the House chamber. The House Sergeant at

Arms, Jeremy Snyder, is standing just inside the chamber doors as he waits for President Kelissa Morrison to give him the okay. "We're good to go. I'm ready," Kelissa said with her beautiful smile.

As the clock showed 9:00 p.m. Jeremy Snyder, now facing the Speaker of the House as he waits for Mr. Speaker to give two hits of the walnut gavel. "Mr. Speaker, the *President* of the United States!" Jeremy projected.

The doors of the House chamber opened—a standing ovation of cheering members of the House. Kelissa's eyes lit up like a star on a Christmas tree. She felt like a Rockstar, slowly walking down the aisle as she shakes hands, giving hugs and kisses to supreme court judges and other members of Congress. Many of the women were in tears as this had never happened before. The first *woman* President in United States history is walking down the aisle. Kelissa was glowing and shining bright in the House chamber. The cheering and applause must have lasted for seven minutes straight as Kelissa was only halfway down the aisle, patiently making her way to the House Clerk's desk. The Members of Congress cheered even louder after she put her John Hancock on copies of the speech. It was as if those copies had now turned into gold.

Ten minutes in, Kelissa finally makes her way to the House Clerk's desk, in front of the Speaker's rostrum, also known as the podium. Kelissa then greets Vice President Harry Griffin and Speaker of the House, Patrick Warner. As the protocol of the House chamber, President Kelissa Morrison handed over *two* manila envelopes that hold a copy of the speech: one copy for the Vice President and one for the Speaker of the House. As Kelissa turned to face the House, the standing ovation continued. She raised her arm to wave her hand. But unfortunately, Kelissa could only lift her arm but so high and for so long, as Ted did yet another number on her late last night, throwing her up against the wall, injuring her shoulder in the process.

As Kelissa saw Ted standing in the box, next to Madeline, Bryan, and other invitees, he blew her a kiss and continued to clap his hands with an endearing smile on his face. Kelissa began to imagine herself giving Ted the finger *right there* in front of everyone. She knew that he could never change his violent ways. He was in too deep of the abuse to change now. But his days were numbered.

The Speaker of the House, Patrick Warner, gave the walnut gavel three knocks on the round sound block to silence the applause. As the people were seated, Mr. Speaker said, "To the Members of Congress, I have the high privilege and distinct honor of presenting to you, the President of the United States." Another round of applause, then another standing ovation. *This* time, the standing ovation lasted five minutes straight. Kelissa was so overwhelmed by such a response. It gave her such a euphoric feeling that she could never explain—seeing all those different faces in the crowd, smiling, and cheering her on. Kelissa relished the undying attention. She could not help but love every second of it. Finally, Kelissa talked into the microphone, saying, "Thank you, thank you. You may be seated—please. Thank you so much." As Members of Congress took their seats, Kelissa took a few seconds to herself before addressing the nation.

After clearing her throat, Kelissa opened her binder and began her speech:

"First, I would like to thank Mr. Speaker, Patrick Warner, Mr. Vice President, Harry Griffin, Members of Congress, respected guests, and fellow Americans. As we mark this extraordinary occasion, I cannot begin to express my deeply rooted gratitude and appreciation for all of you. We have come together in this chamber to acknowledge our agreements, differences, victories, and lost battles. But we've come together this evening to hear the progress we've made in the last year. And we *definitely* have made progress. Our economy has skyrocketed, the best it has been in the last fifteen years. The American people are at work, jobs with respectable wages. Health care has never been stronger. *This* is the America that I've always dreamed of for our children. An America that gives everyone a chance at victory."

Another standing ovation emerged; hundreds of hands were clapping around the House chamber. In her mind, Kelissa was thinking, "*Okay*, so far, so good." A good minute passes before they take their seats. As the House goes silent, Kelissa continues:

"Our nation is shining bright. Small businesses have seen great success. The American people are building empires of their own, creating *their* American dream. And it's never too late to be a dreamer, *never*. But a nation of dreamers who are not *doers*, progress would never be made. And that is why we must *continue* to set an example of encouragement for the children of the future. We must give them the tools they need. We must give them *hope* for *not* just a better *tomorrow*, but a better today, a better *future*, and a better America."

The crowd *rose* again, standing with much applause. As Kelissa waits for the cheers to fade out, she proceeds with her speech:

"Now, we have had our differences, disagreements, debates, and refusals to compromise. But that's okay, there were times when I *did* think twice about certain decisions, but I should have taken that *third* thought before deciding. But I've learned from *my* mistakes that have cost our nation dearly. I admit that now. But one thing I know about this nation, the more we unite, the stronger we become, and the more prepared we are to bounce *back* from our casualties. I can say now that our troops are finally home—our sons and daughters have left Afghanistan, as war with that country has come to an end."

As the crowd applauded again, Kelissa felt slightly lightheaded by the waves of the standing ovation. But now, it was time for Kelissa to speak her mind about what she *truly* wanted to address. And that was her vision of a better America for the *women* of America:

"Our nation still has much work to do. There is certainly room for great progress, which leads me to the hard-working women who sacrifice a great deal in this country. For over two-hundred and forty-eight years, never has this country elected a woman to hold the most powerful chair in office. But thanks to the American people, *we* have remedied that."

Another standing ovation as congresswomen jumped up and cheered for joy. Kelissa had to wave her hand downwards to have everyone seated. Kelissa continued her speech:

"Women have multiple jobs in their lives. *We* are not only career women; we are mothers, wives, supporters, and *also* underpaid. The one-sided salaries where women have been short-changed their whole lives, that, in due time, shall find its remedy. I understand that nothing changes overnight. I understand that a man must be a man. But a man must understand that a *woman* is her own individual self and *NOT HIS PROPERTY*!"

The congresswomen cheered yet again as President Kelissa Morrison spoke on women's behalf. But Kelissa was nowhere near done. The more she said, the deeper she went:

"Women should have total control over their bodies—period. Abortion laws are conflicting, as some states hold firmly on their laws to ban abortion. I've said this before, and I will say that I *am* pro-life. *However*, I hold *no* judgments; I hold *no* grudges towards women who know what is best for them and their future. I don't judge; if choosing *not* to have a child is their decision, *that* is the very right they should have."

As congresswomen stood up again, Kelissa could see the delays of the men standing up. As the men were seated, sexism was rising. But Kelissa knew her voice was compelling and that she *had* to speak for *all* women. Kelissa then continued with her speech:

"I say what I say to say this. This is not to *dehumanize* or *degrade* our men or our sons. Not at all. This shows that *we*, as women, *have* a *voice*, and we have a *choice*. *So*, let us *use* our voice and *respect* our choice. Let us use our voice to speak our minds *and* make our *own* choices for *our* lives and what *we* choose to do with our bodies. 'Hear our voice and respect our choice.' I'll say that again, '*Hear* our voice and *respect* our choice.'

Nothing but tears and cheers as all the women in the House chamber stood tall as they idolized Kelissa standing there at the podium. Members of Congress *slowly* stood up, looking around to see if it was okay to applaud the President's speech. As Kelissa looked around, she saw Madeline clapping and crying; she looked as if she was so proud of her mother. Ted, however, had a different vibration. Kelissa saw the darkness within him from a distance. She knew what would possibly await her back home at the White House.

It was a night to remember for President Kelissa Morrison surely. As Kelissa concluded her speech, The standing ovation she received for such a historical moment in time took her breath away. So many of the congresswomen approached her with hugs and kisses. Nothing purer than love came in Kelissa's direction.

The Kelissa finally reached Madeline. She went straight to her mother, hugged her, and said in Kelissa's ear, "You are my hero, Mom. I know the pain you're going through, but you're the strongest woman I've ever known. I love you so much." Kelissa just closed her eyes as she let that sink in. She was finally able to rekindle the love between her and Madeline. It took some time, but the love was resurrected. Kelissa learned something from the dilemma with her daughter. She realized that the *truth* would always set her free. But Kelissa knew that freeing herself from Ted could and *will* come with a brutal price.

Chapter 44

Tuesday afternoon, February 11th, 2025

A Mother's Closure

As President Kelissa Morrison and the entire ensemble were in prayer, there was a moment of silence. Even though it was months ago, Kelissa kept her word that she would award three Medals of Honor to the children of Robin Vassallo, who lost their lives in both Iraq and Afghanistan.

As the prayer concluded, Kelissa made her way to the podium to make her speech. As Kelissa looked down at her sheet, she said:

"Good afternoon, ladies and gentlemen. Please, have a seat. First and foremost, I welcome you all to the White House. Today, I have an exceptional guest in attendance. I had the honor of meeting and talking with this remarkable, *powerful* human being, Robin Vassallo. Robin sent me this heartbreaking letter, sharing her story about how she lost all three of her children, who served and sacrificed their lives for their country.

Ms. Vassallo's letter reminded me of a woman named Lydia Bixby, who lost her sons in the American Civil War. I remember reading the letter written by President Abraham Lincoln that he sent to Mrs. Lydia Bixby. And I wanted to do the same. So, I sent a letter to Ms. Robin Vassallo and invited her to the White House and award all three of her late children: Matthew, Jessica, and Perry Vassallo, the Congressional Medal of Honor. It's complicated to grieve the loss of just *one* child. But to mourn all three *and* the loss of a husband—that's an undying pain. However, Robin Vassallo has shown me her unending *strength* and *will* to live on and keep her children's legacy alive. I also want to mention that the mental health of our troops is now a top priority, and I will see to it that it becomes a valuable resource for our active *and* veteran soldiers.

I know words cannot always help the pain of a lost loved one. Many parents have had their families changed overnight, hearing the devastating news of their fallen soldiers and living a new reality without them. I feel utterly responsible for the lives of the fallen soldiers, who several months ago lost their lives tragically in a rescue attempt in Afghanistan. A decision that I will forever regret as President.

Deciding to send off our sons and daughters, *knowing* that some may not make it back home, it's enough to make you stay up all night. And I've had *many* sleepless nights in the first year of my first term. As I move forward, I will continue to face complexity and have to make difficult decisions. I just pray that I will not cause the sudden heartbreak of any more families of our brave men and women who put their lives on the line for the liberty and justice of the American people. I also pray for *you*, Ms. Robin Vassallo. As we honor Matthew, Jessica, and Perry Vassallo today, I pray that this will give you a piece of closure and some peace in your heart. God bless you, and God bless the United States of America."

Kelissa then handed Robin Vassallo a two-foot rectangular plaque that held the three congressional Medals of Honor. It brought tears to Robin's eyes, seeing the beautifully decorated plaque with her children's names underneath the medals. Robin was very thankful to Kelissa for the honor of her late children. As the crowd gave a lingering round of applause, Kelissa and Robin held the plaque as the Press pool and White House photographer Georgette Wilson took their photo. As they stood there holding the plaque, Robin looked at Kelissa as she had something to say.

"Madam President," said Robin. "My children would be honored to have met you. Especially my darling, Jessica, seeing the first woman President. I'm forever grateful."

"Ms. Vassallo, it has been an *honor* to meet you. And *I'm* forever grateful to you for sending me that letter," Kelissa responded with a smile.

"You really make us women proud, Madam President. You are truly loved."

Kelissa smiled as she gave Robin a kiss and hug. What Robin said gave Kelissa the confirmation that she was appreciated and respected as a President. It reinstalled the confidence within her and that even though she made some mistakes as President, she was worthy of forgiveness and love.

Chapter 45

Friday Early Morning, February 14th, 2025

Oh No!

It is Valentine's Day once again. Last year's Valentine's Day did not go quite as well, as Ted spat on Kelissa. But *this* year, Kelissa was not planning on being Ted's Valentine. She is three days away from exposing everything she has gone through behind the scenes. All of the abuse: the mental, emotional, sexual, and physical destruction, will soon end.

It was very late, almost a quarter to one in the morning. Kelissa is in Madeline's room, both of them wearing matching white pajamas, listening to music, and spending quality time with each other. They were listening to a sixties rock band called 'The Doors.' Kelissa never heard much of *their* music before, as she is more of a *Beatles* fanatic. But she grew very curious about the lyrics.

"Sweetie," said Kelissa. "What's the name of this song?"

"It's called '*You're Lost Little Girl.*' It's one of my *favorites*," Madeline responded.

"I like the lyrics a lot. I feel like they're speaking clearly about me."

"You mean about telling the truth about dad?"

"Yes, and that's *exactly* what I'm going to do, first thing Monday morning. But I just *know* it's going to be crazy, sweetheart. And I have no idea how your father will react."

"He'll definitely try to deny it. Do you think he'll try to attack you?"

"In front of *Carl*? He wouldn't dare. But you know what? Let's not dwell on it anymore, okay? When Monday comes, I'll sit down with Carl in the Oval Office and tell him the truth. *Everything*. And I'm going to have to tell TJ and Bryan the truth as well. They are the ones who I'm worried about. I don't know how your brothers will respond. I'm just *so* sorry that you kids are involved in this foolishness."

"Mom, it's not your fault that dad has abused you. And he was trying to turn me against you. *I'm* sorry for the things I said to you and how I treated you."

"Aww, *baby*, it's okay," Kelissa said as she hugged Madeline. "I'm just *happy* that we're talking and that we have our bond again."

"I love you, mommy."

"Wow… I haven't heard you call me *mommy* since you were a little girl. I love you more… And for what it's worth, you will *always* be my little princess."

They lingered in time as they gracefully embraced with passion and forgiveness. Kelissa kissed Madeline's forehead and held her tight as they listened to the rest of the song. Kelissa was so happy to rekindle her bond with Madeline. And most importantly, Kelissa was relieved that she no longer had to keep her secret to herself and that she told the one person she *knew* she could trust more than anyone, her daughter.

Now it is 1:11 in the morning. Madeline had fallen asleep, but Kelissa was restless. So, she made her way to the kitchen to make herself a cup of tea. As she waited for the water to boil, she thought deeply about Monday morning. Kelissa felt the liberation running through her veins. The last three years were nothing but pure hell for her, and she was finally ready to escape from the nightmare and put Ted away for a very long time. Even though Kelissa wanted to tell Ted, Jr. about his abusive father, she refused to say a word to him until his father was arrested and in confinement. Kelissa was afraid that Ted, Jr. would try to attack his father for putting his hands on her.

As the water came to a full boil, Kelissa turned the stove off and poured herself a cup of tea. She dipped the tea bag up and down and then pressed it against the spoon to drain the remaining flavors into the cup. As Kelissa took a sip, she closed her eyes, enjoying the enriched peppermint taste.

Walking down the center hall to her private office, Kelissa looked to Bryan's bedroom door. She walked over to his bedroom and opened the door, peeking her head in to look at him. Just as Kelissa knew, Bryan's left arm and leg were hanging off the bed. She smiled as she walked over to Bryan's nightstand, where she put down her cup of tea. She then put his arm and leg under the covers and kissed him on the back of his head. "I love you, my darling boy," Kelissa softly said.

Kelissa then picked up her cup of tea and made her way across the center hall to her office. As she walked in, taking another sip, Kelissa sat at her desk, now in the mood to do some writing in her journal. But her journal was nowhere in sight. Kelissa looked all over in her office, but there was no sign of it. And that's when it hit her. She left it in the drawer of her nightstand in the bedroom from the other night and never took it out. Kelissa then got up from her desk, leaving her tea there as she headed to get her journal from the nightstand.

As Kelissa was in front of her bedroom door, she carefully opened it, as she did not want to wake up Ted. But as she walked into the bedroom, Ted was not there. There was, however, a bouquet of red roses and a heart-shaped box of chocolates on top of the bed. Kelissa looked at the roses and candy for a split second but then made her way to *her* side of the bed, where the nightstand was. As Kelissa stood next to her nightstand, she noticed her Blackberry was on top of it. She checked her Blackberry and saw a text from Ted, Jr. As Kelissa read the text message, it said:

"*Happy Valentine's Day, Mom. I love you to the moon and back.*"

That put such a smile on Kelissa's face. She wanted to respond but thought twice about responding because she did not want to wake Ted, Jr. But then Kelissa said to herself, "Oh, he's a college student; he's up right now." As Kelissa replied, she said:

"*Happy Valentine's Day, sweetie. I love you so very much. Also, I have something very important to tell you on Monday. So, if you can, come home and we'll talk about it. Love you, darling boy. Oh, I'm sorry, you're a man now. Won't happen again. LOL.*"

Kelissa then placed her phone back down on the nightstand and opened the drawer. But then, Kelissa quickly gagged as her journal was not there. "Oh, *God*, no," Kelissa quietly said. Her heart began to race as she knew *exactly* who had her journal. Then suddenly, out of the darkness of the dressing room, Ted appeared with a crazed look on his face. "Looking for *this*?" Ted said, holding up Kelissa's journal. Kelissa did not know what to say or do as she took back steps away from the bed. Ted *then* made his way to the bedroom door as he closed and locked it. Kelissa took one look at his face, and at that moment, she saw no Ted.

"I read *every single page*," Ted emotionally said, "You *dare* to open your fucking mouth? Do you think you're going to take me away from my *kids*? HUH?"

"Maddy knows, Ted. It's all over now."

"Oh, I think your absolutely right, Kel. It *is* over—but it's not over for *me*—it's over for *you*!"

Ted launched Kelissa's journal right to her face and speared her through the coffee table. He got on top of her as he began to choke her with all of his physical might. Kelissa had no physical strength that could compete with Ted. She gagged and gagged as she looked up at his face. He had the eyes of a devil, full of darkness and hatred, no soul whatsoever. Kelissa began to claw her nails into the skin of Ted's arms, trying to get him off of her. Suddenly, she looked to her left and saw a broken leg from the coffee table. It was in her reach to grab it. Kelissa reached for it, got a firm grip, and WHAM! Kelissa whacked Ted across the face with the broken leg.

Ted went tumbling over her. But Kelissa was too weak to get up and escape the bedroom. Ted, now bleeding from above his left eyebrow, picked Kelissa up by her arms, and for the very first time, he threw a haymaker punch, landing *directly* on her face. BAM! Kelissa went tumbling back and hit the floor. In a daze now, Kelissa was bleeding from her nose and lips. But Ted was not done with her. He wanted Kelissa to feel every ounce of pain he could, as his mission was to beat her to death.

BAM! POW! BOOM! Ted punched and kicked as he was *brutally* beating on Kelissa. Her face was becoming unrecognizable, but she still had some fight within her as she lifted her foot and kicked Ted directly in his testicles. "AHHH!" Ted screamed. He then fell to the floor as Kelissa made her way to her nightstand. But Ted grabbed her by her ankle, holding her back from reaching the panic button. He then punched Kelissa repeatedly on her back.

Ted turned her around and got on top of her—multiple slaps across her bloody face. As he was about to slap her for the fifth time, Kelissa grabbed his wrist and, with all her might, took a deep bite into his hand until it bled. "AAAHHHHH! GET THE *FUCK* OFF!" Ted screamed with his bloody hand. Kelissa then took her right foot and POW! Kicked Ted dead in his face as he went backward on the floor. Kelissa finally made it to the nightstand and pushed that panic button repeatedly like a concierge bell. She then grabbed her Blackberry and crawled across the bed, trying to make her way out of the bedroom.

"HELLLPPPPP, MAAAADDDDYYYY!" Kelissa screamed at the top of her lungs.

Kelissa grabbed the doorknob, twisting and turning, too panicky to realize the door was locked. Ted quickly grabbed Kelissa, choking her again so she would not make another sound. Then suddenly, another punch to her face, BOOM! Kelissa fell backward into the dressing room, with the falling Blackberry landing next to the bathroom door. Ted charged her and lifted her back up. Another punch to her body, BOOM! He then grabbed Kelissa by her arms and aggressively *threw* her into the six-foot mirror. Glass shattered all over as Kelissa fell straight to the floor. She instantly had cuts all over her body.

Now lying on the floor, brutally beaten and bloody, Kelissa had minimal fight left in her. But then, Ted did the unthinkable. He walked over to the broken six-foot mirror and tilted the heavy frame so that it would land on Kelissa. Kelissa screamed, "AHHHH!" But she swiftly rolled herself out of the way as the frame hit the floor. She then proceeded to crawl her way to the bathroom. Her white pajamas were torn and stained with her blood as her body was now brutally decorated with open wounds. As Kelissa cried in pain, Ted said to her, "I need you to *focus*, Kel! You're about to *die*! And it's all your fault. I don't care if they kill me too. But by *God*, I will find you in the afterlife, and I'll torment you for *all eternity*."

But Kelissa was not ready to die. There was a large, sharp piece of the shattered mirror beside her right hand. As Ted grabbed Kelissa's right shoulder to turn her around, she grabbed the sharp piece of the mirror and stabbed Ted in the side of his left thigh. "AAAHHHHH, *FUCK*! YOU *FUCKING BITCH*!" Ted screamed. The piece of the mirror was now stuck in his thigh. Kelissa quickly grabbed her Blackberry, crawled into the bathroom, and locked the door.

Kelissa is now stuck in the bathroom as Ted is screaming in pain on the dressing room floor. Kelissa proceeded to stand herself up at the sink. As she briefly looked at herself in the mirror, she was shocked at the horrifying image. She looked as if she was in a car accident or some kind of horror film. But this was reality. The blood was real as it began to freefall down into the sink.

Then suddenly, there was banging on the door. BANG! BANG! BANG! BANG! Ted repeatedly banged on the door as he shouted, "OPEN THE FUCKING DOOR, KEL. COME *DIE* LIKE A GOOD GIRL!" Kelissa immediately called the emergency number for Carl on her Blackberry. Her blood was seeping in between the keys of the Blackberry as she was dialing Carl's number. As Ted continued to bang on the door, Carl immediately answered the phone.

"Madam President!" Carl projected. "We're right outside your door. Are you *okay*?"

"Carl, oh *dear,* God, help me!" Kelissa cries. "Ted's going to kill me!"

"*JESUS CHRIST*!" Carl shouted as he dropped the phone.

Kelissa heard Carl's voice through the phone shouting, "CODE RED, WYRD!" The banging and kicking on the door aggressively continued. Kelissa moved as far away from the door as possible, moving to the far corner as she sat in a cradled position with her ears covered and her eyes closed. At that moment, all Kelissa could think about was her children and what would happen to them if Ted killed her. She began to pray out loud. "Oh, heavenly Father, hallowed be thy name," Kelissa cried. The pounding and kicking continued by Ted as he shouted at Kelissa. He then punched a hole through the door and looked through it.

"AAHHH!" Kelissa screamed. "HELP ME, *PLEASE*!"

"I HOPE YOU SAID YOUR *FUCKING* PRAYERS, BITCH!" Ted shouted with evil tensions.

Then suddenly, there was another loud noise. It was Carl, along with a dozen other Secret Service agents. Carl kicked the bedroom door down with his gun drawn as he was the first to walk into the unknown. As Carl called for the President, Ted knew that this was the end. Without hesitation, Ted picked up a piece of the broken mirror and began to charge at Carl, basically committing suicide.

Five quick shots: BANG! BANG! BANG! BANG! BANG! Kelissa jumped, crying as she heard the gunfire. Now, eerie silence as the five-hundred-pound gorilla in the room has been shot down. Kelissa's ears were ringing; she had no idea what was happening outside the bathroom. Then suddenly, through the ringing in her ears, she heard Carl's voice saying, "Madam President! Are you in there?" Kelissa screamed, "Carl, oh, *God*, Carl. I'm in here!" Kelissa crawled over to the bathroom door and unlocked it. She slowly stood up, dizzy as she opened the door—there was Carl. Kelissa immediately collapsed in his arms.

"H—*He* was really going to kill me, thi—this time," Kelissa said, slipping in and out of consciousness.

"Madam *President*, what do you *mean, "this*" time?" Carl responded.

"*Please* Carl, I—I can't talk anymore. Can you please ta—*take me* to th—the *hos*—hospital, *please*?"

"We're going! We're going right now!"

Agent Sam told Carl that Marine One was a minute away from landing on the South Portico lawn. Kelissa was in the worst shape ever. She could barely stand up as her body was covered in glass and blood. There was *no* time to waste. They had to get the President to the Walter Reed National Military Medical Center as soon as possible. So, Carl and Sam then picked Kelissa up to remove her from the deadly scene. Kelissa saw Ted lying on the dressing room floor, with the five bloody gunshot wounds to his chest, seeing only out of her one eye.

As Carl and Sam carried Kelissa out of the bedroom, Madeline began to scream at the very top of her lungs. She cried, "MOOOOMMMMM! What happened to her? What happened to my mom?" Bryan was hysterical as well. The other Secret Service agents held Madeline and Bryan back from the horrifying image as Carl and Sam carried Kelissa down the stairs, heading outside to Marine One. Kelissa was still slipping in and out of consciousness as they ran out of the White House, carrying her to Marine One. It was freezing as frost breath came out of Kelissa's swollen and bloody mouth. Carl, Sam, and several other Secret Service agents were on board with the President. "Take off, *right now*!" Carl shouted. That door closed and locked, and Marine One took off to the Walter Reed Medical Center. As Carl and Sam strapped Kelissa in securely, she began to speak.

"Ca—Carl?" Kelissa spoke with a broken voice.

"I'm here, Madam President," Carl responded.

"Is h-he, is he de—*dead*?"

"Yes, Madam President, he's dead."

"Te—Tell m—my *kids*, I—I *love* them, Carl. Be—because I'm not going to make it."

"Yes, you will! Just *hold on*, Madam President! We're almost at the hospital!"

Kelissa looked out of the window of Marine One. It was still dark out, as it was 1:55 in the morning. She saw the beautiful lights of Washington D.C., not sure if this would be the last time she would see the enchanted architectural beauty of the nation's capital.

Kelissa began to slip into unconsciousness. Carl and Sam were trying everything in their power to keep her awake. But time was not on their side as she began to drift away. "Madam President, *stay* with me, *please*! *Stay* with me, okay?" Carl projected as he was getting emotional. As Kelissa extended her bloodied hand, the last thing she said to Carl before she went unconscious was, "Go—*Goodbye*, Carl, and Godspeed."

Chapter 46

Friday Early Morning, February 14th, 2025

Life Is but A Dream

Hazy vision as President Kelissa Morrison gained some consciousness. Kelissa, now looking up at the ceiling, blurry light after blurry light as she is being carefully pushed in a stretcher down the Walter Reed Medical Center hallway. The doctors have to work fast as they push Kelissa down to the operating room, where they'll put her under anesthesia.

Because Carl is the head detail leader of protecting the President, he must remain with the President at all times. But Carl was entirely oblivious of Kelissa being abused by Ted—clueless and at a loss for words.

"Wait!" Carl shouted to Sam. "Have the Vice President and the Chief of Staff been notified of our current situation?"

"Yes, they're on their way here right now," Sam responded.

"Oh, Jesus… This is *not* happening; this is *so* not fucking happening."

"What are we going to do now, Carl?"

"Once Mr. Vice President and the Chief of Staff gets here, we have to invoke the Twenty-Fifth Amendment."

The Twenty-Fifth Amendment only becomes a priority *if* the President has been impeached, feels significant illness, is in danger, or has already been declared dead and can no longer fulfill their duties. Afterward, the *Vice* President will be *immediately* sworn in as the President's successor. Kelissa is about to go under anesthesia, so Vice President Harry Griffin has to be prepared to be next in line to take control, just in case things go left.

As the doctors pulled Kelissa into the operating room, they immediately switched her onto another table and placed her under anesthesia. Kelissa is now conscious as the doctor wipes her bloody arm off, sterilizing it to inject the needle. "Madam President, we're going to take care of you. We're going to take *good* care of you, okay? You just hang in there," said the doctor. As the doctor injected the anesthesia in Kelissa's arm, all she could think about at that moment were her kids. Kelissa had no idea if she was going to make it or not.

But her only concern was knowing if her children would be safe if she did not pull through.

The anesthesia was beginning to kick into Kelissa's bloodstream. She felt a sudden calmness as the pain started to fade, and her one eye was growing heavy. All of what she went through, Kelissa had some strength to say one last thing before slipping back into unconsciousness. "Doc—Doctor… *Please* tell my ch—*children*—that I love them."

Kelissa fell asleep and began to dream. She started to see things in her dream that she had not thought about in years. She dreamt about spending time with her grandparents during the summertime at Baker Beach in San Francisco when she was a little girl. Kelissa and her grandfather would fly her kite all day long as her grandmother would take pictures of the two of them, with the Golden Gate Bridge in the background. Kelissa's grandfather would lift her and spin her around. She would laugh and enjoy every second of it. Her parents were always busy with work, but her *grandparents* were the parents she always wanted.

Then another dream occurred. Kelissa was dreaming about the time Ted, Jr. was born. It was the most exciting moment of her life. Kelissa remembered holding Ted, Jr. as his little body peacefully slept in her arms. It was a beautiful June afternoon that day. Kelissa was never happier.

Forty-five minutes into the operation, Kelissa was far away in her dream world. But the doctors were busy at work on her body, as she had suffered *significant* bruises and multiple opened wounds. There were *dozens* of fragments of the glass mirror pierced all over her body that the doctors removed one by one. Her nose was broken, as was her left cheekbone and some busted lips. She also suffered two minor lacerations on the back of her head—from being thrown into the mirror.

As Kelissa was still dreaming, the dreams transformed into the darkest of nightmares. She began to dream about Ted, but the dream was so twisted. At first, her dream of Ted started at their wedding. Kelissa was so beautiful in her exquisite wedding gown, walking down the aisle as Ted waited for her at the altar. And when she finally reached the altar, she reached for Ted's hand, and he reached for hers. As they stood facing each other, they said their vows and kissed. The crowd began to cheer for them. Kelissa smiled, as did Ted. Then suddenly, the cheering stopped immediately. As Kelissa looked around, she could not understand why people stopped cheering and were looking at her in sudden shock. She then looked at Ted, who was no longer smiling but had that same demonic look that he had every time he attacked her. Ted said, "You're bleeding. Don't you like to bleed?" That is when Kelissa looked down and noticed a knife deeply pierced in her stomach as the blood began to turn her white dress completely red. Kelissa then ran down the aisle as she continued to bleed while the crowd started to laugh. Ted then shouted, "You're *dying*! Don't you want to *die*?" The heart monitor began to go rapidly as the nightmare began to haunt her. But the doctors kept working, doing everything in their power to save the President.

An hour and a half later, the doctors were eighty percent complete with the surgery. Vice President Harry Griffin, the Chief of Staff, Andrew Crane, Press Secretary, Lesley Richards, Secretary of Defense, General Blake Talley, and a judge to administer the oath of office were *all* in the waiting room. Since President Kelissa Morrison is in surgery, Vice President Harry Griffin was immediately sworn in as acting President under the Twenty-Fifth Amendment.

As the television was on, *every* news channel went into a complete and utter frenzy. It was non-stop pandemonium as breaking news coverage was an insane, chaotic, catastrophic warzone. People had not a *clue* of what had happened to the President. However, news channels were coming up with *their* conclusions as they showed multiple postings on the showrunners:

"PRESIDENT KELISSA MORRISON ASSASSINATED!"

"THE PRESIDENT IS DEAD!"

"FIRST WOMAN U.S. PRESIDENT, KELISSA MORRISON, DEAD AT 48!"

"MURDER AT 1600 PENNSYLVANIA AVENUE, THE PRESIDENT HAS BEEN ASSASSINATED!"

"ST. VALENTINE'S DAY MASSACRE: THE PRESIDENT ASSASSINATED!"

The entire world was outrageously losing control. No one knew what the hell was going on as there were no available details. Dozens of News vans were parked outside of the White House. White House Chief of Staff, Andrew Crane, had pulled Press Secretary Lesley Richards to the side to speak with her.

"Madam Secretary," said Andrew. "We *have* to make a statement right now. People now believe President Morrison is *dead*."

"I know," Lesley responded. "But the doctors are still operating on her. We have no idea what condition she's in. The press will have a shit load of questions that we *don't* have the answers for."

"We cannot wait any *longer*, Madam Secretary! The *world* thinks the first woman U. S. President is *DEAD*!"

"I *know*, you *don't* have to repeat it. Oh, *God*… This—this just is not *happening*," Lesley emotionally spoke.

"I don't want to believe it either. But it's *real*. And we *really* have to make a statement.

"God, help us all."

Another hour and a half had gone by. The sun had begun to rise, and President Kelissa Morrison had survived. She has a long journey of recovery ahead of her, but she survived. Press Secretary Lesley Richards has stated the President's current situation. She addressed not just the nation but the whole *world* to inform them that the President was, in fact, still alive. But what Lesley left out was that Ted, the First Gentleman, was attempting to kill her. Lesley also confirmed that the

Twenty-Fifth Amendment was invoked, and Vice President Harry Griffin was officially acting President.

Eight Secret Service agents were standing guard of Kelissa as she was now heavily sedated and on the road to recovery. Her face was bandaged up, looking as if she was mummified. The doctors did an MRI and a CT scan to look and see if there was any internal damage, and there was. Kelissa also suffered two hairline fractures to her ribs, but the fractured ribs were actually fractured weeks *prior* by Ted's previous attacks. Kelissa also suffered a sprained neck and multiple contusions in her legs.

President Kelissa Morrison was highly blessed to have made it out of this situation alive. The doctor said that the piece of broken mirror that was deeply pierced in Kelissa's back was an inch away from her intercostal arteries, and had that *one* piece of glass hit that artery, Kelissa would have internally bled to death.

Chapter 47

Friday Morning, February 14th, 2025

The Aftermath of Abuse

The President has come to, as her right eye has opened. Still lingering in the sedation, she could see a blurry vision of the eight Secret Service agents as they guard the room. Even though Kelissa could not see so well, she could hear everything.

As Kelissa lay there in the hospital bed, she heard screams. The louder the screams, the closer the person was getting to her. As she listened, she realized that it was Ted, Jr's voice, *screaming* at the top of his lungs, saying, "WHERE'S MY MOM? I NEED TO SEE MY

MOM, *NOW*!" Madeline and Bryan were right behind him. The Secret Service agents had to do everything to hold the three of them back. Looking through the glass wall, seeing their mother in the hospital bed, they screamed and sobbed at her tormented sight. Secret Service understood their pain but was given orders *not* to permit anyone inside the room except the doctors.

Kelissa heard it all. As she lay there, she became very emotional as a bloody tear fell down the side of her face. She has never been so hurt before in her life. Her kids had to see her *fighting* for her life, and knowing that Ted, Jr., and Bryan had *no* idea of the abuse she was suffering from at the hands of their father. All they wanted to do was hold their mother's hand and comfort her. But since she is the President, she had to be protected, even from her children.

As Kelissa lay there, she suddenly had this overwhelming epiphany. She realized that she had no contact with her parents and that she *knew* her mother and father were probably hysterical and in shock. Barely moving, Kelissa tried to raise her arm to get someone's attention. But the Secret Service agents' backs were facing the glass wall. She then looked around to see if there was a button she could push to get a nurse. But, in the nick of time, a doctor was permitted in the room. As Kelissa raised her hand, the doctor came over to check on her.

"Madam President," said the doctor. "Careful—*hold on*, take it *easy*. Don't move so fast."

"Whe—where… *Where* am I?" Kelissa said, still sedated.

"You're safe now, ma'am. You're in Walter Reed Medical Center."

"My kids, I want m—my *kids*."

"Yes, Madam President. I'll let them know right away. How about some television?"

As the doctor clicked on the television, Kelissa began to watch the news as she waited for her children. Her face was on the television screen as reporters stood outside the Walter Reed Medical Center. The press was creating the most absurd narratives of what happened to her. Some were saying that Kelissa was poisoned, that it was an assassination attempt by Russia, or that it was an inside job. As Kelissa continued to look on at the news, all she could think was, "Oh my God, what have I done?"

Five minutes went by, Kelissa's children had finally come to the room with Press Secretary Lesley Richards, Carl, and now *acting* President Harry Griffin. Ted, Jr. was so upset. He fell to his knees, crying his eyes out as he held onto his mother's right hand while Madeline and Bryan were standing on the left side of her bed. As Ted, Jr. held on to Kelissa's *right* bandaged hand, Bryan held onto Kelissa's left.

Kelissa, now holding Bryan's hand, began to do something. She took her thumb and began to press down on Bryan's thumb. Bryan had no idea what Kelissa was trying to do with her thumb. He looked up at Madeline and said, "What's mommy *doing*, Maddy?" As Madeline looked down at their hands, she cried and said, "Sh—she's playing *thumb wrestling* with you, Bry." An emotional Bryan then kissed his mother's hand and cried his little eyes out. Kelissa did her best to smile, though most of her face was covered by the bandaging.

"Madam President," said Lesley, "We had to invoke the Twenty-Fifth Amendment. VP Griffin is now our acting President."

"My—My parents," Kelissa responded.

"We notified your parents—informed them that you were *not* assassinated. They were placed on the first flight out."

Acting President Harry Griffin walked up to Kelissa, devasted as he said, "I am *so sorry* that you were going through all of this, behind the scenes of everything. But you are *so* strong. The strongest woman I've ever known. You get well, Madam President. I'll take care of everything until you get back on your feet." Harry then carefully leaned down to kiss Kelissa on her temple. Kelissa looked at Harry, grateful to have such a faithful partner to help run the nation.

They all stood there, comforting Kelissa as best as they could. She began to wonder what was next for her. Ted is gone, and her abusive nightmare is now over. As the road to recovery was months ahead, her fate at regaining power as the *President* was a colossal mystery.

Chapter 48

Saturday Evening, March 1st, 2025

Camp David with the Children

It is a snowy Saturday evening at the Camp David resort. Kelissa has been transported to the now heavily guarded Aspen lodge to continue her recovery. Ted, Jr, Madeline, and Bryan stayed with her until further notice. Kelissa also had private doctors and nurses on standby to help assist her, but her children ensured they were there for her. As Kelissa lay in bed, she wanted to speak to her children, one at a time, to let them know what exactly happened. Because Ted, Jr. was the oldest and had no idea of his father's abusive history, Kelissa wanted to speak to him first.

Kelissa's face healed up naturally, and some bandages were taken off. But still, she had a long way to go. She could now see out of both eyes and communicate well enough. As Ted, Jr. came into bedroom number one, the main bedroom, Kelissa was sitting up in the bed, wearing navy blue pajamas, and was ready to have that tough conversation with her firstborn.

"Hey, Mom." Ted, Jr. spoke. "How are you feeling?"

"I'm hanging in there, sweetie. How about yourself?" Kelissa responded.

"I'm not doing too good, mom, to be honest with you."

"I know; you need answers, baby. Come, sit next to me."

As Ted, Jr. grabbed the chair, he sat next to his mother, and she began to explain to him how this all started. "Your father started attacking me back in 2022 when I announced my presidential run. He didn't believe that a woman should have such a powerful position. At first, he begged me not to run. But after a while, the begging stopped, and the beating began. Some nights when you and Maddy and Bryan were having sleepovers at your friend's house, your father would attack me, hitting and kicking me at every chance he had. There were times I was *literally* running for my life in our house. And this has been going ever since." Ted, Jr. looked at his mother with a mask of confusion. Still, he needed more than that.

"But, mom, why would you *stay* with him after all of that? *Why*?" Ted, Jr. asked.

"Sweetheart, that is an answer I'm afraid I don't have," Kelissa responded.

"Didn't something tell you just to leave? Why would you stay with a man who would beat you over and over?"

"I don't know. There was so much going on. I had the presidential run, the campaign, the debates, everything. I guess I was just so determined to make history. I thought I could handle it all. Being President, the abuse, I thought your father would eventually—"

"*Please*, don't *ever* refer to him as my father—*ever* again. He was a goddamn *monster*. And he's lucky that he's dead now because I would have killed him myself."

"Oh, baby, *oh baby*... That is why I kept it all hidden from you, children. I didn't want *anything* bad happening to *any* of you. I didn't want you to attack your own father."

"But *why*, mom? *Why* would you *stay* with such an evil man?"

"Because I was foolish, honey. I cared more about making history as the first woman President. I wanted that more than *anything*. But I was too stupid to realize the reality of that coming with a price to pay."

"Well, he's gone now... But why am I still upset?" Ted, Jr. suddenly cried.

"Oh, baby, it's okay, come here."

Even though Ted, Jr. still had much anger towards his father for what he did to his mother, he still deep down inside misses him. The sudden impact of a man he loved, his first superhero, now dead—Ted, Jr. felt that he lost a piece of himself.

As Kelissa continued to talk with Ted, Jr., she had something vital to share with him, which would stick with him for the rest of his life. "TJ, sometimes in life, we make decisions that will create a terrible outcome that'll change us forever. I decided to stay with your fath—with *him*, and that created a terrible outcome that I will forever regret. When he hit me that first time, that should have been it. He should have been gone by then. But then, where would that leave *you* guys? I would *never* have wanted you guys to grow up without your father. But now, that's exactly what's going to happen… *Goddamn* it!"

Ted, Jr. was startled by his mother's sudden outburst. "Mom, are you okay?" Ted, Jr. asked. As Kelissa wiped her eyes, she said, "I'm sorry, I just feel *so terrible*. I made a *horrible* decision—maybe if I had just *listened* to him. If I didn't run for President, we would still have our family. But I was selfish. *I* destroyed our family because I wanted *power*. I wanted to be a hero to women *all over* the world. But instead, I'm nothing more but a fucking fraud, and I took your father away from us."

A sobbing face as Kelissa cried. But Ted, Jr. had something to get off of his chest. "I can't *believe* you are blaming *yourself*. Mom, he was *abusing* you, *beating* on you. *He* wanted the power, but he couldn't take the fact that *you* had that power. Don't ever, *ever* blame *yourself*." Kelissa looked at her son, smiling as she appreciated his love and care for her.

"I guess I needed to hear that," Kelissa said.

"Mom, you are the bravest woman I know—the *strongest,* and for you to hold onto this secret, even though it was killing you. I don't know if I would have had the strength."

"You know, you look so much like him."

"I would *never* be like him."

"No, of course, you won't. You're going to be the *better* version of who your father *should* have been. But you'll be your own man, and you'll follow your own heart."

"I'll do my very best. I love you, Mom."

"I love you more, and more, and more, every day, sweetie."

As Ted, Jr., and Kelissa finished their conversation, Kelissa told him to send for his brother as she wanted to speak privately with Bryan. A few minutes went by, and Bryan finally came into the room. "Hey, honey. Come sit next to momma," Kelissa softly said. As Bryan sat next to her on the bed, they talked briefly.

"How are you feeling, mommy?" Bryan asked.

"Well, I was doing *fine,* but now my leg hurts," Kelissa responded.

"Oh, do you need ice?"

"No, I need you to get off my leg; you're sitting on it," Kelissa grinned.

"Oh, sorry, mommy."

"That's okay… So, how are *you* feeling?"

"I feel sad and confused. I'm never going to see daddy again."

"Yes, sweetie, I know. I'm sorry, sport. You didn't deserve this."

"Well, neither did *you*, mommy. Daddy was a bad man who hurt you."

"Yeah, he did."

"Why did he do it, mommy? Why did he hurt you?"

"Because I let him. I let him get away with hurting me because of my own selfish agenda. I know you may not understand all of this now. But when you get older, we'll come back to this conversation. Okay?"

"Okay… Are you still going to be the President?"

"Well, Mr. Harry Griffin is now filling in for me until I get back on my feet. And then after I recover, I will step back in as sitting President."

"Being President is tough, huh?"

"That it is, sweetie. Besides being a mother, it's the toughest job I ever had."

Bryan gently hugged and kissed his mother and then headed out. Before Bryan left, he turned around and said, "Mommy, do you regret all of this?" Kelissa looked at Bryan from the bed and responded, "That's a great question, honey. Maybe a few years from now, I'll have an answer for you. Tell Maddy that I want to see her, okay?"

As Kelissa was in bed, her eyes grew heavy as she felt drowsy from the medication. But she still wanted to speak with Madeline. A few minutes later, Madeline entered the bedroom—now laying on the bed with her mother, she placed her head on Kelissa's left shoulder.

"*Ouch*!" Kelissa grunted. "Oh, sweetie, not on my shoulder."

"Oh, I'm sorry, Mom. Here, is that better?" Madeline said as she adjusted the pillows.

"*Yes*," Kelissa sighed. "Thank you."

"So, how are you feeling?"

"Like I was hit by a car a few weeks ago."

"I just can't believe it, Mom. I can't believe he was going to kill you."

"I *knew* it was coming sooner or later. That's why I was going to tell Carl that Monday. But I guess I should have said something years ago."

"I'm just glad he's dead."

"Oh, sweetheart. *No*, no, no. That's a *terrible* thing to say."

"But mom—"

"No! Your father had some serious problems, yes. Problems that *I* didn't even know about. He told me that *his* father used to beat on his mother."

"What?"

"Yeah, he would watch his father abuse his mother consistently—to the point where he thought it was just *normal* for a man to beat on a woman."

"I didn't know that about him."

"Your father went through a lot, sweetie."

"But wait a minute, *no*! He tried to turn me against you. He told me that *you* were the one abusing *him*."

"I *know*, Maddy. But listen, he's *never* going to attack me again. That part of the nightmare is over now. *Now*, we just have to find some healing for *all* of us."

"How are we going to do that, Mom?"

"One day at a time, sweetie. Just one day at a time."

"Is it okay if I stay in here with you tonight?"

"Of course, it is, sweetie. I could go for a *slumber party*," Kelissa smiled.

"One day at a time, huh?" Madeline said as she held Kelissa's hand.

"That's right, baby girl, one day at a time."

Chapter 49

Tuesday Afternoon, March 18th, 2025

Welcome Back, Madam President

The wounds have healed, the physical pain is fading, and President Kelissa Morrison has been granted back her power and duties as President of the United States of America. Because Kelissa had to undergo anesthesia immediately and was slipping in and out of consciousness, there was no time for her to write a letter to the Speaker of the House of Representatives to invoke section 3 of the Twenty-Fifth Amendment of the United States Constitution. But as Kelissa was able to get back on her feet, Harry Griffin gladly returned power over to Kelissa and returned to his role as the Vice President of the United States of America.

Today, at 3 o'clock sharp, President Kelissa Morrison will address the nation. For the first time, she will speak publicly about what happened to her in the early morning of Valentine's Day. As she waits in the Oval Office, she is greeted by Carl. "Madam President, we're soon to head over to the cross hall," Carl said. Kelissa asked Carl to have a seat, as she wanted to have a few words with him. As he sat on one of the couches, Kelissa sat across from him, and they had a conversation.

"Carl, I owe you an enormous apology," Kelissa said with guilt.

"Madam President, you owe me nothing," Carl responded.

"Oh, *yes*, I *do*. In fact, I owe *everyone* an apology."

"No, actually, I owe *you* an apology. I should have known. I should have picked up on all the red flags. Every time he always wanted to speak to you in private. I gave you your privacy because I thought it was about personal things. But I should have known better. All my years in Secret Service, I should have known that *that* was the red flag. But he was your *husband*; there was nothing I could do. I've failed you, Madam President. I'm so sorry."

Kelissa looked at Carl as he began to get emotional. She never saw him or *any* Secret Service agent break down in tears. Suddenly, she realized that even though their job is very serious, these men and women are still human beings at the end of the day.

Kelissa sat next to Carl, held his hand, and said, "Carl, *please* don't blame yourself. I did *not* properly handle this situation at all. I hid it from everyone. *Every* bruise, *every* mark, *every* wound, I wanted *no one* to know what was happening to me. But that was very, *very* stupid on my part. There were many nights where I thought he was going to…"

Carl looked at Kelissa as she stopped talking. "Madam President, you were saying?" Carl said. "Oh, I'm sorry, I completely had a brain fart. I was just saying that Ted was tempting to kill me on multiple occasions, and I said nothing. That was a terrible decision on my behalf, and I'm sincerely sorry. I could have put *all* of your careers at risk. But listen, that part is all over now; he's gone."

As the time was almost three in the afternoon, Carl and Kelissa made their way towards the cross hall. Today, there are even more Secret Service agents guarding Kelissa everywhere she goes. Before going live in front of the world, Press Secretary Lesley Richards had Kelissa step inside one of the powder rooms where Stella and Beatrice were waiting to do her hair and makeup. Even though the wounds on her body were healed, there were still markings and bruises on Kelissa's face that needed to be covered. As Kelissa sat down in the chair, she looked at herself in the mirror and thought, "No more hiding this." She stopped Stella and Beatrice and told them she was not putting on any makeup. Kelissa then went to the sink and began to rinse her face, removing all the makeup so that she could reveal the aftermath of what she brutally endured.

"Okay, are we ready to go—Madam *President*," Lesley said with confusion. "Wait, wha—what are you doing?'

"I'm done with hiding this. The world needs to know what domestic violence looks like—it's *real*."

"Oh... Madam President, I understand where you're coming from, *one hundred* percent. But we *cannot* have you looking like you just left a boxing match. If the world sees *any* sign of weakness, that could cause issues for us in the future. I *strongly* suggest that we cover up the bruises before you go live."

"Madam Secretary, I've been covering these goddamn bruises for the last *three years*. And quite frankly, I'm tired of hiding. I'm *sick* and *tired* of covering up my pain *just* because I'm a woman. The world needs to see this—*women* need to see this. Women need to see that domestic violence can find *anyone*, even the most powerful woman on the planet. This is *no* way for us women to exist on this earth. By showing my face with these bruises, I will put the truth out there and *set* many women free. They'll *never* have to hide their bruises again."

"Madam President, I *beg* of you, plea—"

"That is *final*, Madam Secretary!"

"Yes, ma'am."

"I'm ready."

It was three o'clock, and President Kelissa Morrison was due to make a public speech. As she stood in the Green Room, she took a look at herself in one of the mirrors. At that moment, looking at the mirror, she had a sudden flashback of Ted throwing her into the six-foot mirror that was in her dressing room. From time to time, Kelissa would have those flashbacks. She understood that even though the physical wounds would eventually heal, the mental and emotional wounds would unfortunately take years. "Madam President, you're on. Good luck," said Lesley. Kelissa took a deep breath, exhaled, and made her way out to the podium.

The cameras sounded as if it was fireworks going off. There were literally *hundreds* of people in the Press pool, snapping away at their cameras. As Kelissa walked towards the podium, she had a slight limp to her walk. Her administration wanted to postpone her making a speech. But as Kelissa said, she was no longer hiding the hurt inside. Kelissa opened up her binder and read her speech as she stood at the podium:

"Good afternoon, ladies and gentlemen.

Welcome to the White House. I thank you for coming at such short notice. But I felt that it was important I share with you all the truth. As you know now, I was, *in fact*, attacked, *here*, inside the White House. As you can see on my face, there are bruises. I suffered a broken nose, a broken cheekbone, and some fractured ribs. Now for some of you who created this narrative of it being an inside job. Well, I would say that you were on the right *track*, but it goes even more profound. My husband, the First Gentleman, Ted Morrison, was abusing me for the last three years."

As soon as Kelissa said that, the Press pool was in complete shock, gasping and gagging as they looked at Kelissa in disbelief. Kelissa then continued her speech:

"Yes, ladies and gentlemen, you heard me correctly. My husband was abusing me behind the scenes. Some of the things he did to me are just too graphic, and I'd rather not share them. But I'm here to say that domestic violence is very, *very* real. That is why I show my bruised face, to show you what it looks like. It is not to be taken lightly, but to be taken seriously. I do not wish this onto *any* woman or *man* for that matter. I've been hiding this secret from everyone for the last three years. I covered all of the bruises—hid them under layers of clothing; I hid the pain, I hid everything. I'm not hiding this any longer. My husband is now deceased, as you may already know. He will *never* attack me again.

But I'm very fortunate to have survived that horrible Valentine's Day morning as he tried to kill me. He wanted to kill me numerous times, and I made some very immature decisions by keeping him around. I did that because I was afraid. Afraid to lose everything that I and my campaign worked *so hard* for. I was seduced by the power and wanted to have the perfect image as the first woman President in United States history. I was too afraid to fail. But in the end, I *did* fail. I put a lot of people's careers and lives on the line. Just because I wanted that power, I wanted that power more than *anything*. I wanted the world to see a *woman* do the impossible. And for that, I paid a high price."

There was much eerie silence in the East Room. All you could hear were the clicks of the cameras, nothing more. Kelissa then turned to the last page of her speech and proceeded:

"This is my testimony, ladies and gentlemen. And I say this to you women out there who are dealing with similar circumstances. You are *never* alone; do you hear me? You are not alone. And I understand that it is not *easy* to walk away from domestic violence. Statistically, it takes women on average eight or nine attempts before they finally leave their abuser. I *understand* that it is not easy just to pack your bags and leave him. I understand when your abuser is also the *father* of your children, and he won't leave you alone. I understand how they will *follow* you *everywhere* you go. I know, and I understand. But I *also* know that things will *not* get better if you *stay* with your abuser. They are only destined to get worse. So, I *beg* of you women out there; I beg you to my *soul* to get some help. Tell someone; that's the first step. Tell a friend, a family member, a neighbor, someone you trust. Do *not* stay with him. And when time permits, leave and *never* look back. And for you young women, if your significant other lays a *finger* on you that *first time*, let it be the very *last* time and get away from him. Because I *guarantee* you that there will be more attacks if you stay.

I understand that this is not normal for a President. This is not everyday politics; I know this has nothing to do with democracy. But this *has* to stop. The sexism in our society, treating women as if they are beneath men. This is no way for women to exist in this world. We should not be attacked by the men we once loved, who are also our children's fathers. But to be very clear, this is not to *marginalize* men or assume that *all* men are abusers. I know there are *great* men who are productive citizens in society. There are, in fact, men who are victims *and* survivors of domestic violence as well. And that, *too,* is unacceptable. Women should never put their hands on men.

As President, I will do *everything* in my power to make sure that women *and* men are protected by this behavior of evilness we call domestic violence. As I conclude this statement, I would like to apologize to my children, my administration, and lastly, *all* of you for my lies, deceitfulness, selfishness, and hunger for power. I pray that you all find it in your hearts to forgive me. I thank you all. God bless you, and God bless the United States of America."

Chapter 50

Monday Afternoon, March 24th, 2025

The Second Interview

They meet again; President Kelissa Morrison and journalist Catherine Chang sit down for their second interview. And this time, there is *much* to talk about. No time was wasted as the camera crew and producers were ready to go. Catherine Chang was seated, waiting for the President to enter the East Room. Kelissa is coming into this interview with a chip on her shoulder after asking Catherine to remove the last part of the interview where she cried on camera. But that part stayed in the final cut.

As Kelissa had the final touches of her hair and makeup done, she was ready to get the interview rocking and rolling. "Are we ready to go?" Kelissa said to the producers. The cameras were rolling, and Kelissa began to walk into the East Room and took her seat across from Catherine. "Hello, Madam President, thank you so much. It's great to see you again," Catherine said as she greeted Kelissa.

As they both sat comfortably, Catherine looked at the President, noticing some of the markings and scars on the President's legs. "It's not polite to *stare*, Catherine," Kelissa said as she gave Catherine a stern look. Catherine then apologized and carried on with the interview.

"Madam President, how are you doing these days?" Catherine asked.

"I'm doing better, Catherine. I'm taking it one day at a time," Kelissa responded.

"That's good to hear. *So*, the last time we sat down like this and had an interview was, I believe, over a *year* ago?"

"Has it been a *year* already? Time surely flies, doesn't it?"

"It sure does."

"Yeah, you know, I remember *specifically* telling you to edit out that part where I was getting emotional. But you *didn't*."

"I *suggested* to the editing team to have it removed. But they decided to keep it in because it made you look more human."

"*I* thought it made me look *weak*. But okay, I had a feeling it would make the final cut."

"*So*, not too long ago, you experienced one of the most *horrifying* moments in Presidential history. Your husband was abusing you on multiple occasions."

"That is correct."

"And you were covering it up for the past three years."

"That is *also* correct."

"Why?"

"Well, Catherine, that's a loaded question… *Why*? Because I thought I knew what I was doing. I felt that I could *handle* it—the abuse. But I was very wrong."

"Do you blame yourself for what happened?"

"Are you *only* going to ask me about the abuse?"

"No, Madam President. I have other questions about other topics."

"Alright, just wanted to know."

"Alright, so *obviously*, maybe I owe you an apology about the *first* interview."

"Oh, no apologies necessary."

There was a bit of tension building between President Kelissa Morrison and Catherine. The producers sensed the tainted vibe through the camera and asked to take a break. Kelissa made her way to the restroom to cool herself off.

As Kelissa entered the restroom, she began to pace back and forth with her arms folded, looking down as she was starting to think. Over the years, Kelissa has become less and less of a fan of interviews as she hates *not* having control over the final cut. A few moments later, Catherine Chang entered the restroom. And by surprise, she saw the President was inside and proceeded to have a brief conversation.

"Madam President," said Catherine. "I understand that talking about the abuse you went through with your husband is a very touchy topic. And I don't want to step on any eggshells and offend you."

"No, Catherine—it's not you, seriously. It's me… I've talked with my children, my administration, and they tell me that I shouldn't blame myself. But I *do*. I should have said something a long time ago. And I just don't want my legacy to be remembered as a *weak* woman who only received praise because she was a *victim* of domestic violence. But I don't feel like a victim at all."

Catherine stood there, looking at Kelissa with sorrow and sympathy. But Catherine had a different opinion for Kelissa as she said, "You're *right*, Madam President. You're *not* a victim. *You* are a survivor—*you survived* a brutal, violent, toxic relationship. I can't even begin to *imagine* what your husband did to you behind closed doors. Don't you understand? By surviving domestic violence, you give *millions* of women worldwide *hope*, *hope* that there is a way out of their abusive situation. I don't see you as a victim, and I don't *treat* you like one. I see you as a *survivor*. And I *commend* you for going public with your story. But you *have* to share your story with honesty."

Kelissa was touched by what Catherine said to her. As she looked at her, Kelissa smiled and said, "I guess I misunderstood you. You're *not* just some journalist who is hungry for a story. You actually have a heart." Kelissa hugged Catherine and then headed back out to finish the interview. As final touches of hair and makeup were applied to both Kelissa and Catherine, they were ready for round two.

"Five, four, three, two, one, action!" said the producer. Catherine then continued with the interview. All smiles as the tension between them mellowed down and faded out. Catherine began with this question.

"*So*, are we okay now?"

"We're okay, Catherine. We're okay," Kelissa smiled.

"Okay… *So*, you went through something recently with your late husband, Ted. He was abusing you behind the scenes, yes?"

"Correct, yes."

"And how long had this been going on for?"

"Three years, ever since I started my presidential run."

"Okay, so, take me through what you went through, tell me exactly what your late husband did to you."

Kelissa looked at Catherine and began to think about the dark memories of Ted's abusive behavior. Just *thinking* about her painful past, her body quivered. But Kelissa knew she had to tell her story, and just as Catherine said, she had to be honest. "Ted was a *monster*, a demon at times. There were times when he would beat me so badly that I had to wear layers of clothing just so no bruises would be revealed. I can't recall how many times he punched me and kicked me. Sometimes he threw me to the ground and kicked me repeatedly. I couldn't breathe, I couldn't talk, I couldn't do anything. It was horrible, Catherine… Absolutely horrible," Kelissa said.

As Catherine sat there, looking at Kelissa tell her story of abuse, she could not help breaking her professionalism as she shed a few tears. But Catherine had to continue with the interview.

"Did he *only* beat you with his hands?" Catherin asked.

"No—no, no, no… He beat me with other things."

"What other things?"

"Um, belts, power cords, metal hangers, broken pieces of furniture—*after* he threw me into furniture. One night, he *heated* a metal hanger and burned me with it on my back."

"Oh, *God*."

"Yeah… It was terrible."

"Was there verbal abuse as well?"

"Oh, *dear* God, of *course,* there was. And the things he said to me—I try my best to block it out mentally."

"What were some of the things he said to you?"

"Um, the usual: bitch—*oh*, I'm *so* sorry, I know I can't say that on national television,"

"That's okay, Madam President. We'll *definitely* take *that* out of the final cut. But you were saying?"

"Yes, right, there was *a lot* of name-calling, but mostly threats and very degrading, *sexist* comments."

"Was there any *sexual* abuse?"

"There *was*, yes. Multiple times."

"So, did he ever *rape* you?"

"There were times when I did *not* want to have sex with him, but I didn't really fight him off. It was in the grey area."

"Well, if you weren't giving your late husband your consent, then *yes*, that's rape."

"But Catherine, you *must* understand, there *were* times when I *did* want it, even if it was in a salacious manner. I *wanted* that feeling again, of being loved. I wanted my husband back. And there was actually a part of me that *believed* he would change. I really believed him when he would tell me that he would change."

"Do you miss him?"

"Since we're being honest… *Yes*, I miss him—I miss my husband. The man that I fell in love with long ago. But I *don't* miss the monster he became in these last three years."

"How are your children dealing with all of this?"

"They're hanging in there, to the best of their ability. But it's been difficult. They *loved* their father."

"Did Ted ever abuse the children?"

"No, thank God."

"Then why did he abuse *you*?"

"Well, I thought it only came from his jealousy and resentment of me running for President. But then I realized it was something much deeper than jealousy."

"How so?"

"He told me days before that his father abused his mother when he was a child, which led to his mother's suicide."

"I see… So, it was *learned* behavior?"

"Yes."

"You mentioned suicide—his *mother* committing suicide… Did *you* ever contemplate suicide?"

Kelissa was very hesitant to respond to that question. As she looked over to the far side of the East Room, Kelissa saw her children standing off to the side next to Carl. Kelissa then looked back at Catherine, who was waiting for an answer. "Madam President, did you ever contemplate *suicide*?" Catherine asked again. As Kelissa grew emotional, she slowly shook her head up and down, confirming that she did. Ted, Jr., Madeline, and Bryan looked at each other in disbelief as they had no idea their mother was thinking of killing herself. One of the producers handed Kelissa a few tissues. "Thank you," Kelissa said as she wiped her eyes. After cleaning her face, Kelissa began to speak on the night she was going to commit suicide.

"There was a night when Ted placed duct tape over my mouth and wrapped tape around my wrist. He had me hanging by my arms from the shower rail. He wanted to punish me for sending troops back over to Afghanistan, for the troops who were killed. As I was hanging, he whipped me over and over with his belt and then with a power cord. When he realized that I couldn't handle it anymore, he stopped. After that, I went to my private office and wrote a suicide note in my journal. Then I took a knife and went into the bathroom."

The emotional tension in the room was getting thicker and more profound as Kelissa finished the story. "As I was in the bathroom, I took the knife's sharp point and began to pierce it into my wrist… Oh, *God*… Out of nowhere, Ted knocked on the bathroom door, and that's when I dropped the knife. If he didn't knock on the door, I wouldn't be sitting here right now. I would be dead. I was just so *tired* of it all. All the beatings and verbal abuse made me feel that I was the lowest of the low—as if I wasn't even a human being. I was ready to end it, I kissed my daughter and son goodbye while they were sleeping, and I was going to take my own life."

Kelissa looked over to her children as the three of them cried—*hearing* their mother say she was going to end her life. Kelissa, still sobbing as she said, "I'm *so sorry* to my children for even thinking of leaving them like that. I'm sorry to my administration, as well as the American people. I was just so lost and trapped. I didn't know how to escape the abuse and keep the perfect image. I was in so much pain, and I just wanted all the pain to go away. But I'm sorry… I'm *so sorry* to everyone."

"Cut the cameras," Catherine said as she stood up from her seat and hugged Kelissa. Since the interview was not live, they gave Kelissa a moment to calm herself down. Madeline then walked over to comfort her mother, following behind was Ted, Jr., and then Bryan. "You are *so brave*, and I'm *so* proud to have you as my mom," Madeline cried.

Kelissa had enough for one day and decided to wrap up the interview. Even though she felt better telling her story and letting everything out, the pain was too great for her to continue.

Later that night, Kelissa, just leaving Madeline's bedroom, walked down the center hall to the kitchen to fix herself a cup of tea. As

Kelissa was walking, she looked over to her bedroom, where she had not stepped foot in ever since that night Ted tried to kill her.

As Kelissa fixed herself some tea, she walked back and forth in the kitchen as she thought about going back into the bedroom. She was afraid of stepping inside and awakening those scary, vicious memories she wished she could forget. But something inside of her told her to go in. She took her cup of tea and walked over to the bedroom. Her hand began to tremble as she reached for the doorknob. Kelissa took a deep breath, closed her eyes, and opened the door.

Nothing but pure silence as Kelissa walked in. The broken coffee table had been replaced with a smaller table. The old carpet in the dressing room was removed due to the bloodstains left over from Ted's corpse. It has been over a month since the fatal incident, and this is Kelissa's first time walking inside and revisiting some of the worst memories of her life. But then, Kelissa spotted something dark underneath the bed. She realized it was her journal as she came close to the object. She quickly picked it up, gently holding it in her arms as if it was a newborn baby. Kelissa was surprised at the fact that no one ever noticed the journal.

Kelissa, with her cup of tea in one hand, and the journal in the other, left the bedroom and headed to her private office. She was looking forward to writing in her journal again, as she had so much to say. Kelissa placed her cup of tea and journal on the desk and took her seat. Kelissa then grabbed a pen as she was eager to write. But then, she discovered something alarming. As Kelissa turned the pages, all she saw, in big, bold letters, was: "**FUCK YOU, GO TO HELL, FUCK YOU, BITCH, DIE WHORE, GO FUCK YOURSELF, I'LL KILL YOU.**"

Ted discarded all of Kelissa's writings. Page after page, he wrote the most horrifying, inhumane, unimaginable comments a person could ever say. Kelissa's anxiety was rising like a flame. It felt as if the pages kept him alive. She began to breathe heavier and faster. But as she calmed herself down, Kelissa discovered something even more bizarre. On the very last page of the journal, there was a written note that said, '*Dearest Kel.*' It was a note, obviously written by Ted as she did not write it. He even put the date on top—just as Kelissa did when she wrote. It was the date of February 14th, the morning of when he tried to kill her.

Kelissa was hesitant to read it as she had no idea what he had to say to her. But she whipped up enough courage and began to read the note. As Kelissa was reading Ted's letter, it said:

Friday, February 14th, 2025, 12:13 a.m.

Dearest Kel,

I hope this finds you in time before I kill you. I just wanted you to know that I loved you. I truly, truly loved you very much. I've loved you ever since the very first sight my eyes captured of you. You were so incredibly beautiful to me. You were the undying star in my universe. You were the star that brought light to my darkness. I never meant for this to escalate to the point of me beating you half to death. I never had a chance of staying a good man or a good husband. I was no good for you, Kel. And when I read the pages of all the horrible things I said and did to you, I've accepted the reality that I'm just an awful excuse for a human being.

But you were just so beautiful, Kel. Your face is like this stunning canvas, beautifully natural, and all I wanted to do was make you as ugly as I possibly could. I wanted to torture you, break you down, I wanted to own you, and you be my property. Controlling you gave me great pleasure and happiness. I wanted to make you suffer and suffer some more. It was like a drug to me to control you. A drug that I was addicted to, and I loved it. I became obsessed with you, Kel, and that obsession took a very evil turn.

I know I owe you an apology for my evilness. And I will, but just not in this life. Maybe in the next life, when we are both angels, with our own pair of wings, flying high in the heavenly skies, and we're all together again—one big happy, holy family for all eternity. You must think I'm crazy, huh? Well, you most certainly are right. I'm crazy about you, Kel. I would die for you. Kill for you. There was just something about you that brought out the darkest beast from within me. But the more I abused you, the more you took it. It was as if you were the second coming of Christ. Tough as nails. I guess that's where my jealousy emerged. No matter what life threw at you, you could handle it. You were a warrior, brave, fearless. And I tried to beat that out of you every time. But I couldn't because your spirit shined so bright. I envied that about you, and I hated to love you. Tell my children that I love them with all my heart. I know I wasn't perfect, but I loved those kids to death. That's why I never laid a finger on them. I guess that's all I have to say. Now I can prepare to be reunited with my dear mother in heaven.

It's been real, Kel. And I know Carl or one of the other agents will kill me after killing you. So, I'll see you soon at the pearly gates.

I love you with all my heart and soul.

Theodore Julius Morrison.

Kelissa was speechless as tears poured down her face. She could not move an inch at her desk. After reading Ted's bizarre, psychotic letter, Kelissa decided to rip that sheet out of her journal and destroy it. But shc wanted to make sure that she got rid of the *entire* journal so that no traces were ever found of that letter. That is when she looked over to the fireplace. Kelissa stood up and took her journal to the fireplace, lit a match, holding Ted's letter as she watched it ignite. She then tossed it in the fireplace and watched it burn. And being that her journal was ruined, Kelissa ripped each page, one by one, and threw them into the fire.

Kelissa watched the pages burn into black soot. She stood there as the light of the flickering flames illuminated her teary face. At that moment, she decided to do the one thing she had not done in over a month; she prayed. She got on her knees, placed her hands together, and said, "Heavenly father, you spared my life. You delivered me from evil. I know thou shall not judge, and I won't. But I thank you for freeing me from the abuse that I suffered over the last three years. I don't know why people do evil things. But now I know the reason why you put me in this position. You placed me in the most powerful position because you knew that I was strong enough to survive it. I give all credit to you, father. I *pray*, father—I pray that you continue to watch over my children and watch over me. I have three more years to go in my first term. I need all the strength and mercy you can bestow onto me, father… Amen."

As Kelissa opened her eyes, kneeling in warm silence as the bark of the burning logs continued to break. She then laid on her side, facing the illuminating fireplace. Kelissa's heart was filled with emotion as she lay there having a moment of reminiscing. She looked back in her life, thinking about all that she went through and all that she had survived. And the one conclusion that came to her mind was that she is free.

Chapter 51

Tuesday Afternoon, April 1st, 2025

Madam President

The Press pool awaits President Kelissa Morrison in the James S. Brady Press Briefing Room, located in the West Wing. Kelissa is ready to stand before the press and give them an update on her current condition, her children, and her plans as she moves forward with her administration. Press Secretary Lesley Richards is now up at the podium giving a speech before the President takes the stage.

As Kelissa waited outside of the Press Briefing Room, pacing herself back and forth with her arms folded, she began to think about the conversation she had just finished with her mother over the phone. Kelissa's mother talked about how proud of Kelissa she is for continuing her role as President of the United States of America. Kelissa told her mother how she has been receiving thousands of letters from women all across the country who were survivors of domestic abuse. Even though Kelissa is very much behind with reading each letter, she is doing her very best to read and respond to as many as she can, day by day. Social media has been global with its new hashtag in honor of the President—*millions* of women around the world have been using this hashtag as they share their survival stories of domestic violence:

#IAMKELISSAMORRISON

As Press Secretary Lesley Richards concluded her speech, she introduced the President. "Ladies and gentlemen, the President of the United States," Lesley projected. Once again, the cameras clicked a hundred times per second as President Kelissa Morrison took the stage. Her physical wounds were fully healed, as were the bruises on her face. Kelissa looked better than ever, as mentally and physically healthy as possible.

As Kelissa stood there at the podium, wearing a burgundy suit jacket with the matching skirt, she opened her binder and began to make her speech:

"Good afternoon, everyone. Thank you for coming here today, and I thank you for your patience. I know that some of you are concerned about my mental and physical health. Well, I can tell you that I am doing much better now. I've made *tremendous* progress over the past month and a half. I've been getting bi-weekly checkups from my doctors at Walter Reed Medical Center, and by the grace of God, my physical health is improving day by day. I must say that I don't know where I would be without the love and support of my children.

My eldest son, Ted, Jr., decided to move back home to the White House as he commutes to college to be closer to me for our emotional support during these trying times. At times, it has been a struggle dealing with this new reality. But at the *same* time, it has been a great weight lifted off my shoulders. I survived a horrific, tragic series of events that spanned over three years. However, that is all over now. Ted is gone, and the rest of us are now safe. My nightmare is over. And as I move forward, I tend to make it my mission to prioritize domestic abuse, not just for women but for the small percentage of men who also deal with this serious issue. I do not see domestic violence as a one-sided issue that only affects women. It affects all of us who are involved. Family and friends, specifically our *children*, tend to see this as learned behavior and create a cycle of violence. I'll see to it that I work with my Administration to find a way to protect those who are victims of this secretive epidemic. With *that* being said, I refuse to have the abuse I survived to become my entire legacy.

I intend to leave this in the past as I move forward with my first term as your President. I want to say thank you to Vice President Harry Griffin for his outstanding work as he took over as acting President while I was in recovery. I want to thank Press Secretary Lesley Richards for all the hard work you've done to keep the administration together. And lastly, I want to thank *you*, the American people, for your love and support. I want you to know that I am receiving your heartwarming letters, and I appreciate *every single* one of them. I have not responded to all of the letters but will get to as many as possible. I thank all of you. It means the world to me. And now, I will take a few questions."

Hands shot up in the air as if the reporters were kids in the candy store. "I'll start with *you*, sir, in that shiny red tie," Kelissa pointed.

"Thank you, Madam President," said the reporter. "Fred Dasani, reporting from IDC Press. Madam President, is it true that you have pardoned 365 inmates who were convicted of murdering their abusive boyfriends and husbands?"

"Hello Fred, so that is *part* of my plan. So far, my administration and I are doing extensive research on each inmate's case, just to make sure that their *only* crime was, *in fact*, self-defense," Kelissa responded.

"And just one more question, what are your plans, *specifically*, to help women overcome their domestic violence situation?"

"Well, Fred, as I read the letters of many of these women *and* men, who are victims or survivors, I believe that we need to continue to build non-judgmental communities around the country and make this a more serious conversation. I plan to create programs for the youth, to *educate* them on domestic abuse, being that many cases ties to learned behavior from childhood."

As more hands went up, Kelissa saw this gorgeous African American reporter. The reporter had these piercing brown eyes that could stare right through your soul. Kelissa was captivated by this woman. She quickly pointed to the reporter as she wanted to hear her question.

"Yes, *ma'am*, you, right there," Kelissa pointer to the pretty reporter.

"Thank you, Madam President," said the reporter. "Melissa Brownstone, reporting from *Black Voices Post*."

"Oh, *Melissa, Kelissa*. Is this an April Fool's joke?" Kelissa laughed.

The press had a slight wave of chuckling as Kelissa resurrected her sense of humor. The reporter, Melissa Brownstone, then asked her question. "Madam President, I just wanted to say that I *myself* am a survivor of domestic violence. And I'm just very appreciative of you sharing your story. So, my question is... Well, *first*, I want to *also* say that I'm a Christian. I *do* believe in forgiveness, and I *have* forgiven my abuser. With all that you went through with your husband, do you forgive him? Or can you *ever* forgive him?"

Kelissa, not saying a word, took a moment in silence. After all this time and praying, she never thought about forgiveness. But as the wicked-dark memories began to refresh deep in her mind, Kelissa felt the emotion starting to build up inside of her. As her eyes grew watery, Kelissa remained stuck and speechless as the cameras kept clicking and rolling. Then suddenly, Kelissa took a breath, opened her mouth, and *respectfully* responded with these two words...

"Next question."

Acknowledgments

I would like to take this time to say thank you for going on this complex journey and reading the entirety of this novel. I know this was probably very difficult for you to get through as the topic is very triggering. But you *did* get through it, and I cannot thank you enough for your commitment to finishing this book. And let me tell you, this was not easy for me to write. It took a lot of energy out of me, mentally draining, which is why I mentioned before that I might never write another book like this again. I know that saying, '*Never say never*,' but I believe this story is a once-in-a-lifetime piece of art.

I would like to thank my mother and father for their love and support. I also want to thank my family and the *few* friends I have for *their* support. You all know who you are. I wish to acknowledge and thank some people I had the pleasure of doing business with and who supported me in promoting my books. I want to thank Star from '*The Star Report*,' *Mr. Skinny*, '*Hip-Hop News Uncensored*,' Wavyy Jonez, and Dean Morrow a.k.a. '*Michael Trapson.*' I want to thank my high school teacher, Shea Richardson, who sparked my mind and inspired me to write poetry. I also want to thank my college English professor,

Henry “Hank” Stewart. And lastly, my dear friend, John-Deric Mitchell.

I also wish to say this. Even though this is a fictional novel, I understand that this topic is very real and millions of women, and even some men, goes through domestic violence. In doing the research that I have done; I understand how difficult it is to leave this type of situation. And I am *not* one to judge. However, there is a way to escape.

If you are someone who is suffering from domestic abuse, or you *know* someone who is, help is only but a word away. There is a saying, ‘Misery loves company.” Well, so does buried secrets. And if you leave a secret, such as domestic violence, buried, eventually, that secret will leave you buried underground, right along with it. Do you understand? Don’t wait to get help. You are not alone, and you should not feel embarrassed by seeking help in order to save your life. No one is perfect and *everyone* goes through things that may bring trauma to their lives. Lastly, I will say this about truth. There is freedom in truth, there is *beauty* in truth, and the truth *will* set you free from the ugly darkness that may burden you. Of course, it is easier said than done, but it *must* be done, and you *must* get out before it is too late.

With all of that said, I thank you again for going on this journey with me. And hopefully, I will be able to get you on the next journey to come. You are wonderful; take care, stay safe and stay blessed. Until next time…

About the Author

Jordan Wells was born in Orange, New Jersey, and was raised in East Orange, New Jersey. He graduated from Centenary University, earning a bachelor's degree in business, with concentrations in finance and marketing. He is also a professional actor and a member of the Screen Actors Guild-American Federation of Television and Radio Artists. "*Madam President*" is Wells' second novel. Wells' sixth book, "*It's Fun Being a Human Being*," is Wells' fourth installment of his poetry collection. Wells' fifth book, "*The Ring Pack*," is his debut novel. His fourth book, "*A Lonely Rose*," is an addition to Wells' poetic collection. "*The Healing*," is Wells' third book. "*Mirrors and Reflections*" is Wells' sophomore book. His debut book, "*Logged Off: My Journey of Escaping the Social Media World*," was a monumental achievement in Wells' life, and will continue with his creative writing ventures.

Made in the USA
Middletown, DE
10 November 2022

14558826R00300